LOVE WITHO...

The lightning flash... for a timeless mome... ...ach other. She was wea... ...g, flowery dress, her flame-colored hair was wild about her face, and her eyes were dark with knowledge and longing.

He took a step toward her, waiting to see if she'd run. She didn't. She couldn't. He reached out, sliding his hands up her legs, pulling the dress up her thighs, drawing her toward him.

She came, unresisting, as his hands slid along her bare thighs, pulling the material with them, and her breasts were against his chest. She was damp from the rain, she was hot, and she was his. He moved her head to kiss her, and she tried to turn her face away. "Don't," she whispered, a plea that should have broken his heart.

He had no heart. "I can't afford to be merciful," he said. And he kissed her.

Lightning flared again . . . and she was lost in the blaze of light. . . .

NIGHTFALL

NIGHTFALL

ANNE STUART

AN ONYX BOOK

ONYX
Published by the Penguin Group
Penguin Books USA Inc., 375 Hudson Street,
New York, New York 10014, U.S.A.
Penguin Books Ltd, 27 Wrights Lane,
London W8 5TZ, England
Penguin Books Australia Ltd, Ringwood,
Victoria, Australia
Penguin Books Canada Ltd, 10 Alcorn Avenue,
Toronto, Ontario, Canada M4V 3B2
Penguin Books (N.Z.) Ltd, 182–190 Wairau Road,
Auckland 10, New Zealand

Penguin Books Ltd, Registered Offices:
Harmondsworth, Middlesex, England

First published by Onyx, an imprint of Dutton Signet,
a division of Penguin Books USA Inc.

First Printing, March, 1995
10 9 8 7 6 5 4 3 2 1

ACKNOWLEDGMENTS

I don't usually write these sort of things, since they tend to be a little precious, but this time I couldn't resist. I owe too many people for their help, hand-holding, love, and support. First, to my luscious husband, the finest man of this or any other generation, and my wonderful, monstrous children, Kate and Tim, who did their best to keep me from ever finishing this book in the first place. To my beloved Aunt Beatrice, who provided a place to hide and write, and my writing buddies, Judith Arnold and Kathleen Gilles Seidel.

For the music of Richard Thompson, which inspired and sustained me.

Special thanks go to Sally Tyler Hayes, for her journalistic expertise, and those two little British ladies, Mrs. Whippett and Mrs. Baggit, for their help on the roads of Somerset.

To Maureen Walters, who puts up with my whining and helps me navigate the dangerous waters of publishing.

And most of all, to Jennifer Enderlin, for her vast leap of faith.

PROLOGUE

She dreamed that night. Visions of blood and sex and death, surrounding her, smothering her. She reached out, but there was no one there. No one to hold her, comfort her, tell her it was nothing but a nightmare. No one to promise that the darkness couldn't touch her, couldn't hurt her. No one to make her believe in happy endings. She opened her eyes, and it was still and silent, peaceful, the snow drifting down past her apartment window. She was safe and warm.

He dreamed that night. Lying on the thin mattress, the ceaseless noise of prison pressing down on him. He dreamed of fields and flowers and a woman, calling to him; he dreamed of peace and comfort and happy endings. But when he awoke, cold and sweating in the dark cell, there was no one there. Only the knowledge that darkness was all around him, death lived in his soul, and his hands were stained with blood.

CHAPTER 1

THE NEW YORK POST . . .

Richard Tiernan, sentenced to death for the brutal murder of his wife, was released today on one million dollars bail pending the outcome of his appeal.

In a strange twist, Pulitzer Prize–winning novelist Sean O'Rourke posted the bail, but insists there's no book in the works about the stabbing death of Diana Scott Tiernan fifteen months earlier. O'Rourke has no other known connection to Richard Tiernan.

The special prosecutor, Jerome Fabiani, was visibly angered by the judge's decision to release Tiernan, but said he didn't expect the killer to be free for long.

"He's been convicted, and he's not going to walk away from it. We're pursuing our investigation into the disappearance and probable death of his two children and several other women, and we have no intention of giving up on this one without a fight."

Gulf war veteran and national hero retired U.S. General Amberson Scott, who testified against his son-in-law, expressed his profound anger over Tiernan's release. "I'm just an ordinary American citizen seeking justice," said Scott, who was at the courthouse trying to block Tiernan's release.

Richard Tiernan is scheduled to be back in court within the next two months. He left in the company of Sean O'Rourke, and his whereabouts are presently unknown.

O'Rourke refused to confirm or deny that he had received a seven-figure advance on a book about the notorious Tiernan case.

Richard Tiernan was sentenced to die by lethal injection, the first death sentence in the state of New York since the death penalty was reinstated.

Cassidy Roarke was running late, and she wasn't happy about it. At the age of twenty-seven, she had done her best to make a safe, predictable life for herself. She worked hard at her job, always being careful not to put her heart and soul into it, only her intellect and energy. She was a reliable friend, a shoulder to cry on, a good, decent, determinedly ordinary young woman who just happened to have a notoriously colorful father. She'd moved away from that, from the noise and excitement of her childhood, to a comfortable life in Baltimore, with good if not particularly close friends, a stimulating job, and an existence that other people might characterize as deadly dull.

Cassidy reveled in the dullness. The safe constancy of day after day, with little or no variation. No one needed her here, no one made impossible demands. And if she hadn't knocked over her diet Coke on the way out the door and been forced to change her clothes, she wouldn't have been ten minutes late in meeting Emmie and John for dinner. And she wouldn't have been there to answer the phone.

"Cassidy. It's your da."

It had been months since she'd heard her father's voice, but there was no mistaking Sean O'Rourke's gruff, determinedly Irish tones, even if Cassidy wanted to.

"Hello, Sean," she said carefully, all her instincts alert. He wanted something from her. He always did. And she'd been working very hard at not giving in to his life-draining demands. "What do you want?"

"Can't your father call just to find out how his elder daughter's doing? I've missed you, girl. It's been ages since I've seen you."

"You've been busy," she said.

"That I have. A new book, a new project. Life's been grandly entertaining, Cass."

"If you like child murders," she said wryly.

"You've been reading the tabloids, have you? I would have thought you'd be too well protected in that ivory tower."

"I admit I don't have your tabloid mentality, but even I can't avoid the checkout lines at the supermarket. And working for an academic press doesn't really qualify as an ivory tower, you know."

"And glad I am that you've chosen to follow in my literary footsteps, even if it's on the side of the enemy," Sean said magnanimously. "You haven't inherited my talent for writing, but at least you've got a bit of my love for the written word."

"Sean, I'm late," Cass said wearily, knowing her father would go on all night before he finally got to the point. And there was a point, she was sure of it.

"Faith, you haven't got a moment to spare for your old man? It's your mother's fault. She must have been on to you . . ."

"I haven't talked with her in a week."

"You see, it proves my point. She called to warn you about Richard Tiernan, didn't she? I know the woman. Our married life was a hell I won't soon forget. She must have filled your head with stories about him. You should know better than to believe her melodramatic crap. What did she tell you? That the man's a sociopath, with no sense of right or wrong? That he's one of those charming, evil creatures who's at the mercy of destructive, irrational urges?"

"Why would she tell me any such thing? Sounds like you've been working on your newest book, Sean. As a matter of fact, she called to wish me a happy birthday."

Dead silence on the other end of the line. Finally, "I was never good with dates."

"I know, Sean," she said, her voice gentling. He was doing it to her again. Making her forgive him, when she should be trying to make him feel guilty. "Why should Mother warn me about Richard Tiernan?"

"I can't imagine," Sean said blandly. "Cass, darling, I want to see you."

"Why?"

"Why?" he echoed. "I haven't seen you since last summer, when you came to the Hamptons. I miss my daughter. I'm getting on in years, and I won't live forever . . ."

"Stuff it, Sean. You saw me at Christmas, even if you've conveniently forgotten, and you'll never get old, much less die. So that won't work. What do you want from me?"

"Just a visit," he said, wheedling now, as he was so good at doing. "I thought maybe we could spend some time together. I could make use of your professional services . . ."

Cassidy laughed. "You once told me that all copy editors should be stood up against a wall and shot."

"You're more than a copy editor, Cass, and you know it. And if you just let me put in a word for you, you wouldn't have to be stuck in a place like Baltimore . . ."

"I'm very happy where I am, Sean."

"Come and see me, lass." He started the wheedling again. "You must be due for some vacation by now. Mabry misses you, and so do I. She's worried about me, the fool woman."

Her quiet alarm at Sean's unprecedented phone call began to grow. "Why is she worried about you?"

"A cold that won't go away," he said blithely. "I've told her she's being ridiculous, but she insisted I call you."

That, Cassidy could well believe. Sean never called anyone. "Why do you really want me?"

"Oh ye of little faith!" Sean declaimed. "Come see me, Cass. Before it's too late."

The phone line went dead. Cassidy stared at it, blinking for a moment. "Melodramatic bastard," she said succinctly, slamming down the receiver.

She wasn't going to let him do it to her again. She wasn't going to let Sean manipulate her as he always had. She kept her distance, both physical and emotional, for a very good reason. Sean was voracious—he devoured any soul who came near him, anyone not strong enough to withstand his powerful personality. Cassidy had worked hard at being able to stand up to him, but she kept her exposure to a minimum.

The story about Sean being sick was just that, a story. Sean O'Rourke had never been sick a day in his life—germs wouldn't dare mess with him. A short, fierce bull of a man, he stormed through life, through his five wives and three children and countless best-sellers with an appetite for experience that was astonishing. As a child she'd been terrified of him. Now she was only faintly wary.

And he needed her. It was hard to resist, even though she knew the emotional danger. It probably had something to do with his career—Sean had few real emotions for anything else.

She knew perfectly well she was going to go. Despite her misgivings, she'd survive a visit in Sean and Mabry's Park Avenue apartment. Her father had lost the ability to torment her, and Richard Tiernan was the least of her worries. If he was anywhere in Sean's orbit, she doubted he'd even notice her. She simply wasn't the type to inspire murderous obsessions.

Damn, she was late. It was a March day in Baltimore, and Cassidy had been hoping for spring, not a trip farther north. It couldn't be helped. When it came right down to it, she was still prey to the old emotions that raged through her family, including a hopeless affection for her impossible father, who never failed to let her down. She'd take her vacation time, fly to New York, and see him, making sure he was the same, invulnerable old reprobate. She'd figure out what Sean wanted from her, tell him no, do some shopping, and come home.

Very simple. So why did she have this overwhelming feeling of impending doom?

Maybe she should ignore her family's demands,

book a flight for the Caribbean, and lie in the sun, baking away the darkness that always seemed to invade her soul by the end of the winter.

But she wasn't going to do that. Everything always seemed fraught with disaster this time of year—she'd learned not to give in to her irrational depression. But if she ignored Sean's enigmatic demands, she'd end up spending her entire vacation worrying.

No, she was going, whether she wanted to or not. She just hoped to God she wasn't going to run into Sean's newest pet project.

Murderous psychopaths had never held any particular charm for her. Unlike her father, she preferred the more grisly aspects of modern life between the pages of a book. With any luck, that was as close as she would ever get to Richard Tiernan.

"Leave me alone, Mabry," Sean O'Rourke, born John Roarke, snapped at his fifth wife. "You know how I hate to have anyone fussing over me."

"I'm not fussing," Mabry murmured, tossing her silky straight platinum hair over one angular shoulder. "I simply said that if you don't seem to be feeling better, you should go back to that doctor you're so fond of and stop snapping at me."

"Damn it, I'm not snapping," Sean growled. "I just asked when the hell Cassidy's supposed to arrive."

"This is the third time today you've asked me," she pointed out with maddening calm. "And for the third time I'll tell you, I don't know. I don't even know if she's coming at all. I called her and added my two cents, but Cassidy is her own woman."

"Damn her," Sean said morosely. "You told her I'd been ill?"

"I told her exactly what you wanted me to tell her. That you had a bad cold, you weren't recovering as quickly as I wanted, and that I thought she ought to come see you."

"And what did she say to that?"

"Something noncommittal. You should know, Sean, that if you fail to be there for the people in your life, they might very well fail to be there for you as well."

"Cassidy wouldn't fail me," he said with great certainty. "She's fair and loyal, and she wouldn't hold a grudge."

"You're used to people forgiving you. You'll go too far one of these days."

"Spare me the voice of doom, Mabry, it doesn't become you," Sean said. "I know my daughter better than you. She'll be here. I just want to know when."

Mabry drained her cup of ginseng tea. "For the first time in your life, darling, you'll have to be patient."

Sean glared at her, but she ignored him, her beautiful face serene and distant as she turned to the morning paper. "If you aren't going to fight with me, I'll have to find someone who will," he said in a peevish voice.

Her voice stopped him at the door. "I'd watch it before you tangle with your newest pet, love," she said in a dulcet voice. "He might not be quite as civilized as you think."

Sean's laugh was harsh. "That's what makes him interesting, Mabry. Jackals are far more inspiring than house cats."

"You'll go too far."

"I always have," he said. And there was no missing the pride in his rough voice.

He lay on the bed, letting the white-blue surround him. He'd become adept at disappearing, letting his conscious mind drift free, so that nothing remained, just the shell of his body, the weight of his bones pressing in to the thin prison mattress. There were noises echoing through the vast steel and concrete structure, voices, the slam of metal doors, the jingle of keys and coins, but none of them reached him as he floated, free and formless.

He'd gotten so that he could do it any time he wanted, an instinctive, almost unconscious escape. As an alibi it had been a piss-poor one, but he hadn't been interested in convincing a jury of his peers. He'd only been concerned with ending it quickly.

At one point he'd even considered confessing,

but some stray remnant of self-preservation had stopped him. Once he confessed, there'd be no going back. As long as he kept silent, denied everything, there would always be an element of doubt. No matter how tiny.

He remembered the first time he'd gone into that dark, empty place. It had been automatic, as he knelt beside the body of his dying wife, her blood staining his hands and clothes. When the police had come he'd still been there, silent, lost. Unable to answer their simple questions. Thank God.

It was much better like this. Free and floating, in a vacuum with no sun or wind, no warmth, nothing but a vast emptiness.

He blinked, a tiny movement, and the bright blue of the winter sky invaded his stillness. The bed beneath him was neither thin nor hard. It fit his tall, rangy body far better than the narrow cots in prison, and he supposed he should summon up some kind of gratitude. But gratitude would require emotion, and he had no emotions.

He could hear the two of them arguing, the voices more intrusive than the muffled obscenity of Dannemora. He didn't want to be here. He didn't want to be anyplace at all, but that still, white-blue emptiness. But he wasn't finished yet. He wasn't ready to rest.

He pulled himself upright, barely noticing his surroundings. Sean O'Rourke's upscale Manhattan apartment with its pseudo-Southwestern

decor meant no more to him that the spartan cell
he'd shared with another murderer. All that mattered was getting through the next hour, the next
few weeks. All that mattered was doing what he
had to do. No matter what the cost.

"You're awake, then." O'Rourke stood in the
doorway, his aggressive chin pushed forward.
He was like a bantam rooster, short, bandy-
legged, pugnacious. Tiernan had no illusions as
to what O'Rourke wanted from him, believed of
him. He had every intention of exploiting him
to the fullest.

"I'm awake," said Richard Tiernan. "Where's
your daughter?"

Cassidy was afraid of flying. It wasn't something
she admitted very often, even to herself, but three
days later she blessed the fact that what existed of
the United States railroad system was still working
reasonably well between Baltimore and New York.
She didn't have to mess with getting to and from
airports, and she didn't even have to think about
sitting in a contraption that lifted off the ground
and suspended her in midair for a ridiculous
amount of time.

Unfortunately, it left her with too much time
for distraction, and she'd made the mistake of
grabbing *People* magazine just before she got on
the train. By sheer force of will she'd managed to
avoid any of the media stories involving her father
and a convicted killer, but trapped on a crowded

train with a sour-tempered bureaucrat to her left, there was no way she could resist the temptation, particularly with Sean's pugnacious face on the cover. " 'HE'S INNOCENT,' CLAIMS SEAN O'ROURKE, WHO'S PUTTING HIS MONEY WHERE HIS MOUTH IS" said the teaser. In the corner, over her father's shoulder, was a grainy snapshot of a happy family, a blond, perfect wife, two young, beautiful children, and a tall, dark man standing behind them, a protective hand on the woman's shoulder. Or was it a threatening hand?

Suddenly she couldn't stand even touching the magazine. She dropped it on the floor, but the man beside her immediately scooped it up. "D'you mind?" he asked, not giving her a chance to object. "Disgusting, isn't it?" he leaned over and breathed expensive Scotch in her face. "They let monsters like that go free, just because someone with a little clout talks them into it. He'll kill again, you'll see, and then that asshole O'Rourke will write a book about it. It makes me sick."

Cassidy controlled her trace of amusement in hearing her father called an asshole. She couldn't put up an argument on that front. "Maybe Tiernan didn't do it."

"Have you heard his story? He says he came home, found the bodies of his wife and children, and then went into shock and doesn't remember another thing. They never found the bodies of his children, but his fingerprints were all over the murder weapon. He was covered with her blood. And he's never shown a trace of sorrow or regret."

Cassidy glanced over at the photograph on the cover. They looked so normal, so happy. The perfect family, now destroyed. She leaned back and closed her eyes, turning her face away. She could only hope to God her father wasn't going to want to talk about Tiernan. The whole subject made her faintly ill, the thought of a man murdering his own children. Not that she had any illusions about the sacred nature of the father-child bond. She'd lived with Sean for too long to retain her innocence. Her father could wallow in the mud as much as he wanted, but she wasn't going to let him drag her there with him.

A light snow had begun to fall when the train pulled into Penn Station. She considered calling Mabry and warning her that she'd arrived, then thought better of it. Sean fancied himself an old-fashioned Irishman, one who kept a welcome for any friend or family who happened to stray near him. There'd be room for her in the cavernous old apartment on Park Avenue, and she'd prefer to see Sean without giving him time to prepare. He wanted something from her, she was certain of it, though she doubted it had anything to do with writing. Sean had always ridiculed her lack of creativity, referring to her as his little Philistine. He'd hardly be asking her editorial expertise.

No, he wanted something else, enough so that

he was willing to play sick, to enlist Mabry in his little games. And if he wanted something that much, Cassidy was curious enough to play along. For a day or two.

As luck would have it, Sean and Mabry were coming out of the door just as Cassidy reached the apartment building on Seventy-second Street. "Cassidy, my love!" Sean boomed when he caught sight of her, flinging his arms around her. Cassidy stood within his burly embrace, bemused as always by the rush of love and irritation that swept over her when she was in her father's presence. He pushed her away a moment later, glowering fiercely. "Let me look at you. You've been eating too much again. Don't you know a woman can never be too thin or too rich? Mabry, talk to the girl. I swear, she looks positively voluptuous."

Irritation took over as Cassidy glared down at her father. "What can I say, Sean, I'm hopelessly curvaceous. Nothing short of cosmetic surgery would whittle down my hips, and I'm not sure that would work."

Mabry's cool blue eyes met Cassidy's over her father's head, and she smiled faintly. "You're father's an asshole," she said. "You're absolutely beautiful, as always."

"You're the second person today who's said that," Cassidy said, moving past Sean to hug her elegant stepmother.

"Told you were beautiful?" Sean demanded, not liking to be ignored.

"No, said you were an asshole," she replied.

Mabry laughed. "I wouldn't be surprised if there were more we haven't heard about. How long are you staying, darling? We'll come back up and get you settled."

"No, we won't!" Sean snapped. "You've been harassing me to go to the doctor's for weeks, and now that I have an appointment, I'm not going to miss it. Cassidy can get herself settled in. Take your old bedroom, Cassie. Just make yourself at home—I'm not sure when we'll be back."

"But . . ." Mabry began, a worried expression on her face.

"But nothing," Sean said. "Don't fuss over the girl. Lord, you're becoming an old lady before your time, Mabry, fussing over everyone. You'll be here a good long time, won't you, Cassie? We'll have plenty of time to spend with her."

"As a matter of fact, I wasn't . . ."

But as usual, Sean had no interest in anyone's thoughts but his own. He dragged Mabry down the sidewalk toward Park Avenue, waving an irritated hand. "Later," he shouted, and they disappeared around the corner.

"He never changes, does he, miss?"

Cassidy turned and flashed a smile at the doorman. "He doesn't seem to, Bill. How's he been? Mabry said he was sick."

"Not so's I'd notice. Still getting into trouble, like always. It's good to see you back. Maybe you can talk some sense into him."

"Now, why does everyone seem to think I can do the impossible?" Cassidy demanded with a wry grimace. "Sean doesn't know the meaning of the word caution."

"That he doesn't," Bill said with a sigh, walking with her to the elevator. "Mind you don't forget. Can I carry your bag up?"

"And have Father disown me? We're staunch believers in democracy, remember? No one's allowed to wait on us. Unless it's a bartender."

Bill shook his head. "You watch out for yourself, miss. I'll be down here if you need any help."

"Why should I . . . ?" But the elevator had already closed, and it was making its swift, silent way up to the twelfth floor.

Cassidy wasn't much fonder of elevators than she was of airplanes, but she wasn't crazy about walking up twelve flights, and Sean always wanted to be on the top floor wherever he lived. He and Mabry had been in their current apartment for the last ten years, and it felt oddly like home. She had every intention of kicking off her shoes and walking barefoot through the thick pile carpets, scarfing down Mabry's supply of Perrier or whatever designer water she was currently favoring, and finding something impossibly fattening in defiance of her father's strictures.

She dropped her suitcase in the inside hall, stepped out of her shoes, and took a deep breath. She looked at the wall of mirrors that Mabry, the ex-fashion model, had had installed, and she stuck out her tongue at her reflection.

Sean never failed to make her feel gangly, clumsy, and huge. He didn't like the fact that her five feet nine inches towered over him, and had since she was in her early teens. He didn't like it that she came equipped with an hourglass figure that no amount of rigid dieting, compulsive exercise, or self-hatred could change. He didn't like the calm intelligence in her eyes, he didn't like her flyaway red hair or her choice of professions. In fact, he didn't approve of one damned thing about her.

The odd thing was, he loved her. Cassidy had no doubt whatsoever about that. Which was why she put up with him, for as long as she could stand him.

She tossed her down coat over a chair and began unbuttoning her silk blouse, running a hand behind her neck, freeing her mass of curls that never stayed in a neat bun. She had at least an hour alone in the apartment, and she was going to enjoy every minute of it.

The refrigerator was surprisingly well stocked. Mabry had switched to Clearly Canadian, and Cassidy grabbed a bottle of peach water and a chicken drumstick, shoving the latter in her mouth with relief. She'd been starving, but nothing on earth would make her eat in the train station.

She didn't hear a sound. Indeed, the silence

was so strong that she didn't bother to remove the chicken leg from her mouth as she wheeled around to stare at the far doorway. She simply stood there, her mouth stuffed with food.

He filled the doorway, but the room was in shadow, and she couldn't see his features. She didn't need to. The man standing there watching her with such an unnatural silence could only be one man. Richard Tiernan.

And her father had let her come up to the apartment like a sacrificial lamb.

CHAPTER 2

The man in the doorway took a step forward, into the murky light of the kitchen, and Cassidy finally had the presence of mind to remove the chicken leg from her mouth. She took a faltering step backward, putting a nervous hand to her throat, only to realize that her blouse was unbuttoned.

"I didn't mean to startle you," he said. He had a deep voice, quiet, with a thread of menace like a strand of silk winding through it.

She took another involuntary step backward, away from him, furtively trying to wipe some of the chicken grease from her mouth. "You didn't," she said, her voice shaking slightly.

It was the merest ghost of a smile that danced across his face. Clearly he wasn't a man who found much to amuse him. "I'm not going to hurt you, you know," he said, stopping his advance. He was close enough so that she could get a good look at him in the murky kitchen light, and she didn't like what she saw.

He was attractive. Not handsome in a conventional way—his face was too austere, his narrow nose a bit too forceful, his eyes a bit too haunted. But there was something about him—charisma, charm, perhaps—that reached out beyond the wary cynicism and called to her, even as she knew better than to respond.

He was tall, towering over her own substantial height, and very lean, almost to the point of gauntness. His skin was pale, a prison pallor, she thought belatedly, and his dark hair was cut too short. His mocking, enigmatic eyes were very dark, he hadn't shaved in several days, but he was one of those lucky men who simply looked more appealing when they had a two-day stubble.

He was wearing jeans, a wrinkled oxford shirt, and socks, no shoes. He looked far too much at home in her father's sprawling apartment.

She stopped her retreat, straightening her shoulders, unable to decide whether she was better off buttoning her blouse, or whether that would simply draw his attention to it. "I never thought you would," she said with spurious calm. "I'm Cassidy Roarke. Sean's daughter."

"His name's O'Rourke."

She shrugged. "So he says. He was born John Roarke, but he decided to change it so that he could get in touch with his Irish roots. According to him, he was simply reverting to the name his ancestors used."

"Is it true?"

"Not as far as I know. But Sean adjusts reality to suit his own purposes. You're Richard Tiernan, aren't you?"

There was a quality of stillness to the man that was unnerving, despite the fact that he'd stopped his advance. "Guilty," he said.

If he'd been looking for a conversation stopper he couldn't have chosen a more effective one. Cassidy felt a shiver of pure, superstitious panic wash over her, and then she fought back, hating the feeling, the sense of oppression he brought out in her.

"Really?" she said brightly, buttoning her blouse, realizing with perverse disappointment that he didn't even notice. "I gathered you were insisting on your innocence."

His faint smile should have warned her. "Merely a figure of speech. I didn't realize you were familiar with my case."

She shrugged, refusing to be intimidated. "Actually, I'm not, compared to most of the world. I don't like horror stories, and I was never fond of Stephen King."

"If you think Stephen King is frightening, you should try reality some time."

"I try to avoid it. At least, Sean's version of reality. Life doesn't have to be that unpleasant."

"Sometimes there's no escape."

The conversation was getting odder by the moment, the two of them, conversing in her father's deserted kitchen about death and murder when they hadn't even been introduced. "It's none of my concern whether you butchered your wife and children," she said, her own words shocking her. "I don't want to hear about it."

"Don't worry, I wasn't about to confess," he said in a cool, meditative voice. "You're right, it's none of your business. Unless, of course, I felt the sudden urge to repeat my heinous crime. After all, we're alone in the apartment, and your father won't be back for hours."

"Are you threatening me?"

"I'm suggesting that you might benefit by being a little less trusting."

"I don't trust you, Mr. Tiernan," she said briskly. "I'm not an idiot. I just don't think you're going to take a gun to me. If you've been around Sean and haven't resorted to your murderous ways, then I'd think I'd be relatively safe."

"Maybe I only like to kill women," he said. "And it was a butcher knife, not a gun."

Chicken grease wasn't the best choice on an empty stomach. Cass wondered for a moment what would happen if she threw up, right in front of the rumpled elegance of Richard Tiernan. Probably nothing. He looked like a man who didn't faze easily.

"Did you do it?"

There was nothing pleasant in his cynical smile. "Ask your father," he said.

"Sean doesn't have a great allegiance to the truth." She moved then, reaching behind her to switch on the overhead lights, flooding the room with brightness. It dispelled the physical shadows. It didn't dispel the emotional ones.

"So I've noticed," Richard said. "What about you?"

"Oh, I worship the truth. The one benefit of a typically dysfunctional upbringing—I always say what I think and I never lie."

"I'm not so sure I think that would qualify as a benefit. Lies can be quite useful."

"I'm sure they can." She sounded starched and repressive, like the old maid Sean frequently accused her of being. At least she didn't sound frightened. "What are you doing here?"

"Didn't you realize? I'm living here."

She should have known. It was just the sort of thing Sean would do, give houseroom to a convicted murderer and then fail to tell his daughter about it. "For how long?"

Tiernan shrugged. "Until they send me back to jail, I presume. Your father wants my help on his newest project."

"A book proving your innocence?"

His smile was no more than a faint curve of his mobile mouth. "That would seem logical, wouldn't it?"

"You're not very optimistic about staying out of jail. What if your appeal works?"

"I won't be holding my breath." He moved away from her, heading toward the refrigerator. "Does your father know you're here yet?"

"I met him as he was leaving."

"And he didn't tell you I was up here?"

"He didn't." Cass couldn't keep the aggrieved tone out of her voice. She should have been used to Sean by now. He'd sacrifice his own mother for a good story. A disappointing daughter would be no sacrifice at all.

He closed the refrigerator, turned around, and leaned against it, looking at her. "Interesting," he murmured. "Do you know why you're here?"

Something in his tone of voice startled her. "That's an odd question. I'm here to visit my father," she said.

"Just a spur of the moment thing?"

"No. Mabry called and asked me to come. She said he hadn't been feeling well, but I assumed that wasn't true. Sean's never been sick a day in his life. Are you suggesting there's another reason I'm here?"

"I'm not suggesting a thing." He pushed away from the refrigerator, moving past her toward the back of the kitchen. "Ask your father when he comes home."

"I have a lot of things to ask him."

He looked over his shoulder at her, and his smile was oddly, chillingly sweet. "I imagine you do." And then he left her, without another word.

Cass stood alone in the kitchen, still dazed from the strange encounter. Richard Tiernan was unlike anyone she'd ever met in her life, but then, as far as she knew she'd never met a murderer before. He'd disappeared in the direction of the back of the apartment, and she could only assume he was staying in her half brother Colin's old room. That, or the study, and Sean barely allowed anyone inside the room, much less let them sleep there.

She had a number of options. The first, and most appealing, was to put on her shoes, her coat, grab her suitcase, and walk out the door. Sean was manipulating again, and while Cass had learned to withstand all but his most masterful schemes, she wasn't sure she was up to dealing with the added complication of Richard Tiernan.

Because she had no doubt whatsoever that he had something to do with why she was here. She'd been maneuvered by an expert, and if she had any sense of self-preservation whatsoever, she'd get the hell out of there.

Of course, that would mean not finding out what Sean wanted from her. And if Cass had one abiding weakness, it was her curiosity. She couldn't stand not knowing, even the most insignificant detail.

She also didn't fancy rooming with a man who'd taken a butcher knife to his wife and children. His wife had been pregnant at the time, hadn't she? The thought sent chills of horror through her. Sean might like to flirt with the very edge of madness—Cass much preferred comfort and safety.

She would wait until Mabry and Sean returned

from the doctor. She'd spend the night, make a graceful escape the next morning, and leave Sean to his own devices. If Richard Tiernan decided to continue his murderous rampage, there wouldn't be anything Cass could do to stop him.

He didn't look like a murderer. A butcher, a man who'd committed the foulest crime imaginable.

But he didn't look like the boy next door, either. He looked like a man intimately acquainted with death and horror. A man capable of making a pact with the devil, only to find that the price was too high to pay.

She dismissed the notion, giving herself a brisk shake. She was, after all, her father's daughter, and fully capable of letting her imagination run away with her. Richard Tiernan was another of her father's dangerous characters, in the flesh this time, but nothing to do with her.

Mabry had redecorated recently, and Cass wasn't sure she liked the change to her old bedroom. Gone was the beautiful simplicity of the shaker furniture, which had in turn, replaced her French provincial four-poster. Mabry had gone in for early Gothic, with oversize dark furniture, a dynasty-founding bed, and a green-gilt wallpaper that looked as if it came from a Venetian palazzo. Even the tall window overlooking Park Avenue was swathed in dark green velvet drapes, and the gloom was palpable. She looked around her, knowing instinctively that she was no longer alone.

"How do you like it?"

"Like what, Sean?" At least her father hadn't startled her the way Tiernan had. She turned to glower at him. "Your houseguest, or Mabry's vampire decor?"

"Oh, I tend to think it looks a bit like a Victorian bordello," Sean said airily, sauntering in. "You know I don't interfere with her hobbies."

"What kind of room does Richard Tiernan have? Something with barred windows, to make him feel more at home?"

Sean clucked disapprovingly. "You're getting sour in your old age, darling. Don't you have any compassion for the poor man?"

"I have more compassion for his wife," she said tartly.

"He's the victim of a grave miscarriage of justice . . ." Sean declaimed, but Cass interrupted him.

"I don't think you believe that."

"How do you know what I believe?"

"Let me correct that. I don't think you care, one way or the other. As long as it makes a good book, that's all that matters to you."

Sean's smile was self-deprecating, charming, the sort that would melt the stoniest heart. Cass had learned to resist it years ago. "I'm a slave to my muse," he said. "And that's why you're here."

"I'm not going to be a slave to your muse as well."

"Cassie, darling, you never fail to make me laugh. I need your help, not your disapproval."

"You should have learned by now that one doesn't preclude the other."

Sean beamed at her. "Bless you, darling."

Cass perched gingerly on the high bed. "So what do you want from me, Sean? And don't give me some runaround about you being sick—I wouldn't believe that for a moment."

Sean grinned. "Of course not, love. It's the book that I need you for."

"About Richard Tiernan?"

"Who else? The truth. Complete, simple, compelling. Stark, even. I need an editor . . . God, I never thought I'd admit such a thing. But all the testimony, the witnesses, are such a mess. You should see my office. I need you to organize it, pare it down, while I work with Richard."

"You think you're going to be able to clear his name? I don't know if even the great Sean O'Rourke is a good enough writer to save his life."

"Always the kind word," Sean said. "You let me worry about Richard's part in the book. I understand perfectly that you wouldn't want anything to do with him. You always were such a shy, nervy little thing."

Cass, who was five feet nine and well-rounded, had never considered herself shy, nervy, or little in her entire life, but she didn't bother correcting Sean. Her father had a habit of arranging reality to suit himself. "I've got a job, Sean."

"You've got scads of vacation time, I checked," he countered. "Surely you can give your poor old da a few weeks? Think of the glory of it, the two of us working together on my . . . finest piece of writing in decades. If you don't care about me, how can the professional side of you resist?"

"I care about you, Sean. I just don't want to fall for any of your stunts."

"No stunts, darling, I promise you. Just the two of us, working together."

"The three of us," she corrected sourly.

"You'll do it, then?"

She glanced up at him. If she didn't know better, she would have thought that Sean was almost anxious about her answer. Sean O'Rourke wasn't the kind of man who asked for anything, or allowed himself to care about the answer. He considered himself inviolate, omnipotent, with the women of his family and most other mortals put on earth to serve his genius. That he did so without alienating them was a testament to his brilliance.

But he wanted her. For the first time since she could remember, Sean needed her help, truly needed it. And she was far too human not to respond. "I'll do it," she said. "I can give you a couple of weeks."

"I'll need at least two months . . ."

"A couple of weeks," she said firmly. "And then I'm gone."

"We'll deal with you leaving when the time

comes," Sean said, typically oblivious. "In the meantime, let's tell Mabry you're staying. She bet me you'd have left the moment you saw Richard."

"I should have. Don't you think you should have warned me he was up here?" She followed Sean's sturdy little figure out into the hallway.

"Nonsense," said Sean. "Why would I need to warn you? I'm surprised you even recognized him. You don't usually pay attention to mundane considerations like tabloid murders."

"I saw *People* magazine on my way up here."

"Populist trash," her father sniffed.

"And how will your book differ?"

"Because I'm an artist," he said simply. "Mabry, she's going to stay!" he announced, sailing into the huge living room.

At least this hadn't changed appreciably since Cass had last been there. Still the same clean white walls, the Southwest furniture. Her stepmother lay stretched out on a rustic white sofa that was far more comfortable than it looked. Mabry's endless legs were encased in white cotton as well, her corn-silk hair hung with precision to her broad shoulders, her angular face, which had graced the cover of every major magazine in the world, was ageless. She could have been as young as twenty-five, though Cass suspected forty was more like it. Since Mabry considered her age to be a state secret, she would never know the truth.

"He talked you into it, then?" Mabry murmured, holding out her hand as Cass leaned down to kiss her perfect cheek.

"I never could say no to him," she said, noting with distant concern that up close it was Mabry who looked ill. There were shadows under her limpid blue eyes, a haunted expression on her perfect face, and the hand that held hers trembled slightly. Damn Richard Tiernan, and damn Sean, for putting them in this situation.

"That's your father's problem, Cass," Mabry said easily, and that flash of intensity might never have existed. "No one ever says no to him. He's never had to learn any discipline."

"Bullshit," Sean said, moving to the bar. "Can I get you something, Cassie? None of that white wine crap, I mean a real drink."

"It's early . . ."

"The sun's over the yardarm," he said, pouring himself a tall, dark glass of Irish whiskey, neat.

"Nothing for me," Cass said firmly, taking a seat beside Mabry. "What did the doctor say?"

"He won't tell me," Mabry said.

"Nothing to tell, darling. He said I'm as strong as a horse, and I'd make it another sixty-five years without any problem, as long as I kept on the way I am."

"You're kidding!" Cass said.

Sean's smile was beatific. "Drink in moderation," he said, holding aloft his dark glass, "good food, sex"—he smirked at the elegant Mabry—

"and work. That's what a man needs in order to have a good life."

"What about family? Children?" Cass pointed out.

"Them, too," Sean agreed as an afterthought. "And that's what I have. My older daughter, here by my side. The only thing that would make it better would be if Colin and Francesca were here as well. Particularly Francesca. Your baby sister is a constant delight, Cass. It wounds me that her mother keeps her several continents away from me."

"Alba lives in Italy," Cass said. "Your own fault for marrying a contessa."

"No. My fault for divorcing her," Sean said, momentarily chastened. Then he glanced at the phlegmatic Mabry. "Still, life has been very generous with me. Good company, good work, good food, interesting conversation. What more could I ask?" He wandered back toward the bar, tipping another few inches of dark whiskey into his glass. "Speaking of interesting conversation, I'll leave you two alone to gossip. I know you want to talk about me."

"Believe it or not, Sean, we have other things of interest to discuss," Mabry murmured, but Sean, as always, was oblivious, disappearing down the hall, whistling under his breath.

"It's good to see you, Mabry," Cass said.

Mabry surveyed her silently, ignoring the polite

phrase. "Are you certain you're willing, Cassie? I don't want him putting pressure on you."

"Sean exists to put pressure on people. If I don't like it I can always leave. Sneak out in the middle of the night, taking the silver," she said cheerfully. "What in the world got into you when you redecorated my bedroom?"

"I was depressed," Mabry said flatly.

"Why? You don't usually let things bother you."

"Mortality," Mabry said in a quiet voice. "It affects us all. I'm getting old, Sean is getting old, people are dying."

"You shouldn't have Tiernan around. He's enough to give anyone a case of nervous prostration. The man is quite . . . terrifying."

"I didn't think you were so gullible." There was a faint thread of disapproval in Mabry's voice.

"He's hardly my nominee for family man of the year."

"Don't jump to conclusions," Mabry said. "Anyway, this started before your father's current fascination." She glanced across the room at her reflection. "I'm thinking of getting a face-lift." She stroked her unlined throat.

"It's bound to look better than my room," Cass said.

Mabry managed to smile. "Don't worry about Richard, Cassie. He may be rather intimidating, but he's not going to hurt you."

"You don't believe he killed his wife and children? And weren't there rumors that he'd killed a whole string of women? You think he's innocent?"

"I didn't say that," Mabry temporized.

Cassie felt an involuntary shudder run down her spine, and she wished she'd accepted the drink her father offered her. "You *do* think he killed his family?"

"I didn't say that, either. I really don't know. I just don't think he's going to hurt anyone else. If he did it, he had his reasons."

"Are you crazy? What reason could a man have for slaughtering his family?" Cassie demanded, horrified.

Mabry shrugged her elegant shoulders. "I wouldn't know, and I wouldn't want to guess. All I know is that the man, right now, is no danger to anyone. Except, perhaps, himself."

The image of the tall, haunted figure in her father's kitchen came back to her, with the dark eyes and twisted smile. Danger was exactly the word she would have used for Richard Tiernan.

But then, Mabry had the best instincts when it came to people that Cassie had ever known. She had a rare sense of who you could trust, and who was a danger. If Mabry trusted Tiernan, then perhaps there really was nothing to worry about. If you forgot about the man's eyes. Or the elegant, tortured grace of his body. Or his mouth . . .

What the hell was she thinking about? "All right," she said. "I'll take your word for it that he isn't going to come crawling into my bedroom and slit my throat. Why were you and Sean so determined to get me up here? Why that cock-and-bull story about Sean being sick? It's you, isn't it? Something's wrong with you?"

"Don't be ridiculous," Mabry said. "I don't get sick."

"There's nothing wrong with Sean."

"No," Mabry said, but something in her voice caught Cassie's attention.

"There isn't, is there? Sean's not really sick?"

Mabry shrugged again. "He insists he's fine."

"And you don't believe him?"

Mabry turned her perfect profile to the tall expanse of uncurtained windows, and there was a bleak expression on her face. "I don't know what to believe," she said in a quiet voice. "I'm just worried. I don't like his obsession with Richard Tiernan. I don't like the fact that he was so desperate to have you come up here. And he was, Cassie. He may seem like it didn't matter, but it mattered dreadfully. And I don't understand why."

"Belated paternal affection?" Cassie suggested wryly.

"He's always loved you, Cass. You know it as well as I do. He's just not capable of putting someone else's welfare first. He's got blinders on when it comes to his own needs, his own interests. And I'm just afraid that this time he's going to go too far."

"In trying to prove Richard Tiernan is innocent?"

She turned her sorrowful eyes to Cassie. "I don't know," she said. "And that's what scares me half to death."

"What did you think of her?"

Richard didn't move. He was stretched out across the bed, the sunlight streaming in, but there was no heat in the brightness of the March day. He thought about it, as he'd thought about nothing else since he'd walked into the cavernous old kitchen and seen her.

"She's not the way you described her."

O'Rourke closed the door behind him, moving in and settling his sturdy bulk into the chair in the corner. The glass in his hand was over-full, he slopped some of it, and the room was filled with the sweet-acrid scent of Irish whiskey. "I'm a writer, laddie," he said, affronted. "I've got the awards to prove it. Who the hell are you to tell me I can't describe my own daughter?"

"You said she was tall and plain and unimaginative."

"Did I now?" Sean considered it. "You saw her photograph, you knew what you were getting into. And she *is* tall."

"She is. But she's certainly not plain. And she took one look at me and her imagination went soaring. I think she was convinced I was going to rape and murder her right there on the kitchen floor."

"Now why would the question of rape come

into it?" Sean asked softly. "Did you rape your wife before you killed her?"

Richard ignored the question. "I calmed her down, but she's not too happy with you for sending her up here without any warning. I don't think it's going to work."

"And why not? Don't you think I'm capable of controlling my womenfolk?"

"No one's capable of controlling women," Richard said. "I don't know who'd be fool enough to try. She's going to realize why you brought her here, and she's never going to forgive you."

Sean leaned back, considering it. "I brought her here to help me on the book," he said. "I'm giving her the chance of a lifetime, and if she had an ounce of ambition, she'd jump at it."

"She doesn't strike me as particularly ambitious."

"No, damn it. The girl's a changeling. Her harpy of a mother would have done anything to get ahead, and so would I. But Cassie's more interested in the quality of life, not the quantity."

"I would think that would be admirable."

"You're getting neither, Tiernan," Sean pointed out. "You still haven't told me what you think of her. Will she do?"

Richard closed his eyes for a moment, picturing her. She was tall, lushly built, a far cry from his rail-thin wife. Her red hair had framed her startled face like a halo, and her eyes were bright, wary, and completely vulnerable. He'd taken one look at her, knowing why Sean had brought her, an editorial slave to his muse, a sexual distraction for his reluctant houseguest. He'd seen her, and been consumed with an irrational, unspeakable lust.

It was the first time he'd felt anything even remotely resembling sexual desire in well more than a year. Not since he knelt in the blood over Diana's body.

And the longing he'd felt for Cassidy Roarke had been instantaneous, blinding, overpowering.

Dangerous.

"You're willing to make her the virgin sacrifice?" Richard said.

"She's hardly a virgin, man," Sean snorted. "And I'm willing, yes. Will she do?"

He thought of her mouth, soft, damp, he thought of her unbuttoned blouse that she thought he hadn't noticed. He thought of her long narrow feet.

"She'll do," he said. "God help her."

CHAPTER 3

There was blood, everywhere. The smell of it assaulted her, thick, metallic, the feel of it was black on her hands. There were children surrounding her, crying voicelessly, and the blood poured from their wounds, drenching her.

She knelt, a penitent. The woman stood over her, pale, dying, her mouth open in a silent scream, and she pointed an accusing hand. Cassidy didn't turn. She knew what she would see behind her, looming over her, the knife upraised. She didn't want to watch, to look into his mad, dark eyes as the knife fell, and she joined them, the silent, the dying.

But he was close, so close. She felt the pull, the draw of him, even as she knew that to turn was to face her death. She couldn't resist. She felt his hands on her shoulders, strong, and there was no weapon. She turned, looking up at him, and screamed.

The sound tore her from sleep, and she sat bolt upright. Outside she could hear the ceaseless traffic of the never-ending New York City night, inside the cavernous old apartment her scream still echoed.

She scooted back in her bed, up against the carved headboard, trying to calm her panicked breathing, her racing heart. She couldn't remember when she'd last had a nightmare. Probably when she was a child, still living with her incessantly battling parents. To be sure, in the six years since she'd been on her own, she hadn't been plagued with bad dreams.

This one more than made up for it. It was no wonder—she'd been thrown into the company of a murderer, one who showed absolutely no remorse, and her father's twisted sense of humor only made things worse.

At least she hadn't seen Richard Tiernan again. Sean took his womenfolk, as he termed them, out to dinner to celebrate Cass's defeat, or so she thought of it, and there'd been no mention of his houseguest joining them.

It hadn't helped. She couldn't stop thinking of him. Even eating mediocre food at the Russian Tea Room and watching Sean preen hadn't been enough to distract her from the memory of those haunted eyes.

There was no sign of him when they returned. Cass had curled up in the white sofa, nursing the Irish Mist Sean had forced on her, and wondered what Tiernan was doing. And what he had done.

She shoved her hair away from her face now,

taking deep, calming breaths. Her room was pitch-black—the heavy velvet draperies shut out the light, if not the noise of the city. It felt like a tomb. She leaned over and turned on the lamp, but the sight of all the Gothic splendor surrounding her wasn't cheering.

She dragged herself out of bed, fumbling around for her watch. It was quarter past three in the morning, and there was no way she was going to sleep without a little outside help.

She knew there was any number of choices. Hot milk, the contents of Sean's liquor cabinet, the contents of Sean's medicine cabinet were all available. Hot milk would take the longest and taste the worst, and the kitchen was too close to Tiernan's bedroom. If she had any sense at all, she'd head for the chemical response to nightmares that was a family tradition.

But there was sense, and there was sense. The memory of Sean's drunken brawls was too fresh in her mind. Her mother's slurred whine lay at the back of her thoughts as well. If she had to resort to sleeping pills or liquor to make it through the night, then she damned well wasn't going to stay there.

The kitchen was dark and deserted, the flooring cool beneath her bare feet. Cass leaned against the counter, arms wrapped around her waist, as she watched her mug of milk heat in the microwave while she called herself an idiot.

Richard Tiernan wasn't going to emerge from

his lair, not at that hour of the night. If he did, all she had to do was grab that wreath of garlic hanging on the wall and ward him off.

Her smile caught her in the midst of a yawn, just as the microwave beeped. She pushed her tangle of hair away from her face in a sleepy gesture, reaching for her milk, and then froze.

"Nightmares?" said Richard Tiernan.

She could smell the blood. For one brief, crazy second she could smell death. And then sanity reared its blessed head.

He was standing in the door, where she'd first seen him, watching her. His hands were tucked in his jeans pockets, and his dark hair was ruffled, perhaps from sleep. Apart from that, he looked the same. Lost, dark, and dangerous.

She pulled her oversize sweater around her in what she hoped was a suitably casual gesture. She hadn't underestimated his unnerving effect on her. Damn Sean for getting her into this! "Not really," she said coolly. "I guess I'm not used to the city noise. I seldom have trouble sleeping."

"Lucky you," he murmured.

She put the mug of warm milk to her mouth. It was so hot she could feel the steam burning her lips, and she paused, feeling like a fool. On the one hand, she'd look ridiculous if she put the mug down without drinking. On the other, she wasn't sure she wanted to scald her esophagus in her effort to appear unmoved by his presence.

He solved the matter quite neatly. While she

stood there, uncertain, he walked into the room, crossed to her, and took the mug of milk from her hand. "You'll burn yourself," he said gently.

He was too close to her. She wished this were simply an extension of her nightmare. She wouldn't even mind the blood, as long as it wasn't real. But it was. Richard Tiernan was standing within inches of her, towering over her respectable five feet nine, invading her space, close, too close, and she could feel the heat of his body in the cool night kitchen, smell the faint tang of whiskey on his breath.

She took a step backward, away from him, not caring if she looked like an hysterical idiot. He simply looked at her and smiled, a slow, cynical smile. "Your father says you're going to stay and help us."

Us. It was an unnerving word. She considered denying it, but she wasn't a coward. She didn't run away from her family demands when the going got rough. If she said yes, or said no, she lived with the consequences.

One of which was the man standing far too still in the middle of her father's kitchen. A man whose power to disturb her went far beyond the crimes he was accused and convicted of committing. "Yes," she said.

"We need all the help we can get."

"We" was just as bad as us. "I'll do my best," she said inanely. Maybe that was the way to protect herself from his insidious effect on her. Be

as trite and ingenuous as she could be. As corny,
as breathtakingly guileless . . .

"I'm sure you will," he said, with just the faintest trace of a drawl in his voice. To her horror he
lifted the mug of milk to her mouth, holding it
there. "It's cool enough now," he said.

The challenge was obvious, even with the
unreadable expression on his still, dark face. It
was a challenge she couldn't back away from. Not
with his dark eyes watching her.

She put her mouth against the mug and drank,
when she knew she shouldn't. She should spit it
out, tell him she didn't need it after all, and bid
him a polite but firm good night.

Ah, but she'd been safe all her adult life. She
drank from the mug in his hands, letting the thick
warm milk slide down her throat.

When she'd drained it, she looked at him defiantly. *I'm not afraid of you*, she thought. Knowing
it was a lie.

For the first time his slight smile reached those
dark, haunted eyes. "You have a milk mustache,"
he said.

She took another step back, this time coming
up against the cabinets, as she backhanded her
mouth, wiping the milk away before other, more
troubling suggestions came to her mind. "I think
I'm ready to sleep now," she said brightly, only a
faint tremor in her voice.

"Are you?"

"I'll see you in the morning."

There was only one problem with her firm dismissal. He stood between her and freedom. She was literally backed into a corner, backed by her own nervousness, and he'd advanced on her. She raised her chin, looking at him with completely false calm, and waited for him to move out of the way.

He didn't. Not for an agonizingly long time. He let his gaze fall, travel down the length of her, from her wild mane of hair, down the front of her plain white nightgown to the tips of her bare feet. There was nothing even remotely suggestive about the cotton nightgown or the baggy sweater she'd pulled over it, nothing erotic about bare feet. His eyes slid down her body, and she was burning up.

And then he stepped back. "In the morning," he said. And left her there, disappearing back into the shadows of the night kitchen.

She let out her breath, realizing for the first time she'd been holding it. Just as she'd had a virginal hand at her throat, to ward off demons. She was shaking, she realized absently.

She pushed away from the counter, still tasting the creaminess of the hot milk in her throat. She walked into the darkened living room, reached for her father's bottle of good Irish, and poured herself a stiff drink, tossing it back with only a faint choke, letting it burn its way through the milk, through the memory.

There was no key to the lock on her door. She'd never realized it before, never needed one before.

She needed one now. Not that Richard Tiernan was going to come wandering down the long hallway, past Sean and Mabry's bedroom, to sneak into the Gothic nightmare and have his wicked way with her.

But there was no way she was going to go to sleep without something pulled in front of the door. Even if it was one of those mock-baronial chairs. First thing in the morning she'd go in search of a key.

When she climbed into her bed, the noise from the city seemed to have faded. It was slowly approaching dawn; soon the city would awake in earnest, and there'd be no rest for the weary. She lay back and stared at the carved bed, barely taking it in. She could call Emmie, ask her to manufacture an emergency that would force her to leave on the first train south. She'd even take a plane in order to get the hell away from here.

But as soon as the idea came to her, she dismissed it. She wasn't a quitter, a coward. And Sean, for the first time in his self-centered, misbegotten life, needed her. If she went now, he'd never ask again.

She closed her eyes, listening to the night. The sounds of the old building, the distant roar of the subways deep underground, the squeal of the busses, the clang and rattle of garbage cans. The city was coming awake.

And she was going to sleep. And this time,

damn it, there would be no dreams. Of blood, or death.

Or Richard Tiernan's haunted eyes.

Not a qualm, he told himself, listening for her footsteps in the thickly carpeted hallway. Not a doubt, not a second thought.

He leaned against the closed doorway, thinking about her feet. He'd never thought he could consider bare feet erotic. Everything about Cassidy Roarke was profoundly sensual, from her blaze of flyaway hair to her ripe, luscious body, to her innocent face. Like a Botticelli angel, unaware of the havoc she caused. He'd never felt such lust in his life.

He used that lust for his rationalization. He never thought he'd feel even the faintest trace of interest in sex again, which, considering he was probably going to spend his last few months on earth solely in the company of men, was just as well.

But he'd taken one look at the photo Sean kept on his cluttered desk, and it had been like a physical blow. Feelings, something he'd fought against for more than a year, flooded in before he was able to slam them down again. Something about her face, with the cloud of hair, the stubborn mouth, the wary eyes, the faint, troubled smile had called to him, when he thought nothing could ever reach him again.

He was going to use her. Sacrifice her, if need

be, for his needs. Not for one moment was he going to consider her future, her well-being. In the darkest time of his life, he had seen her picture and with it had come light. If he had to burn her out, he would do so, and not count the cost. Anything to dispel the blackness.

The photograph had disappeared from Sean's desk today. He'd gone looking for it while the happy little family was out at dinner, finally finding it in the bottom of Sean's sock drawer, beneath the mismatched hand-knit argyles from the Auld Sod. Richard had taken it, hidden it beneath his own clothes. He could only draw one logical conclusion—Sean didn't want his daughter to know he kept a silver-framed picture of her on his desk.

He pushed away from the door and pulled out the picture, staring down into Cassidy Roarke's eyes. She'd been mesmerizing in the photo—now that he'd seen her in the flesh the photograph took on an even more powerful significance. He didn't believe in coincidence. She hadn't come into his life for no reason. She was there, for him. And he would use her, no matter what the consequences.

Cass followed the rich smell of French roast coffee, the irresistible, seldom-indulged scent of bacon and eggs. She found those things in the kitchen, filled with light from the bright day and the brightness of the one person she hadn't seen yet. "Bridget!" she cried, flinging her arms around the woman who'd been the bastion of sanity in her childhood.

Bridget put her burly arms around Cass, patting her. She smelled like vanilla and coffee and soap, that familiar-Bridget smell, and for the first time since she'd decided to come to New York, Cass felt a sense of well-being. "And where else would I be, missy?" Bridget demanded sternly. "You don't think I'm the type to retire and sit on my can all day, do you? I've been working all my seventy-six years, and I don't intend to stop now. As long as your father's raising hell and your stepma is more decorative than useful, I'll be here."

Mabry, who was comfortably seated at the kitchen table, smiled sweetly, taking no offense. "Actually, Bridget doesn't come in as often as she used to, but once she heard you were coming, there was no holding her back."

"Faith, they'd let you starve to death," Bridget said sternly, putting Cass at arm's length and peering up at her. "You look as if you'd lost weight already."

"It's no wonder I love you," Cass said with a grin. "Why don't you tell Sean you're worried I'm too thin?"

"That man!" Bridget said with a sniff. Their enmity was long-standing and mutually enjoyable. "You're not going to pay attention to the taste of a man who's been married five times, are you?"

Mabry smiled sweetly. "But it simply took him five tries to get it right."

"True enough. He certainly started out with two of the worst," Bridget said with the brutal frankness that was her hallmark. "And how is your dear mother? Still drinking too much?"

Cass took the cup of coffee Mabry poured for her. "You know mother. Same as ever. She sends her love."

"Not likely," Bridget said, returning to the stove. Bacon was sizzling in the cast-iron frying pan that had been in Sean's household since the beginning of time. "She's never forgiven me for staying with your father."

Cass took a deep, appreciative sip. She never had the energy to make more than instant coffee on the way to work, and she'd forgotten just how wonderful fresh-brewed could be. "I think they fought more over custody of you than me and Colin," she said ruefully.

"It's possible, knowing the two of them," Bridget said. "They never did have their priorities straight. You still like your eggs fried?"

"I still like everything fried," Cass said mournfully.

"At least I'll have someone to cook for. Mabry there doesn't eat enough to keep a bird alive, and your father's been just as picky recently. As for Richard . . ." Bridget rolled her eyes. "That man is impossible to tempt. I'm counting on you, Cassie, love."

Cass sloshed her coffee as she sat. She very carefully avoided Mabry's curious gaze. "How's that?" she murmured with remarkable innocence.

"He won't eat."

"That's his choice."

Bridget turned on her, fist on one sturdy hip. "Now listen here, missy. You know better than to pass judgment on your fellow man. I raised you better than that. He's a good man."

Cass choked on her coffee. She raised incredulous eyes. "Are we talking about Richard Tiernan? The man convicted of murdering his pregnant wife? The man suspected of killing his children as well? A good man?"

"You know better than to read those kinds of newspapers," the old woman said severely.

"The New York Times?" Cass said.

"Things aren't always what they seem."

"He's told you that, has he?"

"In case you haven't noticed, Bridget," Mabry said in her cool, tranquil voice, "it hasn't been a case of love at first sight." She took another sip of her coffee. "Cassidy doesn't approve of Sean's latest project."

"It's not for me to approve or disapprove."

"No," said Mabry. "It isn't."

"Cassidy!" Sean's voice bellowed through the hallways.

"He's up already?" Cass managed to say in a neutral tone of voice.

"He hasn't been sleeping much," Mabry said. "They've been waiting for you."

They. Another one of those inclusive words, as bad as us or we. They were waiting for her. Her father and Richard Tiernan. And avoiding it would only make things worse, make the tension that was clutching her stomach spread throughout her entire body. Bridget and Mabry were already watching her too closely, and she didn't particularly care to have everyone notice how the very thought of Richard Tiernan unnerved her.

She rose, smiling brightly. "Then I might as well take my coffee into the office."

"What about breakfast?" Bridge demanded from her vigil over the frying pan.

"I'm not hungry," she replied with perfect truthfulness, refilling her coffee cup and escaping before Bridget could screech in outrage.

Out of the frying pan, into the fire. Escaping into the presence of her father and his houseguest was no escape at all. The door to Sean's office was open, and she could smell cigarettes, and coffee. She moved quietly, filling the door, hoping to startle them.

Sean was in the midst of some high-flown fantasy, staring out the window at the New York skyline. Tiernan was sitting in the huge green leather chair that had been in Sean's office since the beginning of time. Cass remembered when she was small, curling up in the warm leather arms of that chair, sleeping. It had been her favorite place in the world. Tiernan didn't turn, but she knew perfectly well he knew she was there. He seemed to have a sixth sense.

She wanted to order him out of her chair. Instead she simply stood in the doorway and cleared her throat.

Sean whirled around, an accusing expression on his florid face. "About time you woke from your beauty slumber, Cassie," he said. "You never used to be such a slothful creature. We have work to do, and time's a wasting."

"Is it?" She carefully avoided Tiernan's gaze. He was dressed in jeans and a cotton sweater against the cool morning air. She was wearing the same thing. He had a mug of black coffee in his hand. She drank hers black as well.

"You're the one who's so determined to get back to Baltimore, though why any sane person would choose to live in Baltimore when they have the option of New York is beyond me," Sean declaimed. "We're planning on changing your mind, aren't we, Richard? Make it impossible for you to leave."

"Impossible," Richard echoed.

She couldn't help it, she threw him a wary glance as she moved to her father's littered desk. He met the gaze blandly enough, but she wasn't so gullible she didn't recognize the challenge. The threat.

"I have a job," she said mildly, glancing at one

stack of papers that looked like official court transcripts.

"You could take a leave of absence."

"I could. I don't want to. I have plans, things I want to do with my life."

"Richard doesn't."

Cass glanced at him. He was leaning back in the chair, *her* chair, looking faintly amused at the father-daughter quarrel. "That's hardly my fault, is it?" she said, knowing she sounded childish. "Is it yours?"

She was hoping to provoke a reaction from him. But Richard Tiernan was schooled in the art of concealing his feelings. He simply gazed at her out of those dark, disturbing eyes. "What do you think?"

The silence between them was a palpable thing. She wanted to look away from him, but she couldn't. His gaze caught hers, held it, and in the background Sean was uncharacteristically silent.

And then the spell was broken. "You're not getting through the day without the breakfast I cooked for you," Bridget announced from the doorway. She stomped into the room and dumped the heavy laden tray on the desk in front of Cassie. The eggs and bacon sat in front of her, still sizzling, but Cass's appetite had long fled.

"Cassie eats too much as it is," Sean protested. "Take it away, you fool woman."

Cass immediately picked up her fork. "I'm hungry," she lied, digging in.

"You're always hungry," Sean said with a sniff. "While I fail to see why you don't have a little more self-control, a little more vanity, I'm at least pleased to see you aren't letting your overwrought imagination get in the way of your appetite."

"Sorry, Sean," she said, forcing herself to tuck into Bridget's food with a semblance of relish. "You haven't been much of a role model when it comes to self-control, and I figure there's already enough vanity in this family."

Richard laughed. Cass lifted her gaze, not recognizing the sound, but there was no mistaking the dark amusement in his eyes. "Your shy daughter's got a wicked tongue on her, Sean," he observed.

"She's inherited some of my gifts, at least," Sean said proudly. "Even if there are times when she's hopelessly middle-class. I live in dread of the day she'll decide to get married and have the requisite two point three children. Don't expect me to baby-sit, Cassie, love. I'd probably murder 'em."

The silence that fell was absolute. Cassie put her fork down, telling herself she wouldn't throw up the bacon and eggs she'd just forced herself to eat.

She also had no intention of meeting Tiernan's ironic gaze. There was a limit to her self-discipline, after all. Instead she glanced at her unrepentant father.

Sean simply shrugged. "I've been tactless,

haven't I? I can't spend my time watching what I say," he added. "Richard's used to me. I don't offend you, do I, my boy?"

Cass couldn't picture anyone less like a boy. She forced herself to look at him, but his face was cool, reserved, unfeeling. "You don't offend me, Sean. Though I expect you'll keep trying."

Sean lit another of the thick, unfiltered cigarettes he'd given up years ago. "You know me well."

Cassie pushed the tray away. "When did you start smoking again?"

"Life's too short for self-denial," he announced.

"If you keep smoking those things, it's bound to get a lot shorter."

Sean rolled his eyes. "You see what I have to put up with? Next thing I know, she'll be grabbing the drink out of me very hands and singing temperance songs. I'll make a deal with you, Cassie love. You keep your opinion of my little indulgences to yourself, and I won't make any more remarks about your healthy girlish figure."

He'd done it on purpose. Cass had known her father all her life, she should have been used to it by now. He'd done it to embarrass her, to make Richard Tiernan cast those far too observant eyes over her body and decide just how healthy it was.

She didn't blush, a wonder, given her pale skin and rising temper. She didn't pull the oversize cotton sweater around her, or cross her arms over her chest, or do anything more significant than glower.

"It's a bargain," she growled.

Sean's smile was beatific. "That's settled then. I'm off. You and Richard can start to work without me."

He was halfway out the door before Cass let out a muffled shriek of rage and panic. "Just where do you think you're going?" she demanded.

"Another doctor's appointment, love," he murmured, and Cass knew it was a bald-faced lie. "The two of you will have plenty to do, organizing all the papers."

"But . . ."

"Ask him what really happened that night," Sean called over his shoulder, his cigarette smoke trailing behind him. "And take notes. I want to see if he can keep his story straight."

It took every ounce of Cass's pride to force her to meet Richard Tiernan's cool gaze. "He's impossible," she said.

Tiernan rose, moving across the room. She'd forgotten how tall he was, and what a lethal sort of grace infused his body. He walked to the door, and closed it. Closing them in.

He leaned against it, and there was an ironic expression on his face as he watched her.

"Are you going to take notes?" he asked softly.

She stared at him, bemused, distracted for a moment. "Why?" she asked inanely.

"Because I'm willing to talk."

She wasn't ready for this. She was suddenly very cold, in that elegant, book-lined office that still smelled of bacon and Sean's cigarettes.

She pushed the tray away, hoping he wouldn't notice that her hands were trembling. "All right," she said. She schooled her nervousness, glancing up at him. "Are you going to tell me the truth?"

His smile was devastating. She'd heard that sociopaths had a certain charm, but that was nothing compared to the man in front of her. She could feel the pull, and she wanted nothing more than to smile back, to move toward him.

"No," he said, very gently. And instead of reaching for her, he went and sat down in the green leather chair once more.

CHAPTER 4

Richard Tiernan never thought he'd look forward to spinning that endless pack of lies. He'd told it so often, for police, lawyers, investigators, in-laws. He knew all the details—they were engraved on what passed for his heart. He'd told them to Sean O'Rourke, and watched him try to trip him up. It had become a game between them, one Sean relished and Richard endured. As he endured life.

But faced with the woman sitting at Sean's oversize, messy desk, he found he could summon at least a trace of interest. Just how much could he tell her? How close to the truth could he skate, and when would that reluctant fascination turn to horror?

He needed to find out. He leaned back in the leather chair, stretching his legs out in front of him, watching her. "My wife was a very fragile creature," he said, keeping his voice carefully neutral. That much was the truth, at least. "She was an only child—frail and blond and high-strung. Like a fairy-tale princess."

For a moment Cass just looked at him. And then she pulled a pad of legal paper in front of her and began to write, and if he hadn't been watching her so closely, he wouldn't have seen the frown that wrinkled her brow.

"She was an army brat. But not just any army brat. Her father was General Amberson Scott."

She knew the name—he could tell by the faint pause in her note taking. Most people did. His father-in-law was a war hero, one of the media darlings of the Gulf conflict and a tough-talking man who knew his way around politics far too well. "They were devoted to each other," he said flatly. "Diana's mother is a quiet, unassuming woman, content to follow in her husband's shadow. Diana was their darling, pampered, petted, adored."

"In other words your wife was a spoiled brat," Cassidy said, her eyes meeting his briefly.

"You might say so," he agreed. "But she was a beautiful, charming spoiled brat. We were very happy."

"How nice."

He wanted to grin at the faintly acid tone in her voice. She was surprisingly tough, Cassidy Roarke was, but then, he'd hoped for that much. She'd need to be tough when he got through with her.

"The general approved of me, her mother adored me, and Diana enjoyed being the perfect wife and mother. She loved her children." He kept his voice cool.

She flinched at the mention of his children. He liked that. And then she raised her eyes to meet his, fearlessly. He liked that even more. "You had two," she said.

"Amy and Seth. Amy was five when she died, Seth was three. And Diana was pregnant."

"I remember." Her voice was soft, reluctantly sympathetic. As if she could hear the pain in his voice. Silly, really, when he knew perfectly well there was no pain in his voice at all. No feeling whatsoever.

She dropped her eyes again, looking at the notes. "You lived in Bedford."

"We had a very comfortable life. Diana's mother came from old money, and Diana had already inherited quite a bit from her grandmother. And I worked hard."

"At what?"

"Your research didn't tell you that much?"

"I didn't do research," she shot back. "As a matter of fact, I wanted to avoid hearing anything at all about your case."

"You didn't succeed."

"I know. What was your job?"

"That doesn't make the tabloids too often, does it?" he said calmly. "I was a professor at a small liberal arts college. Generally innocuous profession, even if it kept me busier than my family would have liked."

"I wouldn't have thought you'd make a very good teacher," she said.

"Oh, but I was. Most of the female undergraduates thought I was fascinating."

"Did you do anything about that?"

"Do you mean did I fuck them? Or did I kill them?" he asked, leaning back in the chair and watching her.

"Did you cheat on your wife?"

"Read the tabloids," he suggested. "They have all the answers."

She bit her lip, frustrated, and he stared at her for a moment, his eyes on her mouth.

"What happened the day your family . . . died?"

"Was murdered, don't you mean?" He liked watching her squirm. Not very noble of him, but then, he took what enjoyment he could find nowadays. "I came home early that Friday afternoon. Diana was planning on taking the children on a visit to her parents the next morning, and I wanted to make sure she had everything she needed. The door was open when I got home, which was odd. Diana had always been pathologically paranoid about her safety. She never would have left the door open.

"I walked inside, and I found them."

"Them?"

"Diana was lying at the bottom of the stairs. In a pool of blood, quite dead." The lies were starting now, tripping off his tongue with the ease of long practice. "She had a knife in her heart."

He could see Cassidy shiver. "What did you do?"

"I think I must have gone into shock," he said, used to this by now. "I ran up the stairs, looking for the children. I must have gotten some of Diana's blood on my hands, because they found my bloody fingerprints all over the place. I couldn't find the children. When I did . . ." He'd gotten quite good at this part, at making his voice break as he spun the lies.

Cassidy was pale, suffering. He wondered just how far he could push her. "Their bodies were in the bathroom. Just lying there. I don't know what happened next. My mind went blank. When the police arrived I was kneeling by Diana's body, and the children were gone. Someone had removed their bodies, washed the blood away. I couldn't even bury them."

"That's . . . unbelievable," she said in a hushed voice.

"That was the consensus," he drawled, deliberately breaking the mood.

She'd believed him. Been drawn in by the tale, and now he'd snapped her out of it. She stared at him, white-faced with shock, and he could tell she wanted to run. He had that effect on her. He could also tell that she wasn't going to.

"For a while the family pulled together. The general and his wife flew into New York, and we all faced the media circus. Until the investigation kept coming up blank. No one could find any sign of an intruder in the house, and no one could find any trace of my children's bodies."

She didn't flinch this time, though he knew she wanted to. Already she was toughening up. He was going to have to push harder.

"Once I was officially under suspicion things began to change. At first the general was my staunchest defender. It wasn't until the circumstantial evidence started piling up that he began to pull back. Right now he's waging a one-man campaign to get me drawn and quartered. It was no accident that my case went through the New York judicial system in record time. My father-in-law has powerful friends. He wants my head on a platter, and he wants it yesterday."

"Can you blame him? He thinks you murdered his daughter and grandchildren."

"I lost my wife and children," he said coolly. "My heart doesn't bleed for him."

She considered him for a moment. "You said circumstantial evidence. What was that?"

"Motive, opportunity, lack of alibi, physical evidence," he said. "No one else was seen leaving or entering the house that day. The coroner put Diana's time of death as close to the time I was seen coming home as he could possibly manage. My bloody handprints were on the walls, my fingerprints on the murder weapon, which happened to be a butcher knife from my own kitchen."

"And motive?" she asked breathlessly.

His eyes met hers for a still, silent moment.

"I'm known to have a nasty temper. I had a not very discreet affair, and Diana wasn't going on a weekend visit to her family. She was leaving me, and taking the children, and she'd already filed papers trying to deny me access to my children."

"On what grounds?"

"That I beat them."

"Did you?"

"No."

"Then you had nothing to worry about. If there was no sign of physical abuse, then they couldn't keep you away."

He just looked at her. "Maybe not. Unfortunately the jury didn't tend to think I'd be smart enough to figure that out. The prosecution painted me as a violent man, willing to kill my wife and children rather than let them leave me. There were other disappearances as well. The woman I'd been known to have an affair with disappeared around the same time, and the jury was ready to convict me of anything they could."

"Is it true? Are you a violent man, capable of murder?"

He rose then, and leaned across the desk, close enough so that he could smell the coffee on her breath, the scent of her perfume. Another erotic pulse throbbed. "You're going to have to figure that out, aren't you?" he murmured.

She stared up at him, mesmerized. "Why should I?"

"Because you're curious. You can't help yourself, Cassidy. You look at me and wonder whether I'm some kind of monster, who butchered his wife and children, or whether I'm just a poor victim of a crazy judicial system. Your heart wants to bleed for me, I can see it, and you want to believe me, but you can't quite bring yourself to do it. So you're torn. You don't know whether to comfort or revile me. Do you?"

He could see the faint flush of color on her translucent cheekbones, the aching warmth in deep green eyes. "Would you let me comfort you?" she asked, her voice hushed.

It was like a blow, ripping away the layers of protection, the defenses, so that she struck, straight to that dark, empty place that had once been his heart. He stepped back, away from her, away from the dangerous seduction of her compassion, away from the first real threat he'd come across since that night, endless nights ago, when he'd knelt in the pool of his wife's blood and watched her die.

"No," he said. And he turned and left her, almost running, suddenly, irrationally afraid.

"I'm not certain this was such a good idea after all," Mabry said from the open doorway.

Cass looked up from the neatly stacked files of papers on Sean's walnut desk. She'd been at it since Richard Tiernan had abruptly walked out on her—reading, cataloguing, inuring herself to horror.

The initial police report was there, and the coroner's report as well. Diana Scott Tiernan had died of massive blood loss, caused by a slashed aorta. The fetus was approximately seven weeks old, and had suffocated once Diana Tiernan's heart had stopped pumping.

There were signs of a struggle. She was bruised, with small traces of blood under her fingernails. Blood that had matched the scratches on her husband's arms. Scratches he insisted came from an encounter with a stray cat.

Cassidy had read it all with a kind of shocked detachment. These weren't people she knew, she told herself. If she could just manage to convince herself it was all a fiction, an Agatha Christie murder mystery, then the sick burning at the pit of her stomach would leave her.

She glanced up at Mabry's pale, perfect face. "Not a good idea?" she echoed. "Why do you say that? You're the one who got me up here in the first place."

Mabry grimaced. "Sean was determined that you should come and visit, and who can hold out against your father when he gets in his moods?" She drifted into the room with her unconscious, model's grace, deliberately avoiding the green leather chair. Cass wondered why.

"So he's not really been sick? Never has been?" she asked, leaning back.

"I don't know," Mabry said simply. "I do know he's actually gone to the doctor on several occasions, which would have been unheard of when I first met him. He's refused to let me come with him, and when I asked him what was wrong he simply told me it was constipation. And frankly, if there's one thing Sean isn't, it's anal retentive."

"Do you really think he's sick?"

Mabry shoved a slender hand through her perfectly straight hair. "I don't know. But if he is, I still doubt that has anything to do with his determination to have you here."

"And it couldn't be anything as healthy as simply missing his family." Cass stared down at the desk, her voice neutral. It didn't hurt. She'd stopped letting Sean hurt her years ago.

"I don't think so. If it were, he would have made some effort to get Francesca back here as well. You know he dotes on the child."

"I know," Cass said, stifling her unreasoning sense of jealousy. She adored her baby sister, as did they all. She just wished there'd been a time when Sean had thought she was as bright and quick and wonderful. "And just when did Sean come up with the notion that he needed me here? I don't suppose it happened to coincide with Richard Tiernan's release from jail?"

"What was the reason he gave you for wanting you here?"

"To help him on the Tiernan book. He says he's never done nonfiction before, that it's too detailed for his creative brain, and he needs some editorial help."

"And you believe him?" Mabry asked.

Cassie didn't hesitate. "Not for a moment. Sean isn't the kind of person who asks for help, and I'm the last person he'd come to if he was forced to admit he needs it. As for details and facts, when has Sean ever troubled himself about them?"

"He's got a reason for having you here, Cassie. And I don't like it. I don't trust him, or his infatuation with Tiernan's case."

"What do you mean, infatuation?"

"He's obsessed by it. And by Richard himself. He's got more passion, more interest in his work than he's had in years, and it's all due to a horrifying crime. It's bad enough that Sean is living and breathing murder. I don't want you dragged into it as well."

"You think he did it," Cass said flatly. "You really believe Richard Tiernan slaughtered his family. How in God's name can you bear to have him in the house? To talk to him?"

"I didn't say I thought he did it," Mabry said, tossing her famous head of hair.

"Then if you don't . . ."

"I didn't say that, either. I don't know what to believe. All you have to do is look into Richard Tiernan's eyes and you see things you wished you never had to. The kind of things that will haunt you."

Cassidy felt an answering chill run down her spine. Mabry was the least fanciful human being

Cass knew. It was her serenity, her ability to accept things at face value, that made her so restful, and so important to Sean. If she could see ghosts in Richard Tiernan's dark eyes, then ghosts were most definitely there.

She needed to leave. Turn her back on her father the first time he really seemed to need her, and run for safety.

If only she could.

"You've been married to Sean for almost ten years. Surely you know by now there's no getting him to say anything he doesn't want to. I'm sure he'll reveal his master plan for me in his own good time," Cass said with deceptive ease.

Mabry just looked at her. "You're right, of course. I only hope that he gets around to it before too much time passes. Before it's too late."

Cassidy rose abruptly, needing sunshine, fresh air, smiling faces. She was unlikely to find any of those three commodities in Manhattan. Any more than she was likely to find safety.

"Too late for what, Mabry?"

Mabry shook her head. "I don't know, Cass. I just have a bad feeling about this. And it's only going to get worse."

Richard was lying in the darkened room, stretched once more on the bed that had belonged to one of Sean's children. He never slept much—a few hours here and there, but when the wheels started spinning too quickly, when the lights grew too bright and the pain started, then he had no choice but to shut himself away. He couldn't face anyone right now. Not and be sure he could keep controlling the darkness, the fury that coursed through him.

Sean wasn't the kind of man who paid attention to closed doors. The murky light of the hallway threaded into the room as he stood there, his stocky figure filling the frame. Beyond him the apartment was still and silent.

"The women have gone out," Sean said. "Probably gone shopping."

"Anyone ever tell you you were a male chauvinist pig?" Richard inquired, not bothering to turn his head.

"Any number of femi-nazis," he replied. "I view it as a badge of honor. Name me one woman who doesn't like to shop. Your wife, for instance? Didn't she have staggering credit card bills?"

"You read the trial transcripts, Sean. You know that as well as I do. You never forget anything."

"True enough." He wandered into the room, closing the door behind him, closing in the murky darkness. He sat down in the chair beside the bed. "So what do you think of her?"

He didn't pretend to misunderstand. "You already asked me that."

"What happened this morning? I left the two of you alone, and I expected . . ."

"What did you expect, Sean?" He let the savagery emerge in his voice. "You think I'd have her spread out on the desk, her skirt pushed up to her waist?"

"I'm the girl's father," Sean said coolly. "Watch your mouth."

"You're the girl's father, and you don't have any qualms about handing her over to me."

"Oh, I have qualms aplenty. I'm willing to take the chance."

"It's not you who's taking the chance, is it, Sean? What if I turn out to be a crazed murderer? Another Ted Bundy?" He sat up, turning on the light beside the bed, and Sean blinked like a blinded owl. "You know what they say. That I murdered my wife and children, that I probably killed countless other women. They haven't found Sally Norton's body, but that's the only thing that's kept them from charging me with that murder as well. What if I can't resist? If I have to stab every woman I fuck?"

"Trying to shock me, Richard? I'm a little hard to horrify at this stage in my life. I can understand why you might want to kill your wife. Why on earth would you want to kill Cassidy?"

He sank back on the bed, suddenly weary of the man's obtuse egotism. "Maybe for the simple reason that it would hurt you, and you're beginning to piss me off."

"I've always pissed you off, Tiernan. Let's not pussyfoot around. We've made a Faustian bargain, you and I. My daughter for your story. You want someone to screw, and for some reason you've hit on my daughter. So be it. I need someone to help me with the book, and she's a talented girl. I'm not about to renege. Are you?"

He curved his mouth in a unpleasant smile. "No," he said. "Though I have one question."

"Just one?" Sean said boisterously. "Fire away."

"If we have a Faustian pact, just which one of us is the devil?"

There was a momentary silence. "That, my boy, is what's going to make this book a classic."

She was being watched. It had taken her several blocks of city streets to recognize the feeling, but when she turned and looked around her, no one seemed particularly interested in a tall, well-rounded redhead dressed far too casually for the Upper East Side.

She'd been right about the sunshine and smiling faces. The bright morning had turned dark and glowering, the people around her were striding down the wide sidewalks, their heads down, their perfectly painted faces blank. The air smelled like thunder and exhaust.

She headed toward the park. Not the place to go in search of peace and safety, but she needed trees, even ones that were half-dead from pollution. She needed to watch children playing, to see life, to forget about Richard Tiernan and his twisted destiny.

She was being followed. She entered the park at Seventy-second Street in a small group of people, and she knew one of them was there with her. But whether it was the silk-suited yuppie, the mumbling homeless woman, the cop, or the jogger, she had no idea. It could just as easily have been the pretzel salesman or the elegant gentleman with the military bearing.

And then she knew.

She walked slowly, aimlessly, making it easy for him to keep up with her. She stopped and bought a bag of popcorn, then sat on one of the relatively clean benches. She tossed a piece of popcorn on the ground, watching as a pigeon darted toward her.

He stood at the edge of the path for a moment, watching her as she fed the pigeons. Squirrels with ratty, moth-eaten tails joined battle, and eventually Cassie resorted to throwing vast handfuls out.

"You have a soft heart."

He sat down next to her. She turned to look at him, hoping the sudden tension wasn't as transparent as she feared it was. "I have a passion for justice."

"So do I."

"Justice?" she asked. "Or revenge?"

Retired General Amberson Scott nodded approvingly. "You're smart as well as pretty. I like that in a woman. In this case justice and revenge are the same thing."

He was a distinguished-looking man, Richard Tiernan's father-in-law. He didn't look all that dif-

ferent from the media darling who'd fielded questions on the Gulf war, giving even Norman
Schwarzkopf a run for his money. Despite the tai-
lored British suit, he still exuded a military fair-
ness, a decency, an intelligence mixed with equal
parts determination and compassion. It was little
wonder he'd been such a damning witness for
the prosecution.

"Your father's a fool," he added abruptly.

"No, he's not."

"Then he's playing a very dangerous game, and
he's old enough to know better. Richard Tiernan
is a sociopath, totally without conscience. Any
man who could slaughter his pregnant wife and
children and still sleep at night must be some kind
of monster."

"What makes you think he sleeps at night?" she
asked, knowing it was a stupid, inconsequential
question, unable to banish the memory of his
hands on the glass of warm milk, handing it to
her.

Scott shook his head. "I've talked to your father,
any number of times, and he refused to listen. I
kept out of it—Richard's been convicted, and I
have a strong faith in the justice system of this
country. It's not going to let a man like him go
free. He'll pay for the murder of my daughter and
her babies, and I intend to be there and watch."

It was spoken with calm determination, and
Cassidy had no doubt whatsoever that Scott
meant every word he said. "But what if you're

wrong? What if my father is able to prove he didn't do it?"

Scott shook his head. "Not as smart as I thought," he murmured. "Your father had no qualms about admitting the truth to me—why don't you ask him yourself what his new book is about?"

"I know what it's about. He's going to tell Richard's side of the story. He's going to prove he couldn't have done it." Even as she said it, the words sounded hollow.

General Scott shook his head. "No, he's not. He's going to tell Richard's story, all right. He's going to illuminate the mind of a murderer."

"I don't believe you," Cassie said hotly. Too afraid that she did.

"Sean O'Rourke wouldn't be interested in anything as tame as a true crime story. He's expecting this to be a masterpiece, and he doesn't care what kind of price he has to pay."

"And what kind of price do you anticipate?" Cassidy asked in a frosty voice.

"If Richard runs true to form, it will be the same price I paid. The life of a daughter."

The wind stiffened, catching a piece of torn newspaper and scudding it down the winding pathway. In the distance Cassidy could see the blurred image of Richard Tiernan, and one word of the headline. Murderer.

It would have been simple enough to go with the fear that had been teasing and taunting her

for the last twenty-four hours. Ever since she'd
arrived in New York. But if she started running,
she didn't know when she'd be able to stop. And
she wasn't quite ready to run yet.

She rose, tall, graceful, and he rose with her,
polite, distinguished, a few inches shorter than
she was. "I understand how you must be feeling,
General Scott," she murmured. "And I wish there
was some way I could help, but I think . . ."

"There is a way you can help," he said, and she
braced herself, knowing what would come next.
He'd ask her to spy on Richard, to intervene with
her father, he'd ask her to . . .

"Stay alive," he said. "He's already killed at least
two women, and the police think there were probably a great many more."

"But . . ." Cassie protested, filled with sick horror, but his stern voice overruled her.

"Don't let him kill again." Without another
word he turned and walked away from her, and
the pigeons scattered in his path.

CHAPTER 5

The apartment was still and silent when Cass let herself back in. There was no sign of Mabry and Sean, no sound coming from the bedroom. Cass locked the door behind her, slipped off her shoes, and leaned back against the solid surface.

It was after midnight, but for the first time she had felt safer on the mean streets of New York than she felt in her father's house. The run-in with General Scott had left her shaken, and nothing could rid her of that nagging fear. She'd been trying to tell herself there was nothing to worry about. In a few short minutes Scott had reinforced all her fears. She was living with a murderer. And she was stupidly, irrationally drawn to him. As doubtless his other victims had been as well.

She'd gone shopping, hoping the bright lights and bustle of Bloomingdales would distract her. She couldn't bring herself to buy anything. She went out to dinner, only to find she couldn't eat anything. She went to the movies, and discovered she'd mistakenly made the worst possible choice. She'd been looking for something absorbing and Hitchcockian. Instead she'd ended up with a slasher movie, rampant with elegant erotica, and she'd sat there, horrified, mesmerized at the stylish bloodbath on the screen.

It was no wonder she thought of Richard Tiernan.

She'd delayed even further, stopping for dessert and Irish coffee at a small restaurant around the block from her father's condo. By the time prowling singles started noticing her, she realized she couldn't put off her return any longer.

She pushed away from the door, pulling off her jacket and tossing it on a chair. She moved down the carpeted hallway, tiptoeing. It wasn't until she reached her bedroom door that she heard the voices. Muffled, ominous. Sean's light, bullying voice, carrying the deliberate tones of drunkenness on its Irish lilt. And Tiernan's, slower, deeper. Hypnotic.

She opened her door, prepared to shut out the sound, when her name reached her. And then she was lost—it would take a better woman than she was to resist the urge to eavesdrop.

She moved down the hallway in the direction of those voices. They were in Sean's office, the door ajar, the lights dimmed, and she could smell the peaty scent of the good Irish, hear the faint chink of ice. Tiernan must like his on the rocks, she thought inconsequentially. Her father drank his straight.

". . . Not sure she'll cooperate," Sean was saying, just a little too loudly. "She's got a mind of her own, and always has. Takes after her mother, though she's not the bloody bitch Alice is. Still, I wouldn't put it past her to castrate a man who looked at her the wrong way. She's a fierce woman, I'll tell you that outright."

"Should I be frightened?" Tiernan's voice was much softer, yet Cassidy could hear each word distinctly.

Sean snorted. "I'm just telling you she's not the easy mark you might think she is. And there's no guarantee she'll stay here any longer than she has a mind to. Family loyalty is a forgotten virtue. She looks after herself first, and me and her mother come a long ways behind."

"She sounds like a survivor."

"She's needed to be. Her mother, if you can believe it, is even worse than me."

"It's a little difficult to imagine," Tiernan drawled.

"I've been having second thoughts. Why don't I see what my publisher can do? There are hundreds of savvy, smart women in New York who'd give their eyeteeth to collaborate on a book like this."

"I wasn't looking for eyeteeth."

"Richard," Sean said, sounding even more drunk, "I want you to be good to my girl."

There was a long silence. Cass could feel the color flame in her face, and she waited for Richard to speak. To say something, anything, that would clarify what in hell's name was going on. Why had Sean brought her here? For Richard Tiernan?

Finally he spoke, and Cass could have punched the wall in frustration. "You ought to go to bed, Sean. Your daughter's an early riser, and I expect she's going to want us hard at work by nine o'clock."

"Cassie has a singular disregard for the realities of life, such as insomnia, hangovers, and the artistic muse. These things come on their own schedule."

"I don't think I have a hell of a lot of time to waste," Tiernan said.

"Then the two of you can start without me," Sean said brightly.

Another silence. "Make up your mind, Sean."

"I already have. Mabry blames me, you know. For some reason she's very fond of you. You have that effect on women, don't you? The ability to charm them."

"I don't charm your daughter."

"The hell you don't. I've known her all her life. She's a stubborn creature, and she's fighting it like mad. But I've never seen her look at anyone the way she looks at you."

It was all Cass could do to keep from

screeching a protest. She stayed silent, eaves-dropping, riveted to the spot.

"And how does she look at me?" He sounded cool, only vaguely interested, and Cass could feel her shame and embarrassment rise.

"I've been trying to define it to my own satisfaction. Partly like a child looking at a train set, one he wants desperately but knows he can't have."

"Why can't he have it?"

"The price is too high." Another noisy sip of whiskey, as Sean's voice grew even more maudlin, as his insights drew dangerously sharper. "For the rest, it reminds me of the way people watch the polar bears in the Central Park Zoo. As far as I know, they've never hurt anyone, but people watch them and they remember the one in the Brooklyn Zoo who ate the kids."

Cass listened to his faintly slurred words with a sense of outrage that only increased with the amusement in Tiernan's voice. "So I'm a toy she wants but can't afford, one that will turn around and eat her. Is that it?"

"What do you think?"

"I think it's time you went to bed."

"You're right. Mabry will be wondering what happened to me."

"I doubt it," Tiernan said. "She must be used to you by now."

Cassidy moved quickly, ducking into the nearest doorway. The kitchen was shrouded in darkness.

She waited there, scarcely breathing, as Sean emerged into the hallway.

His grizzled gray hair stood up wildly around his ruddy face, and his raisin dark eyes looked oddly sunken. For the first time he looked old, and Cassie stared at him, unseen, as the mortality that had been looming over her settled on her shoulders.

She didn't dare go back into the hallway and risk running into Richard Tiernan. The layout of the old apartment was circular—she could head through the kitchen and breakfast nook, back out into the front hall and make it safely into her bedroom without anyone being the wiser.

She moved silently, resisting the impulse to open the refrigerator. After a day of picking at her food she was suddenly famished, but she didn't dare risk spending a moment longer in the kitchen. Her nemesis seemed to have a talent for finding her there.

The hall was dark, only the streetlights from the living room windows behind penetrating. She started toward her room, tiptoeing, and then stifled her sudden scream.

"Cassidy," Tiernan said, and his hand clamped around her wrist, stopping her flight. He'd loomed out of the darkness, more silently than she, and in the shadows she could barely see him. For some reason that was no comfort. "Did you hear anything interesting in your eavesdropping?"

She yanked her hand free. "What do you mean?"

"Don't play childish games, Cassidy. I'd thought better of you. You were standing outside the study, listening to your father's drunken fantasies. What did you make of it?"

She wrapped her arms around her body, feeling hot and cold at the same time. "I don't know what to think," she said with perfect frankness. "Exactly what is it that Sean thinks I'm going to provide here? Editorial expertise, secretarial skills, what?"

"What." The word was brief, intensely suggestive.

"Forget it."

"Try telling that to your father."

She was glad of the darkness then, glad it hid the flush that covered her cheeks. "You're right," she said with a shaky laugh. "He doesn't listen to anybody once he makes up his mind. There's no way in hell you'll convince him you're not palpitating with lust for me."

"I am."

The silence was thick, dark, impenetrable. She could feel him, standing too close, not close enough, feel the heat from his body that was somehow icy cold. And then she managed a nervous smile.

"For a moment I thought you were serious," she said, half-afraid he'd tell her that he was. Dead serious.

"Where did you go tonight?" he asked instead.

"Shopping, the movies, dinner," she said brightly. "I don't get to New York that often, and I couldn't pass up a visit to Bloomies. I couldn't find anything to buy, though, and I didn't like the movie much, and of course I didn't run into anyone I knew, even when I was in the park, so it got a little lonely, but then I . . ."

"Then you started babbling," he interrupted her. "Do you have a guilty conscience, Cassidy?"

"Why should I?"

"I can't imagine. You don't strike me as the sort of person who has even a passing acquaintance with evil. Unless, of course, you count your acquaintance with me."

She swallowed. "Are you evil?"

He ignored the question. "Let me give you a piece of advice, Cassidy. If you're feeling guilty, and you're going to lie, the trick is to say as little as possible. There's no reason you need to make excuses. Just answer any direct questions and keep your mouth shut."

"I'll keep that in mind," she said faintly. "Is that what you did when they arrested you?"

Even in the dark she could sense his wolfish smile. "Good night, Cassidy."

She stood, unmoving, as he disappeared down the hallway, and the quiet sound of the door closed behind him. She closed her eyes for a moment, then let out her breath, relaxing her clenched fists. She hadn't even noticed how tense she'd been.

He was a disturbing man. Even under the best of circumstances she would have found him unsettling. If she'd run into him during the course of her work, she would have steered clear of him. That kind of intensity, that kind of subtle, understated power was a direct threat, to the safe, comfortable life she'd built for herself in Baltimore, away from the rampaging demands of her family. It was a threat to her tenuous peace of mind. Perhaps even to her life itself.

But there was no avoiding him in the five thousand square feet of Sean's spacious apartment. No avoiding the pall that hung over the place, over his head. No avoiding the draw that she felt as well, to a man who was . . .

Evil? Or merely troubled and misjudged?

She couldn't save him. She'd learned that early on, with her mother's drinking and her father's self-destructive ways. She couldn't save them, she couldn't save anyone but herself. She thought she'd outgrown the need to try.

But there was something about Richard Tiernan that called to her. And the sooner she learned to shut her ears, block out the noise, the better off she'd be.

She was almost ridiculously easy to play. Richard should have been bored by the lack of challenge, but he wasn't. Everything about Cassidy Roarke fascinated him, even her very predictability. And perhaps she wasn't really that predictable after all. Perhaps it was just that he knew her, in a very elemental way.

If he'd pushed, she would have run. She was a runner, he knew that. He'd barely touched her, resisting the impulse, the need that had swept over him. He had to move carefully, in stages, invading her space, her mind, her soul. If he made a rash, thoughtless move, he could jeopardize everything. And the stakes were too high to risk failure.

He needed to be deliberate, unhurried, stalking her so subtly she couldn't protect herself from the threat. Until it was too late for her to escape.

He'd schooled his impatience. For two days he sat in that green leather chair and watched her out of hooded eyes, listened as she and Sean argued about the form of the book. It amused him to realize she remained oblivious to Sean's plan for the book. She had to suspect, she was too bright not to, but she continued to view it as a means to proving his innocence. Funny, when the only innocence in that entire apartment rested in Cassidy's troubled green eyes.

He'd kept out of her way, hoping to lull her into a false sense of security. He heard her at night, sneaking around on tiptoes, raiding the refrigerator, heating milk to banish her sleeplessness, but he'd stayed in his room, awake, listening to her movements, remembering the way the thin cotton had flowed against her tall, strong body, the way she'd wrapped her arms around her, protecting herself from him. He wanted to go out and drink warm milk from her lips, he wanted to pull that nightgown up around her strong hips and feel her against him. He stayed where he was, listening to her move about in the kitchen. He didn't wonder what kept her awake at night. He knew very well. He'd done his best to keep it that way.

He was running out of time. There was a limit to how long he could wait for her. Sean was writing like mad, like a man possessed, secretly, when he knew Cass wouldn't disturb him. At the rate he was going, the first draft would be finished long ahead of Richard's looming court date. Sooner or later Cassidy was going to get a look at it, and then all hell would break loose.

He needed to make certain he had her first. He needed to test her, tease her, bind her to him, before it was too late. She was the only one who could give him what he needed. It didn't matter that it could require the ultimate sacrifice from her. He was willing to make that sacrifice. He had to ensure that she would be willing, too.

"Bellingham called," Sean announced out of the blue, three days after Cassidy had arrived in New York.

Richard looked up from the book he was reading. They'd made an uneasy trio the last few days, Cassie organizing and reshuffling paperwork, Sean absorbed in his laptop computer, Richard reading voraciously, everything from astronomy textbooks to mystery novels to the true crime books by Joe McGinniss. He'd watch her when she wasn't looking, knowing she'd feel his eyes on her, making sure she couldn't catch him at it. This time he glanced at her openly. Her fiery hair was bundled at the base of her neck, she was wearing little or no makeup, and she had a spattering of freckles across her high cheekbones. She was wearing a cotton sweater, deliberately baggy, he suspected, and khakis. He wanted to see her legs again.

"Who's Bellingham?" she asked.

"Mark Bellingham's my lawyer," Richard replied.

"Not according to your court transcripts. You were represented by Harrison Matthews and his horde of assistants. Pretty impressive credentials—I didn't realize Matthews had ever lost a case."

"You haven't read far enough into the transcripts," Richard replied coolly. "I doubt if Matthews has lost a case. My father-in-law hired him for me. Once he decided I was guilty, he withdrew his financial support, and Matthews withdrew from the case. Mark took over. He was more than competent, and he had the added advantage of being an old friend."

"Why didn't you get a mistrial declared?" Cass demanded. "You must have set records for going through the court system as it was—surely you could have demanded more time . . ."

"I didn't want it."

She stared at him. "Why not?"

"Time wasn't about to make any difference. Either the jury believed me innocent or guilty. Spending two years fucking around with the judicial system wouldn't change it."

"It might have."

"Maybe I didn't care."

It silenced her, if only for a moment. He wanted to pursue it. He could see the reluctant sympathy in those expressive eyes of hers. She was seeing him as a man who'd lost his pregnant wife and children in the most horrible of ways, and she wanted to press his head against her breasts and comfort him. The thought amused him. She'd probably try to comfort a rattler who'd made the mistake of biting a scorpion.

"I tried to put Bellingham off," Sean continued in a faintly fretful voice. "I can't have these interruptions when things are moving so well."

"When do you want me to read it?" Cass asked.

Sean stared at his daughter as if she'd suddenly grown two heads. "Read it?"

"Read it," she repeated with exaggerated patience. "The manuscript. Isn't that why I'm here? Apart from being a glorified secretary, getting your research in order, I thought I was supposed to be editing this as you go."

"You know I can't abide having anyone peer over my shoulder while I work!" Sean shot back. "You'll see it when I'm good and ready."

Cass sighed, rising from the desk. "In that case, I'll go back to Maryland, and you can let me know when you're ready for me. I'm not going to waste my time shuffling papers while you consort with your muse."

"Cassidy, come back here!" Sean thundered, but she'd already vanished into the hallway, and he turned to Richard, frustration on his ruddy face. "Never have children, Tiernan. They're sharper than a serpent's tooth."

"I don't expect I'll have the chance to father any others," he said coolly, dropping the book in his lap. "Are you going to let her go?"

There was a faintly crafty expression on Sean O'Rourke's face, one he didn't make much of an effort to hide. "I don't know if I can stop her," he said with a show of regret.

Richard leaned back, watching him. That regret was only a front. He must have thought better of offering his daughter up to Richard Tiernan, and he was glad of the chance to let her escape.

But he'd reckoned without Tiernan. "If she leaves," he said softly, "so do I."

"Richard, you don't need her," Sean said, trying to hide the fear in his eyes. "I don't know why you think you do. Any reasonably intelligent editorial assistant will do, and I can find any number of good-looking ones who'd be more than happy to go to bed with you. Women tend to be fascinated by notoriety, God bless 'em."

"If I wanted a straightforward fuck, I can find

it for myself," he said. "Certain kinds of women are attracted to the hint of danger. That's not what I want Cassidy for."

"You don't want her?"

"I didn't say that. I just said things weren't all that simple. Are you going to change your mind? Are you willing to give up my cooperation with your goddamned book in return for your daughter's escape?"

Sean's flushed face turned even darker. "You make it sound as if I'm willing to whore my daughter for the sake of my career," he protested.

"Aren't you?"

"I got you out of jail, Tiernan. I offered to stand bond for you, and it was my name, my reputation that convinced the judge . . ."

"Your name and reputation are almost as bad as mine," he interrupted the old man ruthlessly. "Mark Bellingham might not have the clout of Matthews, but he can manage a simple appeal. And I don't have to be here. You and I both know it. We made a bargain, and you're going to keep your side of it."

"Nobody can make Cass do anything she doesn't want to do."

"She'll want to," Richard said quietly.

"I don't like it."

"It's a little late for you to decide that, isn't it? You told me she needed to get out in the world, live a little. You're providing her with the opportunity."

"Why do you want her?" Sean asked. "You've never given me a straight answer. I know it's not a case of love at first sight—you're a cold-blooded bastard at best. What do you want from my daughter?"

Richard leaned back, considering it, considering the man who'd sell his daughter for the sake of his bloody career. "Salvation," he said, with more honesty than he'd ever given Sean O'Rourke before.

But Sean was past the time of recognizing truth when he heard it. "I'll have to trust you," he said heavily. "I hope to God I'm not making a major mistake, but I don't see that I have any option."

Richard smiled faintly. "None that you're willing to accept. Are you going to stop her from leaving? Or am I?"

"I'll talk to her."

"Are you going to warn her about me?" He sounded no more than casually interested.

"Is that against our agreement?"

"Not at all. You can tell her anything you want. I'll take care of the rest."

"My daughter isn't an idiot, Tiernan. She's smart, she takes care of herself. She's not a victim, and she's not the kind of woman who'd look for a fantasy screw with a murderer. Thrills aren't her thing."

"Oh, I thought you decided Cassidy needs a few more thrills in her life. Wasn't that how you justified bringing her up here? I simply intend to provide them." He waited to see Sean's reaction, curious as to how far he could push him.

O'Rourke's brief spurt of paternal protectiveness had already vanished. "This better be a damned fine book," he growled.

Richard only smiled.

There, she'd made the decision, and she'd stand by it. Relief and regreat swamped her in equal parts as she dragged her suitcase out of the closet and began throwing her clothes inside. It was already early afternoon, but she was leaving the Park Avenue apartment within the hour. Mabry was out somewhere—she'd leave her a note. Now that she'd decided to leave, nothing was going to stop her.

"Running away?" The voice was soft, taunting, coming from her open doorway.

Cass met Richard's cool, ironic gaze with a steady look of her own. "Hardly. I just have better things to do than dance to my father's tune. He wants a handmaiden, and I've outgrown the role."

"He wants a daughter. Have you outgrown that role as well?"

"He's always had me, whether he realized it or not. But I'm not going to play the game with his rules. He changes them to suit himself, and I'm too old to get trapped again."

"Such a great age," he said, tilting his head to one side and surveying her. "How old are you?"

"Twenty-seven."

"I was that young once."

"I doubt it."

She wished he wouldn't smile at her like that. With that peculiar bittersweet expression that caught at her heart. "He needs your help, Cassidy. I don't imagine it's easy for him to admit it."

"You're very good, aren't you?" she shot back.

"Am I?"

"You can hone in on a person's weakness. If I stood on my head, I wouldn't be able to win my father's love and approval."

"You already have it."

"Bullshit. My father's love and approval is reserved for himself."

"You're confusing love with attention. He's self-absorbed, and nothing will ever change that. But he needs you. Are you going to turn your back on him?" He asked the question with what seemed no more than casual interest.

"What does it matter to you?"

"The future of the book is of some importance to me."

Of course it was. He must be counting on that book to save him from the bizarre horror of execution. Sean's book would either vindicate him or, if the worst was true, it might explain his actions, enough to keep him from being the first man executed in the state of New York in God knows how long. With a court date on the horizon, Richard couldn't afford any more delays.

"It's a little late to defend yourself," she said,

steeling herself not to feel the wrenching sympathy.

"I'm not interested in defending myself."

"That much was obvious from the transcripts. Why didn't you just tell them the truth and get it over with?"

The silence between them was long and icy cold. "But what is the truth?" he murmured.

"Did you kill your wife and children?"

She wanted, needed to hear an answer. Even if it was the one she abhorred.

But he simply smiled, an eerie, haunted smile. "Don't leave, Cassidy. Don't abandon your father."

"I can't . . ."

"Don't abandon me."

And the quiet words lingered in the air, long after Richard had disappeared down the quiet hallway.

CHAPTER 6

She knew all the buzzwords. She'd read enough, edited enough self-help and psychology books to know that the word "abandonment" was a loaded one, particularly for someone with her family history. All people feared abandonment, by parents, by loved ones, even those who grew up in a safe, "Leave it to Beaver" household. She'd spent years protecting herself from the fear of it, and now it had come around full circle. It was her choice, to abandon those who needed her desperately. Those whom she loved.

She couldn't do it, and Richard Tiernan knew that full well. Lord, he was good, better even than Sean when it came to manipulation. And here she was, falling for it, playing her part.

She stared at her half-packed suitcase. She wouldn't put the clothes away. She wouldn't run like a scared rabbit, either. She's give it another day, another twenty-four hours, before she made a decision.

She stayed in her room, waiting until the apartment settled down into a midday quiet before heading for the kitchen. The last thing she expected to run into was a handsome young man, complete with wire-rimmed glasses, khakis, deck shoes without socks, and a polo shirt with the collar up. He was standing in the pantry, hanging over the open refrigerator door, and when he looked up and saw her, his astonishment equaled hers.

"You must be Cassie," he said after a dumbstruck moment. Then he shut the refrigerator door, held out a hand to her, realized he was clutching a Harp beer, and quickly shifted hands. "I'm Mark Bellingham."

"Richard's lawyer," she supplied, taking his hand. It was cold and wet from the beer, a strong grasp, and her eyes were level with his. "Have you seen him? I can show you where . . ."

"I just came from a conference with him and your father. I gather you're privy to what's going on. I can tell you things aren't looking any too good, but I still have a few possibilities." He glanced at his beer, then at her. "Can I get you one of these?"

She shook her head. "What do you mean, things aren't looking too good?"

"You've read the transcripts. Richard said I was authorized to tell you anything. You know as well as I do that he refuses to mount a defense. He sticks to that same lame-ass story, and it would take Clarence Darrow to get him acquitted. And I'm not Clarence Darrow."

"So you've given up?" She leaned back against the refrigerator, staring at him. He was a very handsome man, with a rumpled, self-deprecating charm about him that was at odds with Tiernan's dark menace.

"On getting him off entirely? Yes. The best I can hope for is getting the death sentence commuted. If he gets life, he could get out in twenty years or so, if he behaves himself. Not that I've ever known Richard to behave himself," he added, half to himself.

"You've known him for a long time?"

"Since we were teenagers. He always was a chilly bastard, but he had a good heart, or so I always thought, and he would have done anything for a friend." He shook his head, taking a long pull on the beer. "Maybe you could talk to him."

She stood up straight. "I can't imagine why you'd think that would do any good."

"He likes you. He trusts you, as much as he's ever trusted a woman, and I can tell you right now those occasions haven't been too often."

"He must have trusted his wife."

"Diana?" Mark Bellingham snorted in contemptuous amusement. "Her least of all. Princess Diana, we used to call her." He drained the beer, then glanced at her. "Look, are you doing anything right now?"

She had the oddest feeling someone was watching, someone was listening. She hated being spied on. "Not at the moment," she said.

"Come to lunch with me. We both care about Richard—maybe between the two of us we can figure out how to save his ungrateful life."

"What makes you think I care about him?" she shot back, appalled.

He looked startled. His sandy blond hair had fallen across his wide forehead, making him look boyish and touchable. She wanted to reach up and smooth the hair back. He was probably used to that reaction, had trained his hair to do just that.

"Don't you?" he countered.

The apartment was quiet, listening for her answer. The heated denial that sprung to her lips would have been more damning than a thousand polite lies. "I care about everyone," she said finally. "Of course I want to help."

Mark Bellingham looked relieved. "There's a wonderful Italian place just few blocks down. But you probably know that as well as I do—you used to live here."

"Not for years," she said. "And Italian sounds fine. Just let me get my purse."

"Don't you need to tell someone you're going?"

"No," she said. Not when they were listening, watching, she wanted to add, knowing she'd sound paranoid.

He was waiting for her in the front hallway, and she told herself she needed this, needed a break from the apartment, from the overwhelming presence of Richard Tiernan. In fact, Mark Bellingham scarcely mentioned his name during lunch, instead going out of his way to be comfortable and charming. There was no reason for her to feel guilty, Cass thought, as she sipped her cappuccino. No need to worry about the people back at the apartment, and what they might think of her. She was free to come and go as she pleased, she owed nothing to anyone, particularly nothing to the man who lived in the back bedroom and haunted her dreams.

She waited until Bellingham had paid the check, waited until the very last moment. "Who do you think did it?" she asked.

He didn't pretend to misunderstand. "I haven't got the faintest idea. Diana was a royal pain in the butt, but no one had cause to hate her. There was no reason for anyone to kill her like that."

"What about the children?"

For a moment he looked blank. And then his golden complexion, probably the result of a tanning bed but appealing nonetheless, turned pale. "I try not to think about the children," he said in a lifeless voice.

They walked the few blocks back to the apartment in silence. The spring afternoon had grown cool and dark, and Cass shivered in her light cotton sweater. When they reached the elevator, he reached out and touched her, and his hands were warm and strong. "I enjoyed this, Cass," he said.

"So did I."

"We didn't talk much about Richard."

"No."

He managed a rueful smile. "That's probably why we enjoyed ourselves. Sometimes our friends put us through hell."

"He's lucky to have a friend like you."

Mark shrugged. "I just wish I could do more for him. But you can't help a man who refuses to help himself, can you?"

"No," she said softly, "you can't."

"Come to dinner with me tomorrow night," he said impulsively.

She had no reason to hesitate. He was handsome, he was charming, he was sane. She needed to get out of the apartment, and he made her laugh. So why did the very thought fill her with a sense of betrayal? What had Richard Tiernan done to her, all with barely putting a hand on her, to make her feel so tied to him?

She ignored the feeling, knowing how irrational it was. "I'd love to," she said firmly. "Call me."

He had a charming smile. Like sunshine on a cloudy day, it should have warmed her soul. "You're sure Richard won't mind?"

"Why should he?" she asked warily.

"Just a sixth sense. Richard's not a man to cross. I wouldn't want to interfere if something's going on between you two."

"Do you think that's why he killed her?" The words came out, before she could stop herself.

"I don't know that he did," Mark said. "He was never a particularly possessive man. Diana was the possessive one."

"But you don't know that he didn't kill her?" she persisted.

"No one knows but Richard."

"And the real murderer," she reminded him.

"And the real murderer," he agreed. "Still, you might not tell him you're going out with me. I'm not certain he'd understand we have his best interests at heart. He doesn't tend to trust people. Not that you can blame him." He looked down, as if he suddenly realized he was still holding her hand, and he released her. "Damn, I'm talking too much, as always. I'll take you someplace fabulous tomorrow night, and the name Richard Tiernan won't cross our lips. How does that sound?"

"Very nice," she said.

She waited until he'd gotten back in the elevator, waited until she was alone in the twelfth floor hallway, before she unlocked the front door of Sean's condo. The place was cool and dark and silent when she let herself in, and once more she told herself she had no reason to feel guilty.

"Enjoy your lunch?" Richard's voice was silken smooth. He was sitting in the Chinese chair in the corner of the hallway, in the shadows, and it took all Cass's concentration not to jump.

"Very much," she said warily.

"Mark's a good man, isn't he?"

"He seems to be."

"Unlike me."

"You aren't a good man?"

He rose, towering over her in the hallway, and she felt her hands clench nervously. She shoved them in her pockets, standing her ground. If she continued to let him terrorize her, there's be no way she could stay.

"I doubt you could find anyone who'd consider me to be particularly good," he said casually.

"Mark does."

"Mark." The word was succinct, dismissive. "He has a great deal of faith in mankind. You'd think a New York lawyer would know better."

"He has faith in you. Whether you deserve it or not."

"Such a reproach," he said softly. "Tell me, did he tell you about his lousy marriage and his dysfunctional childhood? You'd be ripe for a bleeding-heart story like that. Two adult children, adrift on a raging tide of emotions and hormones. It has all the makings of a *New York Times* best-seller."

"You are a bastard," she said.

His smile was wintry. "Tell me something I don't know, Cassidy," he murmured. "Are you going out with him again?"

"I don't think that's any of your business."

"It depends what's drawing you together. If the two of you want to compare rotten childhoods before you go to bed together, go right ahead. Just keep me out of it."

"It's so nice to have your permission," she said in an acid tone of voice. "But I have no intention of going to bed with him."

"His wife wouldn't mind."

"I get the message, Richard. He's married. Yes, he neglected to mention that fact, but you've more than made up for it. And as a matter of fact, we hardly talked about you at all. Sorry to disillusion you, but you aren't the most fascinating thing that ever entered either of our lives."

"I'm glad to hear it," he said, his voice patently disbelieving. "What did you say about me?"

"We talked about whether you killed your wife. And why you haven't made any real effort to defend yourself," she said flatly, wanting to fight back.

But Richard's armor was invincible. "And did either of you come up with any theories? Am I a roaming psychopath who finally snapped and slaughtered his family or an innocent victim of a serial killer?"

"I don't know."

He moved closer, so close his clothes brushed hers, so close she could feel the warmth of his breath. His dark eyes had tiny flecks of gold in them, and they seemed to glow in the gloomy light of the entryway. "Do you think I did it, Cassidy?" he whispered, intense, urgent, demanding. His mouth moved closer, hovering over hers, and she was trapped. "Do you?"

Bright light flooded the hallway, shocking her

into moving, backing away from him. Mabry stood in the doorway, her serene face expressionless as always. "I thought you'd gone back to Maryland," she said, and there was no missing the anxiety and relief in her voice. "Your father said you'd left."

Cass shook her head. "I'll stay a bit longer." She refused to meet Richard's gaze, still astounded that she'd given in. She could tell herself she wanted to pursue the possibility of Mark Bellingham, but she knew that was a lie. For all that she found him attractive, he didn't call to her on any deep, emotional level. Besides, she was old enough and smart enough to know not to get involved with a married man.

She didn't seem old enough or smart enough not to get involved with a murderer, however. She wasn't staying for Mark Bellingham's sake, or for Mabry, or for her father. She was staying because she wasn't quite ready to leave the dangerous fascination of Richard Tiernan.

She was escaping from him. Richard knew it. She was in her room, dressing, humming something beneath her breath, and he could smell her perfume as it slithered down the hallway. The scent surprised him.

Diana had always favored something light, flowery, innocent. It had been part of her allure, the innocence, and the chancre underneath.

Cassidy Roarke favored something richer, muskier, defiantly sexual. It suited her about as well as innocence had suited Diana. A lie, but then, he was used to the lies of women, from their lips, from their bodies, from the very scent they wore.

He'd kept away from her, afraid of what he might do. The darkness was closer now, hovering just beyond the edges of his consciousness, and he was afraid of what might happen if he gave in to it. As long as he held himself remote, no emotions, just cold intellect, then he would win. He would accomplish what he so desperately needed to accomplish, and face his execution with the same cool equanimity.

He found himself wondering whether he might have made a very great mistake in choosing Cassidy Roarke. She was getting beneath his skin, disturbing him, drawing him back into the land of the living, when he was already making plans to leave it as gracefully as possible.

But he really hadn't had any choice in the matter. He'd taken one look at the silver-framed photograph and known, with an instinct that was almost unnatural. It was too late for second thoughts, for guilt, for worrying about the consequences. He would do what he had to do.

He didn't want her going out with Mark. He didn't want her smiling at his friend, her green eyes sparkling, that wariness that infused her entire body whenever she was around him vanishing.

Of course, he went out of his way to put that

wariness in her eyes. He was doing everything he could to terrify her. And he was about to up the ante.

He followed the scent of her lying perfume, aroused by it even as he distrusted it. Sean and Mabry were out someplace, and he didn't expect them to return for hours. It wouldn't matter if they did. He had no qualms about having an audience.

She was in the kitchen, and he stood in the shadows, watching her, as he had so often, waiting until she realized he was there.

She was dressed in something long and flowery, and her red hair was loose on her shoulders. She hadn't put her shoes on yet, and she was on her toes, reaching up, and he could see the long, strong line of her body, the swell of her breasts, the curve of her hip. She was a woman, lush and full, and he wanted to fill his hands with her. It had been so very long since he had touched a woman.

He didn't move, didn't make a sound, but she turned, staring at him, for a moment all her carefully nurtured fear and fascination visible to him. And then she pulled her defenses back about her like a cloak, and she tilted her head back. He could see the nervous pulse ticking at the base of her throat, and he wanted to put his mouth on it.

"You decided to go out with him after all," he said, no accusation, no emotion in his voice.

She flinched anyway. "Is there a reason why I shouldn't?" she countered.

The dress was cut too low. He could see the swell of her breasts above the neckline, see the nervous rapidity of her breathing. He allowed himself a small smile.

"It depends on how fascinated you are with risk."

Her face was pale in the murky light of the kitchen. "What risk are you talking about? You're not suggesting Mark is the one who . . ."

"Killed my wife? Not for a moment. Mark doesn't have a violent, bloody bone in his entire body."

"Then where's the danger?"

Stubborn, she was, and determinedly brave. He should take pity on her. But he couldn't afford to.

"From me," he said gently.

She backed away from him then, coming up against the old-fashioned counter. And because she retreated, he advanced, unable to resist the temptation. If she was going out with Mark Bellingham, he wanted her to go with his taste on her mouth, his touch on her flesh, his heat on her cold fear.

He put his hands on her shoulders, lightly, hesitating for a moment before letting them settle. She felt curiously fragile beneath his touch, and he knew it wouldn't take much strength to crush those bones. He was very strong, he knew it, he used it.

He let his thumbs brush against the hollow beneath her collarbone, and he felt her tremble. Her lids were lowered, as if she was afraid to let him see the sheer panic in her expression. He didn't need to see it or know it. He could sense it, breathe it, smell it. And he knew that mixed with that panic was unwilling fascination.

He bent down, and put his lips against hers. He could taste the toothpaste and lipstick, he could taste the desire. He increased the pressure, gently, and her mouth opened beneath his, unwillingly.

He moved his hands down her arms, capturing her wrists and putting them around his neck, pulling her body up against his. He wanted to groan with the pleasure of it, but his control was absolute, and he made no sound whatsoever as he slowly took her mouth.

The first tremor that swept over her body was fear. The second was something else, as he felt her nipples harden against his chest in the warmth of the dark kitchen, felt the reluctant softening of her mouth. She made a sound, a quiet one, of protest and surrender, and he slid his tongue against hers, pushing her, forcing her to accept him. Or to run. He needed an answer, even as he felt his body harden against hers, even as he felt the call of her, a siren lure, enticing him, calling him to drown in the scented richness of her flesh, to drown and forget the nightmare that haunted his every moment.

He was angry. Angry that she'd reached him again. He'd stalked her, intent on testing her, seeing how far he could push her. And instead she'd pushed back, crawling inside his skin, so that it was his hands that were trembling, his body that was shaking.

She smelled like sex and lies. She tasted like love and truth. He threaded his hands through her thick mane of flame-colored hair, reveling in the texture, and slanted his mouth across hers. He'd never liked kissing much before.

He liked kissing Cassidy Roarke. Liked feeling the passion rise in her, liked feeling the surrender racing just beneath the surface of her heated flesh. He could have her. He could slide his hands down that low neckline and cup her breasts, taste her nipples. He could push her down on the old linoleum floor of the kitchen and pull her dress out of the way, he could fuck her, hard, and she wouldn't protest. She would cry, and she would come.

And then she would run away. Too soon, too soon.

He released her, suddenly, abruptly, taking a safe step away from her, trying to distance himself from the taste, the heat, the scent of her. She looked up at him, her eyes dark with shock and remorse, and he was glad he was so skilled at shielding his expressions. She would be able to glean nothing of his reaction to her.

And then her eyelids fluttered closed, and she

groaned, a soft, despairing sound that would have torn at softer hearts than his.

He could play it out, toy with her, push her. He was tempted to. The need that spiked through his body was strong and fierce, and he needed her, needed her.

But he needed more than the blessed forgetfulness of sex in her warm, lush body. He needed her heart and soul as well.

"Sorry," he said lightly, the prosaic word defusing the situation.

Almost. Her eyes flew open again, and she stared at him. "Sorry?" she echoed, almost as if she didn't understand the meaning of the word.

"I must have been overcome by my baser urges." His voice was cool, ironic, and he could see the flush stain her pale cheeks.

And then her eyes met his, unflinching. "I don't think you allow anything to overcome you. You know exactly what you're doing, and you know why, and there's nothing simple or base about it. Is there?"

He allowed himself the luxury of a faint smile. "I don't usually underestimate you," he said.

"You aren't answering me. You did that on purpose, didn't you? To rattle me. To see what kind of reaction you could get from me. You like playing with people, teasing them, frightening them . . ."

"Do I frighten you, Cassidy?" he interrupted her.

"Yes."

He had to give her credit for her honesty. He wanted to frighten her. He wanted to scare her half to death, and he wanted her to want him anyway. Be willing to do anything for him. "Do you think I'm going to take a butcher knife to you?"

"Did you take a butcher knife to your pregnant wife?"

"Sooner or later I'll answer that question. And I don't think you're going to like what I say."

"Then don't tell me."

"Stop asking."

She bit her lip, biting back the words she no doubt wanted to fling at his head. Her lips were still damp and reddened from his mouth, and he wanted her again, more powerfully than before. "What do you want from me?" she asked with a trace of desperation.

He let his glance slide down her strong, lush body, slowly, then raised his eyes to hers. "What makes you think I want something from you?"

"I'm not a total idiot, even if I act like one on occasions."

"I haven't seen you act like an idiot recently."

"Try five minutes ago. Kissing you in the kitchen was not a particularly smart move."

"Should you have kissed me in the bedroom?" he countered smoothly. "And actually, I didn't notice you doing any of the kissing. Granted, you didn't slap my face and screech 'how dare you?' like an outraged virgin, but I wasn't aware of any enthusiastic participation." It was a lie. He'd felt her response, in a thousand tiny, yearning ways. But she wouldn't know that.

The color on her cheeks deepened. "What do you want from me?" she persisted.

For such a tall, womanly creature she suddenly reminded him of a child. A defiant tomboy, facing her worst nightmare, with fists clenched, trembling, determined not to show it. Maybe that's exactly what he was. The thing every woman feared. A spiritual vampire, ready to drain her of everything for his own survival.

He reached out a hand, waiting to see whether she'd try to duck. She held her ground, but he could see the muscle clench at the base of her jaw, as his long fingers brushed the side of her cheek. "Maybe just a taste of innocence," he murmured.

"I'm not innocent."

He wanted to laugh. "Compared to me you are."

"Compared to you, anyone is."

"Perhaps." He let his fingers play across her lips, and they were soft, faintly clinging. "Perhaps I want to bring you down to my level. Corrupt you, destroy you, and then murder you." He spoke the words lightly, softly, and it took a moment for her eyes to grow cold with fear, for her mouth to tighten, for her to take a step away from him.

"I don't believe you," she said.

"Then what do you believe?"

She wasn't ready for that question. She shook

her head, blindly, and pushed away from the
counter, moving past him, careful not to touch
him. But the long, flowing skirts brushed against
his legs, and the scent of her lingered in the air,
and the taste of her clung to his mouth. And he
stood alone in the darkened kitchen for a very
long time, remembering.

CHAPTER 7

I need your help."

Cassidy looked up from the transcripts she was reading. Sean stood in the doorway, dressed in his favorite Irish wool suit, the one he wore for funerals and weddings. He looked glum, and Cass felt a clutching of nervousness in the pit of her stomach.

"Anything."

Sean grinned. "Don't be so rash, darling. Your da would have your soul if he could, and well you know it."

She considered it. She'd once thought so, flung those very words at him when she'd escaped from his overwhelming presence. "Maybe," she said. "Maybe I'm stronger now."

"Strong enough to stand up to me? It's a good thing—you're going to need your strength."

"What do you need me to do?" She was resigned.

"Bellingham's set up a meeting with the prosecutor, to see if we can work something out. Fabiani's insisting on having General Scott present as well, and Richard says he won't come unless you come with him."

"He doesn't need me to hold his hand," she snapped.

Sean shrugged. "You've been here, how long? A week? You should know that Richard is one very stubborn man. If he says he won't come to the meeting without you, then he won't come. And Fabiani says he won't even consider delays unless Tiernan's there."

"But why Scott?"

"He's a powerful man, politically. He can get what he needs, even from a state's attorney. If he wants to be at the meeting, to make sure things go according to his agenda, then no one's going to be able to stop him."

"You can't stand up to him?"

Sean reacted to the gentle barb as she expected. "Of course," he said, affronted. "The day some retired relic of the industrial-military complex can get the better of me will be the day they put me out to pasture. I'm interested in Scott. He won't talk to me about the book, but the man has secrets, I know it."

"You surely don't think he killed his daughter and grandchildren?" Cass demanded, horrified.

"No."

"He didn't strike me as the kind of man who kept secrets. He seemed to be the sort who put everything on the table, and dared you to accept it or not."

"And when did you meet General Scott?" Sean asked mildly.

She considered lying, then dismissed the notion. She was a lousy liar, always getting caught. "Didn't I mention it?" she said airily. "I ran into him in the park a few days ago."

"Ran into him?" Sean closed the door behind him. "Scott and his wife have a condo on the West Side. Why would he just happen to run across you in the park, and how in hell would he even know who you are?"

So much for airiness. "I believe he followed me."

"I believe it, too." Sean's voice was grim. "What did he want from you?"

"He wanted to warn me."

Sean's reaction was a bark of laughter. "That you were consorting with a convicted murderer? That was hardly news. Did he tell you Richard would kill you?"

"Among other things."

Something in her voice must have caught his attention. "Spill it, Cassie. What else did General Scott tell you?"

She could have asked him anytime during the last few days, and each time she'd considered it she'd stopped, frightened. Frightened of his answer. "He told me you weren't writing a book to clear Richard's name."

"And what kind of book did he say I was writing?" Sean countered, unmoved.

"That you were writing a book, with Richard's help, that would illuminate the mind of a murderer. That you're writing a book about evil, and you don't care what price you have to pay for it."

"You think books about evil shouldn't be written? I didn't know you had such a censorious streak in you."

"You know I don't. Don't try to change the subject, Sean. What's the damned book about?"

"About Richard Tiernan, and the murders of his wife and children. I'm telling his side of the story."

"Are you telling the story of a murderer?" she persisted, not wanting the answer.

She didn't get it. "Ask Richard," he said.

"I'm asking you."

"Don't." The word was short, fraught with meanings she didn't want to consider. "Will you come with him to the lawyer's office or not?"

"Yes."

She'd manage to startle her father, no mean triumph. "You must be more like me than I realized," he said, half under his breath. "Two-fifteen, at Bellingham's office. Richard knows how to get there."

"Why won't he go himself?"

"Beats me. As far as I know he hasn't left this apartment since he got out of jail. Why don't you ask him?"

"Richard doesn't give me straight answers any more than you do."

"Count your blessings," Sean said. "Be ready to leave by two."

"Will he be ready?"

"Your guess is as good as mine."

She sat without moving for uncounted minutes after Sean left. Bridget's wonderful coffee had grown cold in the cup by her elbow, and her stomach, comfortably full of cholesterol, now began to revolt. She should know better than to eat anything but dry toast as long as she lived surrounded by the miasma of Richard Tiernan's crimes.

If they were his crimes. She hadn't seen him since the night before last, when he'd pushed her up against the counter and kissed her. It was just as well. She'd escaped to her room, locking the door with the newfound key and staying there, terrified that he'd come knocking, terrified that she'd let him in.

She hadn't bothered to correct his assumption that she was going out with Mark, for any number of reasons. She wanted him to think she had an escape, even when she knew she didn't. She wanted him to think she hadn't paid any attention to his subtle warnings, when she had. And she wanted him to think that he hadn't become an obsession with her, a constant, peace-destroying presence in her mind.

She flat-out refused to think about the kiss. She'd never realized she had a gift for denial, for blocking things too overpowering to deal with. But every time the taste, the memory came sneaking back, she shoved it away from her with a fierce determination.

He was waiting for her in the hallway, sitting in the Chinese chair. He'd shaved, and his dark hair was beginning to grow from its prison shortness. He sat there in a dark suit, his face thin and shadowed, watching her, and she tugged at her own power suit, something she seldom wore, complete with NFL-size shoulder pads. He rose, slow and graceful, and she wished she'd worn heels. She needed all the defenses she could get against a man who overwhelmed her, physically and emotionally.

"Ready?" she asked brightly, inanely.

"Yes." He opened the door, waiting for her to precede him. That was one thing she could say for him—the man had impeccable manners when he chose to use them. It was hardly reassuring.

She didn't know what she expected as they walked down the broad sidewalks of Park Avenue. He stared straight ahead, his mind seemingly a million miles away, and she hurried to keep up with his long strides. She half expected the people rushing past them to stop and stare, to point out the murderer and his consort. But the people of New York were far too involved in their own affairs to notice the tall, haunted-looking man as he strode down the street.

She reached out to catch his arm, to slow him

down. He stopped, turning to look at her, and for a moment his bleak expression lightened with a look of wry amusement. "Out of breath?"

She was, but she quickly tried to cover it. "We aren't running a marathon, are we?" she countered. "How far away is Bellingham's office?"

"Just another block. We have plenty of time," Once he stopped he didn't seem inclined to move, and the hordes of people simply surged around them, like the Red Sea parting.

"Then why were we running?"

He glanced around them, and shrugged. "I've been in prison too long."

"Is that why you haven't left the apartment since you got there?"

"Is that what your father told you? I haven't become agoraphobic. At least, not yet. I don't imagine I'll have much time to develop the affliction. Unless Mark can manage to pull a rabbit out of a hat."

"If you don't think Mark can get you off on appeal, why don't you hire another lawyer?"

"I don't think anyone can get me off on appeal," he said lightly. "My fate is sealed, and it's a waste of time and energy to fight it. Besides, I have a certain amount of loyalty. I've known Mark since we were in high school, and he's stood by me. How was dinner?"

The change of subject was so abrupt she almost blew it and told him the truth. That she hadn't gone out with Mark and had no intention of doing so. "Fine," she said instead. "Mark's very charming."

Richard made a noncommittal noise. "Let's go see if he's able to charm my father-in-law and the prosecutor, shall we? I expect that's beyond even his abilities."

"Will you tell me the truth if I ask you one question?"

His dark eyes were hooded, and his thin mouth turned up in a taunting smile. "If you can stand the answer."

"Why did you want me to come with you today? You aren't worried about being recognized, and you don't really have a problem with being out on the streets, do you?"

He considered it for a moment. "I'd say I have at least half a dozen reasons. Are you certain you want to hear them?"

No, she thought. "Yes," she said.

"Number one, I didn't want to be out here alone. I've spent too much time being confined during the last year, and the thought of being allowed to walk free in the city terrified me."

"Nothing terrifies you."

"If you want my reasons, don't pass judgment on them."

"Sorry. Reason number two?"

"Number two, your father thought it was a good idea, to make certain I actually got there. Number three, I want Mark to see us walk in together, arm in arm, so that he won't be so sure of his ability to charm anyone he wants into his bed. Number four . . ." he ruthlessly overrode her protest, "I want General Scott to see you with me, to know that all his warnings came to nothing, that another innocent female is in my clutches, and there's not a damned thing he can do about it."

She didn't say a word, shocked into silence.

"Number five," he continued smoothly, entirely aware of her tumbled reactions, "I simply wanted your company, and I knew your father could command it."

She tried to speak for a moment, cleared her throat, and tried again. "That's five reasons, most of them sick. You said there were at least half a dozen."

"Number six," he said, with a charming, predatory smile, "was the irresistible urge to see just how far I can push you. I make you very uncomfortable—you aren't certain whether you despise me, or if I simply scare you half to death."

"You don't scare me."

"Liar. Every time you look at me, you think about what I was convicted of doing."

"And I don't despise you," she continued stubbornly.

"Another lie. You're frightened of me, you hate me, but you're also fascinated by me."

She didn't bother to deny it. "Why do you think I stay on here?" she said, raising her chin to meet his dark gaze. "Apart from helping my father, it happens to be a very interesting case. I think it will make a terrific book."

"You aren't staying because of the case, Cassidy," he corrected her gently. "And it's not my wife's death that fascinates you. It's me."

For a moment she was silent, as mesmerized by his wicked beauty as he'd accused her of being. And then she marshaled her defenses. "I'm fascinated by the size of your ego."

He tucked his arm through hers, his large hand covering hers, and there was no escape. She trembled, but she didn't pull away, letting him draw her down the sidewalk. "You see," he murmured, "just two harmless souls on a stroll down Park Avenue. Who would have thought about the darkness that lurks beneath our pleasant surface?"

"There is no darkness in my life," Cassidy snapped.

He glanced down at her. "Yes, there is," he said gently. "I'm in your life."

The conference room at the office of Bellingham and Stearns resembled nothing so much as an armed camp. Jerome Fabiani and General Scott were sitting on one side of the broad mahogany table, hands folded, faces set in identical expressions. On the other side sat Mark, looking deceptively rumpled, Sean, and Till Elder, Sean's publisher for the last dozen or so years, and a handful of suits Cass didn't recognize, lined up on either side of the table.

Richard didn't release her until they walked into the room, until he was certain everyone had seen his possessive gesture, and Cassidy wanted to scream out denial, fury. She said nothing, taking in each man's expression. Mark looked disturbed, the general, sorrowful, her father, pleased. And she didn't trust any of them.

"Sorry if we're late," she murmured, slipping into a seat between her father and Till.

"Not at all," Mark said genially. "We're not quite ready to begin."

A small buzz of strained chatter began to fill the room, and Till leaned over, putting his hand on Cassie's. "Glad to see you back, Cass," he murmured. "Your father's a reprobate, but he loves you, and he needs your help on this one. I think he's bitten off more than he can chew."

"Why don't you tell him you won't publish it?" she whispered back.

"I'm a businessman before I'm a friend," Till replied with Brahman dignity. "It'll sell like mad."

Richard had taken a seat beside Mark, and he was sitting there, unmoving, as his lawyer whispered in his ear. He was directly across from General Scott, and there was no missing the waves of hatred and fury that were emanating from his father-in-law. Richard met his gaze blandly.

Jerome Fabiani went on the offensive. "I don't know what the point is to this meeting," he announced in the golden voice that had made good use of the newly reinstated death penalty and assured him a future in politics that he was already beginning to work on. "Mr. Tiernan has been tried and found guilty by a jury of his peers. He's going through the appeal process, and despite my best efforts, he's presently free to walk the streets. If his counsel wanted more time to prepare his case then he shouldn't have gotten his client out of Dannemora. Each day that Richard Tiernan is out of custody is a day that society is endangered, and I have no intention of allowing that state of affairs to continue longer than necessary."

Sean dove right in. "A man is innocent until he's been proven guilty, Fabiani."

Fabiani looked at Sean with contempt. "He *has* been proven guilty, Mr. O'Rourke. Once we get through the farce of his appeal, I'm expecting the state of New York to do its duty. Barring any kind of nonsense like the death penalty being repealed again."

"I'm not really worried," General Scott spoke up. "Someone will take care of him in prison. Even the dregs of humanity draw the line when it comes to slaughtering your own children."

Richard didn't show the slightest anger; instead a slow, taunting smile curved his mouth, faint enough to chill Cassidy's blood. Scott's response was immediate, as he lunged across the table, and it took several of the men there to hold him back, as Richard rose, elegant, disdainful. "I don't really know what I'm doing here," he murmured in a

bored voice. "You can work it out among your-
selves. I'm going for a walk." Across the room his
eyes met hers, distant, challenging. "Cassidy?"

She hesitated. She didn't want to go and stand
by him, to leave this room and walk away with a
man capable of such hideous crimes. And yet, was
he capable? Had he done what he'd been convicted of doing? Or was he the most misunder-
stood, most cruelly victimized man in the world?

No, the man standing there, commanding her
presence, was no victim. And much as she wanted
to ignore him, she had no choice. Not with Sean
kicking her under the table. Not with her own
unruly nature calling out to him.

They watched her as she rose and crossed the
room to him. All those men, passing judgment,
some with disbelief, some with contempt. She
went to him, because she had to. And because
she wanted to.

He didn't say a word until they were back out
on the street. He was walking faster than ever,
and she had to break into a half run to keep up
with him, but she didn't try to slow him down.
He needed to move, fast, away from his devils.
And she was willing to go with him.

They ended up in a bar on Sixty-ninth Street.
It was dark in the middle of the afternoon, an old
bar, redolent of ancient spirits and a lifetime of
tobacco, and Richard went straight to a booth
near the back, not bothering to check whether she
followed him. To her amazement she'd no sooner

sat down than a grizzled, elderly bartender appeared with a glass of whiskey and ice. "What would the lady like, Richard?"

He glanced at her. "The same as me, Ed. But not as strong."

She waited until the bartender left, staring at the man opposite her in surprise. "I thought you never left the apartment?"

"There's a service entrance in the kitchen, you know that as well as I do."

"I didn't think anyone ever used it anymore."

"I do," he said, leaning back and staring at her across the table. "Why did you come with me?"

He always asked the most difficult questions. "You told me to."

"You don't usually pay any attention to what I tell you to do. If I'd realized you were so malleable, I would have been more creative. Why don't you stop fiddling with that button and unfasten it?"

She'd been toying with the high button of her suit jacket, and she pulled her hand away. "I don't want to."

"It's warm, you've been racing after me down a crowded street, and you're buttoned up tighter than a battleship. I'm not asking, I'm telling you. Unfasten the goddamned button, or I'll do it myself."

The second glass of whiskey appeared in front of her, lighter in color, and then they were alone again, in the almost deserted bar. She reached up and unfastened the button. "I don't want the drink."

"Drink it."

"I don't want it . . ."

"Drink it."

She picked it up, took a sip, and grimaced. "I hate Irish whiskey."

"How'd you know it was Irish?"

"I'm my father's daughter. Unfortunately." She took another sip anyway, letting it burn down her throat, between her breasts. It stopped some of the panic that had been building up inside her.

He leaned back against the vinyl banquette, staring at her. "So you are," he said, cradling his own glass. "Fatherhood's an interesting thing, wouldn't you say? There are so many different aspects to it. There's your own father, using you for his needs, blithely disregarding your well-being for the sake of his own inflated ego. Then there's a man like Amberson Scott, whose life, outside his career, was entirely devoted to the worship of his little princess." There wasn't the faintest trace of irony in his voice, but the chill reached deeper into Cassidy's soul, and she took another sip of the strong whiskey.

"And then, of course, there's me," he said, staring at his own glass with a cool, meditative air. "If you were to believe the media, and Jerome Fabiani, I'm a man who was so busy with my career and my womanizing that I barely noticed the existence of my children, apart from the act of creating them. Until, of course, the night I decided to kill them, along with their unborn sibling and their mother. I'm not sure what people think I did with their bodies. One theory is that they're buried on a farm in Pennsylvania. I think one of the tabloids suggested that I ate them."

Cassidy drained her glass in one swift gulp. She wasn't used to drinking, and she hadn't been eating much. The alcohol hit her like a sledgehammer. "Did you love them?" she asked, knowing she should keep her mouth shut, knowing she should run.

Tiernan looked at her, his eyes full of sorrow. "More than life itself," he said simply. And she knew for the first time that he was telling her the truth.

He'd made her drunk. It should have amused him, that Cassidy Roarke, the daughter of such a notorious high-liver, couldn't hold her Irish whiskey. It should have made him feel guilty. Or triumphant. He should have felt something, other than the cool, dead feeling in the pit of his stomach, and in the dark hole where his heart had once been.

She'd been close to bringing him alive, and he'd hated her, resented her for that. That cocoon of stillness and death that had shielded him was starting to unravel, all due to her presence, and he'd needed her too much to resist.

He still needed her. But he needed his distance

as well. He should have just left that room, left the fat, smug faces and staring eyes of all those people who looked at him and saw a man who'd committed the foulest crimes against nature. All those innocent, condemning faces. All those fools.

But he wasn't strong enough. He'd considered himself invincible, but he couldn't walk away and leave her there, to listen to the things they would say about him. And he didn't want to leave her with Sean, with Mark, with his father-in-law. Most of all, not with retired General Amberson Scott.

Scott could make a believer out of anyone. He could turn a Quaker into a Green Beret, a democrat into a republican, a dog into a cat. If Cassidy had any doubts at all about his guilt, Scott could wipe them out with the sheer force of his personality.

He couldn't let that happen. He needed to keep Cassidy on edge, confused, doubting, afraid.

Of course, he could always tell her the truth. He watched her as she sat across from him, trying to gather her dignity around her like a torn shawl. How would she respond to the truth that he'd never admitted to a soul?

She'd probably run screaming out of the bar.

He needed to own her first. He needed to have her, body and soul, mind and spirit, before he let her know even an inkling of the truth. He needed her so tied to him that she couldn't run, couldn't struggle, that she'd simply accept, and do as he needed her to do.

The truth was his, and his alone. Sean thought he was getting it, but Sean's ego was blinding him. No doubt he was writing a hell of a book, a landmark of a literary creation. But it wasn't the truth.

Richard was going to die with the truth. If state laws and the vagaries of the justice system gave him a reprieve from his death sentence, he was certain one of his fellow inmates would see to the matter. Scott was right—even the most hardened criminal drew the line when it came to the murder of children, and there were any number of people inside who might think they were buying their own way into heaven by disposing of him.

In the meantime, he had to get Cassidy Roarke back to her father's apartment before anyone else returned. He had to get her back to her Gothic bedroom and put his hands under her skirt. He wanted to touch her, to get her wet, to make her want him. More than she already, reluctantly did.

And then he'd leave her. Aching, wanting, needing him. So that the next time, or maybe the time after that, she'd be ready. And there'd be no turning back. For either of them.

CHAPTER 8

The bright day had darkened considerably by the time Richard steered her out of the bar. He'd managed to get her to drink another half glass of Irish whiskey, mainly by goading her, and she was in a delectably reckless state. One push, one hard push, and she'd fall, on her back, taking him with her.

The hell with waiting. He wanted her, wanted to lose himself in her body, the taste, the smell, the feel of her. He wanted to thread his hands through her wild hair and draw her mouth down his body, he wanted her willing to take everything from him, and then take more.

She stumbled slightly as she followed him into the elevator, leaning back against the burnished walnut and closing her eyes. She hadn't rebuttoned her suit jacket, and he could see the silk blouse that was clinging to her, see the hollow between her breasts. He wanted to put his mouth there.

The elevator door slid open when they reached

the twelfth floor, and he waited, hoping he'd have an excuse to touch her, knowing he needed no excuse. He doubted they'd get past the hallway.

She moved with careful grace, past him, and he let her go. For now. He stood aside while she fumbled with the keys, controlling his impulse to snatch them out of her hands and open the locks himself. The delay simply added to the anticipation. Each level of frustration was a challenge.

The door finally yielded. He followed her into the darkened hallway, closing the door behind them, and put his hand over hers as she reached for the light switch.

"It's dark," she said.

"I know."

"Mabry must be out somewhere . . ."

"Didn't Sean tell you? They were going out to some publishing function, and then on to dinner. They won't be back until late." His hand still covered hers, and he felt the jerk of panic beneath her skin.

"He didn't tell me."

"I didn't think so." He moved her hand away from the wall, using his strength, and she let him. The combination of fear and desire was thick in the air, a potent aphrodisiac. He'd never made love to a woman who was frightened of him, and who wanted him anyway. He was looking forward to it.

He took her hand and placed it on his chest, so she could feel the tempo of his heartbeat, feel his heat. "Do you want to run away, Cass?" he whispered, bending closer, his mouth next to her ear, beneath the cloud of flame-colored hair. "Are you frightened?"

He didn't think she would answer. Probably without the Irish whiskey she would have lied. But she made the mistake of looking at him, and even in the shadows of the deserted apartment he could see everything she wanted to hide from him. Her fear. Her anger. And her desire.

"Yes," she said. And it sealed her fate.

He drew her hand down his chest, to the belt buckle, his eyes never leaving hers. She couldn't look away from him, he couldn't look away from her. He moved her hand lower, covering his erection, and she made a faint sound, one of distress, perhaps.

She tried to pull away then, but he wouldn't let her, pushing her up against the wall, trapping her hand between their bodies, pressed against him, as his mouth caught hers. She made that sound again, and it was something more than distress. It was longing as well, and he tasted it, his tongue in her mouth, as he tasted the Irish whiskey they'd shared, and he was on fire with his need for her.

He slid his hand behind her, pushing the jacket from her shoulders, determined to strip off that suit and have her naked on the hardwood floor of her father's foyer. He felt her fingers curl around him, and he almost came. He reached up and caught her head in his hands, threading his fingers through her tawny hair, and used nothing but his mouth to take her, seduce her, own her, as her body softened and flowed against his hardness.

He pulled away from her, breathing hard, making no effort to control his reaction to her. Her own eyes were lowered, and she leaned back against the wall, waiting. Reaching up, he began to unfasten the silk covered buttons, roughly, wondering what had happened to the deft seducer. He knew the answer to that one. He was living on borrowed time, and he couldn't afford to waste a moment.

He pulled her blouse free from her skirt. Her bra was skimpy, lacy, barely covering her breasts, and he let his thumb trace the darkness of her areolas beneath the lace, felt the nipples bead up. Leaning down, he took one in his mouth, through the lace, swirling his tongue against the textures, sucking it in deep, and he felt her jerk against him, as her hands came up to rest on his shoulders, and she arched back, offering herself, as he needed her. He slid his hand up her thigh, pulling her narrow skirt up with him, when he heard a strangled gasp of shock. Mingled with a snort of amusement.

Cassidy didn't move. He felt the coldness swamp her body, mixed with the heat of embarrassment. He lifted his head, and his eyes met hers for a long, pregnant moment. And then she closed hers, leaning back against the wall and uttering a faint moan.

He pulled her shirt back around her, shielding her body with his, before turning. The three of them stood in the kitchen doorway, with three, varying reactions. Mark looked shocked, even frightened, Mabry troubled. And Sean, curse his black Irish soul, was smirking.

Cass pushed away from Richard, and he tried to reach out and catch her wrist, but she was too fast, moving down the hallway, past the voyeurs, away from him. A moment later he heard her door slam, and it didn't take much imagination to know that the lock had followed.

"Richard," Mark said, his voice shaken.

"Come on, Mabry," Sean said, his voice rich with amusement. "I think the lads have a few things to work out."

"What have you been doing, Sean?" Mabry asked wearily, but there was no answer, and Richard was left alone in the hallway with the only true friend he had.

"What in God's name are you trying to do?" Mark demanded in a hushed voice.

"You're smart enough. You figure it out."

"Don't tell me it's a simple case of lust. I won't believe you."

"Lust is seldom simple."

"Don't play games with me, Richard. I want to know what you have in mind for her. She's an innocent—you don't need to drag her into this mess."

"Who says I'm dragging her into anything? Who

says I want anything more than a taste of that remarkably luscious body of hers? You had your chance a few nights ago—now it's my turn."

"Is this some kind of one-upsmanship? I thought I was the one who had to compete with you, not the other way around," Mark said bitterly. "At least, that's the way it's always been. And she refused to go out with me. Thanks to you, no doubt. What did you do, tell her I was married?"

Richard allowed himself a faint smile. The rage in his blood had quieted, at least for now. He accepted the fact that Cassidy had escaped. For the moment. Sooner or later they'd be alone, and nothing would stop him. "It's the truth."

"Damn it, Richard, the divorce will be final in less than three weeks. I'd hardly call that a lifetime commitment. You didn't explain that, did you?"

"I mentioned you might have some trouble in your marriage."

"Trouble like a divorce that's almost final. Damn you, Richard. What do you want from her? You seemed determined to keep her away from me."

"Now, why should I do that? You're not a serial killer are you? Murdering women once you fuck them?" He kept his voice low and conversational, knowing it was the best way to rattle him.

"Neither of us are."

"How do you know who and what I am?" he countered.

Mark shook his head. "You're wasting your games with me. You forget, I know you. Better than anybody. You have something in mind for Cassie, and her father's in collusion with you. I want to know what it is."

"I'd suggest you use your imagination, but I've already seen how dangerous that can be. If I want anything from Cassie, I promise you'll be the second to know. After the lady herself, that is," he said pleasantly.

"Damn it, Richard, I care about her!" Mark said furiously.

"That was remarkably fast, wasn't it? Since you said she wouldn't go out with you, you must have seen her, what is it? Twice? Don't tell me it's love at first sight."

"I hate it when you sneer," Mark shot back.

"Was I sneering? Sorry. Young love brings out the cynic in me."

"We're not talking about young love, or love at first sight, or any of that bullshit. We're talking about a decent human being who doesn't deserve to be brought into your tortured schemes."

"What makes you think my schemes are tortured? They're really quite straightforward."

"What do you want with her?"

"For the time being, Mark, none of your damned business." He started away from him, down the hall, and Mark's voice followed him.

"I'm warning you, Richard. If you're planning on hurting her, you'll have to look elsewhere for help. Someone else can arrange your legal and financial affairs."

He didn't bother to turn around. "I'm counting on you, Mark." And the faint words were only lightly tinged with threat.

He went straight to Cass's door. He expected it to be locked, so he simply knocked, twice, softly, as he'd heard Mabry do.

In a moment the door swung open, and Cass's face appeared, pale, woebegone, streaked with unexpected tears. "Mabry . . ." she said, and then her voice disappeared as she saw him.

She tried to slam the door shut in his face, but he put out his hand to stop it, forcing it open, moving inside and closing it behind him. He considered locking it, but Cassidy looked at the raw edge of her reserves, and she might very well scream the place down if he tried it.

"Go away," she said.

She refused to look at him, so he simply put his hand on her chin and lifted it, forcing her to meet his gaze. "I didn't know they were here," he said.

"Didn't you?" Her doubt was insultingly clear.

"If I did, I would have taken you to a hotel."

It shocked a reaction out of her, as pink flooded her pale cheeks. "I wouldn't have gone."

"Maybe," he murmured, leaning closer. "Maybe

not. Tell me, Cassidy. What would have happened if they hadn't interrupted us?"

"I would have come to my senses. I stopped being a victim years ago, Richard. I don't do self-destructive things." Her eyes were surprisingly calm despite the flush on her cheeks.

"You're never impulsive? You never ignore what your brain tells you and follow your heart?" he persisted.

"My heart didn't have a damned thing to do with it," Cassidy said tartly. "We aren't talking about romance, we're talking about sex. I'm human, female, healthy as the next person. And you're very good, aren't you, Richard?"

"Good at what?"

"At seduction. At teasing and taunting and drawing someone along, making them do what you want. You know just how to play me. How did you develop such a talent?"

"Lots of practice," he replied in a silken voice.

"It's all a game to you, isn't it? Some nasty, manipulative little exercise in mind control."

"Actually," he said, "it's not only your mind I'm interested in. I want your body and soul as well."

She should have been past being shocked, but she wasn't. She just stared at him, and he moved closer, keeping his hands to himself, so close that his body brushed hers. She didn't back away from him, something he had to admire, even as he knew he had more work to do.

"Leave me alone, Richard," she said, very quietly. "You don't need me, and I'm hardly enough of a challenge."

"Wrong on both counts," he whispered, his mouth brushing hers, just feathering lightly against her lips. They moved beneath his, clinging for a brief, impulsive moment. "Just answer me one thing, Cassidy, and I'll let you be." He spoke against her mouth, barely audible, and he could see the dark torment in her eyes.

"Ask me," she said in a hushed voice, and the movement of her mouth against his was an unwilling kiss.

"Did you like it?"

Her eyes had begun to drift half-closed, but they shot open in outrage, and she jerked away from him. "Get out of here."

He caught her as she tried to get away, hauling her back up against him, and her eyes blazed into his. "Shall I find out?" he murmured, and slid his hand down the front of her skirt, over her mound, pressing.

She hit him. Hard, slamming her wrist against the side of his face, and he felt her ring scrape against his cheekbone, and then she backed away, clearly shocked.

He considered hitting her back. He would have, if it would advance his plan. He would do anything to further his agenda, whether he liked the idea or not. He didn't like the idea of hitting her. Kissing her, teasing her, fucking her, yes. But not hurting her, if he didn't have to.

"It's interesting how easy violence is," he murmured. "Just have someone goad you, and you lose control."

She looked sick. "Is that what happened with your wife?"

"I don't know," he said blandly. "I wasn't there." And he turned and left the room, closing the door quietly behind him.

Cass waited, her fist jammed in her mouth. She wouldn't have heard him walk away—he moved like a vampire, silent, elusive. She counted to twenty, then ran to the door and locked it. When she turned away she realized her knees were weak, and she threw herself on the bed, shuddering.

Her arm ached. She had never hit another human being in her entire life. Even in her childhood, when her elder brother Colin had teased her, she'd never attacked him with pummeling little fists. She hadn't liked the tension, the shouting that had filled her home. She hadn't liked the occasional blows she'd sensed more than seen between her parents. She'd always told herself she'd never lose control, never hit another living soul, never fly into a panic and rage so deep that her defenses crumbled.

But Richard Tiernan had breached those defenses, time and time again, and she had little doubt he'd done it deliberately. He'd wanted to see how far he could goad her, though she couldn't imagine why. Unless he were simply so bored that he was forced to waste his energies playing cat-and-mouse games with the only available mouse in the apartment.

He simply wanted to see what she'd do if he kissed her again. See how far she'd be willing to go, and she, like a brainless idiot, had been ready to do just about anything for him. What would he have done if they hadn't been interrupted?

Except she knew exactly what he would have done. She'd felt him beneath her hand when he'd drawn it down his body, known just how hard he was. He may have been toying with her, teasing her. But he'd been caught in his own trap as well.

She couldn't stay here. How many times had she decided that, how many times had she changed her mind? She wasn't going to pack, she wasn't going to tell anyone, she was simply going to take her purse and walk out the front door. Mabry could send her clothes to her. Sean could survive quite well without her—a semi-competent secretary could handle what she'd been doing.

She glanced in the mirror, intending to put herself in a semblance of order, when she stopped, horrified. Her hair was a tangled mass, a flyaway halo of fiery curves. Her lips were damp and swollen, her eyes huge, and the trace of her reluctant tears could still be seen. Her jacket was somewhere in the front hall, and her silk blouse hung open around her. The front of her bra was still damp from his mouth.

And so was she. He'd known it, he'd done it

deliberately, and all her embarrassment and rage couldn't change simple biology. She was wet for him. Aching for him. Even though he was disaster.

Her hands were shaking as she pulled the blouse over her head. It took her a few minutes to change her clothes completely, dumping the skirt and underwear in the hamper, pulling on a pair of khakis and a cotton sweater and her aging running shoes. She even found an oversize pair of sunglasses to plop on her nose. She was running away, incognito, and she wasn't going to stop until she was safely back in Baltimore.

There was no sign of anyone when she stepped out into the hallway. From a distance she could hear men's voices, low, casual, Sean's distinctive, pseudo-Irish lilt mixing with Richard's slow, dark tones. Mark was probably there as well, damn him, and damn all men.

She almost made it to the front door when Mabry appeared. She looked pale, sick, and resigned. "Running away, Cassidy?" she asked.

"I really need to get back," she temporized. "Besides, can you blame me?"

"Not really. Are you leaving now?"

"I was trying to. Before someone tried to stop me."

"You know us all too well," Mabry said.

For a moment Cassidy had the horrifying thought that Mabry, cool, unruffled Mabry, might start to cry. And then she blinked, her serene smile in place, and Cassidy decided she must have imagined it.

"If you're determined to leave, I won't stop you," Mabry said. "But before you get on the train, we have to talk. Let's get out of this place—it's getting on my nerves. We'll go someplace for a drink."

"No drinks!" Cass said, shuddering, the taste of the Irish whiskey still blending with the taste of Richard Tiernan.

"Tea, then. A nice, soothing English tea, complete with scones and strawberry preserves. And then we can talk."

"About Sean, I suppose?" Cassidy said wearily. "You aren't going to spin me some cock-and-bull story about him being sick, are you? He's as strong as an ox."

Mabry's perfect mouth curved gently. "He's not just sick, darling," she said. "He's dying."

Sean was well into his third whiskey and soda, getting more expansive by the moment. Richard sat back in the chair, watching him, part of his mind preoccupied with Cassidy. She was going to try to run, he knew that. He wondered whether he dared try to stop her. Or if she escaped, could he go after her?

Both those possibilities seemed unlikely. He might have Sean ready to sacrifice his daughter, but Mabry would be on Cassidy's side. If he came up against the two of them, there'd be nothing he could do.

He could only hope he'd brought her far enough along that she couldn't run. No matter how much she wanted to escape him, the strands of his spider's web were too long and sticky, trapping her. Part of her might want to run, but another part was too fascinated to leave. He wondered which part would be stronger.

"Lord, Mabry's gonna tear a strip off my hide tonight," Sean said cheerfully. "And you should have seen Bellingham's expression when we found you two in the hallway. I thought his eyes were going to bug out. It's a good thing I didn't wait a few minutes longer, or he might have had heart failure, and you would have had to get another lawyer."

"What made you decide to come home? I though you were going on to some social function."

"I wasn't feeling well," Sean said blithely. "A bit too much of the grape last night. Besides, I was curious as to what you had planned for Cassie. I expected the two of you would be socked up in bed by the time we made it back here, but you weren't. I must say, I was sorely disappointed in you, laddie."

"Were you, now?"

"I should have known you were just doing things at your own pace. Lord, you remind me of

me when I was a lad. There wasn't a woman who
could say no to me, either."

Richard looked at the man, and calmly thought
about murder. "We aren't at all alike."

"Bullshit. You would have had her panties off
in another minute, and she's the most prudish
little thing I've ever known. Takes after her
mother in matters like that—she'd have the balls
off you before you knew what you were doing."

"We're talking about your daughter, not some
two-dollar whore."

"Didn't know any came that cheap anymore,"
Sean said wistfully, draining his glass. "Are you
trying to tell me you respect the girl? You don't
need to lie to me—I'm not asking your intentions.
You could hardly promise to make an honest
woman of her, now could you? You don't strike
me as optimum marriage material."

Richard surveyed his hands for a moment. Long
fingers, strong fingers. He could choke the life
out of the old man in a matter of moments, and
the world would be a better place. What more did
he have to lose?

He looked up, suddenly shocked. It was that
easy. So dangerously easy, to slip into that kind
of thinking. And only another easy step to act on
it. No wonder there was crime, and capital
punishment.

"Are you all right, boy-o?" Sean demanded,
lumbering to his feet and swaying slightly. "You
look like you've seen a ghost."

Richard summoned the mere trace of a smile. "I have, Sean. And it's yours."

He'd managed to rattle the old man. "Jesus Christ!" he said, staggering backward. "You've got a creepy sense of humor, Tiernan. I hope you know that."

"I do," Richard said gently, staring at his hands again, his murderous hands. "I do."

"Have a scone, darling," Mabry said.

Cassidy stared down at the plate of delicacies with a hopeless sigh. "Somehow I seem to have lost my appetite. Between your melodramatic statements and Richard Tiernan, I'll probably lose enough weight to satisfy even my father."

Mabry took a small, elegant sip of her Lapsang Souchong, while Cassidy clutched her diet Coke grimly. "I wasn't being melodramatic, Cassie," she said quietly. "I meant every word."

"That' what bothers me. You've been around Sean too long—you're seeing everything in extremes. Sean is like an ox, he's tough . . ."

"He's dying. He doesn't realize I know it. The pain isn't bad yet, and the doctor said it probably will stay manageable. That's why he's drinking so much. If he stays just slightly looped he can control it without painkillers. He's got cancer, Cassie. And it's already spread."

The condensation around the glass of soda was wet and icy against her skin. The smell of Mabry's smoky tea roiled her stomach. "How long?"

"Not long enough. He wants to finish the book. He needs to, Cassie. And he needs your help."

"Why does he have to finish the book? It can't be money—I know my father too well. For all his grand auld sod ways, he's always been as close as a miser with his earnings."

"Money doesn't go as far as it used to. And if you're thinking your father has anything as mundane as health or life insurance you can guess again. He's always said he puts his life in the hands of fate."

"And look where it's gotten him."

"It's gotten him me," Mabry said in a gently reproving voice. "And it's gotten him you."

"Rare treats, indeed," she said, fighting down the panic and disbelief that were sweeping over her. "It also brought him Richard Tiernan, so I'm not sure if he's come out ahead. Why does he have to finish that book, if it's not for the money?"

"He wants to go out a legend. You know as well as I do that nothing's ever come close to *Galway Hell*, and Sean knows it, too, for all that he won't admit it. The sales have been fine on some of the newer ones, but the last couple didn't earn out their advance. I don't think it's death he's afraid of, Cassie. It's losing his talent, his reputation . . ."

"He's throwing it away on tabloid trash."

Mabry shook her head. "It's not what you think it is."

"Then how the hell am I supposed to help with the book when I don't even know what it's about?"

she demanded, frustration and denial battling for control.

"It's about Richard Tiernan."

Cassidy took a deep, shuddering breath. "Mabry, I can't stay here. Not with that man. He ... unnerves me."

"Do you think he killed them? More importantly, do you think he's planning to kill you?"

Cassidy grimaced. "It sounds absurd, saying it like that. No, I'm not afraid that he's going to kill me. Nothing so obvious. He wants something from me, Mabry. Something terribly important, and I don't know what it is. And it frightens me."

"You never used to be so imaginative."

"I'm my father's daughter, remember?" she said wryly.

"If you think he wants something from you, why don't you simply ask him?"

"And expect a simple answer? No."

"Is there anything I can do to make you stay?"

"No," said Cassie, quite firmly. "I've had to learn to take care of myself, or my parents would have eaten me up. I'd do anything for Sean, but not at the expense of my own life. I'll come visit, after Richard Tiernan has left, but in the meantime I have to look after myself. I'm a survivor, and I've put the past behind me. I have a safe, comfortable life, and I'm not going to throw it all away."

Mabry leaned back and sighed. "All right," she

said, no longer arguing. "I'll come with you to the train."

Cass didn't move for a moment. It would be so simple—escape. She could run, she could hide, she could forget Richard Tiernan ever existed. After all, she didn't read tabloids, she didn't watch television. She probably wouldn't even hear when he was executed.

Executed. The word burned in her brain, her heart, like acid. She looked up, and met Mabry's knowing blue eyes. "I'm not going anywhere," she said wearily.

Mabry smiled faintly. "I know, darling. I know."

CHAPTER 9

Cassidy couldn't sleep. It didn't come as any sort of surprise—she'd had trouble sleeping ever since she'd made the life-altering mistake of coming up to New York. Just the presence of a convicted murderer under the same roof was enough to unsettle anyone, and after the events of today it was a wonder she wasn't sitting in a corner, babbling.

She rolled over, squinting at the carriage clock Mabry had chosen to fit the funereal decor of her bedroom. At 2:45 A.M. the apartment was quiet—even Park Avenue down below her velvet-curtained window seemed subdued.

She still couldn't believe Sean was going to die. When she and Mabry had returned, Sean was dozing in his office, and she'd stood there and stared at him, seeing the puffiness of pain and illness around his eyes, the graying of his hair, the look of frailty his robust personality had masked. She stared, and knew Mabry told her the truth. He was dying.

And she knew she couldn't say anything to Sean. He thought it was a secret, kept from those who loved him most. God only knew why—perhaps he needed to think himself indestructible, omnipotent. Perhaps he needed denial.

She couldn't leave him. She couldn't even go to a hotel and keep herself away from Richard Tiernan's very real threat. Sean would make a fuss, he wouldn't understand, and Cassidy wasn't in the mood to argue. She just wanted to be with Sean, to do whatever she could for him. If Richard were to hold a knife to her throat, she still couldn't leave her father. She'd made her life, separate, safe, but all those self-protective instincts vanished in the face of her father's need. She hadn't been able to save her parents' marriage, she hadn't been able to make her father into the kind of man she wanted him to be. She wouldn't be able to keep him alive, either, but at least she could make his passing easier. And make some kind of peace for herself.

But she wasn't going to be able to do it with Richard Tiernan stalking her.

She pulled herself out of bed, turning on the light that was too dim for reading. Without thinking about what she was doing, she got dressed, pulling on underwear, an oversize T-shirt, sweat pants, and a baggy shirt, topping it all off with a bulky sweater. She was too hot, and the layers of clothing added ten pounds to her already generous proportions, but she had no intention of considering that. If she was going to survive, to be here for her father when he needed her, she was going to have to make a few things very very clear to Richard Tiernan. And foolish or not, she was not going to wait any longer to do so.

Her bare feet made no noise whatsoever as she moved down the long hallway to her brother's old bedroom at the far end. She walked at a brisk pace, knowing if she hesitated she'd chicken out. If she didn't confront Tiernan now, she'd never be able to. There was something about the middle of the night that stripped life down to its essentials, and she couldn't be bothered with second thoughts.

She didn't knock on his door. Sean, despite or perhaps because of the large amounts of whiskey he consumed, was a light sleeper, and he would be up and spying at the first sound. She reached for the doorknob, wondering if Richard locked himself in at night. It turned silently beneath her hand, and she pushed it open.

She wasn't sure what she expected. She hadn't been in her brother's room since she'd been back, and part of her had pictured satanic rituals or prison-like decor.

In the moonlit darkness it looked much the same as it had the last time she'd seen it. Southwestern decor, narrow beds, clean lines. The twin beds were empty, one neatly made, one in complete disarray. She looked up, around the dark room, and saw him.

He was standing by the window, silhouetted by the moonlight, and the shadow of the mullions looked like bars around him. He was turned toward her, but his face was in the shadows, and all she could see was the glitter of his eyes as he watched her.

She stepped into the room and closed the door behind her. "Don't jump to any conclusions," she said.

He was motionless. She was suffocating in her multiple layers, he must be freezing. He was wearing nothing but a pair of jeans, and the window was open behind him, letting in a chill night breeze. It ruffled his hair, then danced on toward her, playful, innocent.

"I wasn't about to," he said in his slow, deep voice. "I find things are seldom what I expect them to be. And never what I want them to be."

She wasn't about to touch that statement. "My father is dying," she said baldly.

"I know."

"How?"

"He told me."

He couldn't have delivered a crueler blow, and he must have known it. "I don't believe you."

"Of course you do. It's just the sort of thing your father would do. Keep his own family in the dark and tell a stranger. The fact of the matter is, I wouldn't have done this book with him if it weren't his last chance. I knew he couldn't afford to screw it up."

She made a small, unintelligible sound of distress, and he moved toward her through the shadows. "You didn't really expect him to tell either you or Mabry, did you? That's not the kind of man Sean is. He's not the kind of man who asks for help, particularly from the women in his family. Particularly not from the woman he's hurt the most."

"He wouldn't want help from my mother."

"I'm talking about you, Cassidy. He knows how he's failed you, don't mistake that for a moment. It eats at him, as the cancer eats away at his body, and there's not a damned thing he can do about either one. He is what he is, and it's too late to change him."

"I can't leave him."

She could see his smile in the darkness. "Is that what's troubling you? You want to run away from me, but you can't leave him? It's true, right now we come as a package deal. And the big question is, who's going to die first?"

"You're so kind to spare my sensitive feelings," she said with acid-tinged politeness.

"You're tough, Cassidy. Any fool can see that. You can take what your father dishes out, and survive. You can even take my worst behavior and still come back fighting. If someone lied to spare you pain, you'd probably slug them." He took a step closer, into a shaft of moonlight, and she could see his face clearly. He had a scrape along one side of his face, beneath his eye, and she wanted to reach up and touch it.

"What happened to you?" Her voice came out in a hushed whisper, as she clenched her fists beside her.

He reached out and took one hand, gently, making no attempt to force the fingers open. He simply stroked the back of it, slowly, letting his fingertips brush against the claddagh ring she wore. "My just desserts," he said.

She'd forgotten. Blocked out that she'd hauled off and hit him. She hadn't forgotten why. Her blood was thrumming through her veins with a slow, insistent beat, and she swallowed, suddenly nervous. "You haven't asked me why I came here."

"I know why you came here." His smile flashed white in the darkness. "You came to tell me to leave you alone. You're not asking, you're telling. I'm to keep my hands to myself, keep my remarks to myself, and leave you the hell alone. You'll stay on, you'll nurse your father like the dutiful daughter that you are, putting your unrequited love for Daddy ahead of your own sanity and safety, and you want me to stand by and let you do just that. For the first time in your life, you get to be Daddy's girl, and you actually think I'll agree."

She wasn't going to argue with the way he put things. He had a talent for twisting things around. "You have no choice."

His smile was chilling. "There's always a

choice." He still held her hand, gently, stroking. "I'll make a bargain with you."

"No bargains."

He ignored her. "Something we can both live with. We both get part of what we want, even if we don't get it all." he said. "A compromise, a deal."

"You can't give me what I want. Even a part of it."

"You think not? It depends on what it is we're talking about. I can't keep your father alive, but then, no one can. He ignored it for too long, too sure of his own immortality. And I can't make him love you. He already does, to the best of his ability. Far more than you realize."

"Then what can you give me?" She should pull her hand away from him. The gentle touch of his long fingers was mesmerizing, and she couldn't bring herself to break the touch.

"The best sex you've ever had," he said in a low, calm voice. "But you don't want that, do you? You're so busy protecting yourself from hurt that you've stopped living. All your energies go to protecting yourself from pain. Well, life involves pain. And you have to make up your mind whether you're going to choose life or not."

She managed the ghost of a smile. "You're a fine one to talk about choosing life. You've chosen death."

"Are you asking me whether I killed my wife?"

"No. You aren't going to answer, and I don't

think I want to know. I've finished the trial transcripts. Your defense was tantamount to a confession of guilt. You put up no defense whatsoever— I don't know why you didn't just cop a plea and go straight to jail. For that matter, I don't know why you agreed to get out on appeal. From what I can see, you made no effort to make bail while you were awaiting trial. You've accepted your fate with a kind of inhuman passivity, and it's a wonder you aren't dead already."

"Did I have anything to live for?" he inquired gently.

"Has that changed?" she countered.

He looked down at their hands, then met her gaze again. "No," he said. "And it's better that way, don't you think? Considering that I'm not likely to be living for much longer."

"What do you want from me?"

"I want your innocence. I want your blind, unquestioning devotion to your father, your acceptance of who and what he is. I want you to look at me the way you look at him, knowing the worst. I want you to trust me, even when your brain tells you you shouldn't, I want you to ignore common sense and your lifelong need to protect yourself. I want you to give yourself to me, body and soul." The words were soft, silken, hypnotic, weaving a spell around her, one she struggled to break free from.

"You don't ask much, do you?" Her voice came out hushed.

"Everything."

He was mad. Why hadn't she realized it before? A man who could slaughter his family and then go on with his life, a man who could taunt and mesmerize and make her mad as well. She looked at him, and she felt the pull of him, the need, drawing her closer, closer, until she knew she would drown, and drown willingly. Had Diana Scott Tiernan gone to her death as willingly?

She shook her head, trying to break the spell. "No," she said, more a negation of his effect on her than a refusal.

"Of course," he said blandly, "I'd settle for a straightforward fuck."

Her head jerked up to meet his cool expression, and she was furious. "It's all a game to you, isn't it?" She pulled her hand free from his. "Murder must have been the ultimate thrill, and now life is intolerably boring. You have to get your kicks seeing who you can confuse and manipulate."

"Have I confused you, Cassidy? What are you confused about?"

She had never been so angry in her life. So wildly, intensely furious. "I'm calling your bluff, Tiernan. You say you'll settle for a straightforward fuck? If I strip off my clothes and lie down for you, will you leave me alone afterward?"

"How would you define leaving you alone?"

"Don't touch me, don't talk to me, don't tease me."

"No *t* words. No taunting, tickling, or torturing, either?"

God, she hated him. "You turn everything into a mind game, don't you? Can't you ever give an honest answer?"

"Give me a letter of the alphabet, and I'll stick to it," he murmured, unmoved by her whispered fury.

"Go fuck yourself."

"I thought I was going to fuck you."

He stood there, far too close, arrogant, cool, and mesmerizingly beautiful in the moonlight. He was doing it again, playing with her for his own twisted reasons, expecting her to run away again.

She couldn't live in this apartment, with her father, if she didn't face Richard down. Richard, and her fears. "I'm calling your bluff, Tiernan. I go to bed with you, and then you'll leave me alone. Right?"

Damn that smooth, superior curve to his mouth. The unreadable darkness in his eyes. "You love your father that much? That you'll give yourself to the devil for his sake? Or is that it? You need to make a sacrifice. It isn't good enough just being here. You have to prove your love."

"You were the one who started it," she said. "Is it a bargain or not?"

He let his eyes drop down the length of her body. She knew just what she looked like—tangled hair, pale, furious face, and an overlong body swathed in layers of clothes. If the man had any aesthetic sense at all, he'd send her on her way. She was counting on him doing exactly that.

Richard Tiernan couldn't possibly want her. His wife had been a fairy-tale princess. He'd hardly be interested in settling for Sean O'Rourke's oversize klutz of a daughter.

"A bargain," he said lightly. "How did you want to do it?"

She stared at him openmouthed in shock. "What do you mean?"

"How shall we do it? Missionary style, you on the bottom? Or do you prefer the top? We could do it up against the door, with your legs wrapped around me. Or I could take you from the back. That way you wouldn't have to look at me, and maybe you could pretend I was someone else."

"I . . . I . . ." It was one of the first times in her life she was lost for words.

"You're trying to call my bluff, Cassidy," he said softly. "Two can play at that game. Do you want to come first? Do you want me to use my mouth?"

She fumbled behind her for the doorknob, ready to run, when she saw the gleam of mocking triumph in his eyes. She wasn't going to let him win. Too much relied on the outcome of this confrontation. She had to win. She couldn't afford the price if she lost.

She stiffened her back, glaring at him. "Do whatever you goddamn please," she said, and pulled the heavy cotton sweater over her head.

"Oh, but I always take my partners' preferences

into account." He caught the sweater she hurled at him. "Are your breasts sensitive? Do you have a kinky streak? I could tie you up if you think it would make you feel better. That way you could pretend it was rape, and you'd be perfectly free to indulge your martyr fantasy. I think there are a few ties we could use . . ."

She yanked the sweatshirt over her head, her movements sharp and jerky. "Trust me," she said with false sweetness, "I'll be completely passive."

He still hadn't moved. He stood a few feet away, watching her, a faint, mocking smile on his shadowed face, and she wondered what would happen if she hit him again. The idea was as repulsive as it was enticing.

She put her hands under the oversize T-shirt and reached for the waistband of her sweatpants. "You certain you want to go through with this?" she said coolly.

He made no answer, watching her, so she shimmied out of them, kicking them away from her ankles, and then reached for the hemline of the T-shirt before she could chicken out, pulling it over her head. Her underwear wasn't designed to entice. It was cotton, with a modest lace trim, and she hadn't been planning on exposing it to anyone in the near future. Particularly not Richard Tiernan.

"Change your mind, Cassidy?" he murmured, when she hesitated.

Suddenly the reality of what she'd done hit her

with a blinding force. It was the middle of the night, and she was standing in the bedroom of a convicted murderer, wearing only a skimpy bra and panties, and daring him to have sex with her. She must be totally out of her mind.

But he was looking at her with that damn-all, amused smile, and the lingering tendrils of fury wiped out any second thoughts. He was playing a nasty game with her, and the only way she could win was to see it through to the end. "Change yours, Richard?" she countered.

"Why would I do that?"

"You don't really want me. You have no reason to want me. You're just amusing yourself by twisting the lives of the people around you, and you want to see how far you can push me. Isn't that right?"

He seemed to consider it. "Partly right. I want to see how far I can push you. And I like seeing just how twisted other people's lives can become. It's a small solace, but I'll take what I can get."

He took a step toward her, and it was all she could do not to back up. She held her ground, staring up at him defiantly, trying to ignore just how scantily clad she was.

"But you're wrong about one thing, Cassidy, and you know it as well as I do, no matter how you try to tell yourself otherwise. You're too wise, too intuitive not to know the truth, even if you wish it weren't true."

"What?" she asked warily. He was too close,

when she'd been hoping he would have backed down, now that he knew she wasn't about to.

He took her hand in his, and before she realized what he was doing he'd placed her palm against the zipper of his jeans. Against the unmistakable, pulsing hardness of him. "I want you, Cassidy. And you know it. I want you as much as you want me."

"I don't . . ."

He wouldn't let her go. He was holding her hand against him, tightly, rubbing against him. "Live dangerously, Cass," he whispered. "Tell yourself you'll never get another chance to screw a serial killer. Tell yourself you're doing this for dear old Dad. Tell yourself anything but the truth."

"And what is the truth?"

"That you're drawn to me, just as I'm drawn to you. Some dark, hidden part of you wants me, needs me. And is going to take me. Any way you can get me."

His other hand slid behind her neck, pulling her up against his body, her hand still pressed against his erection. His skin was hot against hers, smooth, burning up, and his mouth caught hers in a kiss so devastating, so thorough she wanted to cry. He'd pushed her up against the door, as he'd threatened, and she could feel his ribs, pressing against her, the rough texture of hair, the bone and sinew of him beneath all that heat and fury. His mouth was hard against hers, painfully so, lips and teeth and anger, and the hand at the back of her neck was too tight. She felt dizzy, and she told herself it was with cold, with pain, and she knew she lied. She was dizzy with fear. If she gave herself to him she'd die, she knew it. She wouldn't need him to kill her—she would simply cease to exist, and the thought terrified her.

She shoved at him in sudden panic, and to her momentary astonishment he released her, stepping back, smoothly. "Change your mind, Cassidy?" he asked in a deceptively pleasant tone of voice.

She shut her eyes for a moment, unable to bear the mockery in his face. He had to be some kind of monster, inhuman, to kiss her, to burn for her, and then to stand there, unmoved, and taunt her. She shuddered, then opened her eyes again. "Can I?"

"Of course. It's always a woman's prerogative."

"You're such a gentleman."

"I do try," he said lightly.

"If I go back to my room now, what will you do?"

He appeared to consider it calmly enough. "Go back to bed. Alone, regrettably."

"And what will you do tomorrow?"

"Exactly what I do every day. Haunt this apartment, read murder mysteries, and answer your father's occasional questions. Hardly conducive to an interesting life, but I find I prefer the quiet.

Not that I don't expect to have more than my
share of quiet, sooner or later."

"And what are you going to do about me?"

"About you, Cassidy? Why should I do anything
about you?"

"Will you leave me alone?"

His smile was so sweetly gentle it could have
charmed a rattlesnake. "Not in this lifetime."

She was cold, he could see that. Though the
tremors that shook her lush, magnificent body
could have been brought about by terror, and even
more likely, by rage.

It was that rage that drew him. No matter how
he tried to demoralize her, confuse her, shatter
her, she came back fighting like a mother tigress,
defending her cubs. She was passing every test he
threw at her, passing them all with flying colors,
and he allowed himself a small glimmer of emotion. Of hope.

She was the one. She could do it, she could
fight and keep fighting if it was something
important enough. Now all he had to do was bind
her to him, and that was relatively simple.

He needed to get her on the bed, where she
wanted to be. He needed to get between her long,
wonderful legs and make her feel things she'd
never felt before. He needed to make her come,
again and again, until she couldn't think, couldn't
breathe, couldn't do anything but what he wanted
her to do.

"So what's your answer, sweet Cassidy?" he murmured, moving closer to her. "Yes, or no?" He reached his hand up to her. Her bra fastened in front. Thoughtful of her. He brushed his fingertips against the clasp. "Or if you prefer me to be more exact. Now? Or later?"

A tremor rippled across her skin, and he could feel her heart racing beneath the clasp of the bra, beneath the touch of his fingers. And suddenly it was no longer a game. She stood there, within his grasp, trembling, and all he wanted to do was draw her against him and soothe her. Whisper gentle, calming words, stroking her into quiescence, until she warmed and softened and reached for him, ready for him.

There was no room for gentleness in the short time he had left. No room for compassion, or tenderness, and if he allowed himself to care, even for a moment, he'd be endangering everything.

Her eyes were bright with unshed tears of fury and a thousand other emotions, and he guessed she had no idea. She'd hate to think she was ready to cry in front of him.

He wanted to kiss those tears away, he wanted her to shed those tears for him. And that's what decided him.

He dropped his hand, taking a step back from her, grateful the shadows covered his reaction to her, the tremor that shivered across his own skin. He couldn't take her. Not until he had himself under control. Because if he made love to her when he was vulnerable, even minutely, then all his carefully constructed plans could explode in his face. And the consequences were too horrifying to even consider.

"I assume the answer is later," he said coolly.

Her head jerked up in shock. "What?"

"Go back to bed, Cassie," he dismissed her in a bored voice. "The game has lost its spice. We can start again tomorrow. Unless you think you're going to run."

"I can't run."

He smiled, not bothering to make it a pleasant one. "I know." He scooped up her scattered clothes and placed them in her arms. "Go to bed, Cassie," he said again. "Dream of me."

He opened the door for her, politely, ever the gentleman, waiting for her to take her one chance of escape.

"Not if I can help it," she said in a raw voice, starting past him.

"You can't," he murmured in her ear. And she slammed the door behind her.

CHAPTER 10

Cassidy decided she was a better actress than she would have thought. She was able to meet Sean's gaze with unflinching calm, giving as good as she got. Now that she knew the truth, she was amazed she'd missed all the obvious signs. His color was pasty, and the glitter in his eyes was as much pain as malice. He was subtly more clumsy, his movements dulled by alcohol or drugs or pain, or perhaps a combination of all three. She watched him, when he was absorbed in his work, and wondered how long he had left.

As for Richard Tiernan, she managed to avoid him, no mean feat. He was a man who wouldn't be avoided, not unless it was his choice, so she had to assume he was giving her much needed space. In another man, she might have thought it was a kindness, to spare her embarrassment, to give her time to get used to her father's condition. With Richard, she knew it was simply one more move in his elaborate psychological chess game.

For whatever reason, she blessed her reprieve,

knowing it would be short-lived. She was almost relieved when she walked into the office two days later, a mug of Bridget's black coffee in her hand, to find him there. He was lounging in the green leather chair, a book in hand, and he simply raised an inquiring eyebrow in greeting, a silent reminder of how he'd last seen her.

She had more important things to worry about than Richard Tiernan's mind games. She looked at the book he was reading—Ted Bundy's preppy face gleamed from the cover. She shivered.

"Where's your father this morning?" He set the book down on his lap, deliberately across his zipper, and she knew he'd done it on purpose, to draw her eyes there. "Did he send you in as virgin sacrifice, to distract me?"

"Mabry said he had a bad night. He's sleeping in."

"Sean doesn't give in to things like bad nights," Richard said.

"Don't you think I know it?" she shot back. "Maybe it's a hangover."

"Maybe."

She went behind the desk. There was a pile of manuscript pages sitting there. Sean usually kept his work close at hand, locked in the desk when he wasn't working on it. He must have had a bad night, indeed, to have left it out for her curious eyes.

"Are you going to read it?"

She glanced up. Richard seemed no more than casually interested. "Have you read it?"

"Most of it. It's exactly what he wants it to be. Quite, quite brilliant. It should be a fitting swan song. For both of us."

"Stop it."

"Denial never changed anything, Cassidy."

She stared at the manuscript. She didn't want to touch it, read it, find out things she couldn't bear knowing. Her eyes focused on the first sentence.

Diana Scott Tiernan was every father's dream, a fairy princess daughter, with a delicate, almost ethereal beauty, a wicked laugh, a charm that was as natural as it was powerful. She had only to walk into a room and it would come alive. When she died she was only twenty-nine years old.

She dropped the manuscript, shocked at the rage and jealousy that swept over her. She had never been anyone's fairy princess—there was nothing delicate or ethereal about her. She was an overgrown disappointment to her father, and doubtless a source of amusement to the man lounging in the chair, watching her.

"You don't like the book," he observed.

"Sean makes your wife sound quite . . . wonderful."

"You wouldn't have liked her."

"Why not?" She turned the manuscript over, gratefully, preferring to argue with her nemesis. "He makes it sound as if everyone loved her."

"The skies mourned when she died," Richard said mockingly. "You wouldn't have liked her. The two of you are complete opposites."

"So I noticed," she said wryly. "On the one hand we have the fairy princess, adored by father and husband, on the other, we have . . ."

"On the one hand," he interrupted ruthlessly, with the first real anger she'd ever seen, "we have a preening neurotic who could see no farther than her own selfish needs and twisted longings. On the other, we have you."

She stared at him. "You hated her."

"Intensely." There was no apology in his voice. "It came through during the trial, even though I did my best to hide it. It was that hatred that convicted me, among other things. That hatred that inspired the judge to sentence me to death."

"Did you hate her enough to kill her?"

"Yes." His answer was flat, uncompromising.

"Did you kill her?"

"Read the book." His brief flare of anger was gone, and the manipulator was back.

"I don't believe everything I read."

"Wise of you. Don't believe everything people tell you, either."

"On the other hand?"

There was a gleam of amusement in his bleak eyes. "You want to know how you differ from

Diana? Searching for compliments, Cassidy? Come to bed with me, and I'll tell you everything you want to hear. I'll even tell you I love you if I have to."

She just watched him steadily, refusing to back down. She was getting better at dealing with him, and that knowledge strengthened her. "How am I different from your wife?"

"She was porcelain—fragile, with a hidden flaw that made her shatter. You're earthenware, strong, eternal, solid."

"Lord," she said in disgust, "how could you have been considered a womanizer with a line like that?"

"I'm not trying to seduce you at the moment. I'm telling you the truth, and giving you credit to be able to appreciate it," he snapped.

"Okay, I'm clay, she's porcelain. What else?"

"She was the center of the universe—everyone existed to complement her. She couldn't live outside of the perfect little world she'd spun for herself, with the help of the people who adored her."

"Did she cheat on you? Did she have lovers?"

The smile that twisted his mouth was ugly. "The only person Diana loved more than she loved me was her father."

"Another difference. I'm a minor cog in my father's grand scheme of things."

"Poor girl," he mocked her.

It nettled her, as it was meant to. "You say she

was twisted. Does that mean you consider me to be the picture of mental health?"

"Yes," he said flatly. "Except when you're around me."

"Well, we have one thing in common, apparently. An unfortunate association with you." She leaned back. Her coffee was cold, but she took a delaying sip, just for something to do. "Did you cheat on her?"

"The courts said I did. Any number of times."

"And did you? Did you cheat on this neurotic woman who loved you to distraction?" she pursued.

"Yes."

"The court transcript said one of your lovers disappeared without a trace. There was the hint that there may have been more, but that was stricken from the record."

"Yes."

"Do you kill all the women you sleep with?"

"Only the ones who deserve it," he said. And he picked up his book again, ignoring her.

"You're leaving today?" Cassidy echoed in horror.

"Cass, darling, we have no choice," Mabry said patiently. "Sean wants to get out of the city, and I'm not about to argue with him. There's a party at Chaz's, and it might be the last one he's really up to. I'm not going to tell him we can't go when it's his last chance. Come with us."

"I hate the Hamptons, I hate Chaz Berringer, I hate literary dinner parties," she shot back as she watched Mabry continue to pack, calmly, relentlessly.

"As much as you hate Richard Tiernan?" Mabry countered.

"I don't hate Richard Tiernan."

Mabry raised a perfect eyebrow. "You've been doing an excellent impersonation of hatred, then. I'm sure I thought you despised him."

"Come on, Mabry. You saw the two of us in the hallway a few days ago."

"I also know both you and Richard fairly well, and I can imagine whose fault that little scene was. You've always gone for the safe, unimaginative type. Doubtless a reaction to your childhood. You and Mark Bellingham seemed a perfect match."

"He's married."

"He's divorced. Or close to it. Who told you he was still married?"

"Richard. Who else?"

"Interesting," Mabry said, wrapping silk in tissue paper. She made everything an art, from packing to making coffee to applying makeup.

"So we're agreed that Richard's not my type. I like men who are safe and boring," Cassidy said in a deceptively calm voice. She didn't like how astute Mabry had suddenly become. She did tend to date men who were safe, unthreatening, even boring. And it was a good thing she did. Look what happened when she was exposed to a dangerous package like Richard Tiernan. Her brain and all her self-protective instincts short-circuited.

Mabry's gaze was calm and curious. "So where does that leave you and Richard?"

"There is no me and Richard," she said firmly. "But that doesn't mean I hate him. I feel sorry for him. He's lost his wife and his children, he's been convicted of murder, and he's an outcast of society."

"Somehow I don't think that bothers Richard one tiny bit. I think he's happy to be rid of society," Mabry said wryly. "So you feel sorry for him, do you? The earth mother, gathering the suffering to her noble bosom. Except that you're afraid he might be a viper."

"Do you think he killed them?"

Mabry's eyes met hers for a breathless moment. When it came to people, Mabry's instincts were invaluable, and Cassidy suddenly felt as if her entire future hung on her opinion. If she thought Richard was innocent, then the dark cloud that floated around Cass's head would lift, and there was hope. Though she didn't dare consider what that hope might be.

But life was never that simple. "I don't know, darling. I wish I did." She closed the suitcase, then turned toward Cass. She was one of the few women who could look her in the eye, though her willowy model's proportions made her seem smaller. "Come with us, Cass. You need a break as well."

"Don't you think I'm safe here?"

"Of course I do."

"Even though he's suspected of killing far more than just his wife and children? Not that that shouldn't be enough," Cass added with a trace of black humor.

"There was no evidence about any others. Just rumors. If I thought you were in any danger, I wouldn't have let Sean bring you here."

"Wouldn't you? We're both willing to do just about anything for Sean. Especially now. And what I can do for Sean is stay here while you go to the Hamptons and keep an eye on Richard."

"Why should you need to do that?"

"Because he asked me to."

"Damn Sean," Mabry said wearily. "Richard doesn't need to be watched. If he wanted to take off, it might be better all around."

"Didn't Sean post bail?"

"The money doesn't matter. Estate taxes will probably take most of it anyway."

"Don't talk that way."

"He's going to die, Cass. I need to get him away from here. He's been working too hard, and he'll burn out that much faster if he doesn't get some rest. I just want him at the beach house for a week or so, away from work, away from distraction. I . . . I want him for me. Is that so evil of me?"

She wouldn't cry, Cassidy told herself, her heart breaking for all of them. "Not evil at all," she said softly. "And even more reason for me to stay here. Don't worry, I won't let Richard get to me. He likes the challenge. If I refuse to fight him, he'll get bored and leave me alone."

Mabry looked at her, not bothering to disguise her disbelief. "I can't persuade you?"

"Not right now. I have tons of things I can do in the city—I'll probably hardly be here, and you know Richard seldom leaves. We won't even run into each other."

"Cassidy, you know better than that," Mabry said gently.

"If things get uncomfortable, I'll take the first train out to the cottage. I promise."

Mabry shook her head. "Now, why do I feel things are spiraling out of control?"

"Because the men in this apartment are doing their best to manipulate us," Cass said with deceptive calm. "I, for one, don't intend to let it go any farther."

Richard had developed a deep fondness for thunderstorms in the city. He stood in the open window as the noise rumbled overhead, and the people beneath scurried to get out of the pelting rain. Violence in nature was suddenly attractive, and he wondered if it was a reaction to the violence he had discovered in his own soul. He could watch the lightning sizzle through the thick gray sky, and feel his own blood leap in response.

He had to get rid of her, and quickly. He wondered whether Sean thought he'd been doing him a favor, leaving her behind. He was deteriorating faster than Richard had expected, and he wondered whether the book would be published. It didn't matter. He had the money stashed away, ready to be paid out in discreet, untraceable amounts. No one would ever be able to find it—Mark had helped him cover his tracks too well.

He was running out of time. He needed to dispose of Cassidy Roarke's interfering presence, and then he needed to disappear. Just long enough to make sure everything was well, and then he'd be back, the model prisoner, awaiting his fate with stoic calm.

Thunder racketed through the apartment. It was late, and as far as he could tell she hadn't returned yet. Maybe she wouldn't come back at all, maybe she'd thought better of sharing a deserted apartment with a serial killer who drew her despite her best efforts at resisting.

Maybe he should simply disappear. But he couldn't trust her not to sound the alarm, call the police, and then all hell would break loose. No, he couldn't risk it. His disappearance had to be discreet, unnoticed. Too much was riding on it.

He lay on the bed, listening to the sound of the front door opening, the quiet murmur of voices. Cassidy's, low, throaty, infuriatingly sexy. And a male voice, familiar. Damnably so. Mark Bellingham.

The rage wasn't good for him. The shaft of possessive fury was dangerous. He needed Mark as much as he needed Cassidy. And for the same reason.

A calm man, a sane man would consider alternatives. The practical possibility would be to tell her a portion of the truth, letting her ally herself with Mark, work with him. Together they could provide the perfect answer.

But he was neither calm nor sane. Events had turned him into a conscienceless sociopath, and he accepted that truth with a certain grim satisfaction. He could trust no one, nothing. Not noble resolve, not friendship, not justice. He could only work with what he had. And the only thing he trusted was obsession.

He moved, silently, through the hallway, waiting in the darkened kitchen, listening to them. The conversation was light, flirtatious, innocent, and he wanted to snarl.

He wasn't sure what he would do if Cassidy took Mark back to her Gothic bedroom. He didn't want to think about it. The madness was pulsing in his veins, and he was afraid of it. Afraid of what he might do, whether he was capable of hurting her. He no longer knew his own limits.

The door closed again. If there had even been a kiss, it had been so brief that he hadn't been aware of the momentary silence it had required.

The chains went up, the locks turned, and overhead the thunder rumbled, and the rain pelted the kitchen windows that overlooked the massive apartment building's inner courtyard.

She would come in here, he knew it. And he waited, a trap already baited, waited for her to come to him.

He smelled her first. The ozone and wet rain that clung to her hair, the deceptively erotic perfume. When she appeared in the kitchen door she was barefoot, silhouetted, and he felt a curious pain in what should have been his heart. He didn't want to do this. He couldn't help himself.

The lightning flashed, illuminating the kitchen for a timeless moment, and they stared at each other. She was wearing a long, flowery dress, her hair was wild about her face, and her eyes were dark with knowledge and longing.

The kitchen was plunged into darkness again, and he took a step toward her, waiting to see if she'd run. She didn't. She couldn't. He came up to her and reached out, sliding his hands up her legs, pulling the dress up her thighs, as he drew her toward him.

She came, unresisting, and in the darkness her eyes were wide and frightened as they looked up into his. His hands slid along her bare thighs, pulling the material with him, and her breasts were against his bare chest. She was damp from the rain, she was hot, and she was his.

He moved his head to kiss her, and she tried

to turn her face away. "Don't," she whispered, a plea that should have broken his heart.

He had no heart. "I can't afford to be merciful," he said. And he kissed her.

Lightning flared in the kitchen again, then darkness, and in that moment of time he'd hooked his thumbs inside her panties and yanked them down her legs. Her arms went around his neck, and she kissed him back, as he reached down and unzipped his jeans, releasing himself, before he lifted her, up, up, onto the kitchen counter, pushing her back against the cupboards and thrusting inside her.

She was wet, ready for him, and the sound she made in the back of her throat was dark, entirely sexual, as she wrapped her legs around his hips. She tipped her head back, and he could see the line of her throat, feel the curtain of hair sweep over his arm, and the darkness that was his constant companion filled him. He wanted her to feel that darkness, to know its relentless heat, and he thrust deep, feeling the shivers that swept over her, knowing that he was taking her, owning her, destroying her as surely as he would be destroyed for doing it.

He reached up and ripped at her dress, and her breasts spilled free, against him, nipples hard and constricted, and he could hear the soft, choking sound as she clung to him, feel the ripples of reaction that started to spread.

He knew how to prolong it. He knew how to bring her to the very edge, and then pull back, so that she was clawing at his back, desperate, and each buildup was more intense, until she was soaking with sweat, shaking with need, longing for the oblivion of that exquisite small death that was perhaps worth the ultimate sacrifice.

And then he could withhold it no longer. He lifted her off the counter, holding her against him, as he plunged into her, hard, like a weapon, and she shoved her face against his sweat-slick shoulder and buried her scream, as she shattered, rigid and lost. He had no choice but to follow, to his own small death, feeling his body explode inside her, pulses of life flowing between them, endlessly.

He could no longer hold her. He let her slide down his body, so that her feet rested on the floor, and it took her a moment to find her balance. She swayed, staring at him as if she didn't recognize him.

Her dress was ripped to the waist, and her beautiful breasts spilled out. He wanted to reach for her, to pull her against him, to kiss her high forehead beneath the wild hair, to close her desperate eyes and murmur comfort. To take her back to his bed and do it all again, slower this time, using his mouth, on her breasts, between her legs, doing it all, everything he could think of.

Instead he reached down and calmly straightened his jeans, zipping them. And then his eyes met hers, and he plastered a wry smile on his face. "How does it feel to fuck a murderer, Cassidy? Worth it?"

He expected her to slap him. He expected fury and despair. He should have known better.

She simply looked at him, her eyes wide and sorrowful, her mouth swollen from his. "Bastard," she murmured, a mere token. And then she walked away.

He knew she would leave. He left his door open so that he could be certain she was gone. It took her close to an hour to shower, pack, and leave, the front door slamming behind her. He wondered absently how far she'd run. Whether she'd go all the way back to Maryland, or simply seek the safety of her father's house in East Hampton.

He hoped it was the latter. When he came back, if he came back, he still might be able to salvage something. To use her, as he needed to. He'd given too much time, and for him time was the most precious commodity of all, to preparing her. If she went to Baltimore, Sean could get her back. If Sean was still alive.

It didn't take him long to get ready. He'd packed the moment he'd heard her leave, throwing in just the bare minimum of clothes he might need. The passport Mark had left him was magnificent—it would be simple enough to answer to the name Richard Thompson when he arrived. The driver's license, insurance card, and credit cards were all equally professional. Mark, despite his reservations, had done well. If Richard could trust anyone, he could trust Mark.

But he couldn't trust anyone.

It was past dawn by the time he arrived at JFK. The early morning flight was already boarding, and he'd cut it dangerously close, but he didn't dare take a taxi. Taxis could be traced.

It took him a blessedly short time to get cleared to the plane, and he settled into his business-class seat with gratitude, pulling his alter ego around him. He was Richard Thompson, an insurance executive, on his way to a short holiday. No one would look twice at him, or connect him with the notorious Richard Tiernan. For the next few days, he was safe.

He leaned back as the half-filled plane began to taxi down the dawn-lit runway. He wondered how Cassidy was doing now. Was she furious? He hoped so. She was a fighter, far tougher than she realized. She got that from Sean.

And that was exactly why he needed her. She'd survive the rough sex on the kitchen counter. She'd survive anything he dished out to her. If only he had enough time to make sure everything went as planned.

He shut his eyes, suddenly exhausted. He couldn't remember when he last slept. The drone of the airplane, the comfort of the seat, was enough. He drifted off, and thought of Cassidy. And the despair in her dark eyes when she came.

CHAPTER 11

Cassie got as far as Penn Station, shaken, shattered, confused. She bought her ticket and climbed aboard the first train heading south, out of the city, waiting until the very last minute before she jumped off again, just as it was pulling away from the platform. She didn't know what she was going to say to Richard Tiernan. She only knew she couldn't run.

But there was nothing to say. By the time she returned to the apartment, it was past dawn. And Richard Tiernan was long gone.

At first she panicked, imagining the worst. Remembering all the stories and half truths she'd heard. But he hadn't hurt her. He wasn't the madman the media portrayed him to be. In the middle of her father's kitchen, surrounded by knives, he hadn't hurt her. And he'd let her go.

She searched his room. Most of his clothes were still there, neatly folded, with almost armylike precision. She wondered if he was naturally that precise a man, or whether he'd learned that order in prison. There was nothing of a personal nature, not even a scrap of wastepaper left behind. She sank to her knees in despair on the spotless carpet, and leaned her head against the neatly made bed. And saw the tiny corner of plastic beneath the quilt.

It was a credit card, a gold one with one of those limitless credit ranges. It belonged to a man named Richard Thompson.

She turned it over to look at the signature. It hadn't been signed yet, but it didn't need to be. It was issued from a New York bank on the cutting edge of technology, and the photograph on the back was Richard Tiernan.

It should have come as no surprise. He was a man under sentence of death—he had nothing to hold him here. It wasn't even his money that had provided his significant bond. It was Sean's— every last penny. If Richard Tiernan broke his bond, her father would die penniless.

She figured she had three choices. She could call the police and have them hunt him down before he got too far. She could call Mabry and Sean, and warn them. Or she could go after him herself.

Mark Bellingham's apartment was twenty blocks north, and Cass didn't hesitate. She should have known he wouldn't be surprised to see her. He buzzed her up without question, and when he opened the door, he held out a cup of coffee. "He's gone, hasn't he?"

She ignored the coffee. "Do you have any idea how much money my father posted for him?"

"He'll be back."

"What makes you think that? What's he got to come back for?"

"Nothing," Mark said, closing the door behind her. He was obviously fresh from the shower, his sandy blond hair standing on end, a velour robe around his damp body. "He's been less than honest with me, but I know he'll be back. Six days. I've been ordered to keep your father away from the apartment—the fewer people who know he's gone, the better. You didn't call Sean, did you?"

"I thought I'd better check with you first."

"Good girl," he murmured. "Come on, Cassidy, drink some coffee. We were friends last night— you trusted me. Don't look at me like I'm some sort of serial killer."

"Like Richard."

"I didn't say that."

"Do you believe it? Of course you don't—you wouldn't have helped a serial murderer escape. You did help him, didn't you?"

"What makes you think that?" he said warily.

"Don't be cagey now. You've practically admitted it already. He needed help—someone must have gotten him the credit cards in a phony name. What else did you do for him?"

He threw himself on a white cotton sofa, staring at her with uncomfortably discerning eyes.

"The question is, what did you do for him? There's a mark on the side of your neck, one that's fairly easy to recognize. It wasn't there when I left your apartment last night."

Her hand reached up, instinctively, and then dropped again. "I don't think that's any of your business."

"Unfortunately it doesn't seem to be," he admitted with clear regret. "I didn't realize I needed to warn you about him again. I thought you had more sense than to get involved with a man like Richard. He's dangerous, far more dangerous than you can imagine."

"Then why did you help him?"

"He's my friend," Mark said simply. "Besides, he's not dangerous to me. It's women who are the problem. He draws them to him, like some goddamned high-powered magnet, and they're willing to lay down their lives for him."

"Do they have to?"

He didn't say anything for a moment, and when he spoke his voice was angry. "Go back to the apartment, Cassie. He'll be back. In six days. When he returns you can ask him where he's been, and he just might tell you. It's not my place to divulge Richard's secrets."

"And if he doesn't come back?"

Mark sighed. "Maybe we'd all be better off."

Cassidy took a deep breath, trying to beat down the unreasoning panic that filled her. "Just one question, Mark. Where's he gone?"

"You're better off not knowing."

"Where's he gone?" she persisted.

He tipped his head back, looking at her. And then he rose, moving over to a glass-topped table and his briefcase. He pulled out a file and tossed it at her. "Take this with you. Read it before you decide to follow him."

"I can't follow him if I don't know where he's gone."

"England. To a village on the coast of Devon called Wychcombe. I wouldn't recommend following him."

"Why not?"

"Read the file."

She clutched it against her. "Mark, thank you . . ."

"Don't," he said sharply. "There are times when I think execution is too good for him. Don't let him use you, destroy you, as he has so many others."

"He's not going to use me."

"Cass," Mark said heavily, "it's already too late to stop him."

It had been three years since Cassidy had last been in England. She'd come in the fall, after months of planning, weeks of packing, with a detailed itinerary, and stash of traveler's checks, and enough tranquilizers to ensure that she slept the entire seven-hour flight to Heathrow.

This time there were no tranquilizers, no traveler's checks, and not the faintest idea where she was going.

It was her fault that he'd gotten away. Driven him away, perhaps, though she wasn't sure she was ready to take the blame for that. The scene in her father's kitchen haunted her, and she replayed it over and over again in her mind, trying to see how it could have changed, how she could have stopped him, stopped herself.

Each time she came up with the same answer. It had been inevitable, no matter how much she'd tried to deny it. Richard had made it more than clear, and she'd ignored the very real danger. Ignored it until it was too late.

Sean had asked so little of her. He needed Richard Tiernan, needed him to finish the book that seemed to be his sole reason for hanging on to life. And she'd let him escape.

She managed to get herself on a plane bound for Heathrow by seven o'clock that night. It wasn't until she settled in to her seat that she pulled out the file.

She almost slammed it shut again. It contained newspaper clippings, tabloid articles, all the twisted filth that the press could come up with. A color photograph of a blood-soaked hallway, with the chalk outline where a body had lain. Shrieking headlines, horrifying ones. Richard hadn't exaggerated. The *National Sunset* did suggest that he might have eaten his children.

Those were the most heartbreaking—the family

photos of two beautiful, innocent children, hardly more than babies. The older one, Ariel, was blond and pretty like her mother, though with a look of strength to her china blue eyes that the photos of her mother didn't convey. The younger one, Seth, was dark, mischievous. She stared at the photo, and for a fleeting, hopeless moment she could see Richard as an innocent.

The other charges mounted. He was connected with three different women who'd disappeared, and the articles hinted at satanic rituals, sexual perversions, blood and torture and mutilation. It wasn't until she forced herself to read every word that she found the brief mention that two of the women had surfaced, claiming to have nothing more than friendship with Richard Tiernan. Only Sally Norton remained missing.

She was as different from Diana Scott Tiernan as she could possibly be, if Cassidy could go by the photographs. Small and pixie-dark, with a wry smile and laughing dark eyes, she would have made a perfect foil for Richard. He never denied having an affair with her, and it was all Cass could do not to sit there and hate her.

But Sally Norton had never shown up. She'd disappeared, no one knew quite when, and there'd yet to be any trace of her body. The state had enough evidence to convict Richard of his wife's death—after a while they stopped searching for Sally Norton's decomposing body or the remains of the children. Why waste the taxpay- ers' money?

Cassidy closed the file with a shudder, too sick to even consider that she was trapped on a hated airplane. She was traveling thousands of miles to chase after a man accused—no, convicted—of some of the most heinous crimes imaginable. Would she end up like his children, like Sally Norton, her existence simply wiped out without a trace?

She could turn around when she arrived at Heathrow, fly straight back. There was no need to put herself in danger. She put her hand to her neck in an absent gesture, against the mark he'd made. She wasn't going back. He wouldn't kill her. He had a reason for coming all this way, for putting his appeal in jeopardy, and she needed to know that reason. And if it wasn't good enough, she could always call the British authorities. For a convicted murderer, extradition should be a sim- ple enough matter.

Or maybe it wouldn't. England didn't have a death sentence. Perhaps he'd be kept here, safe . . .

She pushed her seat back, closing her eyes as the thoughts whirled around and around in her brain. She couldn't make any plans, any decisions, until she found him. Until she made him answer the question he'd always avoided. She needed to hear it from his mouth, the mouth that had taken hers with such devastating force. Whatever he chose to tell her, she'd believe it.

She moved through customs in a jet-lagged fog, and when she was asked the purpose of her visit, it took her a moment to come up with a suitable answer. A suitable lie. Because she hadn't the faintest idea what the purpose of her visit to England was. She could hardly tell the matronly looking customs officer that she was following a murderer.

She'd never driven in England, she was lousy at reading maps, she was tired and edgy and restless in a way she refused to recognize. She almost killed herself three times as she drove west from London, forgetting which lane she should be in. A gray drizzle was falling, only to be expected, but it didn't help her mood, and the rental Vauxhall had a manual transmission, when she'd grown too used to an automatic. There was nothing on the radio but funereal organ music, and by the time she reached Somerset she was ready to cry.

She spent the night at a bed-and-breakfast, sharing the loo, eating cholesterol, and drinking lousy coffee for breakfast. By the time she reached Devon in late afternoon the sun had come out, but her mood had darkened considerably. She didn't know what she would find at journey's end, and she doubted she was going to be happy about it.

Wychcombe was a tiny village on the west coast. She parked her car in the marketplace and sat for a moment, stumped. Why in God's name would Richard Tiernan risk everything to come to this tiny town, and how was she going to find him? The police were out of the question, the post office a little too official for Cassidy's state of mind. She settled for the newsagent, buying a diet Coke and a stack of tacky postcards while she fumbled with the British coins she'd exchanged at Heathrow.

In the end, it was surprisingly easy. The woman behind the counter liked to talk, and in late March it was too early for the vast influx of American tourists. By the time Cassidy could tear herself away, she learned the nationality of every guest staying at the two bed-and-breakfasts in town, and none of them were American. She also learned of the elderly businessman who lived down by the cove, who might or might not be American, and the Canadian professor who owned the home farm out by ·Herring Cross. He'd just come for his annual vacation, and his widowed sister and her children would be joining them.

Cass wanted to weep with frustration, but she didn't dare. Once she started crying she had a tendency to weep for everything, and she couldn't afford to give in to it. Her father had always despised tears, and likely Richard felt the same way. The hell with both of them. She'd wait till she found a quiet, deserted spot in the English countryside and then she would howl her heart out.

She started the Vauxhall, stalled out as usual, and then got the wretched thing in gear as she drove aimlessly, down the coast. The roads were very narrow and twisty, the hedgerows blocking the view, and she was driving too fast when another car came careening around the corner. Cassidy jerked the wheel, ending in a ditch, and at that final indignity she did finally burst into tears, resting her head on the steering wheel.

The car that had just passed slammed to a halt, and a moment later a woman's figure appeared at the window. "I'm terribly sorry," she said. "I always take that corner too damned fast. Are you hurt?"

"I'm fine," she muttered wetly, not wanting to raise her head.

"I think you can drive out of the ditch, but maybe I'd better wait and make sure . . ." The voice was uncertain.

"I'll be fine," Cass said. "Please, just leave me alone."

"But I feel responsible . . ."

It took Cassidy that long to realize what was commonplace in her life was not commonplace in Devon. The woman who'd run her off the road wasn't British.

She lifted her head, wiping her tears away, and squinted upward. The sun was too bright, leaving the woman in silhouette. "You're American," Cassidy said.

The woman laughed. "Actually, I'm Canadian. I'd ask you back to the farmhouse for a cup of tea, but I'm in a bit of a hurry. If you're certain you're all right? You've been shaken up, and I feel responsible."

The sun nipped behind a cloud, and Cassidy got her first close look at the Canadian widow. She barely managed to keep her voice steady. "Really, I'm fine. You were on your way someplace—don't let me keep you."

"Are you certain you're okay?"

Cassidy looked up into Sally Norton's elfin face. "I'm feeling much better now," she said firmly.

It wasn't strictly the truth, Cass thought as she watched the woman drive off down the narrow road. On the one hand, she'd obviously found Richard, found his reason for being in England, and discovered that whoever he might have killed, at least Sally Norton wasn't one of his victims.

On the other hand, she found she didn't particularly like his reason for being in England.

The Herring Cross Farm was easy enough to find. A perfect little English cottage, complete with thatched roof and picturesque outbuildings, it rested on the edge of a hillside, not far from the sea. It was hardly the spot for a murderer and his accomplice to retire in style.

She parked the Vauxhall in the narrow lane, sliding out of the driver's seat. In the distance a

dog barked, and she walked through the front yard
with unseeing eyes.

The door was open. The place was deserted.
She didn't know quite what she expected, but
then, she never had with Richard Tiernan. She
walked through into the kitchen, past the clut-
ter of dishes, and looked out to the back garden.

He was out there. Shirtless in the sunshine,
digging in the dirt. Looking for bodies, she wondered? There were scratch marks on his shoulders, and it took her a moment to realize they
came from her. She'd marked him. She wondered
what Sally Norton had thought of that.

There was a straight-backed chair in the corner
of the cluttered, cozy old kitchen. She sat in it,
her arms wrapped around her, and waited.

He didn't see her when he first came in. He was
whistling, under his breath, sounding disgustingly
happy, and the knowledge was like a blow to
Cass's belly. He moved to the sink, and he was
carrying an armload of daffodils.

He shoved them in an old jar, switched to humming, and then turned, reaching for his shirt that
was lying across one of the chairs. And then he
saw her, waiting in the shadows.

It was as if the light had been stripped from his
face, his eyes. His expression went blank, wary,
as he stared at her, almost as if he couldn't believe
his eyes. He pulled the shirt on, and she noticed
it was an old shirt, faded, one she hadn't seen

before. She supposed it was waiting here for him. Along with Sally Norton.

"Are you alone?"

The words almost startled her. "Entirely," she said, her voice deceptively cool.

"Does anyone know you're here?"

"Mark. But he's covered up for you before. He'll probably cover up again."

"What would he need to cover up for?"

"If you decided to kill me. That's what you're thinking, isn't it? Maybe you could stash me in the garden."

"You have your father's imagination." He was back in control once more. That lightness vanished, the wariness, the taunting, back where she remembered it. "What are you doing here, Cassidy?"

"I'd think that would be obvious. I'm here to take you back."

"Against my will? I doubt you could manage. For one thing, I'm bigger than you are. If you have any sense at all, you'll leave. Go back to America and keep your mouth shut. I'll be back in four more days."

"And if I don't have any sense at all?"

He closed his eyes for a moment. "What do you think is going on? I'd be interested in hearing just how your fevered mind works."

She leaned back, looking at him. He was remote, a stranger. A very dangerous stranger, but she was past the time of being careful. "There are a number of possibilities. Obviously you aren't a serial killer."

"Why do you say that?"

"I ran into one of your victims down the road."

"Which one?"

She vaulted out of the chair. "Don't mock me, Richard. I won't let you run out on my father. You mean too much to him at this point. I won't let . . ."

"You won't have any say in the matter," he said coolly. He was buttoning his shirt with deceptive ease. "I don't mean a goddamn thing to your father except as the means to an end. You know why he won't let you see the manuscript? He doesn't want you to know the truth. That he's writing my story. How I spent my adult life killing women who were foolish enough to fall in love with me."

There was a knife on the table. A large, sharp-looking butcher knife. She hadn't noticed it before. She noticed it now. "You didn't kill Sally Norton."

"Is that who you saw? She's my partner in crime." His eyes followed her wary gaze, and he leaned over and picked up the knife. "Not a very good specimen," he murmured, running his long thumb against the blade. "Too dull to cut. It hurts more when the blade is dull. Did you know that, Cassidy?"

She didn't move. "I knew that."

He turned the knife over. "I should sharpen it,"

he said dreamily. "There's a whetstone out back. Maybe I'll go do that, right now. It would give you time to leave, you know. You could get away from here, before I had a chance to stop you, before I had a chance to hurt you. You could take your adventurous little ass back to New York and forget you ever came here."

She was mesmerized by the knife in his hands. And by the elegant, deadly beauty of those hands. "And what would happen to you?"

"Oh, I'd be back when I said I would," he said, waving the knife airily. "I always keep my word, don't you know?"

"And I suppose you never lie?"

"Oh, no," he said calmly. "I lie all the time." He started toward her, the knife still held in one hand, and it took all the courage she possessed to stand her ground. He wasn't going to use that knife on her, she knew it. Even if he wanted to convince her that he would.

"You aren't going to hurt me," she said.

He brought the knife up, letting the dull edge stroke the side of her face. "Why do you think that, Cassie? Don't you think I like to hurt women? I've hurt you already, and I've enjoyed doing it."

"You aren't going to frighten me."

"You're scared shitless." He turned the blade, so that the sharp edge touched her delicate skin.

"You have no reason to kill me."

"Madmen don't need a reason. We just do it

because those little voices in our head tell us to," he said, his eyes glittering. "And I have a reason. You'll tell people where I went. The fewer people who know about this place, the better. It might be worth killing to keep it a secret." The tip of the knife trailed down her throat, a steely caress, and she couldn't keep herself from swallowing convulsively.

"You're not a madman."

"I'm doing my best to convince you that I am," he said with eerie calm.

"I know. And I wonder why."

They heard the car at the same time, pulling to a stop outside the house, the sound of laughing voices, the slamming of several doors. All Richard's taunting malice disappeared, wiped clean, and he looked pale, almost sick.

"Get out of here, Cassie," he said, and it sounded almost like a plea. "Just get the hell away from here before it's too late."

She didn't know what she expected to burst through the door. What hounds of hell, what evil personified to race in.

Richard had dropped the knife, taking a step away from her, and his face was set, pale, unreadable. As the door opened, and two small figures hurtled toward him, flinging themselves in his arms.

"Daddy!" they shrieked, a babble of noise almost too much for two children. Ariel and Seth, showering their father with kisses, with questions, with demands and with love.

Cassidy stood there, numb, when she felt a hand on her arm. It was Sally Norton, looking up at her, an unreadable expression on her piquant face. "I should have known," she said wearily. "Another American out here was too much of a coincidence." She tugged at her. "Let's leave them alone for a bit, shall we? They haven't seen each other in more than a year."

Cassidy followed her, too shocked to hesitate. The side garden was just coming into bloom, and Sally pushed her down into a chair, then sat across from her.

"They're not dead," Cass said.

"No, they're very much alive. And thriving. As you can see, I'm not dead, either."

"And Diana?"

"Diana's quite dead," Sally said emotionlessly. "Rotting in hell at this very moment, if there's any justice." Her sudden smile was almost a shock. "You're not what I expected."

"Expected?" Cassidy echoed, still reeling.

"Then again," she continued, "it makes a certain amount of sense. I'm just surprised he didn't bring you when he came. He said you weren't ready yet."

"Ready for what?"

Sally Norton's eyes narrowed in sudden concern. "Exactly why are you here?"

Cassidy shook her head. Jet lag, confusion,

postcoital dementia, had melted her brain. She was surrounded by Richard Tiernan's victims, each of them alive, healthy, and she didn't know what to think. Her mind refused to function.

"I don't know," she said simply. And she rose, walking out of the garden without a backward glance, back to the hated confines of the rental car.

CHAPTER 12

She'd run away again, Richard realized. It was to be expected, Cassidy Roarke had an unfortunate habit of always being in the wrong place at the wrong time. Why the hell couldn't she have gone to the Hamptons with Sean and Mabry? Why the hell did she have to come back to the apartment when he'd finally reached his limit? Why did she have to follow him here, when he needed just five days alone with his secrets? And then, why the hell did she have to disappear again, after she'd blundered in and jeopardized everything?

He couldn't go after her. He had to trust that she wasn't about to go off half-cocked, that she'd simply needed to run away and hide. She was tougher than she realized, but she knew her limitations, and he expected she'd simply gone to ground someplace, to lick her wounds and try to make sense of what she'd seen.

He doubted she'd be able to. It wouldn't make sense to her, that a man would stand by and willingly go to his death for the murders of his wife and children, when he knew his children were very much alive and thriving. Hidden from sight, hidden from danger. In the safe, capable hands of Sally Norton.

They were thriving, indeed. Seth, after his initial exuberant welcome, grew a little hyper, ending in exhausted tears. Ariel was uncertain, watching him out of blue eyes that were identical in color to her mother's, if completely lacking Diana's eerily calm expression. By the time Seth had fallen apart, Ariel had started talking, and she prattled away, nonstop, tucking her small, delicate hand in his and looking up at him trustingly.

No one had looked at him with any kind of trust in well over a year. It was a novel experience, shattering, reminding him of just how he had come to this desperate, barren place in his life. Reminding him, if he had any chance of forgetting, just what his priorities were.

It was past eleven when they were finally bedded down and sleeping. Past eleven when Richard was finally alone again with Sally, ready to ask the questions that had been waiting patiently.

She handed him a tall glass of whiskey. "You look like you need it," she said, throwing herself down on the shabby chintz sofa in the sitting room.

He liked this place—he always had. 1 looked much the same as when he'd first bought it, three years ago, hoping to talk Diana into moving, away from the States, away from her family. She'd hated it.

He sat down beside Sally. She was looking calm, beautiful, and she'd done more for him than any other human being. He took her capable hand in his. "I do."

She pulled her hand away, smiling at him. "Don't, Richard. That's history, and you and I both know it."

"Sally . . ."

"I know," she said gently. "You'd do anything for me. Even convince yourself you were in love with me once more. There's no need, darling. You don't owe me anything."

"I owe you my life."

"It doesn't look as if you're getting out of this mess with your life," she pointed out.

"I'm getting what's most important to me."

"It's important to me as well. I just wish things hadn't taken such a turn. Perhaps I don't need . . ."

"Don't even think it," he said, his voice tight. "You've sacrificed enough."

"I'd do more."

"I know you would. I'm doing my best to ensure that you don't need to. What did you think of her?" He asked the question casually, taking a sip of the dark whiskey, wondering if he could fool her.

Sally knew him too well. "Don't worry, Richard. She'll be perfect. You know it as well as I do. But how much have you told her?"

"Nothing."

"Nothing? She didn't even know about the children?"

"Or you. You're one of my many victims, you know. In the states they pretty much put every missing female to my account. I'm suspected of more crimes than Ted Bundy."

"That's ridiculous."

"I traveled a lot. And Diana dropped more than a few hints. They don't need to convict me of the others—Diana's death is enough to make certain I get the death penalty. The tabloids can just enjoy themselves."

"Are you so very sure you can't tell the truth?"

"Very sure," he said, leaning his head back on the shabby sofa. He wished there was some way he could bring himself to want Sally. To love her again, if he'd ever really been in love with her. But all he could see, all he could think about was Cass, with the wounded eyes and the soft body, and not the woman who had already given up everything for the sake of his children. He wanted one break, damn it. One tiny little advantage.

He thought he'd gotten everything safely settled. He'd been ready to go to his death, either by official hands or by a murderous fellow inmate, when Sally had gotten word to him. And suddenly an appeal was necessary. He had more to do.

He only hoped the appeal wouldn't screw things up too much. His complete lack of interest in his defense had ensured that things moved along very quickly especially with his esteemed father-in-law pulling the strings and calling in favors. As long as he hadn't put up any argument, his fate had been sealed.

He didn't want to spend years in and out of courts. He wanted it finished, over and done with. He wanted punishment, he wanted the end.

But not until everything was taken care of.

"What did you tell her?"

"She asked if they were your children. I said yes. She asked if I was Sally Norton. I said yes. And then she left."

"That simple? Do you know where she went?"

"Are you going after her?"

"Not now. I only have a limited amount of time with the children."

"Will she call the police? Do you trust her?"

He thought about it. Thought about her warm green eyes, her soft mouth. Thought about what he needed from her, and what he wanted from her. "I'm not quite sure yet," he admitted. "I needed more time. I didn't need her to follow me here, before I was ready . . ."

"I think you'd better go after her."

"The children . . ."

"The children are delighted you're here, but they know your time is limited. I've talked to them, they know to take what they get and be happy. Children are resilient, Richard."

"They shouldn't have to be."

"True. But it's a little late to change things."

He grimaced. "Can't you stay here?"

"You know we can't. You don't want to endanger everything we've worked for, do you? We'll head back down to Cornwall in the early afternoon. If things seem safe enough, you could come down in a day or two, for another short visit. The children have school, and they need to keep up a normal life. Bring her back with you, if you think she's ready."

He managed a faint smile. "You've gotten bossy in your old age, Sally."

"It comes to all of us, when the stakes are high enough. Will you go after her?"

"I have no choice."

"What are you going to do when you find her?" Her voice was hushed, edgy.

He glanced over at her. At the face he'd once loved. "It depends. If things go as I wish, then I'll tell her a small part of the truth."

"If not?"

"Then I'll have to kill her."

Her brain had ceased to function, Cassidy decided. It wasn't surprising, she was operating on a major case of jet lag, on top of one of the most devastating twenty-four-hour periods immediately preceding her abrupt trip to England. That twenty-four hours had included very little sleep and far too much emotional and physical upheaval. To come face-to-face with Richard Tiernan's murdered mistress and children, very much alive, was a shock she wasn't ready to assimilate. So she didn't even try.

She drove, far too rapidly for the twisting, narrow roads, but fortunately with the approaching dusk, the traffic was nonexistent. She was too tired, too distraught to read a map, and she didn't give a good goddamn. She just wanted to get as far away from Wychcombe, from Richard Tiernan and his inexplicable lies, as she could.

She headed toward London, toward Heathrow and Gatwick and escape. To get away from the mind games and confusions she was willing to get back on a hated airplane, and as far as she was concerned, Richard could stay hidden in England. Mabry was right, Sean wouldn't live long enough to miss the money he'd forfeit. And Richard's disappearance would probably only help the sales of the book.

She didn't even know the name of the town where she stopped for the night. She paid no attention to clocks, to time. Her dreams were fitful and haunted. It wasn't until she reached the outskirts of London the next morning that she slammed on the brakes, turned the car around, and nearly got herself killed in the process.

A born victim, she thought as she sped back toward Wychcombe. A glutton for punishment, a masochist, a fool, and an idiot, who should have known better. She'd spent her adult life protecting herself, from dysfunctional relationships, men who were no more than grown babies, people with draining needs and hidden agendas.

So why in God's name wasn't she smart enough not to fall in love with Richard Tiernan?

It was dark when she reached the edge of Wychcombe once more. She'd spent the day in the car, finally coming to terms with right-hand driving and steering wheels and rearview mirrors. She was ready to confront Richard, in front of his mistress and children if need be. She was ready to demand answers.

The farm at Herring Cross was harder to find in the dark. The narrow, winding roads seemed ominous, and the distant hush of the sea, mixed with the wind rushing through the newly budded branches overhead, seemed to warn her. She was past listening to any warnings, and had been for weeks.

She pulled into the driveway. An ancient, gorgeous Morris Minor sat there, and the lights in the old house were minimal. There was no sign of the larger sedan Sally had been driving when she drove Cassidy off the road, and she had to accept the fact that Richard Tiernan might very well be alone.

She wasn't going to let it stop her. She was tired of running. Tired of being a coward. She thought she'd gotten braver, more resilient in the last few years, but Richard had taught her the error of her ways. She wasn't going to let him defeat her. She wanted answers. She needed answers. And she was willing to risk anything to get them.

The door was unlocked, the living room deserted when she let herself in. She looked around her, taking a deep breath to calm herself. It was a beautiful room, shabby, chic, with faded chintz slipcovers, comfortable old chairs, scratched, ancient furniture, a rose-colored rug, and piles of books everywhere. The vase full of daffodils stood in a corner, and she stared at it. Surely a man who picked daffodils was no danger to her.

But he was, and he proved it time and time again. He was alone in the house, she knew that with sudden certainty. The night was dark, no one knew she was there. Even Sally Norton, his obvious partner in crime, thought she'd left. He could bury her in the back garden, hide the car . . .

She shook her head, forcing the vicious thoughts to recede. He hadn't murdered Sally Norton or his children. He hadn't murdered anyone, and he wasn't going to start with her.

She turned, slowly, to see him standing in the doorway, watching her. He was wearing black, and his face, his expression was in the shadows.

"You came back," he said, his voice enigmatic.

She didn't move, and when she spoke, it seemed almost an errant thought. "I ran away from home for the first time when I was eight years old," she said. "I got as far as the Port Authority Bus Terminal, where a policeman found me and brought me home. My mother gave him a tip, me a slap, and locked me in my room for three days. I ran away the first day she let me out. Sometimes it seemed like the only answer."

"And you never stopped running?"

"Oh, no," she said. "I thought I'd outgrown it. Learned to face my fears, face whatever threatened me. Until I met you. And then I started running again."

"Do I threaten you?"

"Of course you do. You do it on purpose, but I'm not sure why. Will you ever tell me?"

"Perhaps." He moved into the room, toward her, and she hoped she'd see some kind of possibility in his dark face. All she saw was danger. And desire.

"Your children aren't dead."

"No," he agreed.

"Neither is Sally Norton."

"Obviously. She's been taking care of them. Keeping them safe."

"Safe from what?"

He smiled, a brief, terrible smile. "From the dangers of modern life."

"I came back to find out why."

"Why what?"

"Why you haven't told the truth. Why you allowed the prosecution to accuse you of murdering your children and your lover and you never told anyone they were alive."

"Why should I? I wasn't convicted of their murders. Diana's death was enough to send me to death row."

"Why didn't you fight it?" She heard the desperation in her voice, ignored it. "If you'd told the truth, you could have had a fighting chance. Diana's parents could have taken the children. Instead you let those poor people believe their entire family had been wiped out, when the children could have provided comfort for the general and his wife . . ."

She was unprepared for his reaction. His face drained entirely of color. Only his eyes blazed with anger, and her own life hung by a precarious thread as he moved toward her, slowly, sinuously, and she was mesmerized, willing to die, unable to move, as he reached his hands up to cup her throat.

"It's easy to kill," he murmured, and the pads of his thumbs stroked the fragile hollow of her neck. "Did you know that, Cassidy? Just a certain amount of pressure, and it would crush your throat. You'd suffocate, fairly quickly. It wouldn't be very messy, at least at first. But then, when someone dies a sudden, violent death, their bladder and bowels empty. Diana stank when I found her."

She tried not to swallow convulsively. He would have felt her fear against the faint pressure of his thumbs. "You found her?" she echoed, trembling slightly.

"Haven't I always said so?" He let his thumbs

trace the line of her neck, and his hand, his elegant, murderous hand, paused for a moment as it traced the mark he'd left, less than forty-eight hours earlier.

"Why would you kill me?" she asked, with far more bravery than she felt.

His thumbs kept up their gentle stroking, and she realized with sudden shock he'd been drinking. There was a glitter in his eyes, a faint deliberateness in his speech, and the smoky tang of whiskey was on his breath. She knew, to her sorrow, what people did when they were drunk. The emotional, the physical hurt they could inflict.

Richard Tiernan was far from drunk. But he was already dangerous. The whiskey he'd drunk that night might be enough to push him over the edge.

"Why would I kill you?" he murmured, considering it. "Maybe I like to kill. Maybe Sally and I have a grand plan, and I'd be afraid you'd expose it. It might be worth murder for that."

"Those are two possibilities," she allowed, watching him. "But I don't believe them."

"More fool you," he said softly, moving his thumbs back to the front of her throat. "I could kill for what I want."

"You aren't going to kill me," she said.

"Why not?"

She could see the cynical, frightening curve of his mouth. She could see the torment in his dark, haunted eyes. She could feel the faint tremor in his hands as they circled her neck, and she knew. "You didn't kill your wife," she said with sudden, complete certainty, and the relief and joy that filled her heart was explosive. "And you're not going to kill me."

He dropped his hands as if burned, stepping back from her. "Stop it, Cassie."

"You didn't kill her. I don't know why you've let things go on like this. Why you haven't tried to find out who really did it. Unless you know, and you're shielding him. Or her."

"Stop it," he said again. "I'm not interested in your romantic theories. You don't know anything about it."

"I know that you never killed anyone in your life, and you're not about to start now. You're innocent, Richard. I know that as well as I know my own name."

He made one last attempt to fight her. "You're in over your head. Leave it alone . . ."

"I'm in over my head because you dragged me here. You want something from me, and I can't imagine what. Is it trust? I trust you. Is it belief in your innocence? I know you're innocent, Richard. Is it love? Maybe I can give you that, too. But that's not what you want from me, is it?"

He'd moved away from her, going to stand in front of one of the mullioned windows, his back toward her. The room was dark, only one light glowing, and the sun had set, plunging the room into shadows. "You're wrong," he said, not bothering to turn around.

"Wrong about any number of things, no doubt." She moved into the room, closer to him, unable to resist, drawn to her fate, to her doom, to her love. Close enough to feel his body heat, to see the tension that rippled through his lean, elegant frame. "To which were you referring?"

He turned to look at her, and this time it wasn't death in his eyes, in his face. It was life. Blazing. Frightening. Complete. "I want your love."

She swallowed. "And what would you give me in return?"

His smile was wry. "Till death do us part?" he suggested.

"Will you fight your conviction?"

"No." It was flat, inexorable.

"Did you kill your wife?"

"I thought you believed in my innocence," he mocked her.

"I do. I want to hear you say the words. Did you take a knife and stab your wife in the heart?"

"No," he said.

She believed him. "This is the last time I'll ask you. What do you want from me?"

"I want you to love me more than you've ever loved anyone. I want you to give up everything for me. And I want you to let me die."

She stared at him. "You don't ask much, do you?"

"Eternity. And your soul."

"And how do I give up everything for you?"

"By taking care of my children."

She took a deep, shocked breath. "It all comes down to that, doesn't it? Your children are at the center of this, somehow. What about Sally?"

"Sally's sick. She's got a kidney disease. She needs treatment as soon as possible, and she's not going to get it here. She's living here under a phony name, with no national health card and no medical records. The paperwork Mark got for her and the children has been good enough so far, but when it comes to something as expensive as dialysis, the bureaucracy is going to look a little more closely, and that's just too damned dangerous. She's got to go back. In the meantime, my children still need someone to take care of them."

"And I'm that person?"

"Yes."

"I passed the tests? That's what they were, weren't they? You were trying to make sure I was strong enough, devoted enough to watch over them? What if I hadn't been?"

"Then I would have had to find someone else."

She didn't move, suddenly very cold as reality washed over her in ugly waves. "Why me?" she asked. "Was I a random choice? Have you had any other contenders?"

He ignored her sarcasm. "I saw your picture."

"Where?"

"Sean keeps it on his desk."

"Don't be absurd—I've never seen it."

"He hid it when you arrived. But it was there when I first met with him. I took one look at you and knew you were the one."

"And if I say no?"

"You won't."

"Why not?"

"Because you love me. You're good with children, even Sean admits that much. You'd do it for me, and you'd do it for them."

"You're suddenly very sure of me. What if I get tired of them? Tired of living a lie? What if I decide you're beyond seeing what's right for everyone, and I take matters into my own hands?"

"I'll kill you."

She believed him. Totally and completely. "You aren't quite sane, you know."

His smile was small consolation. "I know. Will you do it? Will you take care of my children, love them? Be their mother? Will you let me die, without putting up a fight? Will you do everything I ask of you? Will you give me everything? Will you promise, and never break that vow?"

She stared at him. "How long do I have to decide?"

"Thirty seconds."

She was beyond thinking clearly, beyond considering the consequences. "Yes," she said. She reached up and touched his face, before she could change her mind. "I'll do anything you want me to do. I love you."

The words came unbidden from her, a revelation, a benediction. She heard them with astonishment and a sense of rightness. She didn't know how long she had loved him, she didn't even want to think about it. There was no sense to it, morally, emotionally, and she'd always prided herself on her good sense. That had vanished when she walked into her father's kitchen and looked into his haunted eyes. She loved him, and if loving him made her crazy, so be it.

She was unprepared for the sudden change in him. He'd been holding himself very taut, and suddenly the tension seemed to leave his body. He sank to his knees in front of her, his arms around her waist, his head pressed against her belly, and he was trembling. She reached down, in wonder, to cradle his head against her, and she felt the heat of tears against her skin, and her heart broke.

She dropped to her knees in front of him, pulling him into her arms, pressing his face against her shoulder, holding him, like a mother, like a lover, holding him as he shook. The anger, the danger, the demon lover had vanished. This was a man in need, this was her man, and there was no sacrifice that was too much for her to make.

Even if it meant watching him die, something far worse than simply dying for him. He had asked it of her, and she would give it.

She put her hand against his face, feeling the dampness. She wanted to see him, to soothe him, but it was too dark in the room, and his mouth sought hers, blindly, like a child seeking its mother's breast. She kissed him, and the darkness shuddered and fell around them like a blanket, wrapping them tight.

Outside in the distance she could hear the roar and rush of the ocean. The faint call of a night bird echoed in the sky and then was hushed, and Cassidy sank to the floor beneath him, clinging to him, holding him, maternal, unquestioning, unasking. There was no question where this night would end, no question that she had given herself to him, body and soul.

Tomorrow would be time enough for regrets. Or perhaps next year. Or another lifetime. She had given herself, and she had promised.

There was no turning back.

CHAPTER 13

The floor was hard beneath her back. Cassidy didn't mind. The roughness of the wood beneath her was a reminder of reality, of the inevitable pain that was part of joy. She welcomed it.

She couldn't see his face in the shadows, and she was glad. There in the night they were safe, together, defenses and lies vanishing into the beneficient darkness. She put her hands up to his shoulders, clutching them beneath the loose black T-shirt, and closed her eyes.

There was no anger in his mouth as it touched hers. She opened her own to him, willingly, tasting his tongue, as she felt his hands slide up her thighs, bringing her skirt with them. He lay between her thighs, and she could feel his erection against the rough zipper of his jeans, and she lifted her knees, bringing him tighter against her, as she threaded her fingers through his hair.

His hands reached up to cover hers, and then he pulled away, sitting back on his heels in the darkness, kneeling between her legs, looking down at her. "Take off your clothes for me, Cassie," he whispered. "Do it this time and mean it."

He knew her too well, that was one of the many frightening things about him. He knew she wanted him to seduce her, to strip off her clothes like the accomplished lover he was reputed to be, so deftly she was barely aware of it happening. Instead he was asking her to be a willing participant. He had told the truth, more times than she could remember, when she'd asked him what he wanted from her. Everything.

Her hands were shaking when they went to the row of tiny buttons down the front of her dress. He didn't help. He knelt there, huge and dark and powerful in the shadowy living room, as she fumbled with the buttons, one after another, down the center until she reached the spot where the skirt pooled up around her thighs, resting against his crotch as he knelt between her legs.

He waited, with endless patience, and her fingers brushed against him as she unfastened the last few buttons. She felt him leap and pulse against her fingertips, and it was all she could do not to let her hand linger. Instead she spread the dress open, feeling the coolness of the night air kiss her skin, mixing with the heat of his gaze.

She'd dispensed with her plain white cotton underwear. For this innocent visit she'd somehow ended up wearing teal green lace, and even with his hooded expression she could read his reaction.

"Go on," he said, not touching her, when she longed, needed to be touched.

The bra fastened in front, and it took her several tries to undo it. Even undone, it still clung to her full breasts, and she wasn't sure whether she should flick it aside. Whether he thought she was too voluptuous, too full-blown, too . . .

He reached out and separated the bra, pulling it away from her. Leaning forward, he put his mouth on her breast, and she could barely control her response. She cradled him against her breast, stroking his face, reveling in the deep, sensual pull of it. She felt glorious, erotic beneath him, as he suckled on one breast, and then the other, drinking from her, devouring her, strengthening her and draining her.

He let his mouth drift down, across her belly, pressing his face against her womb. She reached down for the lacy waistband of her bikinis, and his hands covered hers, and together they pulled the wisp of cloth down her legs.

She reached for the hem of his T-shirt, wanting to pull it off him, but he stopped her. "Not yet," he murmured, his voice low and sinuous in the darkness, as his elegant hands moved back up her legs, pulling them apart, cupping her hips.

She knew what he was going to do. She knew she ought to make some token, girlish protest. She wanted to give to him, not take from him.

But she closed her eyes and leaned back, silent, as his mouth found her. Her heels dug into the wood floor, her hands fisted, and she bit down on her lip as he used his mouth, his lips, his tongue, his teeth, to take her, claim her.

It was dark and frightening, it was like nothing she'd ever experienced before, and if a small, angry part of her soul resented his power, his skill, her body was beyond reason. He was taking her someplace she'd never been before, someplace brilliant and terrifying, and she fought against it for a moment, pushing against his shoulders.

But he was strong, and he was relentless. She began to whimper, helpless little cries of distress, and even as his mouth drove her, his hands stroked her thighs, soothing her, comforting her, holding her, as the madness began to swirl and escalate, until she convulsed, in an endless, silent scream, as he took her soul.

He wouldn't stop. It was as if he knew she could take no more, and he was determined to prove to her that she could. On and on he pushed her, tongue thrusting deep inside her, all the while his hands cradled her hips, holding her captive, fingers stroking, soothing, tongue pushing, taking, until she was sobbing, begging him, her head thrashing back and forth on the wood floor, her hips arched, her fists pounding at his shoulders, as she fought it, fought him.

And then it was too late. She was lost, and she knew it. Her scream was no longer silent, it was an unearthly, high-pitched wail. As he took what he wanted from her. Everything.

She was crying. She wasn't quite sure why. All she knew was that he'd slid over her, covering her with his fully clothed body, wrapping her in his arms as his mouth met hers. He tasted of love and sex, he tasted of whiskey and of her. His arms were strong and comforting around her, and she never thought she would have sought comfort from him.

She closed her eyes, knowing that the tears were still pouring down her face, unable to do anything about them. He kissed her tears, kissed her eyelids, and kissed the side of her mouth, his lips lingering, and after a moment she turned her face, putting her mouth against his, willingly.

He kissed her very slowly, carefully, teeth tugging at her trembling lower lip, tongue sliding delicately inside her mouth, meeting hers, coaxing hers. It wasn't until a shudder rippled through her body, and she began to kiss him back, that some of the darkness began to recede.

He sat back on his heels, taking her with him, her dress still hanging from her shoulders. With seemingly no effort at all he rose, pulling her with him, and she staggered for a moment, her knees weak, until he pulled her up into his arms, and then he was carrying her through the dark house, up the stairs, and her newly sensitized body thrummed with panic and desire.

The bedroom was low-eaved, shrouded. The moon had risen, shining in the open window, and the cool breeze carried the scent of daffodils on the air.

The bed was small, the sheets were white, and he put her down carefully, pushing the dress from her shoulders and tossing it away, so that she lay there, cool and naked, vulnerable and afraid. But not afraid enough to run away again.

She could see his eyes glitter in the darkness, but she couldn't read his expression. He stripped off the black T-shirt and sent it sailing. He unzipped his jeans and then hesitated, lifting his head to look at her.

"Have I frightened you yet?" he asked, and there was a wealth of tension, of banked emotion beneath the casual words.

She was surprised she was able to speak so calmly. "Were you trying to?"

He considered it, moving to stand next to the bed. "I don't know," he said with devastating honesty. "I may have been. Did I succeed?"

He only deserved equal truth. "A little."

"Do you want to run?"

"A little," she said again.

He reached out his hand and slipped it under her tangled mane of hair, and he was impossibly, heartbreakingly gentle. "Are you going to?" he whispered.

"Never again." And she turned her face against his palm, and kissed him.

Richard looked down at the woman sitting on

his bed. Her hair was a fiery mass around her pale face, her mouth was swollen from his, and her eyes were filled with panic and love. Quite simply, she was going to be the death of him.

He'd wanted to push her, and he had. He'd wanted to see whether she'd turn and run, whether she could take what he could give her, whether she had what he needed, and he was willing to sacrifice everything in the discovery.

He hadn't realized it would involve sacrificing his own tenuous state of mind. He hadn't realized that giving himself to her would wrench him out of that dark, empty place where he'd survived for so long. That she'd drag him into feeling again, when he thought and hoped that he'd lost the ability. That she'd make him care about her, not for the sake of his children, not for the sake of his goddamn plan, but for her.

He knelt on the bed beside her, pressing his face against the fragrant hollow of her shoulder. She put her hands up and held him there, comforting him when he deserved no comfort, giving herself to him when he deserved no gifts.

He shuddered, the pain rippling through his body, and her hands were smooth and cool as they soothed him. He could taste the heat of her tears, and he wanted to make her laugh. He wanted her in sunlight, in joy. But there were only shadows and sorrow left in his life.

He was so tight with desire that he was afraid to touch her. He tried to hold himself very still, to calm the raging need that swept over his body. He'd played it all so carefully up till now; he couldn't afford to make a mistake at this point. She was his, she would do what he needed her to do, and she wouldn't fight. He just needed a moment or two to . . .

She touched him. Her hand against the open zipper of his jeans, long fingers sliding inside, encircling him. He jerked, pulling away from her, out of reach. Crossing the room and standing by the moonlit window.

"Give me a minute," he said in a harsh voice.

"No." It was simply spoken, enough to make him turn his head and stare at her. She looked like a pagan goddess, a wanton angel, with her fiery cloud of hair, her pale, voluptuous skin, her calm expression.

He struggled fiercely for his distance, for his cold, protecting humor. "No?" he echoed. "I would have thought I made you come enough to keep you satisfied for at least fifteen minutes."

It didn't work. She climbed off the bed, moving toward him, gracefully unself-conscious. "You know me very well," she said, moving in and out of the moon shadow as she approached him, and she looked predatory, magnificent in the silvery light. Far removed from the little girl he'd married, he reminded himself, deliberately, trying to squash the raging lust that rippled through his body.

Even the memory of his dead wife couldn't

affect him. He stood and watched as Cassidy approached him, and for the first time he understood the need to run.

She came up to him, and he could smell her skin, the fragrant scent of perfume, mixed with the headier smell of fresh daffodils on the air. And the scent of her arousal. "But you haven't realized," she continued calmly, "that I'm beginning to know you. You've spent the last few weeks trying to frighten me. And I only just realized that I frighten you as well."

He just managed a cynical smile, as his heart was pounding in his chest. "Are you going to take a knife to me, Cassie?" he murmured.

"No," she said. She sank to her knees in front of him, like a penitent, her hair like a veil around her shoulders, and her cool, deft hands released him from his unzipped jeans. He was full and throbbing in her hands, and she was trembling slightly, despite the sureness in her movements. "Something far more dangerous," she said. And she put her mouth on him.

He reached down and threaded his fingers through her tangled hair, meaning to pull her away, but instead he held her closer, imprisoning her, though she had no wish to escape.

He didn't want to do this. He wanted to own her, take her, enslave her. But he was beyond control, as much her slave as she was his, and he pushed into her mouth, unable to help himself, knowing only the darkness and the warm, seeking wetness of her.

This was no faceless solace. This was Cassie, with the beautiful smile and the wary eyes, with the compassionate soul and a fierce maternal instinct that could battle the world and win. This was the woman he needed, this was the woman he loved . . .

He tried to pull away, before it was too late, but she refused to let him go, her hands digging into his hips, her mouth inexorable, inexperienced, and quite the most erotic experience he had ever had in his entire life. And then there was no longer any alternative, as he thrust into her mouth, and gave her what he had never given another woman.

He knew, without asking, that it was something she had never done before. And something she would never do for another man. She took him, and everything he had to give her, without a murmur, and when he was finished he sank to the floor beside her, pulling her into his arms.

She was hot, she was trembling, and her arms slid around his waist as she buried her face against his shoulder. She had won, but she had lost as well. He belonged to her now, but that only made her bonds tighter. He wondered if she realized it.

She started to pull away, and he let her go, hoping he'd manage to disguise his reluctance. In the moonlight her face was pale, with a flush of color on her cheekbones. She wasn't used to being a wanton. It was very becoming.

"The bathroom's in there," he said, rising, taking her hand and pulling her upright. It was a good thing she was suddenly shy. If she looked down, she'd see that he was getting hard again, already. He should be used to it. Her presence had induced an advanced case of satyriasis in him that he'd been unable to combat.

"Thank you," she murmured in an absurdly polite little voice, moving past him toward the door. He controlled his urge to touch her.

"You're welcome," he said wryly, just as polite. The door closed behind her, and he wondered idly whether she was going to throw up. He didn't think so.

She didn't like to drink—he remembered that. She got drunk easily, and the notion of the things he could do to her in bed if she were a little bit sloshed was undeniably appealing. He zipped his jeans, with difficulty, and went back downstairs to pour himself a drink. And to wait until she was brave enough to emerge from the bathroom, like a bride on her honeymoon.

For a brief, sour moment he remembered his own wedding night, and he forced himself to probe that memory, like an old wound. Why hadn't he read the obvious signs? How naive could he, a self-proclaimed cynic, have been?

But that was years ago, when he believed in the power of love. Of one man, one woman, bonding, passion and eternity. That, and the sacred, unshakable innocence of children.

He no longer believed in love. In bonding, in passion or eternity. But he still believed in the resilience of children.

Things weren't going exactly as he had planned, and he had to accept that fact with as good grace as he could muster. He cared too much for her. He needed her too much. She sneaked beneath his defenses even as he tried to shatter hers.

It didn't matter. Whether it made it harder or easier for him, in the long run it would make no difference. The bonds were there, spiderweb fine but infinitely strong, and growing stronger all the time. By the time he returned to jail, the children would be safely ensconced with Cassie. Even Sean's impending death would work to his advantage. There would be nothing to call Cassie back to her life in the States.

He carried the glasses back upstairs and set them on the table by the bed. She was still in the bathroom, and he wondered idly what she was doing. She'd come out sooner or later. And he was more than ready for her.

He stripped off his jeans and kicked them away, then stretched out on the pristine double bed. He pulled the white sheet up around his middle, more to preserve Cassidy's sudden shyness than as any protection from the cool night air flooding in the open window. He took a shallow, meditative sip of his whiskey and water. And waited for Cassidy.

*   *   *

She was afraid to leave the bathroom. She'd spent as much time as she possibly could, washing her face and stealing his toothbrush to brush her teeth. She'd considered taking a shower, and then thought better of it. He might very well join her in there.

She was afraid. Not of him this time. Or at least, not much. She was afraid of her reaction to him. Of the fever that was running through her body, one that was bordering on sickness, bordering on madness. Her body burned and shook for his. And she was afraid to see him until she could regain some tiny portion of self-control. Some tiny piece of Cassidy Roarke that didn't belong, blood and bone, to Richard Tiernan.

It was a losing battle. She knew that. She could see her reflection in the mirror over the sink. She looked like an Irish witch. She looked like a woman in need. She looked like a woman hopelessly, wrongly in love. And it was a waste of time and energy to fight it. Especially since time was at a premium.

The room was darker when she opened the door, the moon having moved farther across the sky. He was lying in the bed, waiting for her, watching for her, and it was just as well his expression was shrouded in the shadows. It meant hers was as well.

It took all her self-control not to scamper across the room and dive beneath the sheets. She was self-conscious about her body, and without his hands on her she felt awkward, overgrown. The man had actually carried her up the stairs, and he hadn't even been breathing hard. Well, he had been breathing hard, but it wasn't because of her weight.

She forced herself to cross the room slowly, to slide beneath the sheet next to him, trying to be casual about it. Of course it didn't work.

"You're still nervous," he said, a statement more than a question, and she could hear the amused disbelief in his voice.

"Of course not," she said in a damnably shaky voice. The pillows were piled high behind them, and she'd pulled the sheet up to her shoulders. If he just gave her a little time, she'd probably calm down, she told herself. After all, they'd already done more sexual variations than she'd indulged in during her entire, admittedly limited, sexual history. Her affairs had been few, short-lived, and relatively unsatisfying, and they'd never gotten past the most basic of positions.

If she'd survived this much, the rest should be fairly straightforward. In a bed, him on top, just like the few other occasions when she'd tried unsuccessfully to fall in love.

And pigs could fly.

He held out a tall glass filled with amber liquid and ice, and she took it, reluctantly, accepting the need for Dutch courage.

She took a deep gulp, and she was lost.

"Coke?" she whispered in awe and delight. "Diet Coke? I thought it was whiskey."

"Only the best for you, Cassie love," he said lightly, putting his own half-empty glass of Scotch beside the bed. "I know you don't like to drink."

"You haven't let that stop you before. I thought you'd want me drunk and pliant."

"Oh, no," he murmured. "I want you wide-awake and very observant."

Cassidy swallowed nervously. "Maybe you'd better give me some of your whiskey."

He touched her face, his fingers long and smooth and delicious against her skin. She looked into his eyes, the unfathomable darkness of them, and she could see her own reflected in them. And then she could see nothing at all, as he blocked out the light and his mouth covered hers.

The tang of whiskey was sharp and cool on his tongue as it sought hers. She made a faint, whimpering sound as she slid down beneath him, and the pristine white sheet was swept away from them both, leaving them naked in the moonlight, amid the scent of spring flowers.

He moved over her, covering her with his large, strong body, and she was so caught up in the sweeping pleasure of his tongue in her mouth that she was scarcely aware that he was lying between her legs.

His mouth left hers, and his deep thrust took her by surprise. She made a startled noise, clutching his shoulders, but she was wet and ready for him. He pushed all the way, then sank his head against hers, his breathing deep and rasping, as she tried to accustom herself to his size, his presence, his unexpectedly sudden invasion.

After a moment he lifted his head, and his faint smile and glittering eyes were as triumphant and possessive as his body. "I didn't want to give you a chance to change your mind."

"And if I did?"

"Too late." He withdrew, just slightly, then thrust deep again, and she couldn't control her tiny sound of dismay.

"Am I hurting you?"

"No," she said, a lie. Then, "Yes. A little. I'm not used to . . ."

"Men? Or me?"

"Both," she whispered, wishing the darkness covered them, wishing he couldn't see her face.

"Don't fight it, Cassidy," he said. "Don't fight me." And the next thrust was powerful, demanding, as long fingers caught her thighs and pulled them around him, bringing him deeper still.

She wondered if this was another test. One she would fail. What did he want from her? And did it really matter?

She wrapped her arms around him. His skin was hot and slick, and she could feel the tension in his muscular frame. For the first time she realized the effect she was having on him, and it soothed her initial panic.

The first wave hit her with the force of an electric shock. She hadn't been expecting it, and her body convulsed beneath his with short, sharp tremors that seemed to draw the very life out of her. She couldn't breathe, and she didn't want to, as her body seemed to take on a life of its own, trembling and shaking and dissolving, colors and blinding light blurring before her eyes as she gave herself up to it, and tried to pull him along with her.

But he was having none of it. When her tremors finally began to fade he pulled away from her, and she found herself bracing for him to plunge inside her again.

But instead he pulled out completely, and she clutched for him, panicked. "No," she gasped. "Don't leave me."

The room was darker now, the moon had set. His hands on her body were sure and strong, and his voice came out of the darkness. "This way," he said, turning her over on her stomach and lifting her high on her knees.

She didn't object. She was beyond second thoughts or self-consciousness. For the first time in her life, she had given herself over completely, and he could do anything he wanted with her. She buried her face in the cool white sheets, feeling his hands on her thighs, positioning her, coming up behind her, pushing into her, deep and sure and powerful, and her hands clutched the mattress as she wept, soft, mindless cries of pleasure and despair, of pleading and surrender, of total, eternal acceptance.

There was no tenderness now, and she didn't want any. The bed shook beneath them, her body shook with the force of his thrusts, and she reveled in it, terrified and renewed at the same time. His hands slid from her hips, up her back, and she met each thrust with eagerness, ready for him, ready for oblivion.

He leaned over, his body wrapped around hers, his arms holding her tight. One hand slid between her legs to touch her. The other to her mouth, his fingers sliding inside, taking her that way as well.

It was enough, it was more than enough. She shattered, into a thousand pieces, as his mouth sank down on her shoulder, biting hard, and his body filled hers, pulsing deeply, filling her with everything that was his. Life and death, commitment and final abandonment. Giving and taking, and none of it mattered, as she dissolved, into the night, into his arms, losing the very last of herself in the sweep of darkness and the pulse of life.

There was gentleness in him after all. His hands were tender as they settled her down on the mattress, and his body wrapped around hers, warming her, calming her. She realized she was trembling, a belated, almost absent thought, and then she heard his voice, the soft, murmured words of praise and pleasure, as his hands stroked her body into calm, into warmth, into sleep.

She tried to fight it. There wasn't enough time,

enough time in the world for them, but she couldn't resist. His words, sex words, love words, senseless, wonderful words in his deep, soothing voice couldn't be resisted, and she closed her eyes, only for a moment.

When she slept she dreamed. They would kill him, and they would make her watch, and she cried, reaching out for him. When she awoke she was sprawled across him, the room was still in the complete darkness of early morning, and he was buried deep inside her. She opened her eyes to look down at him, and the orgasm that shook her was powerful, instantaneous, and shared.

He closed his eyes, his strong teeth bared in a grimace, and she watched him. And she knew she owned him, as much as he owned her.

CHAPTER 14

The sun was blazing in the window when Cassidy awoke. She was alone in the bed, something which didn't surprise her. The sheets, both top and bottom, were tangled around her, and the mattress was half off the bed. She was sticky and sore, physically and emotionally exhausted. And she was smiling.

Wrapping one of the sheets around her, she moved toward the open window. Richard was digging in the garden, and not for one moment did she allow herself to consider that he might be digging her grave. She looked down at the daffodils beneath her, at their cheery yellow bells. There was a worm inside one, eating.

She never had, and never would, accustom herself to English showers. She scalded herself, she froze herself, she barely managed to get the soap out of her long, thick hair. By the time she emerged she was shivering, and she glanced at her body in the wavery mirror above the pedestal sink. She stopped in shock. There were rough patches of red on her fair skin, doubtless from the roughness of his beard. There were dark marks on her breasts, on her hips, on her neck and shoulders from his rapacious mouth, and she could see the faint bruising on her back were his teeth had sunk in deep.

She looked lush, wanton, and well-loved. She looked like a woman fresh from her lover's bed, and more than ready to go back there. Her lips were red and swollen, her eyes dazed and dark with remembered passion. She could barely recognize herself.

She found her suitcase in the bedroom, and she wondered when Richard had brought it in for her. She dressed quickly, throwing on a long full skirt and an oversize cotton sweater, and made her way downstairs, barefoot, to the kitchen.

He was drinking a cup of coffee. He turned to look at her, slowly, his dark, unreadable eyes sliding over her body, and she waited for some teasing, offhand remark.

He said absolutely nothing. He simply put his coffee down and came toward her, slowly, deliberately, and she stood her ground. He took the hem of her sweater and pulled it over her head. By the time he'd lifted her skirt and pushed her underwear down her legs, she'd already managed to unbuckle his belt, and when he pushed her down on the cluttered farm table amid the dishes, he was hard and ready for her, pushing inside her before she'd managed to lean back.

It was fast, silent, and inexorable. She barely noticed her discomfort, as each succeeding thrust shoved her farther across the table. Dishes shattered on the floor, but neither of them paid any attention. She came first, unable to stop herself, and he followed, quickly, sinking his head on her breast in panting surrender.

"It must be something about kitchens," he said in a thoughtful voice after a few moments.

She shoved at him, and he moved away from her, his jeans down around his thighs. He simply pulled them up and fastened them, then reached out a hand for her to help her off the table. "Mind the broken dishes," he said casually.

She looked up at him, at his outstretched hand, and wanted to scream or cry. She had given herself to him, willingly, but the reality of that was beginning to hit home as she lay spread-eagled on the kitchen table, still trembling with the aftermath of her brief, powerful orgasm. She had no defenses left. And the thought terrified her as nothing had before.

She ignored his hand, scrambling off the table with a fair amount of awkwardness, feeling like a fool. But Richard was having none of her avoidance. He reached out for her, and the awkwardness vanished, as it always did when he touched her. "You have a demoralizing effect on me," he added wryly.

She closed her eyes briefly, knowing that color was flaring in her face. Stupid to be embarrassed after all they'd done in the last twelve hours, stupid to be embarrassed with his semen dripping down her legs, but there it was. "As do you on me," she said in a quiet voice.

She didn't expect his response. The tenderness of his mouth against hers. Her eyelids fluttered open, and she looked up at him, completely vulnerable. "Good morning," he said softly.

And finally the humor of the situation hit her, and she managed to smile in return. "We already went a little past that, didn't we?" she said.

"We can always go back," he whispered, and kissed her again. And this time she put her arms around him and kissed him back, sweetly, with the doomed love that had taken possession of her heart.

"We're going down to see the children," he said. "Sally's expecting me, and I doubt she'll be surprised when she sees you. She always was a perceptive woman."

Cassidy felt the sharp stab of jealousy with something akin to wonder. She'd never considered herself a jealous, possessive person. She found she was a great deal more elemental than she'd ever thought. "Were you in love with her?"

"No. And she was perceptive enough to know that as well."

"But you had an affair with her. After you were married?" She was hoping he would deny it.

But the time for lies were past. "Yes," he said.

"And what did your wife think of that?"

"It made her insane." The words were lightly, eerily spoken.

"I don't think I want to hear about this," Cassidy said, moving away from him to pour herself a cup of coffee.

"Then don't ask," he said calmly enough. "We'll leave in half an hour. It's several hours' drive from here, and I want you to have time to get to know them."

"What about you?"

"What about me?"

"Don't you want to see them? You don't have much time here before someone realizes you left the country. Don't you want to spend as much time as you can with your children? Don't you love them?"

"I'm planning to die for them," he said with icy simplicity. And he walked out of the room before she could take back her questions.

It was a glorious spring day. By the time Cassie changed and met Richard by the Vauxhall she'd left in the driveway, she'd made up her mind. She looked at him warily, unable to read his expression as he tossed a picnic hamper in the backseat of her car.

"What about a truce?" he said in his deep, slow voice.

"I hadn't realized we were still battling."

"We're always battling. On one level or another. Just for today, don't ask me any more questions.

You aren't ready for the truth, and I'm sick to death of lying. Why don't we pretend we're a normal American couple, going for a peaceful drive in the English countryside? No deaths, no lies, no secrets. Just for today?"

She wasn't sure if she'd ever gone to him of her own accord before. She crossed the drive and put her arms around him, leaning her head against his shoulder. His arms came around to hold her, lightly, possessively, and she could hear his heart beating beneath her ear. Just as her own heart was pounding, in silent counterpoint with his. "Yes," she said.

It was lambing season. As Richard drove her rental car down the narrow lanes, they passed field after field of sheep and their new offspring. The hedgerows were still more twigs than leaves, but the daffodils were everywhere.

They drove in silence, listening to the BBC and the weather in Welsh. They drove in amiable conversation, speaking of childhood and loved books, of college years and favorite movies. Neither of them mentioned the past two years, neither of them mentioned family. Cassidy leaned back, watching as they sped down the narrow, twisty lanes, and wished it could go on forever and ever.

They reached the tiny town of Neatsfoot by late morning. Sally and the children seemed cozily ensconced in a cottage at the edge of the village, and while Cassie wondered why they didn't live in Richard's house at Herring Cross, she didn't

ask. She was determined to keep her curiosity at
bay for as long as she could. What she most
needed to know she could discover simply by
observing.

When she fought her irrational jealousy, she
could see that the affection between Richard and
Sally was no more than that. At least on Richard's
side. He greeted his old friend easily enough, with
a casual kiss that nevertheless felt like a knife in
Cassie's belly. She wanted his passion, his obsession. She wanted his casual, comfortable affection
as well.

His children were all over him, dragging him
into the cottage, chattering at a rapid-fire speed
that left Cassie dazed and smiling. She stood by
the car, watching as they disappeared, then
turned to meet Sally Norton's wary brown eyes.

"You came back," she said.

"I did," Cassie agreed.

Sally watched her for a long, thoughtful
moment. "Come with me," she said abruptly. "I
want to show you something."

No questions, Cassidy reminded herself, nodding her agreement. Not unless you can handle
the answers.

Sally led her through the house, past the living
room where the chatter of excited voices danced
with the lower, calmer registers of Richard's deep
voice. He was a good father, Cassidy realized with
absent surprise. Calm, loving, totally involved.
Though why she should have doubted that, when

he was already willing and ready to die for them, was something she didn't bother to consider.

The garden was small, gray, with only the bright splash of yellow from the daffodils brightening the gloom. Cassidy took one last, longing glance at the house before she sat, waiting to hear what Sally had to say.

"You're not to betray him," she said abruptly.

"I never would."

"So you say. But he's not an easy man, and things are never what they seem to be."

"I know that."

"You think you know him so well?" Sally said with just a trace of bitterness.

"Yes."

"And you're in love with him, aren't you? Poor, silly girl," she said, the bitterness growing stronger.

She didn't deny it. "Tell me what I can do. How I can help."

Sally shook her head. "He's got you well and truly trapped, hasn't he? Just as he trapped me. He never pretended to love me, you know. That's part of his danger. He doesn't promise anything he's not willing to give, so you can't comfort yourself with the thought that you'd been misled. You have to accept the fact that you went into it, deliberately blinding yourself to the truth."

"What is the truth?"

"He'll never love you. I don't think he's capable of it. Oh, he's good in bed, as I'm sure you've very well aware. But his heart is in the grave, with his bitch of a wife. He worshipped her, you know. Everyone did. Sweet, saintly Diana, the little princess. Everyone was devoted to her. Even her children thought she was some kind of magical creature, though they rarely saw her."

"What do you mean?"

"She was too emotionally frail to take on the burden of children. She had a live-in nanny, and Richard did the majority of the child care. Little Diana could simply bask in the glow of maternity without doing any of the work."

"What about you?"

"I do the work, all right. I love these children, as much as if they were on my own. I don't want to give them up. I told Richard that my treatment could wait, but he wouldn't hear of it. I should have kept my mouth shut in the first place," she said bitterly.

"Why did you tell him?"

"Because if I hadn't, he'd probably be a dead man already. He wasn't fighting his death sentence, you know. He thought he had everything settled, between me and Mark Bellingham. It wasn't until I got sick that he accepted the appeal, accepted the fact that there was still something worth fighting for."

"Why? Why hasn't he told the truth, why is he letting them do this to him when you and I both know he didn't kill his wife?"

Sally Norton's smile was twisted. "Don't speak

for me," she said. "I know what happened that night. He told me. If you want the truth, ask him."

It was icy cold, the panic that swamped her. "He didn't kill her," she said again, hearing the uncertainty in her own voice.

Sally ignored her. "You're not to break your promise," she said fiercely. "If I leave the children in your hands, you're not to go back on your word. Richard will be beyond stopping you, but I won't. If you do anything stupid that endangers those children, I will kill you. Do you believe me?"

Cassidy had no doubts whatsoever. "I would never anything to hurt them."

Sally stepped back, the fury vanishing from her, leaving her pale and sick-looking. "Good," she said flatly. "I trust you. God knows, I have no choice." She turned, starting back toward the cottage, when Cassie found words that surprised her.

"Do you love him?"

Sally stopped, but she didn't turn around. Her back was narrow and very straight, and she looked both strong and fragile. "I did once. To the point of desperation. He's good at that, you know. Getting a woman to love him."

Cassidy ignored the implications. "Do you still love him?"

Sally turned to look at her, and there was death and darkness in her eyes. "Not since he told me what really happened that night."

*   *   *

If Richard had any doubts about the very real danger Cassidy Roarke posed for him, that day would have wiped them out. He couldn't stop thinking of her. Remembering the taste of her skin, the scent of her neck, the texture of her nipples. He was like a randy teenager with a perpetual erection, and it had taken all his considerable willpower not to pull over by the side of the road and haul her onto his lap during the trip down to Neatsfoot.

He'd deliberately left her alone with the children, watching from a distance as they tested her, as only a five- and a seven-year-old can test. His children were nothing at all like their mother, thank God. They were resilient, fierce, openly demanding. Seth had already taken a fancy to her, climbing into her lap and chattering away amiably, and he suspected that Sally wasn't too pleased with how easily they were adapting. He couldn't let himself think about that.

He couldn't worry about Sally's well-being, or Cassidy's, or his own. All that mattered was his children's welfare. Cassidy had passed almost every test. He had one more for her, the most difficult of all. He wondered what he'd do if she failed.

Things had gone too far to pull back. If she backed out, betrayed him, then he would have no choice whatsoever.

At least then he would go to his death knowing he was getting no more than he deserved.

Odd, how Sally's clean, orderly kitchen left him unmoved. He leaned against the counter while she assembled sandwiches, surveying her neat movements, her trim figure.

"What did you say to her?" he asked casually.

Sally didn't pretend to misunderstand, nor did she waste their time by lying. "I warned her about you."

"I thought you might have. You don't like her, do you?"

"That's where you're wrong. As a matter of fact, I like her very much. Enough that I regret what you're asking of her."

"You were willing to give the same."

"But I didn't think I was in love you."

He said nothing, allowing her that fiction. He knew women, and he knew Sally. For all Sally's insisting that their short affair had come to a mutual conclusion, he knew she still wanted him. Still wasted her emotions on an impossibility. It would have grieved him, if he had any emotion to spare.

"You haven't told her the truth yet, have you?" Sally asked.

"No."

"Are you going to?"

"If I have no choice." He pushed away from the counter, going to stand by the window. The weather had shifted, darkened, from a glorious spring day to the promise of an angry storm. "I think I have to get back to the States."

"So soon?"

He'd learned to shut off his emotions two years ago. The presence of his children brought them forth again, combined with Cassidy Roarke's wild passion. It was all he could do to hide them from Sally. "The sooner I get back, the sooner I can have Mark make the final arrangements. You need to begin treatment, we both know it, and you've already waited too long."

"She'll just disappear? As I did?"

"If I can persuade her. Her father is dying. Once he goes, which I imagine will be fairly soon, she'll want to get away. By the time she realizes what she's done, the ties she's severed, it will be too late."

"Or so you hope."

"It will be too late," he said, his voice icy to hide his fear.

"Once I finish treatment, I can come back . . ."

"No. They've been disrupted too much in the last few years. First the loss of their mother, then their father."

"Not to mention their grandparents."

He said nothing for a long moment. "They'll stay with Cassidy. If I work things well enough, they'll assume she's just another victim of mine."

"What are people going to say when I show up again? Don't you think they'll ask questions?"

"I doubt anyone will notice. They're more inter-

ested in rumors than facts. If anyone asks, just
say you were in an ashram in India, and that you
didn't know I'd been accused of murder. Tell
them you think I'm entirely capable of slaughtering my wife and children."

"Richard . . ."

"Do it," he said, his voice tight with tension.
"It's the one last thing you can do for me. My
children are dead. As long as the world believes
that, they're safe."

"I can't . . ."

"You've done this much for me already, Sally.
Don't let me down at the last minute."

She looked at him, her dark brown eyes filled
with love and hopelessness. "I'll do it," she
promised.

His children wept when they left, early that evening. He lied to them, because he had to, telling
them that Daddy had to go back and work, but
that he'd be coming back by summer. It was small
comfort. He'd be dead by summer. He would
never see his children again.

"May I come again?" Cassidy asked them, her
voice slightly unsteady, her green eyes bright with
unshed tears. "If your father can't make it, do you
mind if I come alone?"

The response was everything he could have
hoped for, and it was enough to keep him from
losing his tenuous grip. They would survive. They

would thrive. He was leaving them in the best of hands.

He didn't say a word as they drove back north. He was driving too fast, and he knew it, and he didn't give a damn. The mindless rage was simmering through his veins, and there was no way he could vent it, apart from driving much too fast in Cassidy's car.

She sat next to him, eyes closed, face shuttered. He could see the white streaks her tears had made on her pale cheeks, and the sight of that enraged him even further. He could feel the blackness closing in around him, and it frightened him. He'd been fighting it for so long. Now, when things were finally in place, he couldn't allow the darkness to destroy everything. One final lie, and everything would be safe.

If he could trust her. If he could trust his power over her, that power he'd worked on so painstakingly. It had been an assault, long and well-planned, and she'd succumbed, just as he'd expected her to. She was his, now and forever, completely, and if he'd made the fatal mistake of being caught in his own web, then there wasn't that much time to suffer for it. If loving her made his eventual punishment that much harder, it was the least he deserved.

She said nothing as he drove faster and faster, the demons pushing him toward the edge, dragging her along. The speedometer crept higher and higher, the rain lashed against the windshield, and the roads were slick and narrow. He didn't care. He wasn't going to die, not this way, not with her beside him, even if some crazy part of him wanted it. Wanted her death, with his, tied together in a kind of mad eternity.

He took a corner too fast, the wheels lost their purchase, and he felt the car begin to slide. Slide toward the cliff, and he watched it go, calmly, wondering whether they'd tumble, end over end, down into the fierce and angry sea. He was entirely willing.

And then, at the last possible moment, he jerked the wheel. The car stopped its death slide, skidding around on the wet, deserted pavement and ending up against the bank of the far side, headlights spearing crazily into the black rain.

The car stalled out. He dropped his hands, closing his eyes, and in the dark of the silent car, he could hear her breathing, rapid, panicked, he could hear the pounding of her heart.

He wanted to feel her heart against his hand, he wanted to lick her skin, he wanted to taste her tears. He opened his eyes in the darkness, to meet hers.

She looked like a woman who had faced death, willingly. Her face was pale, her eyes huge, and her car was too goddamned small.

He stumbled out into the rain, dragging her with him. They tumbled down the hillside, slipping in the mud, her hand tight in his, and when they ended up beneath a twisted yew tree, it took less than a moment for him to find her, with his mouth, with his hand. She was wet and ready for him, she would do anything he wanted, and he knew it. She would go down on him in the rain, kneeling in the mud, if he wanted it. He could take her any way he wanted, and she asked for nothing in return. Nothing but his soul, which she'd stolen when he hadn't been looking.

He wanted to push away from her, but he couldn't. He was caught, just as she was, and her breasts were cool and damp in his mouth as he pushed her down in the mud, ripping her clothes open. She was slick and ready, but this time, in the cold, in the rain, he perversely wasn't going to rush it. He was going to screw her, long and slow, in the mud, in the night, so that when he finished with her she would be beyond defenses, beyond help. She would be his, body and soul.

She thrashed beneath him, trying to hurry him, hot and eager, and his power over her made him feel both cruel and alive. He slid his fingers between her legs, testing the heat and dampness, then moved farther, between the dark cleft, so that she jerked beneath him.

He kissed her, hard, and she kissed him back, arching against him. He put his jeans-clad knee between her legs, pressing against her, rocking against her, and heard her faint whimpers, felt her fingers clutching against his shoulders, as the rain poured down around them.

He caught her hands and forced them back,

into the mud, as he rocked against her. He hadn't even unzipped his pants, and he could feel his cock pressing against the rough denim, a pleasure pain that equaled what he was doing to her. She was beyond coherent thought, her hair was wet with rain and mud, and he was so far gone he wasn't sure if he'd be able to shuck off his pants and finish.

She was crying now, making small, helpless sounds of distress beneath him as she writhed, and he took pity on her. And on him. Levering himself off her body, he unfastened his jeans, releasing himself into the cool night air.

"Tell me," he whispered low, a dark, cruel force driving him. "Beg me."

Her only response was a harsh, choking noise, as he put his cock against her, feeling the heat and dampness and need of her. He sank in, hard, filling her, and the sound she made would haunt him until the day they killed him. A low, keening wail of despair and completion, as her body tightened around him, waves and ripples of reaction as she climaxed.

He came immediately, not regretting it, shoving her down into the mud, exploding inside her with the pent up fury and obsession that had been simmering all day. He was only vaguely aware of the long, endless orgasm that shook her, clenching him tightly within the milking depth of her body, and when he finally collapsed on her, he could still feel the ripples caressing him.

He could do it again, he knew it. He was still
hard, and he wanted to, he wanted to just keep
fucking her until there wasn't anything left of
either of them.

And then he heard it. The faint sound of smoth-
ered tears.

He rolled off her, into the mud, shocked.
Shocked at the guilt, the sorrow that swamped
him.

"Cassie," he whispered, his voice harsh. "Baby."

The endearment was another shock, one he
wouldn't have thought he could utter. He pulled
her into his arms, tight against him, as she shook,
sobbing. He didn't know why she cried. Because
he'd screwed her in the mud, because he'd hurt
her. Or something far more frightening.

"Did I hurt you?" he asked urgently, pushing
her hair away from her tear-streaked face. Her
eyes were tightly shut, but tears were streaming
out, mixing with the rainwater and the mud from
his hand. "Cassie, baby, tell me what's wrong."

She just kept crying. Diana had been a master
of crying—he'd learned to hate women's tears,
and the various manipulations they hid. He'd
learned to ignore it, to listen to a woman sob and
wail and not feel anything at all. Cassie lay in his
arms, weeping, and he couldn't bear it.

"Cassie, love," he said, and his own voice was
breaking, his powerful control was breaking.
"Don't." He kissed her, kissed her tear-streaked
cheeks, her mud-streaked brow, her chin, her

nose. "Don't cry, baby. I won't hurt you again, I promise. Just don't leave me. Don't run this time, Cassie, God, don't run."

He was scarcely aware of when the sobs halted. Her arms were tight around him, her eyes were open, swimming with tears. "I won't run, Richard. I swear it."

And fool that he was, he believed her.

CHAPTER 15

They called it a bed-and-breakfast, but as far as Cassie was concerned, it was the closest she'd come to an American motel since she'd set foot in England. The long low whitewashed structure was hidden behind the old coaching house, its newness artfully disguised by darkened timber and texture paint, but the beds were queen-sized and new, the televisions in each room had remote controls, and she could even work the shower.

She needed it. Mud plastered her hair, was ground into her skin. Richard had tugged her clothes back around her with impatient, yet gentle hands, then pulled her back up the slippery hillside to their abandoned car. It seemed as if they'd been down in the mud for hours, but during that time no one had driven by and noticed the car halfway off the road. Or at least, no one had bothered to investigate.

Once in the car she'd leaned back and closed her eyes, ignoring the mud that settled into the cloth seats. When Richard parked behind the old inn, she barely managed to rouse herself, and it wasn't until she found herself standing beneath the shower in their room that her brain began to work once more.

The knowledge shattered her. Standing alone beneath the lukewarm stream of water, the mud pooled at her bare feet like blood. She felt battered, raw and aching, and she leaned against the wall of the fiberglass stall and closed her eyes, searching for a trace of pride, or self-control.

She had none. She'd rutted in the mud like a sow in heat, she'd lain beneath him in the rain and begged him. She'd done what she always swore she wouldn't do. She'd given herself, body and soul, to someone who was worse than bad for her. He was death and disaster, and she'd welcomed his possession, no questions asked.

I don't think he's capable of loving anyone, Sally Norton had told her. *I haven't been in love with him since he told me what really happened that night.*

Cassie knew she had two choices, and two choices only. She could go back into that bedroom, lie down on the bed, and let him do whatever he wanted to her. Let him take her heart and soul and mind, and most of all her body, over and over again, until she was completely helpless.

Or she could ask him what happened the night his wife was killed.

In the end, she had no choice at all. The survival instinct, one she'd nurtured all her life, came back to life. She'd survived her childhood, survived Sean and her mother, survived the careless lovers and the wrong choices, until she'd built a safe life for herself, where people couldn't hurt her, use her. She couldn't throw it away now, out of blind, misguided lust she kept wanting to call love.

He was sitting in a corner of the small room. He'd managed to find a shower of his own, she couldn't imagine where, but she could be glad he hadn't chosen to join her. His hair was wet, slicked back from his dark face, and he was wearing a black T-shirt and jeans. Even so, he looked oddly British, as if he'd taken on protective coloring.

He had a glass of whiskey and ice in his hand, and he looked up at her with no expression whatsoever. She wanted to slap him.

She dressed hurriedly, pulling on a pair of jeans and an old sweater, and he watched her, his dark eyes never leaving her. "Going somewhere?" he asked pleasantly, when she started pulling on her shoes.

The very evenness of his tone startled her. She'd been so intent on her own confusion, her own needs, that she hadn't noticed that somehow, at some point, Richard had disappeared. Slipped back into the dark, distant world of his, where no light entered. Where she was locked out as well.

"Would you try to stop me?" she countered.

"Ah," he said, leaning back. "You *are* leaving. I

should have known. The moment you promised never to run away, you began planning your escape."

"Would you let me go?"

"Of course." He took a sip of his whiskey, and he seemed no more than idly interested in her. "Just out of curiosity, where are you going?"

"I'm not necessarily going anywhere."

"I see. I have another chance, apparently." The very notion seemed to amuse him. He was distant and chilly, the manipulator who'd toyed with her in the apartment in New York. "How am I going to persuade you to stay? Get down on my knees and swear my undying love? That I'll be faithful till the day I die? That's not much of a promise in my case."

"Stop it."

"What do you want from me?" he asked, taking another sip, and she realized he was mildly, dangerously drunk. Just enough so that he was balancing on the edge. Now was the time for her to push.

"The truth. No more evasions, no more lies. Simply the truth."

"You won't like it."

She felt a chill dance along her backbone. "I can take it."

"I doubt it."

"What happened that afternoon?" Her urgency was suddenly overwhelming, and she knelt next to him, her hands on his arm, beseeching him. "Tell me the truth, Richard."

He turned his head slowly, and there was death and sorrow in his eyes. And Cass was very, very frightened.

"She was going to leave me," he said, quite simply. "She was going to take the children and leave me. I couldn't let her do that."

The chill intensified, and unwittingly she tightened her clasp on his arm. "Tell me, Richard."

"She was pregnant. My lovely, delicate, indisputably crazy wife hadn't allowed me near her bed for more than a year, but she was two months pregnant by the man she'd always loved more than me. She was taking the children and going to him, and I wasn't about to let that happen.

"I picked the children up at the day-care center early that day. Diana seldom bothered with the mundane details of motherhood—I rather think she was expecting me to bring them home to her before she left. I wouldn't be surprised if she expected me to drive her there as well."

"Drive her where?"

"To her lover's. I didn't realize quite how bad things were. I didn't mind her going, but I was damned if she'd take my children. I took the children to Sally and asked her to hide them. No matter what happened, she wasn't to come forth until I told her to. One of the few times in my life when my instincts were right."

He took another sip of whiskey and glanced

down at her hands clutching his arm tightly. "I
went home, and Diana was there. She told me
about the baby then—I hadn't known she was
pregnant, or even that she was sleeping with anyone. She told me there was no way I could keep
custody of the children, that she was taking them
with her and I'd never see them again. She'd been
very clever, I realized that belatedly. The accidents, the trips to the emergency room for broken
collarbones and cracked skulls weren't accidents
at all. She'd hurt the children. And she was ready
to tell the authorities that I was responsible."

Cassie knelt there, sick inside. His arm was like
a band of steel beneath her fingers, the tension
so strong that he hardly seemed human. "What
happened next?"

"She told me to try to stop her." His voice was
slow, almost drugged. His eyes met hers. "I picked
up a knife, and did just that."

The night was very still. She could hear the
distant sound of laughter from the pub, the noise
of traffic as it rushed by outside, the gentle patter
of rain against the windows. "You killed her?"

"I knelt beside her on the hall floor and
watched as she bled to death," he said simply. "It
was very quick. Even if I'd tried to get help, it
probably would have been too late. But I didn't
try. I just sat there and let her die."

She found herself outside in the rain, and she
couldn't remember how she got there. She must

have somehow risen to her feet and walked away from him, and he couldn't have tried to stop her. If he had, she would have been no match for his strength, his determination, his lethal seductiveness. So he must have let her go.

It was late at night, but she could hear the noise of laughter from the pub, the raucous sounds echoing through the mist. She was leaning against the wall, and her face was cold and wet.

No more denial, and no more hope. It was just that simple. He'd warned her not to ask if she wasn't able to hear the truth, but like a fool she'd gone ahead, praying there'd be some reason, some secret, some magic formula that would make it all right.

Why hadn't he lied to her? Why hadn't he kept up that enigmatic silence that had served him well enough in the time since Diana had been murdered? Why tell her?

She closed her eyes, leaning her head back against the plaster wall, and she wanted to howl out her misery and pain. Her body felt ripped apart—she wanted to run, as far and as fast as she could. She wanted to jump in the car and drive away, away from the cold-blooded killer who sat silently in the room, away from the self-destructive need that was tearing her to pieces.

She wanted to run, before she made the impossible, deadly mistake of running back to him.

He hadn't come after her. He let her go. And

she had no choice but to leave. While she still could.

He finished the whiskey after she left. The final test, and she'd failed it, quite miserably. He should have known. He'd found the perfect woman, against all odds, and then he'd gone and blown it. Blown it by making the dire mistake of falling in love with her.

It was the most absurd thing, and he almost thought he could laugh. At this point in his life, facing death because of the dark, miserable soul of one woman, he jeopardized everything by falling for another.

He hadn't even been in love with Diana, he'd known that fairly soon after their marriage. He'd been infatuated by her beauty, entranced by her frailty, manipulated by her world-class obsessions. He hadn't been in love since he was in the third grade and planned to devote his life to Marcy Connors, with the fat blond pigtails and the freckles.

That was his problem. Since entering puberty he'd been chasing after short, skinny little girl/women. Cassidy was a throwback to Marcy, with her lovely curves and her good-hearted nature.

What a fool he was. What an absolute fucking idiot, to have gone and blown everything, the only hope he had for the future, because he couldn't keep his mind and his body separate. Why the hell did it have to be Cassidy Roarke?

She was running home to Daddy as fast as her long, luscious legs could carry her. He should be used to that by now. She would go and tell Sean the hideous truth, as she thought she knew it, and Sean would send her someplace to keep her quiet. Cass's version of the truth was too tame for the likes of Sean O'Rourke. The real truth would be even less appealing.

No, Sean could have whatever truth he wanted, Richard wasn't about to stop him. But he would have to stop Cassidy. Before she told the wrong person, trusted the wrong man. He had to be fully prepared to do anything necessary to protect his children. Including murder.

If he'd had any sense at all, he wouldn't have let her escape in the first place. No one knew she was in England besides Mark and Sally, and he'd covered his own tracks very well. He could get away with it. People might suspect, but he could only be executed once.

He'd go after her, of course. But he wouldn't do anything rash. He knew better than she did why she ran. She'd panicked, looking for an excuse, and he'd given it to her, giving her one final test. She'd failed it, which should have come as no surprise. He should feel liberated.

Instead, he felt consumed with a dull, angry ache. He'd have to make other plans. The last few months were for nothing.

Or perhaps not. When they finally managed to strap him down on the gurney for the last time, he'd think of fucking Cassidy Roarke in the mud, in the rain. Of doing her every way he could possibly think of, and her begging for more.

And he'd die smiling.

CHAPTER 16

The 737 developed engine trouble somewhere over the north Atlantic. Cassidy didn't give a damn. She sat in her window seat, staring out into the billowing clouds, feeling the plane buck and shudder, and she didn't even break out in a sweat. She doubted she'd ever be afraid of flying again.

She doubted she'd ever be afraid of anything. She'd gone beyond that—nothing had the power to hurt her, frighten her, humiliate her. She had looked into the face of love, and seen death and despair, sickness and betrayal. There was nowhere else to go.

She was almost disappointed when the plane landed safely at JFK. The other passengers let out cheers and whoops of relief. Cassie simply unfastened her seat belt and prepared to deplane.

Customs was a simple matter. She had no luggage. She rented a car with little trouble, and by seven o'clock that night, she was heading out toward the Hamptons and Sean's country cottage, that was more like a small mansion.

The traffic was deadly, but Cass ignored it. The talk radio program was about men who loved too much, and for a moment she thought of Diana, and how Richard's devotion to her must have driven him to murder. She turned off the radio, letting the air-conditioned silence wash over her.

Sean was throwing a party. She shouldn't have been surprised—Sean was happiest with an audience, and Mabry was happiest providing that audience. She parked the rental car three streets over, behind a Jaguar that in other days she would have coveted, and walked to the cottage, bracing herself as she stepped into the noise and light.

Sean was holding court, surrounded by a group of old friends, new acquaintances, hangers-on, and the like. He spotted her immediately, waved an airy hello, and continued with his anecdote. She stood and stared at him for a moment, assessing. He looked vibrant, alive, robust. He wasn't going to die, damn it. He'd always known he was invincible, and he'd convinced her of that fact as well. He'd just needed time away from Richard Tiernan. As did she.

Mabry appeared beside her. "I'm glad you changed your mind, darling. I've called the apartment several times, trying to talk you into coming, but I've always gotten the machine. I was beginning to worry."

"I was visiting friends upstate," Cass murmured absently, the lie coming easily. She still hadn't decided what she was going to tell Sean and

Mabry, how much she was going to warn them. Maybe she simply wouldn't say anything at all.

If only Richard would stay in England. Take his children and hide, where no one could find him. Where she wouldn't have to see him again, but she'd know he was alive and well, and that his children were loved. There was no reason on earth for him to return and offer himself as a sacrifice to the bizarre ritual of execution. But then, none of his actions had made any kind of sense to her. Including his determined seduction of her.

There was no other word for it. She'd never been seduced in her life, but that was what Richard Tiernan had accomplished. He'd come on to her, mentally, emotionally, and physically, and he'd taken her on all those levels. She just wondered how long it would take her to reclaim herself.

Why hadn't Richard told the truth? He'd been convicted of premeditated murder, and the cold calculation of it had worked against him. If he'd told the truth, that he'd picked up the knife in a moment of blind rage after learning his wife was pregnant by another man, surely he would have gotten off with a lighter sentence.

There was no understanding why he did the things he did. She could only hope and pray he'd have enough sense to run, farther and faster, taking his children with him.

She glanced at Mabry. "Have you spoken to

Richard in the last few days?" she managed to ask in a casual voice.

"Richard's not the type for casual phone conversations," Mabry said wryly. "I imagine he's enjoying his solitude."

"I imagine so."

"By the way, I have a little surprise for you. Actually, not so little nowadays, but I think you'll be pleased."

"I don't know if I'm in the mood for surprises," she said slowly.

"You know Sean. He loves mixing things up. What made you decide to come here after all?" Mabry asked curiously, pushing her perfect sheath of white blond hair away from her strong-boned face. "You never liked these free-for-alls."

It had seemed so very simple when she'd left England. She'd find Sean and tell him the truth about Richard.

Now she wasn't so certain. "I was worried about Sean," she said with a faint smile, avoiding the issue. "Besides, it's off-season. I mistakenly thought things would be quiet around here."

"You should have known better. Your father's determined to live life to the fullest." Unspoken, the knowledge of how short that life could be hung between them. "You can sleep in your old bedroom, though you'll have to share it. We've got a full house this time."

"Who's here?"

"The usual suspects," Mabry said lightly. "Pick

the most unlikely houseguests you can imagine, multiply that by ten, and you have our current guest list. It makes for an interesting cocktail hour." She drifted away, graceful as ever, and Cassidy watched her go.

Even in the best of times, Mabry made her feel oversized and rumpled. After a transatlantic trip and a monumental case of jet lag, Cassie felt like a bag lady. She wanted nothing more than to disappear to her room, to her shower, to a peaceful night's sleep. Mabry had already made it clear that that was an unlikely prospect.

If she wasn't going to tell them the truth about Richard, then she had no real reason to be here. No reason not to run away, back to Maryland. She would never have to see Richard Tiernan again. Never feel his cool, elegant, murderous hands on her flesh again, never know the deadly delight of his mouth . . .

"Penny for your thoughts."

She didn't want to turn. She couldn't believe that she recognized that voice. But there was no avoiding it. She managed to plaster a bland, social smile on her face before she turned. "General Scott."

"Your family was worried about you," he said. "They were afraid you might have gotten into trouble."

"I never get into trouble," she said with deceptive calm. "I must say I'm surprised to see you here. In the enemy's camp, so to speak."

"Oh, I don't consider your father the enemy," he said blandly. "Not at all. Merely misguided, and even on that I'm not so sure. I think we both want to make sure Richard gets what's coming to him, though our motives aren't the same. Your father wants to make a fortune on his book. I simply want revenge."

Cassie looked at him, trying to control the little shiver of fear that slid beneath her backbone. The general was dressed in civilian clothes, in a suit that fit his trim, middle-aged body to perfection. He was tanned, fit, with a determined gleam in his blue eyes and a set to his chin, and Cass had no doubt he was a man who wouldn't allow defeat. "What if your revenge is misplaced?" she found herself asking, ignoring what she knew in her heart.

His expression darkened, to one of profound disappointment. "He's managed to fool you as well, has he? He was always good at getting women to believe in him. To do what he wanted. My poor Diana was just one in a long line of vulnerable women. What did he tell you? That she was spoiled, neurotic, faithless?"

"He said she was insane."

The words fell into the noise of the party like crystal drops of acid. Amberson Scott didn't even blink, and yet he seemed to grow, to intensify, like a deadly summer storm. "If she was," he said finally, "then he made her that way."

He reached out a blunt hand and gently

touched her hair. A father's touch, paternal, soothing, and Cassie found herself longing for it, longing for the parent she had always dreamed of and never had. "Don't let him do the same to you, Cassidy," he murmured. "He's destroyed too many little girls. Don't let him destroy you as well."

"Amberson." A pale gray lady appeared by his side, and for the first time Cass recognized General Scott's wife. Diana's mother. A ghost of a creature, with none of her late daughter's fragile beauty or her husband's vivid personality.

"Essie, you haven't met Cassidy Roarke. Our host's daughter. Cassidy, this is my wife, Esther."

Cassie just managed to drag forth a polite smile. It wasn't reciprocated. Essie Scott looked at her out of gray, lifeless eyes, murmured something scarcely intelligible.

And suddenly Cassie needed to escape. From the general's formidable presence, smothering and intractable and yet oddly appealing, and from his wife, with her dead eyes. "I really need to see my father," she murmured. "If you'll excuse me."

"Of course, my dear," the general said. "We'll see you at breakfast."

"Breakfast?" Cassie said, trying to hide the horrified disbelief that washed over her.

"You know your father. He was kind enough to invite us to be houseguests for the weekend. As well as Mark Bellingham. Now all we need is to entice Richard from the apartment in New York, and we'd really be an odd assortment." There was no humor in the general's voice. "He *is* still in New York, isn't he, Cassidy?"

"I assume so. Where else would he be?"

He wasn't a man who could be lied to. "Where, indeed?" he echoed. "You should get some sleep, dear girl. You look like you have a monumental case of jet lag."

She had schooled her reactions enough not to betray anything. "You don't get jet lag from a drive down from Connecticut," she said.

"I thought I heard you say you were visiting friends in upstate New York?"

"I have friends all over."

"I'm sure you do. And I'm sure you know how to protect yourself. You wouldn't let anyone use you. Hurt you. Would you, Cassidy?"

"Sonny," the pale lady, already forgotten, hissed. The general ignored his wife.

"I'm a survivor, General Scott," Cass said. "I know how to take care of myself."

"I'm glad to hear it. Quite often one finds that the person you most want to trust is the one who'll betray you. Remember that, child."

Cassidy, five feet nine in her size ten stocking feet and a ripe one hundred and thirty-five pounds felt far from childlike. But there was something about the general that made her feel fragile, delicate, and very feminine. She wasn't certain she liked the feeling.

"I'll remember," she said coolly, wanting to move away from him.

But he'd caught her hand in his, and he was stroking the back of it. A soothing, paternal stroke, that nevertheless made her want to snatch her hand back, to run. "If you want to talk to me, I'll be here," he said, so quietly his wife couldn't hear.

Cassidy looked at him, startled. There was an oddly seductive air to him, and yet she knew perfectly well that he had no interest in seducing her. Perhaps it was just the natural aphrodisiac of power and charisma. She was drawn to it, even as it roiled her stomach.

"You're very kind, General," she said stiffly.

"Tell me where he is, my dear," he said, his voice urgent.

She didn't pretend to misunderstand. This was a man who'd lost his beloved daughter to a murderer's knife, who believed his grandchildren had been wiped out as well. It was no wonder he was so intent on revenge, no wonder that he'd mounted a very powerful one-man crusade to have Richard Tiernan die at the hands of the State.

If he knew he could salvage something out of this, that his grandchildren were alive and well, would he let go of his vengeance? Would he settle for having his grandchildren back, and drop his need to see Richard crucified?

She opened her mouth, ready to tell him the truth, ready to trust him. And then it was too late, as a human whirlwind dashed between them, flinging herself into Cassie's waiting arms.

"Francesca!" Cassie caught her half sister, staring down at her with mixed shock and pleasure. "When did you get here?"

"A few days ago. I was going to surprise you, but I couldn't wait anymore," she said merrily. Francesca O'Rourke was thirteen years old going on thirty-five, with Sean's irrepressible nature and her mother's, Contessa Alba Finanieri O'Rourke da Rimini, astonishing beauty. "Mabry said Sean was sick, and I wanted to come and see for myself. Besides, Mother's thinking of remarrying, and you know how tedious people are when they think they're in love."

Cassidy could feel the sudden flush that covered her fair skin. Francesca didn't notice, but she was certain the general was far more observant. He was also just as likely to guess why. "Very tedious," she said lightly. "What do you think of Sean?"

"Oh, he seems fine. A little tired, of course, but then, he's getting old."

"He's younger than I am, young lady," the general remarked in an avuncular tone brimming with indulgent humor.

Francesca turned and tucked her arm through the general's, smiling up at him with innocent adoration. "But he doesn't have time for me. He never has, for any of us. Cassie can tell you that much. I think I'll adopt you instead, Uncle Amberson. At least you're interested in me."

Uncle Amberson. The phrase struck Cassie as

extremely odd, but the general was beaming down at her irrepressible younger sister with a fond smile. Essie Scott stood in the background, pale gray, her expression unreadable.

"I take it you're my roommate," Cassie said, for some reason wanting to reach out and yank Francesca's hand away from the general's. "Why don't you come with me and help me get settled? I want to hear about school, about your mother, about everything."

"My mother's a bore, school's a bore, everything's a bore," Francesca announced with an impish grin. "I'll come with you, and you can tell me all about your love life."

Once more the color swept over Cassie's face. Once more the general watched.

If it weren't for the jet lag, the exhaustion, the emotional upheaval, she thought. If it weren't for a number of things, she'd be more in control. Right now all she felt capable of doing was flinging herself down on the bed in her room and crying.

"No love life," she said flatly. "I never meet the right kind of man."

Francesca moved away from the general, graceful, with her endless, coltish legs beneath the white cotton shorts, the halter top exposing her tanned shoulders and still flat chest. "Then I'll tell you about my love life," she said cheerfully. "Ciao," she called over her shoulder to the general.

"Ciao, my child," he murmured, and Cassie could feel his eyes, following them as they left.

"So tell me about Richard Tiernan." Francesca couldn't even wait until she'd closed the door to their room. Fortunately Cass had her back to her half sister, so she had a moment to school her reactions. By the time she'd shut the door and sunk down on the twin bed, she knew she looked bland enough to fool the most discerning eyes.

"What about Richard Tiernan?"

"Is he a monster? That's what the press here say, and that's what Uncle Amberson says. Sean says to wait until his book is published, and Mabry said I should ask you."

"Why do you want to know?"

"He seems to be the center of our mismatched family right now. He was the main reason Mother didn't want to let me come, but when she had to balance sending me into the arms of a child murderer against having time alone with her teenage lover, you can guess what won out."

"Teenage lover?" Cassie echoed.

"Well, actually Carlo's in his mid-twenties, but he's still young enough and pretty enough to be her son. But we're not talking about Mother, we're talking about Richard Tiernan. Did he do it?"

"Francesca," Cass protested wearily.

"Come on, Cassie. You've never lied to me, at least as far as I know. You're the one member of my family I can count on to tell me the truth.

Mabry had a funny look in her eye when she talked about you, and I've been around enough to recognize what that means."

"Francesca, you're only thirteen!"

"Women mature early in Italy," she said with great solemnity, throwing herself down on the bed beside Cassie and stretching out her long, slender legs. "So tell me the truth, Cassidy. Have you fallen in love with a child murderer? Uncle Amberson seems to think so."

"He's not your uncle," Cass snapped. "And no, I haven't fallen in love with a child murderer."

"Let me rephrase that. Have you fallen in love with Richard Tiernan?"

She was too tired, too emotionally overwrought for this, Cass thought, looking down at her little sister's dark, vibrant eyes. Francesca was right— she'd never lied to her, a bastion of truth in a family full of secrets. She couldn't start now.

"If I have," she said carefully, "it would be a very great mistake."

Francesca digested this, nodding sagely. "Isn't that the way it usually is? As far as I can tell, falling in love seems to be a major mistake. Look at the messes my mother is always getting herself into. Did you know Uncle Amberson is afraid Richard is going to kill you?"

Cass bit her lip. "The general is very bitter."

"Who can blame him? He's lost his daughter and his grandchildren—it's no wonder he wants a blood vengeance. We Italians can understand such things."

"You're half-American," Cass pointed out wryly.

"Not if you ask Sean. According to him, I'm half-Irish, half-Italian, a very dangerous combination."

"I tremble at the thought of you reaching puberty," Cass said.

"Not for another couple of years, thank God," Francesca said cheerfully. "The da Riminis are late bloomers. So what are you going to do about this Richard Tiernan?"

"Nothing."

"Do you think he did it?"

Cass could see the dark, haunted eyes, the elegant fingers clutching the glass of whiskey. She could still hear his low, husky voice, telling her what she hadn't wanted to hear.

"I don't know," she said. And realized that despite everything, it was the truth.

Francesca nodded. "It's all very sad," she said. "I'm doing my best to make Uncle Amberson feel better. He laughs when he's with me. He says he feels like he has a daughter again."

Cassidy looked at her sister, at the adolescent, boyish frame and the wisdom and caring of an ancient. That clawing sense of anxiety was building once more, smothering her, and she couldn't pinpoint its cause. It probably had no cause, other than the massive upheaval her life had undergone.

"Sean is ill, you know," she said carefully, changing the subject.

"I know. That's one reason why I insisted on coming. If it weren't for that, I might have wanted to stay in Milan just to interfere with Mother and Carlo. She has a difficult time fawning on young men if I'm around watching."

"You're a monster, Francesca."

"So Mother informs me. Is he going to die, Cass?" The question was abrupt, allowing for no answer but the truth.

"I think so," Cass said gently.

"Soon?"

"Probably."

There was silence in the room, and when Francesca looked up again her dark eyes glittered with tears. "But he looks so well."

"I know he does, darling. We can be grateful for that. And maybe the doctors are wrong. Lord knows, they make mistakes all the time. But Mabry doesn't think so."

"Uncle Amberson says that Richard Tiernan is driving Daddy into an early grave. That Sean's death will be another murder caused by him."

"No!" Cass said sharply. "If anything, Richard is keeping him alive. Giving him a will to live. He's obsessed with the book, Francesca. If he didn't have that, I'm not sure what kind of shape he'd be in. You know Sean—his work and his fame always come first."

"With his children trailing a respectful ten

paces behind," Francesca added, with the wisdom of her youth. "That doesn't mean we don't love him, does it?"

"It doesn't mean we don't love him," Cass agreed. "And it doesn't mean he doesn't love us, to the best of his ability."

Francesca sighed. "I wish I could have had a father like Uncle Amberson. Someone who looks out for you, puts your welfare first, is willing to hound someone to the ends of the earth to avenge you."

"First of all, I don't think you'd want to be in a position where you needed to be avenged," Cass said dryly, trying to inject a note of common sense into the conversation.

"Oh, I don't know. I am thirteen, after all, and full of romantic daydreams. Not to mention the fact that I'm half-Italian, half-Irish."

"Half-American," Cass corrected.

"I mean, I don't want to be murdered or molested or anything. But I rather fancy the idea of being greatly wronged," she said cheerfully.

"I think you might find the general's kind of love rather smothering. You've always been remarkably self-sufficient."

"So have we all," Francesca said. "I only hope when I grow up that I take after you and not my mother."

"I make the same stupid mistakes your mother makes."

"Not really. My mother chooses men to assuage

her vanity, to make her feel younger, prettier. She'd never put herself at risk, even for me."

Cassie managed a smile. "Whereas I try to avoid choosing men in the first place."

"You don't make the right choices. The safe choices." She grinned. "I can't wait to meet Richard Tiernan."

The sudden pounding on the door was shocking, disruptive. Francesca moved swiftly, but the door was flung open before she could reach it, and Mabry stood there, white-faced, tears streaming down her face.

"Your father's collapsed," she said. "They're calling an ambulance. But I think . . . I think it might be too late."

Richard leaned back in his seat, closing his eyes as the jet hurtled itself through the skies. He'd done an excellent job of shutting everything off. He'd held the children, played with them, not for one moment letting them see that his heart was breaking.

They'd asked about Cassie, and he'd lied, damning himself and her. She'd already touched them, she would have saved them, and instead she'd run. She'd failed the final test.

He couldn't, shouldn't blame her, but he did. There was no room in his life for compassion, for mercy. He would sacrifice anyone for his children, but in the end Cassidy had made her choice.

He wondered idly what he'd face when he

returned to the States. Had she alerted the police? Would he be met with an armed escort?

Somehow he didn't think so. Any more than he thought she would have told Sean what she thought was the truth. She would have run to him, of course. But in the end he owned her, more than Sean did. She might be able to fight it, enough to run, enough to protect herself. But not enough to betray him.

It was a close thing. He had kept himself wrapped in darkness, safe, invulnerable, for so very long. She'd begun to seep through the cracks, getting to him in ways he couldn't afford to let happen.

She *had* gotten to him. But he was busy fighting it, concentrating on what needed to be done. By the time he saw her again, if he saw her again, he'd be invulnerable once more.

Damn her. And damn him. Damn them all, the great, sorry, stupid bunch of them, with their twisted lives and their obsessions. Somehow, out of all of this mess, he needed to salvage a safe haven for his children.

That was what he needed to concentrate on, that was what he needed to remember. The hell with Cassidy Roarke and her wary eyes and soft mouth.

He'd find a woman he could trust with his children, one he didn't want to fuck. Someone he could pay enough, trust enough, to keep his children safe. And then he'd finish it all, quickly, neatly.

Maybe he'd take Cassidy Roarke with him.

He didn't know whether he'd gone that far. Sunk that deep into conscienceless madness, that he could contemplate murder and suicide. All his humanity, his faint veneer of civilization had vanished, leaving him with nothing, not even the will to survive.

What mattered was the children. Always had, always would. Cassidy Roarke had been a momentary distraction. He could forget about her, leave her to the likes of Mark Bellingham.

And maybe, just maybe, after they killed him, he'd haunt her dreams. So that whatever bed she shared, there would always be three of them there. And she could never lie beneath any man without thinking of him.

It would be enough.

CHAPTER 17

There's nothing we can do." Mabry's voice was cool, emotionless, colorless. As if she were the one who was dying.

"What do you mean?" Cassie demanded.

"Dr. Ryman says he's stabilized. For now. All they can do is watch him and see what happens. The next twenty-four hours should make the difference. He's not strong enough to undergo any more tests at the moment, but if he continues to gain strength . . ."

"And if he doesn't?"

"Then he'll be dead," Mabry said flatly.

"No!" Francesca shrieked, and Cassie immediately turned and wrapped her arms around her, holding her tightly.

"Hush, darling," she murmured, stroking her midnight tangle of hair. "It won't do any good to weep and wail. We just have to hope for the best."

Francesca suddenly looked very young, indeed, less than her thirteen years. Tears were streaming down her pale face, and she shook her head. "I didn't know. He wasn't supposed to be that sick. He told me he'd just had a cold."

"Sean's a liar," Cassie said flatly. "He didn't want us to worry about him."

"Oh, Cassie, he can't die," Francesca wailed. "Don't let him."

It struck her with the force of a blow. She had always been the strong one among her motley assortment of half siblings, trying to protect them from the vicissitudes of life. If it were up to her she'd change the world, but this, like so many other things, was beyond her.

"It's not in my hands, love," she said gently.

"Do you want to see him?" Mabry asked. "They'll let us in for ten minutes, every hour. Francesca can take the first visit if she wants."

"No!" Francesca sobbed. "If he's going to die on me, I'll never forgive him."

"Dear girl." General Scott moved up behind her, his voice gentle and soothing. Cassie hadn't even realized he'd come to the hospital with them. "Let me take you back home. This is too much for a sensitive child."

Francesca pulled herself out of Cassie's arms and flung herself at the general, sobbing her heart out, all the while the general stroked her, whispering soothing, avuncular phrases.

"That's the best thing for her," Mabry agreed wearily. "Take her back to East Hampton. We'll probably be here all night, and it would remove a great deal of worry from me to know she was well looked after."

"I'll treat her as if she were my own daughter," Scott said solemnly.

Cassie didn't move, didn't say a word. A sudden feeling of dizziness and dread washed over her, and she swayed, disoriented, confused. Too little sleep, too much emotion, monumental jet lag had thrown her instincts into an uproar. She looked at her little sister, wrapped in the general's strong, paternal arms, and tried to shake herself.

The general turned to glance at her. "Trust me, Cassie," he murmured. "I'll take good care of your little girl. Tell Richard if you see him."

"Why should Richard care?" she summoned up the energy to ask.

The general's smile was bland, but the expression in his eyes was suddenly, shockingly intense. "Richard, in his own way, is as protective of children as I am."

Cass could feel the color flood her face, deep, revealing, and there was nothing she could do but stare at him, hoping he wouldn't read the knowledge in her eyes.

He moved closer, and he smelled like peppermints and wool and safety. "Where are they, Cassie?"

He was far too observant, and guilt and denial swamped her. "I don't know what you're talking about."

"Where are they?"

He knows. Cassie stood in the middle of the hospital hallway, watching as the general led her little sister away, and tried to digest that information. He suspected his grandchildren were still alive, and it had been her own stupid reaction that had convinced him.

Maybe he'd always guessed. If so, why hadn't he done something about it? What bizarre, complex game were the two men playing, fighting over Diana's children? What did those two innocents have that both father and grandfather were willing to go to such lengths?

"You can see him first, if you want," Mabry offered.

Cassie roused herself to look at her stepmother. "You don't want to see him?"

"Not yet. I saw him for a moment, and he . . ." she shuddered. "He has all sorts of tubes and wires sticking out of him. He looks like he's already dead. He wouldn't know whether I was there or not."

"What do you want to do then?"

"Go back to the apartment. Essie and Amberson will look after Francesca. For now I just want to go home and hide."

Back to the apartment. She didn't say the words out loud, didn't warn Mabry that the apartment would be empty. Richard Tiernan was gone.

Mabry probably wouldn't even notice. "We'll go home," Cass said, tucking a comforting arm beneath Mabry's. "We'll come back first thing in the morning and see how Sean is doing. He's not going to give up without a fight, you know. He's not going to die without one hell of an exit line."

Mabry managed a rusty-sounding laugh. "You're right. Sean never could resist a scene. He'll rally. By tomorrow he'll probably be sitting up, signing autographs and working on a new book deal."

"He needs to complete the current one first, doesn't he?"

Mabry looked at her curiously. "Didn't you know? He finished it more than a week ago, just before we left for East Hampton. It's ready to go to his editor."

"No," Cassie said slowly. "He didn't tell me."

"I think he was afraid to let you see it. Knowing how conflicted you are about Richard."

"Conflicted?" she echoed. "Hardly. My feelings for Richard Tiernan are completely straightforward."

"And what are they?" Mabry asked curiously.

"None of your damned business," she said lightly. "Let's find us a taxi."

"Don't you want to see Sean before you go?"

"Not likely. If I see him, I'll kill him. It would save a lot in medical costs, but then we'd have to deal with legal fees. I think it's better to let him be."

"Why are you so mad at him, Cass? You've always known the way he is, manipulating people to do what he wants. You must have known he'd have a hidden agenda for you and Richard," Mabry said.

"I've known," Cass said flatly. "I just don't like it when I get incontrovertible proof."

"He's always loved you very much, you know."

Cass looked at her. "Not the way I define a father's love," she said.

"Perhaps your definition is a bit too strict."

Cassie just shook her head. "He wouldn't dare die before I get a chance to tell him off," she said. "Let's go."

It was still in the predawn hours when they arrived back at Seventy-second Street. Cassie slid from the taxi, remembering the last time she'd arrived here, in the same early hours, expecting to confront Richard, only to find the place deserted. At least this time she didn't have to worry about coming face-to-face with her nemesis.

She'd never thought the heart of New York City to be particularly silent, even in the middle of the night, but the old prewar apartment building felt like a tomb, as the walnut-lined elevator carried them upward.

The apartment smelled freshly aired. Bridget must have come in to clean during the last few days, something Cass could only view with relief. She had no idea how she'd left the place when she'd taken off for England, chasing after Richard. She'd never had any secrets from Bridget, and she wouldn't now.

It was easy enough to get Mabry settled into the huge king-size bed she usually shared with Sean, tucked up under a duvet, a glass of straight whiskey, without ice, in her hand. "I could sleep for days," she murmured, leaning back and closing her eyes.

"Lucky you," Cass said. "I think I've gone beyond exhaustion. I only wish there was a simple cure for jet lag."

The silence deepened. Mabry opened her eyes, when Cass had been hoping she'd drifted off to sleep. "Why do you have jet lag, Cass?"

It was a simple inquiry, calmly asked. Cass stared at her, unable to come up with any kind of sensible answer.

And then she didn't have to. Mabry set the glass of whiskey on the nightstand, closed her eyes, and went instantly to sleep.

She didn't dare get up from the end of the bed for a few minutes, afraid that the slightest movement might jar Mabry from her sleep, might bring back the unanswerable questions. By the time she moved, her muscles were stiff and aching, and she tiptoed from the room, so tired she wanted to weep.

She stared down to the end of the long hallway. The door to Richard's room stood open, darkness beyond. Sometime, tomorrow perhaps, she'd steel herself to go down there and check, to see

whether he'd left anything incriminating behind.
Whether she liked it or not, she was now an
accessory to his escape. She wasn't about to tell
anyone where he'd gone, or let him leave anything
that might yield a clue. She wanted him healthy,
safe, and continents away from her.

She needed sleeping tablets, or whiskey, or
warm milk. She had moved beyond exhaustion
into some dark, anxious place, and sleep seemed
no more than a pipe dream. In the end she
decided to go for warm milk, the safest choice,
as always.

Until she walked into the kitchen.

He was sitting at the table. The mug of warm
milk sat in front of him, a bottle of Irish whiskey
stood open beside it. "I think you'd do better if I
spiked this," he said, his voice calm, reasonable,
as if there was nothing more than wary politeness
between them. As if she'd never lay beneath his
body and cried out with the wonder of it.

Without waiting for her answer, he tipped a
goodly portion into the mug, then poured some
into his own glass of ice. For a moment Cass was
gripped with a strangling, powerful rage. She
wanted to scream, to throw herself at him and
shake him, to smash the whiskey and ice and hot
milk across the room.

And he knew it. He watched her, remote,
observing, reading all her emotions far too well.
It took every ounce of strength she had left to pull
herself together, to wrap a false calm around her.

"I don't like whiskey," she said, and she was shocked to hear her voice, smooth, unemotional.

"I know you don't. Drink it anyway." He kicked a chair away from the table for her, and she knew she should walk away.

She moved carefully, taking the chair and sitting down, away from him. The milk sat in front of her, the faint amber of the whiskey leaving a shadow on its creamy surface.

"Is Sean going to make it?"

She lifted her eyes to meet his. "Do you care?"

Richard shrugged. "It depends whether he's finished the book or not."

"He's finished. He was done before he left for the Hamptons."

"Did you know that?"

"No. What does the book matter to you? It doesn't have the truth in it, does it? You didn't tell Sean what happened that night. You didn't tell him your children were still alive."

"You know Sean writes fiction. I gave him enough to weave elaborate tales. I imagine it will be a very powerful book." He leaned back in the kitchen chair, watching her. "However, he's paying my estate a very considerable sum of money for my cooperation."

"What about the Son of Sam law? I thought a criminal couldn't profit from books about his crime?"

Richard's smile was faint and chilling. "Mark Bellingham is a better lawyer than you might think. The money doesn't go to me, it gets put in a blind trust to be administered by Mark, Sally Norton, and a third party to be named by Mark."

"It's for the children."

He said nothing.

"That's what it's all about, isn't it? You've done this all for the children." She reached out for the mug of milk, then pulled her hand back again, not surprised to see it was trembling. "Is that why you killed your wife?"

"Drink your milk, Cassie," he said gently.

She stared down at it once more. She knew too much, far too much for his safety. She'd abandoned him, ruined his plan for his children, and now, instead of staying in England, he'd come back, and in all likelihood he'd come after her. To silence her.

Would he poison her? He was already under sentence of death, and he seemed to have no interest in having that sentence commuted. They could only execute him once. If she were dead, there would be no one to tell about the children. Mark had a professional vow of silence, Sally was risking her health and her very life to take care of them.

She was the only wild card. He'd killed for them before, she no longer had any doubt. Would he kill for them again?

"What's going to happen now?" she asked, delaying.

"It all depends. Sean will live or die. If he lives,

you'll be so caught up in being the perfect daughter, trying to prove your love for him, that you won't have any time to waste worrying about me and mine. Sally's health seems to have stabilized for now, and in the meantime Mark will be on the lookout for someone to take her place. Someone trustworthy. Someone willing to put the lives of my children ahead of anything else."

It shouldn't have hurt. But he was so adept at twisting her around, even his lightly spoken words were like a knife, stabbing at her.

"And if Sean doesn't regain consciousness? If he dies?"

"Then I think you'll be very dangerous, indeed. You'll be torn apart by grief and unfinished business, and you'll probably say the wrong thing to the wrong person. I can't let that happen."

"How are you going to stop me?"

"I'm not certain. Drink your milk, Cassie."

Old movies danced through her head, a poisoned drink taken from the hands of a lover. She could accidentally knock it over. She could flatout refuse—he wouldn't hold her down and force it down her throat.

She reached out for the mug, and he watched her. It had cooled considerably, and she could smell the tang of whiskey. Did she smell something else as well, something lethal?

"What did you put in here?" she asked, stalling for time.

"Milk. Low-fat, I'm afraid, that's all that was here. A shot of whiskey. Almond extract."

"Almond?" Wasn't there a poison that smelled like bitter almonds? Something immediately lethal.

"Almond," he said. "Oh, and of course, there's the rat poison Bridget left behind. I hope it won't taste too terrible. I was hoping the almond and whiskey would cover the taste. Maybe I should have added some sugar as well."

Cassie swallowed nervously. "I'm glad to know you find this all so amusing."

"I find you amusing," he said, darkness in his eyes. "Particularly your definition of love and trust, right before you run away. Drink the fucking milk, Cassie, and see whether you drop dead or not."

"Why don't you have the first sip?"

He shook his head. "Not on your life. Suicide was never my thing."

She looked at him. At his dark, defiant eyes, the bitter cruelty of his mouth. His elegant hands, the bleakness of his soul. She took the mug of milk and drank.

She almost drained it. She set the mug down again, and met his eyes defiantly. "How long does it take to work?"

"I don't know. You're my first poisoning. I usually stab my victims."

"You're enjoying this, aren't you?" She sat there, waiting for the first cramp to hit. "Do you always

punish people who are crazy enough to fall in love
with you?"

"Falling in love with me isn't your crime, dear
heart," he said lightly. "You can't convince me you
even committed it in the first place. Love isn't
great sex, and jumping to conclusions, and
believing the worst, and running away when
things get nasty."

He leaned closer, close enough to kiss her, and
she could taste the whiskey on his breath, the fury
in his soul. "Your crime was making me love you.
Trust you. Believe, for a few, crazy hours, that
there was something to fight for, after all." His
lips brushed hers, heartbreakingly gentle. "Your
crime was giving me hope, and then taking it
away again."

She didn't move from the table. He was long
gone—she heard the door close behind him, but
she sat there, unmoving, as the first gray light of
dawn filtered into the kitchen. The doctored milk
sat in her stomach, curdled there, and she wanted
to get up and vomit in the sink. She wouldn't let
herself do it.

She put her head down on the table, her hand
clutching the empty mug of milk. Astonishingly
enough, she slept.

Richard leaned against the door, his eyes closed
in the darkness as he fought it. Fought his rage,
his fury. Fought the murderous frenzy that he

thought he'd finally quelled. Could he kill someone? Someone he thought he'd loved?

Hadn't he already done just that? His moral responsibility to his children put him on the wrong side of the law, but he wasn't going to worry about it. He didn't make excuses, or try to hide from what he knew was the truth. He had made an irretrievable decision, and Diana was dead. Excuses and justifications wouldn't change that.

If only he could scour his soul of the anger, the rage, the stupid, lingering hope that Cassidy Roarke brought out in him. He thought when he saw her again, he'd feel nothing but rage. He was wrong.

She looked at him and the mug of milk he offered, and she thought him capable of murdering her. For that very belief moment, he wanted to kill her.

But he saw the pain and the panic in her silvery green eyes. He felt the longing and despair in her soul. She was a coward and a fool, she'd run from him when he needed her to trust him. And yet he'd known that despite everything, despite believing the worst of him, she still loved him.

It made life so much more complicated. It kept him tied to her. He couldn't hate her. He couldn't turn off his feelings, as he'd learned to do years ago. He was enmeshed in her, wrapped tight, and there was only one way to slash free.

He waited until first light. When he walked

back into the kitchen, he'd thought it was deserted, until he saw her at the table, sound asleep.

Another mistake on his part. He remembered her lying curled in his arms, her pale skin with the faint dusting of golden freckles, the utter stillness of her. Vulnerable, sexual, and he wanted her with a sudden fierceness that threatened to wipe out everything.

It took him a moment for sanity to rear its ugly head. By the time he put his hands on her he was calm. She didn't wake when he lifted her up in his arms, her solid weight settling against him. Or if she did, she didn't want to admit it. He carried her through the apartment, into the Gothic monstrosity of her bedroom, and lay her down on the neatly made bed. She reached for him, murmuring something unintelligible, but he carefully released her hands from behind his neck and set them beside her, pulling a cover up around her. She pouted for a moment, then with a sigh she curled up, one hand tucked beneath her face, flame red hair spread out around her.

Her body trusted him, even when her mind couldn't. He should take that as some kind of comfort, but he wasn't in the business of looking for comfort. Or for justice. Lies were his only protection now.

He stared down at her, imprinting her on his mind. For a moment he allowed himself to reach out, to push a tangled strand of hair away from her face, to caress her with a feather-light touch. He wouldn't put his hands on her again, he knew it.

And then he left, closing the door behind him.

"Get up. Cassie." She heard his voice through a fog, calling to her. She struggled to open her eyes, as she'd fought to do for the last few hours, but the mists of sleep and exhaustion were powerful foes.

"Get up," he said again, impatient. "Mabry needs you."

She stirred. She couldn't remember where she was, what house, what state, what country even. Richard's voice, cool and impatient, the bed beneath her, soft and smothering. Had he drugged her after all? Or had life finally caught up with her? She didn't want to open her eyes—Mabry could cope by herself.

"Your father is dying, Cass. Wake up."

She opened her eyes. It was late afternoon, raining, and she was lying in her bed at the Park Avenue apartment. She hadn't the faintest idea how she got there. For the moment she didn't care.

"What did you say?" Her voice was raspy with sleep and denial.

"Mabry's going to the hospital. Sean's in a coma, and they don't think he's going to pull through. Do you want to go with her?"

She didn't bother to answer him. She simply scrambled out of bed, kicking the covers away.

The floor swayed beneath her, and she felt herself falling. His hands were there, elegant, deadly, impersonal, catching her, holding her until she regained her equilibrium. A small, treacherous part of her wanted to sink against him, to close her eyes and take warmth and comfort and strength from him. He held her at a distance.

"Too much rat poison, Cassie?" he murmured.

She looked up at him. "Not enough," she said, and pulled away.

It was rush hour by the time they made it down to the lobby, but Bill had a taxi waiting, the meter running. Mabry looked pale and still and cold, and it took Cassie a moment to realize that Richard wasn't just seeing them into the waiting car, he was coming with them.

The backseat of the taxi was small. Richard's long legs pressed up against hers, his thigh measured against her own, and she felt the heat and strength of him.

It was just as well he was with them. For once, Cassie's calm, maternal instincts failed her. She simply let Richard lead the way through the maze of bureaucracy that was Sloan-Kettering. She trailed along behind him, her arm around Mabry's suddenly frail figure.

It took her a moment to realize the looks they were getting, once they reached Sean's floor. People weren't staring at her and Mabry. They were looking at Richard Tiernan, the murderer, and there was fascination and horror in their faces.

Mabry went first. Richard and Cass sat across from each other in the small, private waiting room. She wouldn't look at him, afraid of what she might see. Her nerves were on the raw, screaming edge, and if she looked at him, saw the cool, murderous contempt in his eyes, she would shatter.

When Mabry joined them, her face was pale, tears streaming down her face. Cassie reached for her, but then Bridget was there, appearing out of nowhere, folding Mabry against her ample bosom, murmuring soft, soothing words as she drew her away. "You go on in, Cass," she called over her shoulder. "I'll see to your stepmother."

She couldn't help it. She allowed herself a brief, worried glance up at Richard.

His face was entirely impassive. "Do you want me to go?"

She hadn't expected it. "Do you want to see him?"

"Not particularly."

"Then why are you waiting?"

"For you."

It was that simple, that complicated. More than she could cope with. She simply nodded, then followed the nurse down the long, silent hallway.

"Ten minutes," the woman whispered, ushering her inside. "He probably won't know you, but you never can tell."

The door shut silently behind her, closing her in. The noise was constant, jarring, machines beeping, ticking, wheezing, breathing for Sean, pumping blood through his veins, living for him.

She walked over to the bed, steady, calm. "You always have to make a production out of everything, don't you?" she said in a quiet voice. "Did you have to be so goddamn dramatic? Collapsing at your own party?"

His eyes were closed, sunken in his paper-white face. He looked bruised, skeletal, already drained of the vibrant life that had washed through him. Cassie reached out and touched his hand, the one without the IV. "You aren't finished yet. I don't know why you think you can just give up, when there are so many things left undone. So you finished the book. So what? What if I told you it was all a bunch of lies? Would you care?

"Probably not. You were always more interested in a good story than the truth. It'll make a fortune. That's why you did it, isn't it? To make sure Mabry is taken care of."

There was a faint tremor behind one eyelid, but the monitoring machines kept their steady, relentless drone. "Of course, you wanted a masterpiece as well. I wouldn't make the mistake of thinking you were capable of a selfless act," she said wryly. "You'd be insulted if I did. You want to go out on a blaze of glory, don't you? You want another Pulitzer, even if it's posthumously. Or better yet, how about a Nobel? I could pick it up for you, make a touching speech about you and Richard. He'll be dead as well, you know. Do you believe in hell? If you do, you'll be there together."

She almost thought she saw a faint reaction on Sean's face. She clutched his hand, leaning closer, angrier than she'd ever been in her life. She didn't know why she was crying—probably just a leftover symptom of jet lag. "Don't you dare die," she said furiously. "You haven't told me you love me. Damn it, you haven't let me tell you I love you."

He didn't move. "Listen, you son of a bitch," she hissed, "I'm not going to let you die without some goddamn sign."

His eyes opened. Only for a brief moment, resting on hers. His nose and mouth were covered with a respirator, he couldn't say a word. But she could see the gentle, bemused expression in his eyes. Feel the faintest pressure on her hand. And then his eyes closed once more, and his hand went slack beneath hers.

She let him go. Backhanding the tears from her face, she walked from the room, back straight, shoulders squared, hoping to God she wouldn't see anyone, hoping that Richard had abandoned her.

He was alone, standing in the middle of the waiting room, watching her. She stopped in the doorway, disoriented. "The bastard," she whispered beneath her breath. "He's dead."

He watched her for no more than a heartbeat. And then he was across the room, pulling her into his arms, pressing her face against his shoulder, holding her so tightly her bones ached. It was no wonder she sobbed, she thought absently. She was only clutching him so tightly because she wanted him to release her. Only weeping against him because . . . because . . .

It no longer mattered. She needed whatever comfort she could find. And the dangerous comfort of Richard Tiernan was the only thing she wanted.

CHAPTER 18

He took her back to the apartment. She didn't say another word, and neither did he. He didn't know when she'd eaten last, he didn't know when he had, either. What they both needed was a decent meal, some time alone, some sleep.

He locked the door behind them and kissed her, sliding his arms around her waist, pulling her tight against him. She didn't fight. She went to him, openly, willingly, trustingly, and he didn't even want to consider the ramifications of that willingness, that trust.

He wanted to make love to her, slowly, tenderly, kissing every hollow and pulse. He didn't stop to consider that doing just that was the most dangerous thing in the world for him. He was past that point. All he could think of was Cassie, her need, her pain, her sorrow. He wanted to soothe her, heal her. Even if it meant destroying himself in the process.

He didn't pick her up, though he wanted to. He wanted to give her every chance to escape. He took her hand in his and drew her down the hallway, past the kitchen, the row of bedrooms, down to his own. He didn't want to make love to her in her Victorian funeral parlor of a room. He wanted her in sunlight and warmth. Failing that, he wanted her in his bed, where he'd slept alone, thinking of her.

She closed the door behind them. The apartment was dark, only the streetlights illuminating the room. A light rain was falling, but he paid no attention. She leaned back against the door and looked at him, quiet, vulnerable, waiting.

He reached out and began to unfasten the row of tiny buttons that traveled down the front of her denim shirt. She'd dressed quickly before they left for the hospital, and she hadn't bothered with a bra. There was a God, after all.

He pulled the tails of the shirt out of her jeans and let them hang, as he began to undo her zipper. She didn't stop him. Her eyes were wide, shocky, her mouth pale and resigned. Suddenly he couldn't help it. He sank to his knees in front of her, wrapping his arms around her waist, pressing his face against her belly.

She never hesitated. She put her arms around his head, holding him close, and he could feel the despair and love pulse through her body.

He was adept at undressing women—he had done more than his share, and he'd mastered the art of denim when he was still in his teens. For some reason his hands shook when he wanted to be so deft, and her jeans, loose on her hips, suddenly decided to cling, so that he had to tug, leaving her in no blissful doubt as to what he was doing.

She didn't stop him, didn't help him. She simply leaned back against the door and let him strip her clothes off her.

Her body was flushed pink, trembling, when he finally managed to get her naked. He stripped off his own clothes, quickly, and then he did pick her up, carefully, and set her down on the unmade bed. She looked up at him, and there was no doubt, no fight, in her beautiful green eyes. Only quiet acceptance.

He kissed her then. He tasted her mouth, slowly, carefully, drawing her response with all the expertise at his command. He kissed her eyelids as they fluttered closed beneath his mouth, he kissed the side of her neck.

He slid his hand between her legs, and she was damp, weeping for him. She arched back again, and he covered her mouth with his, silencing her, as he slid his long fingers deep inside her, using his thumb, driving her toward an oblivion she desperately needed.

He didn't give her a chance to fight him. She came almost immediately, convulsing in his arms with a wild cry, burying her face against his shoulder as her body shimmered with fierce response.

He wanted to be noble enough to leave it at that. To soothe her down, to calm and love her, and then to walk away. But he couldn't do it. He needed her, needed her far more than life itself, and when he eased her onto her back she went willingly, pulling him with her, legs spread to cradle him, to take him deep inside, to drain and renew him, to make him alive again, when he'd wanted so much to die.

There was such sweetness in it, when he hadn't known it existed. They were together in the darkness, a slow, tender joining that was unlike anything he'd ever experienced before. It was love, not sex, and that knowledge shattered him more than his powerful climax.

She must have heard the voices first. Her body was soft, warm, pliant, covered with a sheen of sweat, and then suddenly it was stiff with anxiety. For a moment he thought it was the inevitable second thoughts, until he heard the voices. Coming closer.

He didn't recognize them. A man and a woman, though the man was low-voiced and scarcely able to get a word in edgewise as the woman declaimed in the loud voice of someone just faintly drunk.

"We'll take Colin's bedroom," her voice announced. "I'm sure Mabry won't object, and I wouldn't be caught dead in that Victorian mausoleum. I don't know what got into Mabry to choose such a ghastly decorating scheme. Her interior designer must have been crazy."

"Don't be ridiculous," the voice continued, after

a mumbled protest. "Colin's in Africa, and God only knows when someone will get word to him that his father has gone to his just reward. In the meantime I know that Mabry wouldn't think of having us go to a hotel. It's a good thing I have a key. Besides, Cassie will want her mother around for comfort in her time of mourning."

Richard raised his head, looking down at Cassie's stricken face. "Your mother?" he inquired in a whisper that he couldn't keep free of amusement.

She was beyond noticing, lying beneath him, his body still tight within hers. "My mother," she said in a strangled whisper.

"Did you lock the door?"

"No."

"Neither did I. And I don't think I have time to get up and do so now." He reached down and flicked the sheet over them, still keeping her pinned to the mattress, her face rosy from love and embarrassment.

The blasted woman was still talking when she opened the door. There was a dead silence, but Richard wasn't interested in taking a glance at his unwanted visitors. He was far more concerned with the mute, stricken expression on Cassie's face.

The silence, unfortunately, didn't last long. "Good God!" the woman shrieked. "Cassidy Roarke, what the hell do you think you're doing?"

He rolled off her then, though he didn't want to, keeping the sheet around her. He looked up at the harridan standing there, in her designer suit and real pearls, her flushed face and glittering eyes, and the pale man behind her.

"What do you think she's doing?" he inquired mildly enough, putting his arms around Cassie's head, letting her turn her face into his shoulder.

"I hardly think *that* is an appropriate activity at a time like this. Her father has just died." She managed a convincing sniffle. "And just who the hell are you?" the woman demanded, taking a slightly staggering step into the bedroom.

Faced with a mother like her and a father like Sean, it was no wonder Cassie had developed a habit of running away when things got rough. It was even more surprising she'd held still long enough for him to penetrate her defenses.

He rolled onto his back, staring up at her with a deliberate smirk. "The man who just made love to your daughter," he said blandly.

Cass made a soft little sound of distress, and then was quiet. He suspected that if she could, she would have dived beneath the covers.

"And who may that be?" she demanded.

To his amazement Cassie stirred, emerging from her haven. "Go away, Alice," she said. "This is hardly the time for introductions, and if you think Mabry wants you here, you're crazy. There are any number of decent hotels in the area. *Go away.*"

Alice turned with majestic rage, only slightly marred by the wobble in her gait, and stalked toward the door. She paused, leveling an accusing gaze at her daughter. "I must say I would have thought better of you, Cassie. I thought you cared about your father. Obviously I'm the only one who ever really loved and understood him. It was no wonder our relationship was doomed. We were too young, too much alike."

"You were twenty-three when you got married, Alice, and he'd already been through one wife. You were old enough to know better," she said wearily.

"I must say," Alice was weaving faintly, as the man behind her tugged on her arm, "that I am sorely disappointed in you." She slapped at the restraining hand. "Leave me alone, Robert. Can't you see I'm having a discussion with my daughter?"

"Not the time or place, Alice," the man muttered, obviously much embarrassed.

"Yes, Alice," Richard said in a deceptively mild voice. "Go away, or I'll climb out of this bed and throw you out the window."

"Don't be ridiculous. You wouldn't dare lay a finger on me." Alice yanked her arm free, stormed back into the room and sat her ample butt down on the chair.

"Er, Alice," the man referred to as Robert said nervously. "I wouldn't count on that."

"Why not?"

"Because the man your daughter's in bed with is Richard Tiernan. You know, with the murder trial and all? I doubt he'd think twice about getting rid of an interfering old woman." There was just a trace of satisfied malice in the man's voice, as Alice surged to her feet in horror.

She sputtered, but nothing intelligible came out. By the time she began making sense, Robert had led her all the way down the hall, and her shrieks of outrage echoed through the apartment until the front door slammed.

Richard looked down at Cassie, wondering what he'd see. Her eyes were closed, her face pale, with two bright spots of color on her cheeks.

"You've got a helluva mother," he observed calmly enough.

Her eyes shot open. "Tell me about it," she said in a strangled voice. "Between her and Sean, it's a wonder I survived."

He wasn't sure what he expected. That she'd dissolve in tears once more. That she'd run screaming from his bed. Instead she simply lay there, looking up at him, steadily, expectantly.

He cupped her face. "Are you all right?" It was the best he could offer. He couldn't say the words—there was too much at stake, and they were both too vulnerable.

She smiled, a sweet, sad smile, and her hands covered his. He kissed her then, before she could answer, and she kissed him back. "Go to sleep," he whispered against her mouth.

He half expected her to argue. But she seemed worn out by emotion. She closed her eyes obedi-

ently, and in moments she was sound asleep, his
body still covering hers, his hands still caught in
hers.

Cassie could hear the shower running. She
didn't move, didn't want to. The bed was warm,
soft, comforting, and as long as she didn't leave
it, reality wouldn't intrude.

She'd made up her mind. Sometime, she wasn't
sure when, the last doubt had fallen. Maybe it
was when he'd held out his arms to her in the
hospital waiting room. Maybe it was when he'd
threatened to throw her mother out the window.
Maybe she'd always known it, and just been trying
to deny it.

It no longer mattered what he had done. She'd
lost the ability to judge between right and wrong.
All that mattered was that she loved him, needed
to be with him. If there was something evil and
sinful about that, so be it. She was willing to pay
the price.

She knew she would be paying, for the rest of
her life. She didn't care. She would take what
little time fate had to offer them. She wouldn't
fight it, or him, anymore.

She must have dozed off for a while. When she
awoke, he was sitting on the bed, wearing jeans
and a black T-shirt, his face remote, wary.

"Do you think your mother will be back?"

She considered it, sliding back against the pillows. "Not likely. She's a devout coward, and if I

know Robert, he'll encourage her to think you'll kill her. Heaven only knows, she brings out murderous impulses in the gentlest of people."

"And I hardly qualify as that, do I?"

Testing again. She wasn't going to let him do it to her anymore. "Has there been any word from Mabry?" She changed the subject.

"I talked with her about fifteen minutes ago, while you were sleeping. She's busy with paperwork, and then she'll be back. She wanted to know how you were doing."

"I shouldn't have left her," Cassie said guiltily. "I should have gone to find her . . ."

"You weren't in any shape. For God's sake, can't you think of yourself for once, instead of everyone else? Mabry's a grown woman, she can take care of herself."

"I should have been there . . ." she said stubbornly.

"No. You should have been with me."

There was no way she could argue with him, when it was simply the truth. "Sean would have hated dying like that," she said. "Drifting away in a hospital bed. He would have wanted to go out in a blaze of glory."

"Do not go gentle into that good night?" Richard said softly.

"Exactly."

"We don't always get what we want, and life isn't particularly fair."

She managed the faintest of smiles. "There's a

news flash." She sat up. "I should get back to the hospital and bring Mabry home. She needs some rest. If the damned paperwork can't wait, I'll take care of it."

"Do you want me to come with you?"

She thought of the wary, frightened looks the hospital personnel had given him. She thought of her need to burrow deep and hide in her sorrow. To isolate, to get through tough things alone. "Yes," she said.

She was unprepared for his reaction. He'd been guarding himself, shielding himself, waiting for her rejection. For her to run. "Yes?" he echoed.

"I need you."

They were words that she'd heard, but never spoken to another living being. She spoke them to Richard.

The effect was astonishing. For the first time she saw real vulnerability on his dark, shuttered face. And then he put his arms around her, holding her tight against him, not saying a word. She could feel the tension, the tightly leashed power in his muscles, she could feel a thousand things rushing through him, things without a name. And then, before she could say another word, he released her, left the bed, and moved toward the door. "Take your time," he muttered, not turning back. "I'll have some food waiting."

The shower went part way toward making her feel human, and she had little doubt food would take her the rest of the way. The kitchen was deserted when she walked in, but the table was set with steaming soup, a cold can of diet Coke, and croissants. She had no appetite, but the man definitely had his good points.

"Hullo, darling," Mabry said from the doorway as Cass sat down to wait for him.

"Oh, Mabry," she said brokenly, rising.

"No tears, darling. Sean would hate it," Mabry said, shaking her flaxen hair. She suddenly looked decades older, but her eyes were clear and dry. "We can make a suitable fuss at the wake, of course, but for now he'd prefer something a little more elegant."

"I'm afraid I've given up on pleasing him," Cass said. "I never could be the daughter he wanted."

"You were exactly the daughter he wanted," Mabry said fiercely, giving her a shake. "And he knew it, even if he never told you so." She moved away from the doorway to lean with her hands on the windowsill, looking out into the dark afternoon.

"Have you talked with Francesca yet? How's she doing? And has anyone been able to get in touch with Colin?"

"Lord knows where your half brother is. I've set your mother and stepfather to tracking him down. It'll keep her occupied." She sighed, pushing her pale blond hair away from her face. "Francesca knows, but she doesn't seem to want to deal with it. Amberson suggested he take her up to their summer place in Vermont, and I said that was probably wise."

Again that odd feeling of uneasiness. "Are you certain that's a good idea? Shouldn't the family be together . . . ?"

"I trust the general. He's raised one daughter, poor man, and I think he sees Francesca as a substitute. He'll take good care of her, and we won't have to worry about how she's handling things."

"I'd like to talk to her."

"Honestly, Cass, I don't know what you're fussing about. I don't know their phone number—he gave it to me but I was too addled to write it down. We'll just have to wait until he calls in."

Cassie picked up a croissant, slowly, deliberately, trying to stuff her unreasoning feeling of panic. "She's only thirteen, Mabry. She may act like she's older, but she's really just a child."

"All the better that she be with the general and his wife. I've never had children, and neither have you. You don't want her around Richard, do you?"

The question was shocking, point-blank, and Cassie's response was instinctive. And unexpected. "I'd trust him with Francesca."

Mabry managed a crooked smile. "Love has made you blind, Cass. I never thought to see the day. Or is it lust?"

"Mabry . . ."

"Forgive me," she said, contrite. "Alice was kind enough to tell me where she found you when she barged in here. I'm a bit over the edge, but I shouldn't have said that. Obviously you've decided that Richard never killed anyone. I'm glad."

"I didn't say that. I can only go by my instincts. And my instincts tell me that he wouldn't hurt an innocent child."

"But do you have any right to endanger another human being on the sole basis of your instincts?" Mabry asked.

"You know I can't make that decision."

"Then let's leave it alone," Mabry said wearily. "Leave Francesca where she is."

"Leave who where she is?" Richard appeared in the kitchen doorway, and Cassie felt the familiar, treacherous warmth filling her, despite his distant expression, his failure to come close to her.

"Cass's sister," Mabry said briskly, getting up and moving past him. She paused, looking at him, and there was both dignity and warning in her cool gaze. "You got what you wanted, Richard. She loves you. She's obsessed by you, willing to believe and do everything you want her to. Sean would be proud of you."

"What are you talking about?" Cass demanded.

"I would have thought you'd caught on by now. You were Sean's virgin sacrifice. Richard saw your picture on Sean's desk and said you were part of the deal. He'd cooperate with the book, give Sean everything he wanted, but in return Sean had to deliver up his daughter."

"Don't be ridiculous," Cass snapped. "Sean couldn't have done any such thing. I wasn't his to deliver."

"You're here, aren't you? You were in Richard's bed. Sean said he'd get you up here, and the rest was up to Richard. As far as Sean was concerned, you needed a little change, a little excitement in your life. Don't be naive, Cass. You knew something was going on."

Cass had gone numb, a small blessing. "Like fucking a murderer? That was supposed to broaden my horizons?"

Mabry shrugged. "You know Sean. But you don't have to go along with it anymore. The book is finished, and it's a masterpiece. Sean is dead, and he doesn't need you or anyone to dance to his tune any longer." She moved past Richard, cool and graceful. "I thought it was about time you knew the whole truth." And then she was gone, leaving them alone in the kitchen.

Cassie stared down at her meal. Her soup was cold, her diet Coke was warm, the croissant ripped into a thousand tiny pieces. "The truth," she said in a quiet voice. "Just how much more truth is there?" She raised her head to meet his oblique gaze. "You didn't kill your children or Sally Norton. You did murder your wife. You seduced me for the sole purpose of taking over the care of your children. You said you fell in love with me. You made a bargain with my father. I'm surprised you didn't make a bet as well. How long would it take to get beneath my skirts. How long it would take before I'd go down on you. How long . . ."

"Cassie." His voice was cool, emotionless, as hers was overwrought.

"I should be used to it," Cass continued in a musing voice. "I shouldn't feel so damned sorry for myself. My father has never been anything other than what he's appeared to be. And you certainly never tried to convince me you were a white knight, falsely accused of monstrous crimes. If anything, you've encouraged me to believe the worst of you. Why, Richard? Why won't you defend yourself? Why won't you tell me I'm wrong, that I wasn't just the means to an end, a mother for your children and an easy lay? That my father wasn't ready to barter my heart, my body, and even my life for the sake of his own ego and some goddamn book?"

"It doesn't matter what I tell you. You're going to have to decide what you want to believe."

"And if I believe that you're a manipulative, uncaring bastard, what would you say to that?"

"That you're probably right."

"That you have no qualms about killing in order to further your plans. And that's to see your children taken care of, isn't it? A noble enough motive. Is that why you killed your wife? You didn't think she was a good enough mother?"

He didn't answer. He simply stood there, leaning against the cupboards, watching her.

"Or was it simple jealousy? She was carrying another man's child, and you couldn't stand it. Were you always pathologically possessive? You'd rather be accused of murdering your own children than let them fall into anyone else's hands. It must be one more revenge against Diana for cheating on you. Keeping her children away from their grandparents was the final, cheap shot."

He blinked, just a flash of expression, and then it was gone again. "Whatever you choose to believe, Cassie," he murmured.

"You're so good," she said in a wondering voice. "So damnably good at twisting people. At twisting me. I look at you and know what you're capable of, know the lies, and yet I keep thinking there has to be an excuse. A reason, behind all of this, that justifies everything. That justifies lying and cheating and manipulating, that justifies murder. But for the life of me, I can't imagine what it could be."

Something cracked. Some glimmer of an emotion so fierce that it robbed Cassie of her breath and heartbeat. He moved, quickly, coming close to her, his hands on the arms of the chair, imprisoning her, his face in his, so that she could see the bleakness of death in his eyes. "Can't you?" he whispered, his voice raw and cracked. "When you figure it out, come find me. If it's not too late."

"How can I fight it if you don't?" she demanded fiercely. "How can I make sense of it if you go running after death just as hard as Sean fought it?"

"That's your problem." He backed away, quickly, heading toward the door, leaving her. And then he paused, and she could see the strength that surged through his tall, lean body, as he pulled some semblance of control back around him. When he turned, his eyes were black and glittering in his face, his expression distant, impassive, chillingly polite. "By the way, what were you and Mabry talking about?"

Cassie stared at him blankly. "What do you mean?"

"You and Mabry were talking about Francesca. That's your younger sister, isn't it?"

"Yes. And don't start thinking she can take my place. You can't seduce her and make her take care of your children."

"Why not?" he said coolly, taunting her.

"Because she's only thirteen years old," Cass shot back. "Besides, she's safe and sound up in Vermont. With luck she'll never have to meet you."

She was unprepared for his reaction. All color left his face, and he looked like death. "In Vermont?" he echoed hoarsely.

"Your ex-father-in-law is looking after her. He's very fond of her."

"Oh, God," Richard moaned. "Jesus fucking God, no!" And he staggered from the room like a man who'd been struck by lightning. Leaving Cassie behind, all her horrified instincts in flame.

CHAPTER 19

The old man had won. He should have known, when it came to evil as monumental as retired General Amberson Scott, there was very little anyone could do to retaliate. He was an experienced campaigner. Each encounter was met with a devastating counterattack, and he'd struck the final, decisive blow.

Richard could go to any lengths to protect his children. He could barter his soul, kill, destroy, corrupt, all for the sake of Seth and Ariel. But he couldn't let another innocent be sacrificed.

Scott knew it. It was only a wonder he hadn't played his trump card before now. But then, there hadn't been any need. Richard had been planning to go to his death quietly, without any degree of fuss. Scott would have his revenge, and there the matter would end.

He could thank Cassie for the change, he knew it. Somehow she must have let something slip about the children, damn her soul. The general now had something to live for, besides revenge.

And Richard had something to live for as well. He was the only one who knew the truth. Even if he tried to tell someone, he wouldn't be believed. What little he'd confided in Mark had been met with guarded doubt.

He had to go after Cassie's sister himself. That was what Amberson wanted, he had no doubt of that. A final, deadly confrontation, with the old soldier meting out justice. But Richard was going to bring the general down with him. The last defenses had fallen—he was no longer a cool, dangerous automaton, moving through what was left of his life, manipulating fate. He was alive, furiously, wildly alive, and it was too late to change.

Mabry stared in shock when he barged into her bedroom. "Do you have a car?" he demanded.

She yanked her shirt back around her too skinny body. "I beg your pardon?"

He caught her by her scrawny arms and shook her. "Goddamn it, do you have a car in the city? I can't waste time renting one."

"Waste time?" she echoed. "What in God's name is wrong with you, Richard? What do you need a car for?"

"To go after the general. When did you last hear from him?"

"You're not making any sense. The general and his wife have taken my stepdaughter to Vermont for a few days, so she doesn't have to go through the upset of Sean's illness."

"How long ago did they leave?" He shook her again, taking his fury and panic out on her and not caring.

"This morning, I think. For heaven's sake, Richard . . ."

"Leave her alone." Cassie's voice was almost unnaturally calm.

He turned and snarled at her. "You told him, you stupid bitch. You must have let something slip. And now he's taken your sister, and God only knows what will happen if I don't get there in time."

"What are you talking about?" Mabry demanded, yanking herself out of his angry clutches. "Why should the general hurt Francesca? Why, he absolutely dotes on her."

The wave of nausea that washed over him made him sway for a moment. "He'd hurt her to get back at me," he said flatly.

"I still don't understand."

"You don't have to understand. You just have to tell me where you keep your fucking car."

"Seventy-fifth and Lexington," Cassie answered for her, moving to one of the tall pine dressers and fetching a set of keys. "It's a grey BMW . . ."

He snatched the keys out of her hand before she could finish, turning on his heel.

"Wait a minute," she called after him, and he could hear her running to catch up with him. "I'm going with you."

He stopped at the front door, long enough to

turn and look at her. She looked pale, disheveled, and frightened, and he felt not the slightest pity for her.

"If your sister is hurt," he said in an icy voice, "it will be your own fucking fault."

She flinched, almost as if he'd hit her. "I'm coming with you," she said again, grabbing his arm.

"The hell you are." He didn't even stop to consider his options. Cassie was a strong woman, a determined woman, and he'd reached the end of his endurance.

He hit her. Hard. A sharp jab to her chin, forceful enough to knock her on her butt, to knock the breath and the sense from her. By the time she regained her equilibrium, he'd be long gone.

She went down like a felled oak. He was aware of several things, the delicacy of her bones beneath his fist, the sheer astonishment in her eyes, the grace with which she fell, the lashing regret that seared through him. And then he was gone, slamming the door behind him, before he could let his damnable, renewed conscience attack him again. He didn't have time for morality, for a conscience, for anything but driving north to Vermont as fast as Mabry O'Rourke's BMW could take him. And he didn't need Cassie along for a distraction.

He grabbed the first taxi he found, though he probably could have run the distance in a shorter time. He browbeat and bribed the attendant into letting him get the car himself, shoving a handful of twenties into his grubby fist. By the time he swung around the final curve of the parking garage and aimed the headlights into the city night, his adrenaline was popping, and nothing was going to stop him.

Including the figure of a tall, lone female with a cloud of hair, silhouetted against his headlights.

She could see him, see the car, and she didn't move, standing there. He didn't hesitate. He was more than adept at playing chicken—the last year of his life had been an elaborate game of it, and he wasn't about to be bested by Cassie Roarke. He shoved his foot down on the accelerator and headed straight for her.

He saw her, she knew it. The headlights illuminated her, and she didn't budge, still trying to catch her breath after her wild race to the parking garage. She'd almost missed him. It had taken her a moment to regain her bearings when he'd hit her. She'd scrambled to her feet and gone after him, not even taking the time to consider what he'd just done. She used the stairs while he took the elevator, coming out on the street just in time to see him disappear around the corner in a taxi. She started after him, at a sprint.

She could hear the roar of the engine, feel the heat of the headlights spearing through her. He might very well kill her. He'd looked at her as if he'd wanted to. If he thought she'd put his children in danger, then he was more than capable of it, she'd realized that about him. She shut her eyes, breathing deeply, and didn't move.

The engine roared. The tires squealed. She could feel the air rush toward her with the force of a speeding train, and she squeezed her eyes more tightly shut, bracing herself.

The BMW screeched to a stop beside her, close enough that the door handle brushed her clothes. The electric window opened. "Get in," he said from the darkness inside the car.

She opened the door and got in.

She barely had the seat belt fastened around her when he tore out into traffic, just missing an oncoming truck. The drive through midtown would have been horrifying if she were in any condition to care, but she simply sat there, clutching the leather seat, and let him drive.

She didn't speak until they had crossed the George Washington Bridge and were heading north. His elegant hands were clenched around the leather-covered steering wheel, and his face, reflected in the dashboard lights, was set in frightening lines.

"I'm sure you're not in the mood to hear any advice," she began in a carefully neutral voice.

"You've got that right."

"But if the police stop Richard Tiernan for speeding, I don't think they're going to let you keep driving. Are you even supposed to leave the state of New York?"

"No," he said flatly, but the BMW slowed down marginally.

"What's the general going to do to Francesca?" she forced herself to ask.

He didn't answer.

"Damn it, I have a right to know. She's my sister, I didn't say anything when he offered to take her, even though I had a funny feeling . . ."

"A funny feeling," he echoed in an odd voice. "Did he say anything to cause that 'funny feeling'?"

The memories came flooding back, along with a guilt strong enough to strangle her. She'd forgotten. In her jet-lagged, sleep-deprived, grief-shattered, lust-engorged mind she'd forgotten all about the general's cryptic words and subtle threats.

"He said to tell you that Francesca was in good hands," she said.

"Did he, now?" Richard said in a distant voice. "Didn't you think that was odd? Considering I've never met Francesca?"

"Yes. I asked him. And he said you were protective of children."

"Damn him," Richard said quietly.

"And he said something else. A moment later," she said, misery in her voice. "He asked me where they were."

"Ah," said Richard, and she could see his long fingers wrap tightly around the steering wheel,

and she imagined her neck in his deadly grip.
"And what did you say to that?"

"Nothing."

"No, I'm sure you didn't," he said smoothly.
"You just jumped, and looked guilty, and probably
blushed, didn't you? Didn't you?" His voice was
vicious.

"Yes," she admitted.

There was a long silence. "And to think there
was a time when I thought your blushes were
charming."

"I didn't tell him they were alive!" she shot
back fiercely.

"You didn't need to. He's a very clever man, the
general. Your face told him all he needed to know.
That's why he's done this. He's holding Francesca
hostage. He wants me dead. He wants his
grandchildren."

"Did he kill her?"

He turned to look at her for a moment, and the
amusement on his face was macabre. "Still looking for a scapegoat, Cassie? I thought you knew
who killed Diana. I thought you had it all figured
out, blame apportioned, motives examined, judgment passed."

"What happened that night?"

"I told you everything."

"I don't think you did. I think your confession
of guilt was just one more part of this massive
test you've been running on me, a test I keep fail-

ing. It's a long drive to Vermont. Why don't you tell me what happened?"

"Trust me, you don't want to know."

"Tell me, damn it. There's no reason to hold anything back," she cried. "For God's sake, just tell me."

She could feel his hesitation, and she wanted to hit him. "You don't want to know," he said finally, "but you don't have a choice anymore. I'll tell you. And then you can see whether you can still sleep at night."

The house was quiet when he came home. Deceptive of course, the house was always quiet on the outside, and inside storms and furies raged, alternating with quiet, drugged despair.

Diana stood motionless, waiting for him, and he could see in the glitter of her mad blue eyes that she hadn't taken her pills that day. He'd never decided which was worse, the taking of the pills, or the forgetting. He tried to get her into treatment, even managed to get through a nine-month period where she was only on mild tranquilizers. Until her father returned from the Middle East, and found a new doctor for her. And she was gone again.

Thank God for his instincts. He'd taken the children to Sally, asking her to keep them until she heard from him. He was used to Diana by now, by the way the storms built until they exploded in a poisonous rage. He could trust

Sally. She wouldn't turn the children over to anyone except him.

"Where are they?" Diana asked. Her voice was clear and childish, eerily like that of a six-year-old, and her beautiful blue eyes were opaque.

"They're taken care of," he told her, calm, soothing. But she was already past the point of listening.

"They're coming with me." She was standing on the stairs, and she moved down, deliberately graceful, deliberately coquettish, dressed in pink, with ruffles and bows. Something too young for her. Something her father bought.

"Where are you going, Diana?" He was very calm, already knowing the answer.

"To my father. He's the only one who really loves me. He always has. People don't understand about us. The bond we have."

"I understand." And he was beginning to. Finally.

"I promised him I'd bring the children," Diana continued in a wheedling little voice. He half expected her to twist a curl around one finger and shuffle her feet. He half expected her to be wearing shiny black Mary Janes.

"No."

The trusting expression vanished from her face, leaving it white with rage. "They're my children!" she shrieked. "They come with me."

"No."

Her eyes were suddenly crafty, and her voice

softened into a gentle murmur. "They won't stay with you. My father is very powerful. He's a national hero, beloved by everyone. He has friends. Judges, lawyers. You're already under suspicion, you know."

"Suspicion of what?"

"Seth's broken collarbone," Diana said sweetly. "They didn't think it was accidental. I mentioned that you were capable of frightening rages."

"You said what?" He took a step toward her, fury overriding any concern.

"Taken on top of Ariel's fractured arm, and the bruising their teachers noticed, I think an investigation is finally under way. They weren't sure whether to believe me or not. But I convinced them."

He closed his eyes with sudden guilt and horror. How did he let this happen? Hadn't he been protective enough? He never realized just how very dangerous Diana could be.

"Why did you hurt them, Diana?" he asked carefully, afraid he might kill her.

Diana's pout was horrifyingly innocent. "They're horrible to me. They deserve it." She moved past him, graceful, closing the front door behind him. "They don't do what I ask them to. They don't love me. They only love you. And you love them. More than you ever loved me."

He controlled his fury with the last of his strength. He hadn't known what it felt like, to want to kill someone with his bare hands, to rip their heart out. Now he did. "Then why do you want to take them with you?"

"My father wants them."

It was a shot in the dark, torn from his deepest, most terrible suspicions. "What's the matter, Diana? Are you too old for him?"

"Yes," she said simply. She turned, and for the first time he saw the knife. A butcher knife, large, recently sharpened.

"Diana," he said softly, warily.

"You were supposed to protect me, you know. You were supposed to love me to distraction, and keep him away from me. But you didn't. You didn't think I was a little princess at all. You got tired of me. You said I was spoiled, that I had tantrums. You put the children ahead of me. That wasn't fair. It was no wonder I turned back to Daddy."

"Not fair at all," he said in a sick voice.

"Are you going to try to stop me?" she crooned. "My father wants my children. I'm going to provide them for him. After all, I should be a dutiful child. I've always been a dutiful child, ever since I was five years old and he started coming to my room. I was his little soldier, waiting for him when he came home, brave and strong. I never cried. No matter how much it hurt, I never cried."

He wanted to throw up. He stared at his fairy-tale princess of a wife, the one who froze in bed with him, who hadn't let him even touch her hand for more than a year. "I would have done anything he wanted," she continued, surveying the knife with a fond air. "But he only likes children. I'm pregnant, you know. Because sooner or later Seth and Ariel will be too old for him as well. And this child will be our special one, just Daddy's and mine."

"Oh, God," Richard moaned, as the full horror sank in. "Diana, angel, you need help . . ."

"Don't call me that!" she screamed. "I'm not an angel! I'm not anybody's angel. Tell me Richard, does it make you sick? To know that you can't measure up to my father? But then, you always knew that. You just didn't realize that you didn't measure up in bed, either." There was spittle coming down the side of her cupid's bow mouth, and her eyes were totally mad. But still cunning.

"Are you going to try to stop me, Richard?" she cooed, moving closer, the knife clutched in her hand. "It won't do you any good. I'm good at fooling people, you should know that by now. My father will take us into his home, protective, paternal, and you'll be charged with child abuse. You might not be convicted, but the stigma will remain. You'll never see them again."

"I'll see you in hell first."

Her smile blossomed, and he knew suddenly that this what she wanted. "Will you, Richard?" she asked. "Be my guest." And she held out the knife, handle first, daring him.

He lunged for it, but she held tightly to the blade, and he could see the blood spurt around her fingers. She was grinning wildly. "It will look like a struggle, Richard. I grabbed the knife, trying to stop you from killing me, but it was no use. You were crazy, determined to kill me because I'd betrayed you. They'll put you in jail, Richard, for a long, long time. They may even kill you. And my father will have the children."

He jerked at the knife, but she held tightly, oblivious to the blood. Suddenly their macabre battle stilled, and she looked up at him, trustingly, beautifully. "What do you want from me, Richard?" she asked.

"I want you to get help," he said desperately, feeling the hatred welling up inside him.

She shook her head. "No, you don't, Richard. You want me dead."

Because it was the truth, he backed away in horror, jerking the knife away from her. But she clung tightly to it, stumbling forward and landing in his arms. He felt the shudder of her body as the knife sank in, deep, through flesh and bone.

She held him, smiling so very sweetly. "Thank you, Richard," she murmured, as she began to slide toward the floor.

The knife was in her chest, deep, and the blood welled out, dark and pumping. Her eyelids fluttered closed, and he sank to his knees beside her in horror, reaching out to touch the pulse at the side of her neck. It was faint, fluttering, fading. She was dying.

He stared down at her, and his hands were wet

with blood. He should get up, find the phone, and dial 911. There was a chance, a very slim chance, she could still make it. He knew he should get up, try to save her.

He didn't move. He knelt beside her, watching, as her life blood flowed into a deep black pool around them. He watched her die, so quickly, and he thought of their children, safe, hidden. He picked up Diana's limp hand and held it, gently, tenderly, as she died, and he thought he could see the ghost of a smile on her face.

The police found him there, still kneeling beside her. His fingerprints were on the murder weapon, but it didn't matter. In his own mind he killed her. Degrees of guilt were a waste of time. All that mattered was that his children be kept safe. In the dark confusion of shock, he could think of only one way to ensure that General Scott never put his filthy hands on them. And that was if they were presumed dead.

He found that he'd gone into a dark, safe place where nothing could touch him. At times during the next few months he wondered whether he made the right choice. Whether he should have simply confessed, to the premeditated murder of his innocent wife and children.

He watched the general from a safe distance, almost amused at the rallying support from the old man, the determination to find the truth and free him. Until he began to believe that Richard must have murdered his wife and children, that there was no other possible explanation. And doubtless he'd guessed why. Scott had explained it all so well during his testimony, looking like the quintessential war hero, a grief-stricken father, betrayed by his much-beloved son-in-law. It had been common knowledge that Diana was planning to leave him, planning to take her abused children with her, home to the safety of her parents' house. It was no wonder that Richard had finally snapped, and slaughtered the bunch of them rather than let them go.

But wise or not, Richard never confessed. He kept his secrets, emerging from his self-imposed darkness to trust only two people, Sally Norton and Mark Bellingham. Between them they got the children out of the country, and he never bothered to consider whether they believed him or not. At least they believed him enough to help him. Everything would have been fine, if Sally hadn't gotten sick.

And suddenly he could no longer simply accept his fate. There was only one way out, and he took it, telling Mark to accept Sean O'Rourke's constant offers of help. Anything in order to ensure that there'd be someone to take care of his children, even if it meant having to spin an elaborate network of lies for a skeptical Sean O'Rourke. Even if it meant telling him the truth.

But he was mad, as mad as Diana had been at the end. That bloody confrontation in his hallway had turned him psychotic. He had to be, to think he could make a deal with fate. That he could look at a silver-framed photograph and find the answer he needed.

And sure enough, fate had had the last laugh. Instead of proving to be his salvation, the woman in the photograph turned out to be the most disastrous thing that could have happened, after he'd been so very very careful. She endangered his children, and she endangered her own sister.

There was no longer anything else he could do. The choice was out of his hands. He would face the general, finally, for the confrontation that should have taken place in hell. The black ice that had encased him since the night Diana died had cracked and fallen away. And Richard stood there, wounded, bleeding. Ready for battle.

The car was silent, the finely tuned motor of the BMW a quiet purr. Cass sat in the passenger seat, eyes closed, hands lying loosely in her lap. She knew there were tears staining her face, but she figured he wouldn't notice. And wouldn't care. He was someplace else, remembering, reliving what he wanted to shut away.

He didn't want her words of comfort. He didn't want her justification, her reassurances. He'd faced things, passed his own judgment, and meted out his own punishment.

She'd screwed up his careful plan. His stupid, noble, bullshit plan, and she'd messed it up. She would be furiously grateful that she had, if it weren't for one reason.

Or actually three. Seth, Ariel, and Francesca.

The little ones were safe for now. But now that he knew they were alive, the general could find them, Cass had no doubt of that. As long as that evil, monstrous old man lived, he would use all his resources to track them down, to take them.

She knew what Richard planned to do when he found the Scotts. And if she found that the old man had put one filthy hand on Francesca, Cass would beat him to it.

She glanced over at Richard. He was somewhere else, his eyes on the dark, shrouded interstate heading north, his strong, elegant hands on the steering wheel, seemingly at ease. She knew it was deceptive. He wasn't a murderer, despite his guilt-ridden belief.

But before the next twenty-four hours passed, he would be.

CHAPTER 20

It began as fog when they crossed the Vermont border. By the time they reached White River Junction it had turned to the deadly click of freezing rain. Richard didn't alter his speed. Cass didn't care. Fear no longer had a place in her life. She was putting her trust in Richard completely. He might not care whether they lived or died, but he wasn't going to leave Francesca to the mercy of Amberson Scott. He would drive as swiftly as he dared, and Cass would trust him.

The snow should have been a relief by the time they reached Montpelier. Without a word Richard leaned forward and flicked on the radio, but the local weather report was far from reassuring. A spring storm, complete with snow, sleet, and freezing rain, had blown through the Northeast. In another forty-eight hours it would be spring again. In the meantime, northern Vermont was in for it.

"Shit." The first word spoken between them since he'd made his confession, Richard muttered it tersely as he started down off the interstate highway. As far as Cass was concerned, it was appropriate enough.

He pulled into a McDonald's and parked, the BMW sliding gently to rest against the curb. "I don't know about you," he said, "but I need a bathroom and some coffee."

It was disturbingly normal. Cassie managed a fitful smile. "Me, too." She wanted to ask questions but she didn't dare. She followed him in to the bright, noisy atmosphere.

By the time she emerged from the bathroom, he was nowhere in sight. She panicked, certain he'd abandoned her in the middle of the snowy night, until she looked out into the parking lot. He was already back in the car. She bought a huge cup of coffee and a danish and ran out, half-afraid he still might take off again. He watched her impassively, waiting until she refastened her seat belt before pulling into the slippery drive.

"I thought you'd left me," she said, carefully opening the plastic top and taking a sip. It was hot and strong and oily, and it was close to heaven.

"I considered it."

"Why didn't you?"

"For the same reason I allowed you to come in the first place. Your sister might need you."

It was no more than she expected, and no more than she deserved. "I do have my uses," she said coolly. "I can take care of children, as long as people explain to me what kind of danger they're in. And I'm good at going down on convicted murderers."

He shot her an impassive glance. "True enough."

The coffee slopped onto her jeans, burning her. "Do you happen to have any idea where we're going?"

"Yes."

Cass shut her eyes, mentally counting to ten. "Would you feel like telling me?"

The silence lasted just long enough to make Cass want to scream. "The Scotts have a house near Smuggler's Notch. I'm sure they're there."

"Why?"

"Because he told Mabry he was taking your sister to Vermont. And he wants me to follow. He wants me to find him. I would think that would be fairly obvious."

She ignored his vicious tone of voice. "Why obvious? What does he want from you?"

"Revenge. I killed his daughter, remember? His precious, fairy-tale princess."

"But you didn't!" she was fool enough to protest. "It was an accident, one she brought on herself. You didn't . . ."

"Shut up!" he said fiercely. "Just shut the fuck up. I don't need your explanations, your justifications. She's dead. I don't know whether she landed on that knife by accident or on purpose, and I doubt I could have saved her. But the fact is, I didn't try, and all the rationalizations in the world won't change that basic fact." He slammed his fist against the leather-covered steering wheel. "Damn! I told myself I wouldn't let you do this to me again."

"I'm not doing anything to you."

"Cassie," he said in a cold, angry voice, "after spending the last few weeks with you, the death penalty is beginning to look like a reprieve."

"I'm not going to let them kill you."

His laugh was as cold as the snow-fogged night. "You can try to stop them. You can see if anyone will believe you. It might be a moot point by then. Scott is up there in his mini-fortress at Smuggler's Notch, and once I get up there, one of us won't come down. I'll either be dead or a killer, and the state won't look kindly on either option."

"I won't let them kill you," she said again, her voice fierce and stubborn.

There was a moment of silence. "Cass, don't you know a losing proposition when you see one?"

"No," she said. "I still believe in people. I still believe in you."

"Then God help you," Richard said.

Richard had lost track of time. Cassie was curled up on the front seat beside him, asleep, as he started up the mountain road in Stowe, heading toward Smuggler's Notch, and the first greenish gray light of dawn began to penetrate the darkness. He'd been driving all night.

He glanced over at her. Her eyes were shadowed, her red hair an angry tangle around her pale face, and she wasn't dressed for this weather. The jeans and sweater wouldn't provide enough protection against the stinging cold of the spring storm, and her sneakers would be soaked within minutes of starting up the trail to the house.

Why the hell had he brought her? He'd swerved at the last minute, and it would have been easy enough to take off into the New York City night, leaving her standing there. Safe.

Instead he'd taken her with him. He must be a glutton for punishment. A masochist, to keep tormenting himself with her presence. Because even now, with his adrenaline popping, his nerves on the raw edge, his fury with her still strong, he wanted to pull the BMW over to the side of the snow-covered road and pull her into his arms. He wanted to kiss her eyelids, the sensitive spot beneath her ear, the pulse that beat so strongly at the base of her neck. He wanted to love her, not just now, but for always.

There was no such thing for him as always. He'd lied to her when he said either Scott or he would be dead. He wasn't leaving it to chance, or to the state. They'd both be dead by the time the day was over.

She made a faint, sleepy sound of protest, almost as if she'd heard his thought in her dreams. She knew him so well, and yet not at all. He knew one thing. His instincts had been right. She was the one. She'd go to England and watch over his children. Mark would take care of it for him—he'd left the necessary papers. There would no longer be any danger—Scott would be dead. There was simply no alternative.

He should have done it sooner, rather than let that danger hang over the heads of his children. But the plain and simple fact of the matter was, he wasn't a murderer. That dark, dreadful place that had closed in on him after Diana had died hadn't allowed him any action at all. He stayed there in the darkness, only seeing that he had to protect his children. Not realizing that one simple act of violence would protect them forever.

He knew that now. He could thank Cassie for liberating him. Making him breathe again, hurt again, hate again. Making him love again.

He wasn't going to tell her. He'd considered it coolly, during the long hours of the night drive. Originally it had been part of his plan, to lie to her, to convince her he loved her, so that she'd be tied to him, body and soul, past death.

The damnable thing was, he did love her. And loving her, he couldn't tell her. Couldn't tie her to a dead man. She would love the children, take care of them, without that kind of emotional blackmail. She'd heal that much faster if she never knew.

She stirred again, frowning. He wanted to see her in the summer, with freckles across her nose. He wanted to see her in a bathing suit, that lush, gorgeous body that she was so self-conscious of kissed by the sun. He never would. He'd never make love to her in a field of daisies. It was mud and darkness and rain for the likes of them. Sleet and snow and eternal night.

Fields of daisies were for other people. For Cassie and another man. Not for him.

His hands were clenched tightly around the steering wheel, and he was driving too fast. He slowed down, deliberately. He had to let her go. He knew that, and the sooner the better.

"Damn."

She stirred, looking up at him sleepily, disoriented. There were motels and ski lodges all the way up the road, and for just a moment he was tempted to stop, to take her inside one and just hold her. Just for an hour or two. Was he so evil that he didn't even deserve that much comfort?

"What's wrong?"

"The road is closed."

"What do you mean?"

"The road over the Notch is closed. It's usually snowed-in for most of the winter, but by this time of year they open it. Apparently they've closed it because of the storm."

"Where does that leave us?" she asked.

"Heading up the Notch without snow tires." He waited for her protest.

She made none. "All right," she said, leaning back.

He jerked the wheel, too suddenly, and the BMW skidded over to the side of the road, sliding several feet before coming to a stop. She turned to look at him through the early dawn, her face composed. He wanted to rattle that composure. He wanted to shake her, to scream at her, to . . .

He saw the bruise. It was a beauty, dark purple, beneath the right side of her chin. He'd forgotten. He stared, sickened, at the mark. He'd never hit a woman in his life, no matter how much Diana had pushed him.

"What's wrong?" she asked. "What are you staring at?"

He couldn't help himself. He reached out and touched the bruise, and she flinched. "Oh," she said in a dull voice, turning her face away from him. "I'd forgotten."

He wanted to push, to punish himself. "Are you used to being hit?"

She kept her face averted. "Not since I was a child."

"Hit?" he said. "Or spanked?"

"Hit."

Again the dark rage. At whoever had hit her, a helpless little girl. And at himself. "Who hit you? Sean?"

"Whoever was drinking the most at the time," she said. "You don't have that excuse."

"I don't have any excuse."

To his astonishment she managed a faint trace of a smile. "True enough. What are we waiting for?"

"I can take you to a motel. You could wait there . . ."

"No. And don't think you can clip me again. I'm coming with you, and there's nothing you can do to stop me. I'm your albatross," she said with a fierce kind of humor. "Your barnacle, your worst nightmare."

He stared at her. At her pale, defiant mouth, her sorrowful eyes. "I'll dream about you in hell," he murmured.

"See that you do."

The barricade at the foot of the Notch road was feeble enough—just a couple of highway sawhorses with flashers attached. He stopped the car, but before he could move Cassie had jumped out, moving swiftly through the slush to pull one of the barriers out of the way. He drove through, waiting for her, squinting at the slowly lightening sky. The stuff coming down was something between rain and snow, wet, but not icy, and the gritty stuff beneath the tires had at least a trace of traction. Cass jumped back into the car, and he started up the twisty road slowly, keeping up enough speed to maintain his steady climb.

They made it farther than he would have thought. The tires spinning, BMW traveling sideways, they slid their way up the hairpin turns, until the slush turned to ice and the car ended up sideways in a ditch. He switched off the motor, turning to look at her. "You're not dressed for this," he said in an even voice.

"Neither are you." She was already out of the car, a determined expression on her face. She looked like an Irish Valkyrie, an amazon, ready to do battle. That strength would have to carry her through whatever they faced at the top of the hill.

He pulled himself out of the driver's seat. He was wearing Nikes, not the best for climbing an icy mountain trail, but then, he didn't have a choice. The mist that was falling had already coated Cassie's hair and sweater, and she blinked. He wanted to kiss her eyelids.

"Let's go," he said in his coolest voice, starting the rest of the way up the road.

She trudged behind him, silent, steady, no complaints. Her feet would be wet and soaking, blocks of ice. He knew, because his were. She was having trouble keeping up with him, but he didn't slow his pace. He didn't dare. Too much time had already elapsed.

He almost couldn't find the trail. He'd climbed it years ago, when he and Diana had first married and they'd come up here for a family visit. Even then there'd been trouble, and he'd gone for long hikes, discovering the back trail up to Scott's mountaintop retreat. It looked different, years later, in the snow and ice, than it had in the height of summer, but for once his instincts were working.

The trail was slippery, the rocks coated with ice. He heard her scrambling behind him but he didn't dare pause, dare help her. He had to concentrate on what lay ahead.

Her voice came from behind, breathless. "What do you think he'll do to Francesca?"

"You don't want to know," he said grimly.

"I have to know. If I'm going to make it up this goddamn cliff, I need to have a reason," she snapped, panting.

"How old is she?"

"Thirteen going on thirty. She's precocious, very Italian, very loving . . ." her voice cracked for a moment, but Richard kept on walking.

He took pity on her. She needed fear and rage to keep her going. She also needed hope. "I don't think he'll have touched her yet," he said, hoping it wasn't a lie. "I think he'll be waiting for me."

"What about his wife? How could she stand by . . . ?"

"She'll be drugged. She's been an addict as long as I've known her, and Amberson keeps her well-supplied. I never realized why. With luck he'll have knocked your sister out with something. She might never have to know what happened to Amberson."

"What will happen?"

He paused, turning to look down at her. The evergreens were shorter and more scraggly as they climbed higher, but the trail was dark and brooding, making it hard to see her expression. He knew it in his heart anyway. "You don't need me to tell you, Cassie. You know."

"Richard, you can't . . ."

"I no longer have any choice."

She looked up at him, and he felt her despair echo in his veins. "Richard, I love you."

"I know," he said. And he started back up the mountain.

Cassie had never been so miserable in her entire life. Her feet had gone beyond numb to a kind of stinging pain, the cold had seeped into her bones along with the liquid air, and her sweater hung wetly around her frozen jeans. The rocks were icy, the dirt was mud, and for every few steps she took, she slid back at least one.

Richard moved ahead of her, tall, unyielding, untouched by mortal concerns. It was always possible she hated him, even as she followed him, turning her mind off, turning her fears off, simply enduring, as the icy needles of mist coated her, seeping through the cotton sweater, encasing her arms.

She barely felt it when her ankle twisted beneath her. She went down again, scrabbling for a handhold, sliding in the ice and mud a few feet until she ended up against a stubby pine tree.

She lay there for a moment, catching her breath. Richard hadn't stopped, moving relentlessly upward, and cursing silently, Cassie struggled to her feet.

Only to collapse again, as the pain sliced through her in white hot waves, and she couldn't stifle her soft moan of agony. She sat back, pulling her foot out from under her, carefully, leaning against the tree, watching as Richard climbed back down to tower over her.

She tilted her head back to look up at him. "I blew it," she said.

"Do you think it's broken?"

"I have no idea. I heard a crack. I know I can't stand on it, at least now. Go on ahead."

He stared at her, and she waited for some token protest. She got none. "All right," he said. "The path is well-marked. If Francesca doesn't come to find you, the police will find the car abandoned on the road and send out a search party. They'll find you before long. Make sure they check at the general's house. They probably have orders to leave him strictly alone—Scott has that kind of power—but make up some story. About your friend going on for help."

"You aren't coming back down?"

He knelt down beside her in the rain, and she wasn't sure what she expected. Not the gentleness of his hand, touching the bruise at the side of her face. Not the tender brush of his lips, against her eyelids, her cheekbone, her lips. A benediction. A promise.

A farewell.

She watched him until he disappeared into the woods up ahead. Listened until the sounds of his climb were swallowed up in the mist and rain. She sat back, shivering, miserable, still feeling the warmth of his mouth on her. She trusted him. He would save Francesca. He would stop the general. He would . . .

He would die. Her eyes shot open in sudden horror as the final realization hit her. He wasn't coming back down. He wasn't planning to survive. He was going to kill General Scott, and stop the threat to his children forever. But he was going to die as well, to expiate his sin, his crime—a crime no court would recognize.

She sat up, screaming his name, but the sound was swallowed up in the mist. She couldn't let him do it. She was a fighter, a survivor. And right now her survival depended on Richard's. Her life, and any possibility of happiness.

She started after him, crawling, scrambling, dragging her wounded ankle behind her, her fingers sliding in the mud, her face scratched by branches. She was as relentless, as determined as he had been. Nothing was going to stop her.

She reached a rise, a leveling off of the steep terrain. She had no idea how long she'd been scrambling after him—she'd lost all track of time. Suddenly everything began to look a little less wild, a little more ordered. Military order. She had to be getting closer.

She slid again, landing on her stomach in the mud, and she lay there, panting, trying to catch her breath. Listening to the sounds of the forest. The drip as the mist condensed and dropped off the trees. A distant, quiet hum. And the sudden, horrifying sounds of footsteps, coming closer.

She lifted her head, ready to roll into the bushes and hide, but it was already too late. The general stood there, dressed in impeccable fatigues, a walking stick in his hand, looking down at her as she lay in the mud, an amused expression on his kindly face.

"I'm quite impressed, Cassidy," he said. "I've been watching you for quite a while. You would have made one hell of a soldier. Most new recruits start whining the moment things get tough. A sprained ankle would have them screaming for their momma. But you just kept crawling up this mountain."

"I had a reason."

"So you did," he said pleasantly. "I expect you're wondering how I knew you were here. This place is a fortress, but I'm not interested in having a private army interfering with my personal life. The security system is the best in the world. I can watch anyone who gets within a mile of this place. That's why I'm wondering where Richard is."

The hope that flooded her was warming, strengthening, and she struggled to sit up. "He's not here."

"Don't be ridiculous. You would never have found this place without him. I don't like liars, Cassidy. I have to discipline them."

"Where's Francesca?"

"Safe."

"Safe?" she echoed. "In your hands?"

"Ah," General Scott murmured. "I gather Richard told you the truth. Or what he considers to be the truth. Did he tell you how he murdered my little girl? He didn't understand the bond we had. He was jealous, he always had been. Diana and I used to laugh about him, about his efforts to make her what he wanted her to be. Diana knew who she was."

"Diana never had a chance. Not with a monster like you for a father."

His expression didn't alter. "No one understands," he said lightly. "I don't expect them to. Come along, Cassidy." He leaned down and hauled her to her feet, putting an arm around her waist. "I'll help you up to the house, and we can wait for Richard."

She tried to push him away, to free herself, but he was almost unnaturally strong. He half dragged, half hauled her up the mountain, oblivious to the mud and filth, oblivious to her struggles.

The house was just over the rise, a peaceful, sprawling mélange of wood and glass. "My little aerie," the general murmured, not even out of breath, as they started across the stretch of ice-rimmed lawn leading to the deck.

"I don't see any state-of-the-art security system," she muttered.

"I have all I need. Cameras, so I know who's coming. And a high-powered sniper rifle. I was an expert marksman when I was younger, and I believe in keeping up my skills. The moment Richard appears in one of my surveillance cameras, I'll be ready for him."

"You'll kill him?"

"Eventually." He was panting now, a fact that gave Cass only faint satisfaction. He opened the sliding glass door and shoved her inside. She collapsed on the pure white carpeting, smearing it with mud. "I want answers first."

Cass was silent for a moment, listening. "Where is Francesca?" she demanded. "Where's your wife?"

"Both sound asleep." He shrugged out of his fatigue jacket, moving over to the bar. "I'm more than aware of the value of pharmaceutical aids. Can I get you a vegetable drink? It has excellent restorative properties."

"Will I need them?"

"Actually," he said in an apologetic voice, "no."

"You're going to kill me."

"I'm afraid it's necessary. And your sister as well. In the army you learn to face the unpleasant task, and not to waste your time lamenting over the inevitable." He poured two glasses of a greeny-orange mixture and brought one over to her. For the first time in her life she longed for whiskey.

"Why?"

"I have to make absolutely certain that Richard is known for the monster he is. I'm afraid of your father's book. I'm afraid of the appeal. As long as he didn't fight it, I was content. But I know about the justice system in this country. Despite my best efforts, he could spend the rest of his life in some place that's a hell of a lot more hospitable than an army barracks. I can't let that happen. He has to be punished for what he did. If he won't die for Diana's murder, then he'll die for yours and your sister's."

"You're going to frame Richard?"

"Of course. I'll need an excuse for shooting him, won't I? I'll say he took you hostage, dragged you up here, and shot both you and Francesca. I had to kill him like the mad dog that he is." He held out the glass. "Take this. It'll make you feel better."

She knocked it out of his hand, and the green slime landed on the white carpet. "I'm not into drugs," she said.

The general smiled. "A perfect little soldier," he murmured. "You want it the hard way. You know where my grandchildren are. Tell me."

She didn't bother to deny it. "Where you'll never find them."

"Don't be ridiculous. I can find anything I want. If I'd had any idea they were still alive, it would have been a matter of days, maybe hours, before I had them with me. Richard was very clever about that. I never even guessed. I thought he must have found out that Diana was carrying my child, and gone mad. Of course, madmen can be very crafty."

"You're a prime example."

The general shook his head. "I'm not mad, child," he said reprovingly. "I do what needs to be done. It's just that simple."

"That simple," she echoed.

"Would you like to clean up a bit? See your sister?"

"I thought you were going to kill us?"

"If you're dead when Richard appears, I'll have very little bargaining power. And I need to find out what happened that night." There was a faint crack in the general's facade, one that made his paternal calm all the more frightening.

"I want to see Francesca."

"I thought so." He helped her to her feet, solicitous, and handed her his walking stick. "This should help. This one belonged to the great General Dwight D. Eisenhower himself. I've always treasured it."

Cassie's fingers curled around the handle of it, and she looked into the general's face. She didn't have the strength to use it as a weapon. Not yet. But she would.

"Take me to Francesca," she said again.

"Gladly."

Richard was glad Cassie had fallen. She never would have made it up the sheer face of the cliff, and he knew her well enough to realize she wouldn't have accepted being left behind. He didn't think he could have hit her again—he still

felt sick at the memory of it. Though if he had
to, he would have. He'd learned he had the ability
to do just about anything.

The cliff was the only way to approach the
house without Amberson's damned video cameras.
There'd been no way to mount them over the cliff,
and supposedly no need. No one would approach
the place by such a suicidal method. No one in
their right mind.

Richard no longer considered whether he was
sane or not. Oddly enough, it was his return from
darkness that made him realize how very much
over the edge he was. Sanity and madness were
no longer issues in his life. He knew what he had
to do, and intended to do it, and pay the price.
He'd never been one to avoid the consequences.

He'd done rock climbing before, but he'd done
it with the proper equipment, and the rocks
weren't covered with a film of ice. He wondered
briefly what would happen if he fell. And then he
dismissed the notion. He wouldn't fall. He
couldn't. He was going to kill Amberson Scott
with his bare hands, and he was going to make
it hurt.

And then he was going to kill himself.

CHAPTER 21

"You bastard," Cassidy said.

Francesca lay on the bed, so unnaturally still that for a moment Cassidy had been afraid she was already dead. She was wearing something pink and frilly, exposing her long, coltish legs and budding breasts, and Cassie's hand gripped tightly around the walking stick.

"I haven't touched her," Scott murmured. "Just to get her changed. I've watched her though. She's very pretty, your little sister. Very innocent. Do you know if she's reached puberty yet?"

It was all Cassidy could do not to lash out at him. "Yes," she lied.

"A shame. I like them when they're still pure. Unsullied by blood. But I might make an exception in her case. Like Diana. I never could give her up. Don't look so distressed, Cassidy. She'll never know. I fed her enough of Essie's drugs to make sure she won't accidentally regain consciousness. When I finish with her, I'll see to it that a single bullet to the temple will take care of things. Immediate, painless. I'm not a cruel man."

She glared at him. "I thought you only liked your own children," she spat.

The general chuckled. "Don't be ridiculous, child. I'm a soldier. Where do you think I learned my taste for children? Battle zones provide human casualties of every age and degree of innocence. I only turned to my daughter because I was home, back in so-called civilization. And because she wanted it."

"I don't want to hear this."

"She was five years old," the general continued, unperturbed. "The bathroom's in there."

She made it to the toilet in time, throwing up. Her stomach was empty, and dry heaves followed, wracking her body, until she collapsed on the cool tile floor of the bathroom, too sick and miserable even to think.

He came and stood over her, turning on the blinding fluorescent light. "You should have had the vegetable drink, Cassie," he said kindly. "Compazine is good for the stomach as well."

"Go away," she groaned.

"Certainly, my dear. I just wanted to add my condolences on the death of your father. I gather he passed away yesterday. We were enemies, but we shared one thing. The devotion of our daughters." And he closed the door silently behind him.

It was a long time before Cass could move. Could struggle to her feet, leaning on the sink.

Her eyes were dry—there were no tears to shed for Sean right now. No tears for anyone.

She grabbed a snowy white towel and began to wipe the mud and dirt from her face. She looked like death—a fitting comparison. Hobbling over to the edge of the bathtub, she sat, carefully unfastening her mud-caked running shoe. The pain was agonizing as she tried to ease it off her damaged foot, and pulling off the wet sock, she could see her ankle was swollen and purple. She had no idea whether it was broken or not, and she didn't care. If need be, she'd walk down the mountain, carrying Francesca's drugged body over her shoulders.

She emerged from the bathroom, still cold and wet but marginally less muddy, and moved to the bed. Francesca lay there, still and cool, her jaw slack, all the bewitching adolescent vitality drained from her.

"Oh, baby," Cassie murmured, stroking her forehead, "I won't let him do this to you. I promise. I'll get you out of here."

Francesca's eyelids twitched, just faintly, and her mouth barely moved. "I'm okay." The words were so quiet she thought she imagined them. And then Francesca's eyes opened for a fraction of a moment, and she could see the fierce light in them before she closed them again. "I tried to spit out most of the drugs he gave me when he wasn't looking. But be careful, Cassie. He's got cameras everywhere."

"Francesca . . ."

"Shhh," Francesca whispered drowsily. "Go for help. He's left me alone so far. I'll be okay. I didn't take that much. Just find help." She closed her eyes again, slipping back into unconsciousness.

"Sonny." Cassie heard the voice, calm and soft, echo from the living room. She rose, pressing Francesca's hand in silent comfort, and hobbled toward the noise as a wave of hope washed over her. Only to have it ebb, as she saw the general's wife.

Essie Scott was wandering around in a soiled dressing gown. Her gray hair stood out around her head, her eyes were vacant, her tongue busy as she licked her lips, over and over again. "Sonny?" she called plaintively.

"Mrs. Scott," Cassie said, limping forward.

Essie tried to focus. "Who are you, dear?" she murmured. "You're not one of the maids. We don't have maids here, do we?"

"No, I'm not one of the maids."

"And you're not my daughter. My daughter's dead."

"I'm not your daughter. Mrs. Scott . . ."

"And you're not one of Sonny's little friends. You're much too old." She sighed, moving around to the bar. To the lethal green concoction. "Why are you here?"

"Mrs. Scott, we need your help. Your husband isn't well . . ."

"Nonsense," Essie murmured, pouring herself a

glass of the vegetable juice. "He's perfectly fine. He's a national hero. I'm the one who's not well. I need my medicine. He's protected me, but he knows how I get. I imagine things. Terrible, terrible things. But my Sonny couldn't do such things. He's a war hero."

"Mrs. Scott . . ."

"No, I won't listen to you," she said firmly. "I know who you are now. Sonny warned me about you. You're the enemy. You're going to confuse me, tell me lies."

"They aren't lies. Your husband is a monster. He rapes children. He raped your daughter, Mrs. Scott. And he'll keep on, unless you help me."

"No! I won't let you say these things! Go away." Her voice began to rise in a hysterical shriek. "Go away!"

"Come, dear." The general appeared, freshly dressed in a spotless uniform. "Don't let her upset you. You know they're nothing but lies. Come and lie down. You need your medicine. You know what happens when you forget your medicine."

She looked up at him, dazed, trusting. "They *are* lies, aren't they, Sonny?"

"Of course, dearest." He patted her hand, leading her tenderly away. He paused in the doorway. "In case you're wondering, Cassidy, there's no way Richard can sneak up here when I'm not looking. Along with video cameras I have heat sensors activated. An alarm would sound if he came anywhere near the perimeter of the grounds. There's no way he can get up here without my knowing."

"How reassuring," she said acidly.

Amberson Scott only smiled.

She watched him go, leading his wife away, murmuring soothing, solicitous phrases. The door shut behind them.

Cassie hobbled back to Francesca, but her sister had ingested more drugs than she'd realized. Shaking her, slapping her did no good whatsoever—she simply blinked and sank back into a stupor. "Damn it, wake up, Francesca," she cried. "We've got to get out of here. Fast. Before he comes back." Francesca didn't move.

Cassie froze suddenly, as a shadow loomed up behind her, silent, deadly, and she knew it was too late. Hands reached down, catching her shoulders, dragging her away from the bed, and she started to scream, as she felt herself pulled up against a large, hard body, and his hand covered her mouth, stifling that scream. In the distance she could hear the general coming, and the man behind her dragged her into the darkened bathroom, closing the door behind them, and she heard his voice hissing in her ear. "What in Christ's name are you doing here?" Richard demanded.

She tried to struggle, but he simply pushed up against the tiled wall of the bathroom, and she was unable to fight him. He reached over and turned on the shower, full force, the noise and heat of it filling the room, and she fought him in mindless panic, unable to breathe, until she heard the sharp rapping on the door.

"Decided to take a shower after all?" General Scott's voice came through the thick door.

Slowly Richard released his hand from her mouth. It took her a moment to be able to speak, but she managed a creditable job. "Yes."

"A wise idea. You're probably chilled to the bone, and who knows how long it will take before Richard realizes he's not going to be able to sneak in. He's going to have to walk right in, and there's no need for you to be uncomfortable, waiting. There are some clothes of Diana's in the closet when you're finished. I couldn't bear to throw them out."

Cassie leaned her head against the tile, Richard's body still pressed tight against hers. "They wouldn't fit me," she murmured.

"Certainly they would," the general said cheerfully. "They fit me."

Richard's hand came over her mouth again as she began to struggle once more. They fought, in the steamy darkness, until he simply flattened her against the wall, immobilizing her. "Stop fighting me," he said in her ear. He waited, damnably long, and then removed his hand.

"Let go of me. He's going to hurt Francesca . . ."

"He's not going to touch her. Right now he's far more excited by the game of cat and mouse he's playing with me than he is by the thought of another child to molest. Amberson's interests are simple. He finds the hunt to be the most appealing. After that he'll settle for sexual perversions."

"You can't be sure . . ."

"No," he said brutally. "But there's nothing we can do about it right now. I don't have any weapons, and he does. We're going to have to figure out a way to distract him. If I know him, and I do, he's gone back to sit in the living room with his gun across his lap, just waiting for me to put in an appearance. He doesn't know I managed to get through the heat sensors and the cameras by coming straight over the cliff, but he's smart enough not to rule it out. He's waiting for me, and he'll be ready. It wouldn't do to underestimate him. He's a formidable opponent."

"What are we going to do?" she whispered. "How can we stop him?"

"I'm not sure. I know one thing, we're only going to get one try at him. You're going to need to get your sister out of here while I go for him. It's our only chance."

"No," she said fiercely. "He'll kill you."

"Probably. But not before I take him out."

"I don't want you to die." It was a cry of pain, of despair, and his reaction was immediate.

His hands slid up her body, to cup her face, and his mouth covered hers in the darkness. It was a long, slow, gentle kiss, as his mouth slanted across hers. He took his time as he took her mouth, with tenderness and longing and a promise of love that was no more than a dream. He gave her more in that kiss than he'd given her in half a dozen sexual encounters. He gave her his soul. And she took it, willingly, gratefully, knowing without words that she was loved.

The rap at the door was sudden, shocking. "Still in there, my dear?" The general called. "I think you've had a long enough shower. We wouldn't want to waste energy, now would we? Come out."

Richard leaned over and turned off the shower. "I'll be out in a minute," she called, knowing her voice shook.

"I have keys to every lock in this house. You're not my type, Cassidy, but that wouldn't stop me from . . ." His voice halted abruptly, and through the thickness of the door the sound came, soft, whispering.

"Sonny. Where are you, Sonny?"

He didn't curse. "Coming, Essie," he called, ever patient. "You've upset my wife, Cassie," he said. "I'm afraid I'm going to have to punish you for that."

Richard had already moved away from her, the tenderness vanishing. "You've got to get out of here. Now." He yanked open the door, and the murky light of the stormy day filled the room. Francesca lay on the bed, unmoving.

"I can't leave her."

"You won't need to." He moved to the bed, hauled Francesca into a sitting position, and slapped her across the face, twice. Francesca blinked, opening her eyes, her mouth agape with drugged outrage.

"You're developing a talent for that," Cassie said furiously, still shaking.

He glanced back at her. "I don't expect to have a chance to do it again." He rose, moving away. "Get her out of here."

"Come on, Francesca," Cassie murmured, hobbling to the bed and putting an arm under her sister's shoulder. "We've got to leave before the general comes back."

"Yes," Francesca murmured docilely enough, struggling to her feet. The two of them stumbled toward the sliding glass door, pushing it open. Cassie turned, looking for Richard, but he'd disappeared. Without a goddamned word.

The mist had turned to snow once more, coating the lawn, scumming the wooden deck. But neither of them noticed as they staggered across the lawn toward the woods and the steep, treacherous path down off the cliff.

Cassie felt the sudden burn in her shoulder, like a fist punching her, knocking her away from Francesca, throwing her to the ground, the walking stick still clutched in her hand. A moment later she heard the noise, felt the warm and wetness of blood, and she realized she'd been shot.

"I can't let you interfere," the general shouted, walking toward them. Francesca was on her knees in the snow, swaying slightly, and Cassie reached out, trying to protect her, to hold her, when the general fired again.

Her sister's frail body recoiled, and she fell, rolling over the rocks and ice, falling down the steeply sloping lawn. Falling toward the edge of the cliff.

Cassie screamed, lunging for her, but Francesca was moving too fast. She clawed out, desperate, but there was nothing to hold on to. Her sister made no sound at all as she hit the rock ledge, and then she went over, tumbling through the air to oblivion.

The silence was deafening. Cassie struggled to her feet, ignoring the heat and wetness of the blood from her shoulder, ignoring the pain and weakness of her ankle. She clutched the walking stick as she advanced toward the general.

"You killed her," she whispered.

"Richard is to blame," he said calmly, unmoved. "For all of this. If he'd just left us alone, everything would have been fine. Now I'm afraid matters have been precipitated. I can't wait until he shows up. You're going to have to die now, my dear, much as I regret it. You know I admire you very much," he said, advancing on her, slowly, the small, deadly gun in one capable hand. "Your devotion to your father, your blind loyalty to Richard. Your stamina. As I said, you would have made a hell of a soldier. You would have made a hell of a daughter."

"I'm not your type, remember," she shot back, waiting for him to get within range.

"Who knows what would have happened if you were my child?" he mused, coming closer. Almost within reach. Within a few, dangerous yards of the cliff that had taken her sister. "But that's impossible. A weakling like Essie could never have given birth to an amazon like you. The best she could offer was Diana. Lovely though she was, she was hardly worthy of me. I should have had sons."

Cassie looked up, past Scott, and an unearthly calm settled over her.

Richard had found his weapon. A human one. He appeared on the snow-covered deck, Essie Scott's dazed, drugged figure standing limply beside him.

"Would that have made the difference?" Cassie deliberately pitched her voice to reach the deck. "Would you have molested your sons as you molested your daughter?"

"Undoubtedly," said the general calmly, and stopped. "This gun has a greater range than that walking stick, and I have no intention of coming any closer. I'm sorry, my dear." And he raised the gun.

Her next moves were instinctive. She hurled the stick at him, with all her force, ducking and rolling on the ground as the gun spat. In the distance she heard the high, keening wail that came to an abrupt halt, and when Cassie came to a stop she looked up, to see Richard and the general wrestling in the snow, sliding and struggling, moving toward the cliff that had taken Francesca. There was no sign of Essie Scott.

She tried to rise, but couldn't. Blood was everywhere, her blood, and she had used up the last of her reserves. She lay in the snow, watching the vicious confrontation in horror.

It was like nothing she'd seen in the movies or on television. It was violence, scratching, clawing, murderous violence, and despite Richard's youth and size, they were evenly matched. The general had expertise and evil on his side, and they rolled toward the edge of the cliff, coming up hard against the stone barrier. Cassie held her breath, unable to move.

The general struggled to his feet. There was blood on the snow, and he reached down to touch the kitchen knife protruding from his chest.

He yanked it free. Blood was everywhere, but he simply didn't notice, advancing on Richard. "Fitting, don't you think?" he wheezed. "You should have learned you can't win, Richard. I think I'm going to cut your heart out before I toss your body over the cliff. If they ever find you, they'll assume the wolves got to you."

He leaned down, the knife steady, when he jerked. A look of great astonishment covered his face. And then he dove forward, over the barrier, falling end over end down into the valley, the back half of his head blown away.

Essie Scott stood in the snow, gray hair flying,

rifle in her hand. "He did lie," she said simply. "He did." And she turned and went back inside the house. In the distance, in the deafening silence, Cassie thought she could hear her humming beneath her breath.

And then she heard another sound. A soft, feminine cry. "Cassie. Help me."

"Francesca!" she screamed, struggling to her feet, but Richard had already moved, leaping over the wall. By the time Cassie had managed to drag herself to the edge, Richard had already reached her. She was caught up against a small clump of trees, her frilly pink outfit stained with blood. But she was alive, and Richard was with her, and it was going to be all right. Everything was going to be all right, she thought, sinking back into the snow. Everything was going to be just fine, as the icy blackness closed in around her, and she surrendered to it, running away for the last time.

CHAPTER 22

You need to speak to your stepmother, Cassie," Alice announced. "She's being completely unreasonable. And why she's allowing that dreadful contessa woman around is beyond me. Francesca is just fine, she's made a better recovery than you have, and the two of them ought to head back to Venice or Naples or wherever they come from. It's not as if Sean is leaving her a thing in his will. Everything's in trust for the girl."

"As it should be," Cass said wearily. "Alba is Sean's fourth wife, and as such, has just as much right here as you do. And what is Mabry doing that has you in such an uproar?"

"She's starting a fire in the library fireplace, and I was trying to read. It's a blistering hot day, and she's doing it just to drive me from the place. I won't have it. She can't drive me out of here . . ."

"She certainly can. It's her apartment. Don't you think it's time you went back to Florida? Robert must be lonely without you."

"Robert can take care of himself," Alice said

with a sniff. It was just past noon, and she'd only just started drinking.

"Oh, I'm sure he can. I was just worried about your friends."

"My friends?"

"All those widows. Those very attractive, very well-off widows, who'd find an unattached male irresistible. I'm certain they're taking very good care of him. After all, they're used to looking after men."

Alice sat there, dumbstruck, and Cassie wondered why she hadn't thought of it earlier. Lack of energy, doubtless. It would have rid them of Alice's noxious presence days ago, leaving them in blessed peace.

"I need to get back," she said abruptly. "You're absolutely fine, and we both know it, despite your acting like a Victorian heroine, lolling around in bed. It's only for your sake I've been staying, but honestly, Cassie, I think it's time you pulled yourself together. No need to mope. I do think it outrageous that Richard Tiernan had his conviction overturned, but at least that should have pleased you. I think I should be entitled to know why, but no one seems to trust me."

"You were the one who told me he'd been released," Cassie said, leaning back in the bed. "You said new evidence had come to light, and her death was ruled accidental."

"And I don't believe a word of it. I'd like to know why he didn't seem any too happy to be released. You probably even know where he is right now," Alice said accusingly.

"I don't think it matters, do you?" Cass murmured.

"It shouldn't," Alice said shrewdly. "I'm going to pack. Tell your precious stepmother to put out the goddamned fire; I'm leaving."

Cassie pulled herself out of bed, slowly, pulling a robe around her. It had been five weeks since she and Francesca had been taken off the mountain by helicopter. She'd missed her father's funeral, she'd missed Richard's hearing. She'd seen him only once since he'd climbed up the cliff, her sister's wounded body in his arms. He'd left the moment his release had come.

The whole sordid mess had been covered up quite neatly—Cass imagined Sean would have howled in outrage. He'd never believed in discretion, and even the future of two innocent children would probably be fair game in return for publicity.

Richard had been released and the charges had been dropped, she knew that much. Esther Scott had been surprisingly informative in her drug-dazed ramblings, and Jerome Fabiani had had no choice but to let Richard go. That, or have the whole ugly mess come out, and no one was particularly interested in having the details spread across the tabloids, least of all an up-and-coming district attorney who'd been instrumental in convicting an innocent man of murder.

The press had been far from appeased at the vague information released. New evidence had come to light, Fabiani had announced. They were pursuing their investigation.

But Cassie knew that the investigation had been quietly closed. Diana Scott Tiernan's death had been ruled an accident, and no one was willing to push it any further.

And so Richard had left, disappeared from public view, and the tabloids already had a new murder to keep them busy. The tragedy of General Amberson Scott's untimely death merited a discreet three inches in *The New York Times*. No mention that his wife had been institutionalized ever sullied those pristine pages.

She limped down the hallway. Oddly enough, her sprained ankle bothered her more than her gunshot wound. The general had either been a worse shot or a better one than he believed. The bullet had passed through the fleshy part of Cass's upper arm, causing no damage but a nasty scar. Francesca had gotten off even more lightly. The bullet had grazed her scalp, giving her nothing more than a few stitches and one hell of a headache.

Mabry was sitting in front of the fireplace. The room was beastly hot, but unlike Alice, Cassie didn't have any illusions about the reason for the fire. She closed the door behind her and curled up in her favorite green chair, watching, as Mabry fed sheets of manuscript to the flames.

"Are you certain you want to do that?" she murmured.

"Yes." She didn't bother to turn her head. Her silky blond hair glinted in the firelight, and she still looked incredibly graceful, youthful. It was only her soul that was drained.

"Did you read it? Was it any good?"

"It was the best thing he'd done in years. Absolutely brilliant. Richard told him enough of the truth, and Sean figured out the rest. He let the general come into the house, with Francesca there, knowing what he'd done to his own daughter." Mabry shivered for a moment, then managed a weary smile. "No one ever said your father had a speck of decency in him."

"Not a speck," Cassie agreed wryly. "Are you certain you want to do that? It would make a fortune."

"I don't need it," Mabry said. "And I don't want it. Do you?"

"No. Sean will be remembered for *Galway Hell*. He doesn't need this for his literary legacy." Cassie leaned back, closing her eyes for a moment. "Alice is leaving."

"Thank heavens for small miracles. Alba and Francesca are going, too."

"Are they? I'm sorry about that."

"Francesca needs to get back to her own life. She's resilient, but her treatment at the hands of that monster still gives her nightmares. She needs to get back home to a place where she can heal."

"He didn't touch her, did he? That monstrous old man . . . ?"

"She says no. I think she might not be ready to deal with it. I'm not sure I trust Alba to make sure she gets counseling."

"I don't trust Alba at all. But I trust Francesca. I think she got all the good sense and self-preservation in the family."

"Not all of it," Mabry said slowly. "You know, I wondered whether you might want to go with them."

"Trying to get rid of me as well, Mabry?" she murmured wryly. "I can go back to Maryland anytime. My job is open if I want to come back. Just say the word."

"They're leaving for Milan this evening. The plane makes one stop. In London."

Cass closed her eyes for a moment. "I can't just up and decide to go to Europe, Mabry."

"You've done it before."

"I thought you liked having me here."

"I want you to be happy, Cass. You're not going to be until you face what you left."

"I didn't leave him. He left me. He came to my hospital room, kissed me on the cheek, and said good-bye."

"And what did you say?"

"What could I say? He didn't need me anymore. What was I supposed to do, beg him to stay? He couldn't. There'll always be a cloud over his head. His best bet is just to fade into the English countryside, out of public view. His children need some kind of normalcy, constancy. He can provide that now, but not if he comes back here."

"So go to him."

"It was his choice. He doesn't want me."

Mabry tossed the last hundred pages or so onto the fire, and the flames burst around them, throwing off a shower of sparks. Rather like a funeral pyre, Cassidy thought absently.

Mabry sat back on her heels, watching it burn. "Your father loved you, you know," she said, seemingly a non sequitur.

Cassie considered it for a moment. "I know," she said softly.

"Go with Francesca and Alba," Mabry said. "You don't even need to get off the plane when it stops in England. When it lands, you'll know what to do. Some things are worth fighting for, darling. Life is too damned short."

"I can't."

"Why not?"

"Because he has to give. Something, anything, I don't know what. But I can't run after him, I can't throw myself at his feet, I can't keep giving to him. He has to give something back, or there's nothing there. And right now he's too caught up in making a normal life for his family to have time for me. Maybe in a few months. A few years. Maybe never."

"And you're just going to sit around and feel

sorry for yourself?" Mabry spun around, looking up at her.

"Hey," said Cass lightly, "I come by it honestly. My mother is the queen of self-pity."

"Cassie . . ."

"No more, Mabry. I need time. Please." Her voice cracked slightly.

The severe, beautiful lines of Mabry's face softened. "You've got it, sweetie. But what am I going to do with the extra ticket I bought for you?"

Cass managed a smile. "How long has it been since you visited Italy?"

It was only the third time she'd left the apartment since she'd come home from the hospital. Alba, used to going first-class, hired a limousine, and they drove out to JFK in merry style, with Francesca and Cassie going through the tiny refrigerator's stash of diet Cokes while Alba and Mabry went through a bottle of Moet champagne in record time. She stood at the customs barrier and waved good-bye, a fixed smile on her face.

Her cheeks hurt when they finally disappeared. She turned, moving back through the crowded airport, moving blindly. She needed this time, desperately. Time alone in the apartment, time for an orgy of grief and suffering. Time to wail and scream and cry and pound her fists against the wall. Time to face the fact that she would never see Richard Tiernan again.

She had two choices. She could try to deal with

the fact that he was gone. That he wasn't coming back. Or she could wrap herself into a safe little cocoon of denial. And she wasn't sure which would hurt more.

The driver was waiting when Cassie came back alone, and the stock of diet Cokes had been magically replenished. She sat back in the plush leather, letting the air-conditioned silence close around her during the long drive in from Long Island. It had been so long since she'd been alone.

Maybe she'd go home to the apartment and eat absolutely everything she could find. Comfort food like macaroni and cheese, fresh bagels, and nachos, washed down by gallons of diet Coke. Then she could start in on the Ben and Jerry's Super Fudge Chunk, a stack of waffles, maybe even a glass of warm milk . . .

She shut that line of thought off quickly, sharply, putting a hand against her mouth to stop the sudden whimper of pain that bubbled forth. She was going home to the empty apartment. To silence, and healing. To not answering questions or smiling when she didn't want to. She was going to learn how to live again. If there was any way she could.

"Good to see you out and about, Miss Cassidy," Bill the doorman said when the limousine pulled up. "You call if you need any help, now."

She remembered the last time he'd told her that. Richard Tiernan had been waiting for her, up in her parents' apartment, and he was worried for her.

The apartment would be empty tonight. "Thanks, Bill," she murmured, as the elevator doors slid shut.

She closed and double locked the front door to the apartment behind her, kicking off her shoes. Her ankle was still giving her trouble, and she moved slowly toward the kitchen, her long skirts swaying around her. She'd lost weight in the last five weeks. Sean would have been proud of her.

She stopped in the hallway, closing her eyes. Sean. Why did she have to wait so long to come to terms with him, now that he was dead? Why couldn't she have made peace with him while he still lived? When they could have salvaged something?

But Sean O'Rourke wasn't the man for a peaceful existence. He'd died as he lived, stirring things up. She wondered if he'd hate the fact that his last, brilliant manuscript would never be published. And she knew he'd probably approve of Mabry's dramatic gesture.

She wandered into the kitchen, heading for the refrigerator. She was leaning over it, staring without enthusiasm at the gourmet contents, when she suddenly grew very still.

She turned, slowly, very slowly. Richard Tiernan was standing there in the dark, silent, watching her. Waiting for her.

She was afraid. More terrified than she'd ever

been of him. This was the last chance, the final choice. There were no more excuses, no more running.

"Why are you here?" she asked, her voice barely a whisper. The chill of the open refrigerator didn't help matters, and the cold air stirred her dress against her legs. She knew she was crying, and she couldn't help it. She was expecting every kind of excuse, every kind of manipulation, and she didn't know how to protect herself. How to ask him for what she needed.

"For you," he said, very simply.

And it was enough.

If you enjoyed
Nightfall,
you'll love Anne Stuart's
next romantic thriller,
Moonrise.

Turn the page
for a special preview
of *Moonrise,*
coming from Onyx
in the Fall of 1995.

The woman didn't know she had just come closer to death than most people did in their entire lives. She stood outside the door of the ramshackle cottage, her white cotton clothes creased and rumpled from the long trip. In another lifetime the upraised hand that had just knocked on his door would be wearing a spotless white glove, and there'd be a hat on that soft sweep of hair.

He stood in the shadows, watching her. He'd chosen this cottage, this tiny island off the gulf coast of Mexico, for a reason. No one could anywhere near him without him hearing them from miles away. There was no approach from the rocky beach, and the narrow drive that led through the thick underbrush led nowhere else.

He'd been lying in his hammock, working his way into a bottle of José Cuervo, when he'd heard the taxi turn toward his place. Teo's ancient Buick was unmistakable to a man of his training, no matter how drunk he was. They wouldn't be coming after him in a taxi, he thought, as he moved silently, swiftly through the house. He took only one gun with him. One would be enough.

The slender white-clothed figure climbed out of Teo's taxi, and she carried a case with her. He wondered exactly what kind of weapons she had in that case, and how she'd managed to get them through the surprisingly rigorous customs on the tiny island.

She had to be carrying as well, but as far as he could see there was no room for anything but the smallest gun on that slender body. She could have a knife strapped to her thigh, but she didn't hold herself like someone good with knives, and his instincts, honed over time, were infallible.

The taxi left, and they were alone in the clearing. Night had already fallen—it came early in October—and the moon was beginning to rise, covering the area with a silver light.

In the moonlight, fresh blood would look black.

He stood in the trees, loose, relaxed, alert. He could take her out in a matter of seconds. It was what he was trained to do, what he did best. He could send a bullet into her brain, just behind her ear, judging the distance within a fraction of an inch, and her skull would explode.

Or he could move up behind her, and she wouldn't hear him. Even if her training matched his, she wouldn't be as good as he was. No one was.

And she was too young. Even if she had his talent, she didn't have his years of experience.

He wondered why he hesitated. There was no reason anyone would have come after him, would have gone to the trouble of finding him, unless they were planning to kill him. And he had a cardinal rule—get the bastards before they got you.

He raised the gun. He didn't want to put his hands on her—it had been too long since he'd had a woman, and he wasn't a man who mixed sex with killing. One was a basic need, to be ignored if it grew inconvenient. The other was a job.

She climbed up the sagging front steps, and he noticed she was wearing an incredibly stupid pair of white shoes. High heels. No killer would come after him in high heels.

He slowly uncocked the gun and let out his breath.

He hadn't realized he'd been holding it. She knocked on the door, and he could read her body language in the silver light. She was nervous. No, beyond that. She was scared.

So she must know who and what he was. What did she want with him?

Curiosity was a luxury in which he seldom indulged. He started to back away, tucking the compact Beretta into his belt, feeling the coolness of metal against his hot skin, when she turned her head. And a flash of memory hit him, like a fist in his gut. He knew who she was.

Win Sutherland's daughter. Cherished only child of his mentor, his foster father, the man he'd trusted and loved most in this world.

The man who'd betrayed him.

What the hell was Annie doing here? He hadn't seen her since the funeral, and he'd stayed in the distance. She'd been so lost in grief she hadn't seen him, but then, he'd always made sure she seldom noticed her father's protégé. He was good at that, at blending in. It was one of the reasons he'd managed to stay alive for so long.

But now she was here. And he didn't know what the hell he was going to do about her.

I'm a fool to come, Annie thought, rubbing her sweaty palms against the lean line of her skirt. It had taken her more than twelve hours to get here, she was exhausted and hungry and her head ached.

But most of all, she was scared shitless.

She couldn't imagine why she was frightened of someone like James McKinley. She'd known the man most of her life—he'd been a family friend, her father's confidante, a pleasant, polite man who'd pose no threat to anyone.

The man who knew the secrets. That's what her father had said, years ago. If ever anything happened, anything questionable, she could go to McKinley for the answers, Win had told her in a rare burst of openness.

It had taken her months to remember. But remember she had.

She banged again. It was getting dark, and she'd sent the taxi away, afraid that if she'd asked him to wait, she might chicken out. "Hello?" she called out, still avoiding using his name. "Anyone home?"

"Right behind you."

She whirled around, hitting her elbow on the door. She hadn't heard him approach, and in the moonlight she knew an instant's panic as she looked up into the face of a complete stranger.

"What are you doing here, Annie?"

Not a complete stranger after all. She knew that voice, cool and distant, infuriatingly calm. But she didn't know the man who stood far too close to her.

He was McKinley's height, tall, much taller than her own five feet eight inches. But there all similarity ended.

She'd never really looked that closely at McKinley when he'd been with her father. She knew he was tall, ageless, anonymous, dressed in neat dark suits.

This man had nothing to do with that memory. His hair was long, shaggy, tied back from his unshaven face. His eyes were dark, glittering, and he was wearing cutoffs and a grubby tropical shirt that hung open around his chest. This was an animal, feral, trapped, and very dangerous. He smelled of alcohol.

"Jamey?" she said in disbelief, instinctively using her father's name for him.

He flinched as if she'd hit him. And then he seemed to straighten, and that sense of danger disappeared. "Your father's the only man who got away with calling me that," he said.

She smiled uncertainly. "Win got away with a lot of stuff," she said.

"Not always. What are you doing here, Annie? And how did you find me?"

"Martin told me where you were."

She could see some of the tension in his shoulders relax. Muscled shoulders. She'd thought he was close to her father's age. She began revising her estimate downward by twenty years.

"Why?" he said again, his voice brusque.

"I want to find out what really happened to my father."

He just stared at her for a moment. "He died, Annie. Remember? He had too much to drink, he fell down the stairs and broke his damned neck."

"I don't believe it."

"They did an autopsy. I'm sure you can read it if you've got the stomach for it—"

"I saw it. I still don't believe it. I think he was murdered."

It was growing darker, and the faint slivers of moonlight filtered down around them. His face was composed of planes and shadows, and she couldn't see him clearly. Just the glitter in his dark eyes. "What do you expect me to do about it?"

He hadn't denied the possibility, which shocked her. "You were his best friend," she said. "Don't you want to know the truth? Don't you want revenge?"

"Not particularly."

She looked up at him, frustration making her grim. Reckless. "Well, I do. And if you don't want to help me, I'll have to take care of it on my own. I'm going to find out what happened to my father. And I'll be damned if I let them get away with some cover-up."

He didn't move. She had the sudden, eerie feeling that she was in danger. Very great danger. She didn't dare look behind her—instead she kept her back straight, even though McKinley was close enough that she could smell the alcohol on his breath. She could feel the tension in the air, emanating from his body.

And then it seemed to dissolve. "All right," he said in a cool voice, putting one hand under her elbow in what should have been a polite gesture. "You might as well come in and we'll talk about it."

She jerked away, then held still. "Does that mean you'll help me?"

"That means," he said in his deep rasp of a voice that held the faintest memory of East Texas, "that you'll tell me everything you know, everything you suspect, and then we'll see what we have to do about it." He pushed open the door into the shadowy cottage, and she had no choice but to precede him inside. Once more resisting the impulse to look over her shoulder.

She looked around her as he flicked on the electric light. It was a small room, untidy. The furniture was frayed and broken dishes were piled on the table. She turned to glance at him in the soft light.

"Why are you living here?" she asked. "This doesn't seem like your kind of place at all."

Just the faintest trace of a smile curved his mouth. It was hardly reassuring. "And you know me so well, don't you, Annie?"

"I've known you for most of my life," she said, defensive.

"How old am I?"

She blinked. "You're drunk."

"I didn't ask that. And as a matter of fact," he said, grabbing a chair and straddling it as he poured himself a glass of tequila, "I'm not nearly drunk enough. I've barely made a start on the night's ration." He poured a second glass, pushed it across the table toward her.

"I don't drink."

"You do tonight," he said. "How old am I?"

She took the glass of tequila and allowed herself a faint sip. She hated tequila and always had. "I used to think you were my father's age," she admitted.

"Your father was sixty-three when he died."

"I know that," she said irritably, taking another sip. "Maybe late forties?"

"Maybe," he said. "So why don't you think your father's death was an accident?"

"Instinct."

"Christ," he said weakly. "A woman's intuition. If

that's all you've got to go on, sweetheart, then you're wasting my time."

"My instincts are excellent. Win always said so."

"Yeah," he said, draining his glass.

"When did you become a drunk?" she said sharply. "You never used to be like this."

"April second."

The reply hung between them. It was the day her father had died.

She moved then, skirting the table, coming around to his side and kneeling down in front of him, not even hesitating. "You loved him," she said. "As much as I did. We can't just ignore what happened. Someone killed him, and we have to find out who. If you won't help me, I'll do it myself. But you will, won't you?"

He smiled down at her. Annie wasn't reassured. She didn't know this man—she kept looking for McKinley beneath the stubble and the danger, beyond the tequila and the unexpected look of him

"Oh, I'll help you, Annie," he said softly. "You'll get the answers to all those questions. But I'm not sure you'll like them."

"Liking has nothing to do with it. I'm not going to stop until I find out."

He looked down at her, and there was an odd expression in his eyes. "I know you won't, Annie," he said gently. "And I'm sorry about that."

He was going to have to do something about her. She knelt at his feet, all sweet-smelling innocence and trust, staring up at him. Her father's age? Christ, he was thirty-nine years old. He'd done his job too damned well.

She was right—he had known her for most of her life. And he knew just how tenacious, how stubborn, how bright she was. She wouldn't let it go. Not until she learned the unpalatable truth, about all of them.

Win wasn't around to cloud her mind anymore. And she'd inherited his brains, even if she'd never used them in the same arena. It would only be a matter of time before she began making some very dangerous enemies.

It wasn't his concern, he reminded himself. He was a dead man already—so what if Annie Sutherland was added to their list of victims?

He looked down at her. She probably had no idea of the thoughts racing through his brain, that no amount of tequila could deaden. He looked down at her slender, delicate throat, and thought about how much pressure he'd need to exert to break her neck. It would be simple, easy, no more than a flick of the wrist, and she and her questions would be no threat to anyone.

She wasn't a particularly beautiful woman—Winston had seen to that. He wondered what she'd do if he put his hand behind her head and pulled her mouth toward his crotch.

She probably didn't know what to do with that mouth, he thought sourly. Win had scared off any but the most harmless of her lovers, including that idiot she'd been married to for three years.

In the end, he didn't touch her, because he wasn't certain what he'd do. There was no hurry. No one could approach this place without him knowing, and so far they'd done a piss-poor job of coming after him. Annie being there would up the ante, of course, but they'd already let her get this far.

"Why didn't you ask Martin for help?" he said suddenly. "Or did he turn you down?"

"I wanted you," she said.

The words hung between them. He watched, with drunken amazement, as a faint sheen of color mottled her cheeks. She was actually blushing.

"Annie," he said, suddenly weary, "go to bed."

She glanced around. "Where?"

"There's a bed upstairs. Take it. I've had too much to drink tonight to deal with you. We'll talk about this in the morning."

"Does that mean you're going to help me?"

He rose, caught her arms and hauled her up. She was slender, the white suit was wrinkled, but she still smelled like some faint, sexy perfume. Not the kind of perfume Win would have chosen for her.

"Maybe," he said. "For the time being, get your butt upstairs and out of my sight."

She smiled at him then. Christ, he'd forgotten Annie Sutherland's smile. It had been a long time since he'd seen it, an even longer time since it had been directed at him. It was still just as powerful.

"I knew you wouldn't let me down," she said. She leaned over and hugged him, an exuberant, sexless hug, backing away before he could make a drunken swipe at her.

"I didn't say—"

"I'll see you in the morning," she said, escaping up the narrow stairs. Not knowing how close that escape was.

It was too damned small a house. The upstairs bedroom was nothing more than an open balcony. There was no door on his bedroom either.

He knew, deep in his heart, what he was going to have to do, and all the tequila in the world couldn't change that.

He was either going to have to do his damnedest to convince sharp-eyed, quick-witted Annie Sutherland that her father was a harmless bureaucrat who'd died in a freak accident.

Or he was going to have to kill her himself.